THE DISAPPEARANCE OF
IRENE DOS SANTOS

THE **DISAPPEARANCE** OF **IRENE DOS SANTOS**

Margaret Mascarenhas

GRAND CENTRAL
PUBLISHING

NEW YORK   BOSTON

Grand Central Publishing
Hachette Book Group
237 Park Avenue
New York, NY 10017

Visit our Web site at www.HachetteBookGroup.com.

Printed in the United States of America

First Edition: June 2009
10 9 8 7 6 5 4 3 2 1

Grand Central Publishing is a division of Hachette Book Group, Inc.
The Grand Central Publishing name and logo is a trademark of Hachette Book Group, Inc.

Library of Congress Cataloging-in-Publication Data
Mascarenhas, Margaret.
The disappearance of Irene dos Santos / Margaret Mascarenhas. —1st ed.
    p. cm.
Summary: "A novel set in Venezuela about the search for individual truth, love, and belonging, embodied in a fifteen-year-old girl"—Provided by publisher.
    ISBN 978-0-446-54110-7
    1. Teenage girls—Fiction.   2. Venezuela—Fiction.   I. Title.
PS3613.A794D57 2009
813'.6—dc22
                                              2008037862

Book design and text composition by Stratford, A TexTech business

For Saryu and Vinod

It is better to die on your feet
than to live on your knees.

—Spanish writer, communist, and politician
Dolores Ibarruri, also known as
"La Pasionaria" ("Passion Flower"),
who formed the Spanish communist party

THE DISAPPEARANCE OF
IRENE DOS SANTOS

The passiflora edulis produces an exquisite and fragrant flower, with five white sepals and a fringelike corona that is deep purple at the base. Pollination is best under humid conditions.

Lily

In Lily's dream it is raining and Irene thunders past on what appears to be a giant wild boar. "Vamos, vamos!" She leans down, arm extended, hand reaching to pull Lily up in front of her. Lily also reaches, but their hands are wet, their fingers slip, the grasp does not hold. In that split second, just as their fingertips separate, a lightning bolt strikes Irene full on the chin; she falls back against the rump of her mount, which continues galloping away into the forest. The dream ends as the honeyed song of the golden-winged Maizcuba announces the break of dawn in the postcolonial city of Tamanaco.

As the first light filters through the windows of the freshly whitewashed Quintanilla residence, Lily opens her eyes and stretches her arms. Using her elbows as leverage, she laboriously hoists her body, over eight months heavy with child, into a sitting position. She leans over to kiss Carlos Alberto, who is still asleep, but her belly gets in the way. She will kiss him later, from a more comfortable position.

Easing herself awkwardly but quietly out of bed, she slips on an ankle-length kimono, black and white, and pads barefoot to the kitchen. Her mother's voice, the voice of her childhood, light and bright, accompanies her down the hallway, reminding her not to mix too much water in the Harina P.A.N. for the arepas.

The sounds of cooking in the large, airy kitchen with the speckled gray Formica table, where Lily had dutifully done her homework as a child, are the most comforting sounds she knows. It is in the kitchen that her mother reigned supreme, creating the perfect arepas, buoyant and filling at the same time. Lily is certain she has never tasted arepas comparable to her mother's. Or cachapas. Or hallacas. Or mondongo. Or anything gastronomic. Although she has learned eight of her mother's most familiar recipes, executing them with military precision, the result is never as delicious. She suspects Consuelo of withholding a secret ingredient, but Consuelo, laughing, says the secret is love. "When you are cooking you should pour your love into the pot. You are too distraída, mi amor, thinking of other things."

It was in the kitchen that Consuelo taught Lily to dance to the music of the transistor radio, which her father, Ismael, had installed on the wall over the counter. Merengue and salsa—un, dos, tres...un, dos, tres—Consuelo's full, rounded hips swirling sensuously, Lily's bony ones jerking, awkward. Afterward, their faces flushed with pleasure, they would go out to the garden and pluck passion fruits from the loaded vine that Ismael had brought all the way from the rain forest. It took twelve passion fruits to make enough juice to quench their thirst. Then her mother would teach her to draw, the subjects selected from items at hand—a jar full of carnations, a bowl of fruit, her mother's face. Lily could never quite master the art of shading, and her renditions lacked depth.

Consuelo tells her daughter that the preparation of a meal

is as much a creative act as drawing or painting. I won't be around forever, she says. Debes aprender. But since Lily does not acknowledge the possibility of a world in which her mother is not, Consuelo might as well have said nothing at all. In any case, there is Marta, who cooks almost exactly like her mother.

Marta, an immigrant from Cuba, has been with the family almost as long as Lily can remember, first working for Consuelo and now for Lily. Marta thinks of herself as Venezuelan first and Cuban incidentally. Every Sunday morning she takes an hour-long bus ride to Caracas to visit her Trinidadian friend José Naipaul, who is dying of lung cancer, returning by noon.

On Sundays, Marta is not expected to cook; Lily is in charge of breakfast, Carlos Alberto of lunch, and dinner is comprised of sandwiches from the week's leftovers. The only food Carlos Alberto knows how to prepare is steak, which he marinates in olive oil and parsley, sears, and serves rare, accompanied by heart of palm salad, chilled beer, and a butter-yellow rose from the garden. After dinner they play cards, or sometimes dominoes, which Marta prefers to cards. By now their Sunday routine is established, automatic; they never give a single thought to a different type of Sunday.

Though it is from her mother, a painter, that she learned to draw, it is architecture that Lily has chosen as her profession. Architecturally, and in spite of her self-inflicted culinary deficiencies, the kitchen is her favorite design subject as well as her favorite room in the house. When designing a house, she always saves the kitchen for last, like dessert. She works out her preliminary drawings, freehand, on the kitchen table, an arrangement that works well, since it gives

Carlos Alberto full occupancy of the tiny study, where he pens his stories for the producers of telenovelas. Since Lily's best childhood memories are from her mother's kitchen, she has designed her own as almost a replica of Consuelo's, separated from the living room by a wide, open arch instead of a wall, though her kitchen table is wood, not Formica. Thus, the living room and the kitchen are one. There is no dining room.

Lily doesn't like it when Marta points out similarities between her own life and her mother's, certain that her taste in kitchen layout is where the resemblance ends. For example, Lily would never allow her husband to roam the countryside as he pleases, spending more time away than at home.

It is not that her father doesn't love her mother, she knows this. It is just that he has other, perhaps equal, loves. Poetry. Music. The Gran Sabana. The life of one such as her father, who is constantly traveling for inspiration in the jungles or the plains, is unpredictable. Lily does not appreciate unpredictability. She reads the endings of novels first and never watches telenovelas, not even those written by her husband, which undergo many nerve-racking twists and turns, and take too long to come to a resolution. In her work and in her life, she likes straight angles and areas with well-defined, proportionate boundaries, efficiency of space. She has installed hidden storage units in her kitchen, stocked with utensils and household supplies, in neat, regimented rows. She stows her passions and desires in the same way. Spontaneous, unexpected bursts of emotion are quickly reined in, put in their place, though she finds such exercise of control increasingly difficult ever since she became pregnant. But this, she believes, is simply a matter of hormones; it will pass as soon as her body is her own again.

"Why don't you let me make the breakfast today; I'll be out in a moment," calls Consuelo.

"Don't worry, Mami, I can manage," she says.

She pours the milk and the water for coffee into separate pans to boil. She lightly fries the arepas until they have formed a skin, places them on a brightly hand-painted plate, a souvenir from her father's travels. She likes this plate because, besides being cheerful and attractive, it can go in the oven with the arepas.

She squeezes fresh orange juice into a glass pitcher and heaps coffee into the old-fashioned French percolator, which she received as a wedding present from her godmother, Amparo Aguilar. From the refrigerator, she removes butter, queso blanco, and ham, and places them on another, less dramatic plate. Around these, she symmetrically arranges slices of avocado sprinkled with salt, pepper, and a dash of lemon juice. She sets the table for breakfast. Pouring two cups of coffee, to which she adds frothy boiled milk and a single spoon of sugar, she takes her seat at the table. While she waits for her mother to join her, she slips her hand into the pocket of her kimono, draws out the letter from Irene, reads it again.

Consuelo enters the kitchen, eyes still puffy with sleep, and kisses her daughter lightly on the lips.

"Buenos días, Mami," says Lily, placing the letter back in her pocket.

"Buenos días, cariño. And what were you reading just now with such concentration?"

"I found a letter yesterday in a box of old school things. It revived so many memories."

"Good memories, I hope?" says Consuelo. "Are you glad

I didn't throw all your things away in spite of all your criticisms about hanging on to old junk?"

"Yes, you were right, I'm glad you kept them. The letter is from Irene. Do you remember her? Te acuerdas, Mami?"

"Ay," sighs Consuelo, "who can forget her?"

"I wish I knew what happened to her."

Not knowing what happened to Irene bothers Lily in the manner of a faint itchiness. Without that knowledge, she feels incomplete, unresolved, part of a never-ending story. But her mother changes the subject abruptly, "Have you heard from your madrina? She promised to be here in time for the delivery of your baby."

"I'm sure she'll be here; she knows we're depending on her. Anyway, Mami, about Irene—"

Carlos Alberto comes into the kitchen, sniffing the air hungrily. He is already dressed in brown corduroys and a black pullover, his Sunday uniform. Carlos Alberto kisses his mother-in-law good morning and moves behind Lily's chair. He bends and plants a wet, sucking kiss on her neck in the special place that gives her goose bumps. He smells of lime soap and shaving cream. She turns her head to catch his lips with hers, but the kiss is interrupted by the doorbell.

Carlos Alberto opens the door. It is Marta's daughter, Luz. Returning her quick embrace, Carlos Alberto says, "You're just in time for our special Sunday breakfast." He ushers Luz toward the kitchen, where Lily and Consuelo are seated at the table.

"¡Ay, qué bueno, Luz!" says Lily, pulling herself to a standing position, opening her arms in welcome. "What a lovely surprise!"

"So, what are you cooking?" asks Luz, smiling, as she walks toward her embrace.

"We are cooking up life!" Lily says, patting her belly, just before she slips on a patch of spilled milk and crashes to the floor.

The new girl stood out like a neon sign in her white frilly dress with pink ribbons on the first day of school. Cinnamon skin, and green eyes far older than her ten years. Her long dark brown hair was primly pinned back from her face on both sides of her middle parting with delicate gold-plated barrettes, making her look quaint and old-fashioned, a girl from another era. But what struck Lily was the contrast between the daintiness of the girl's attire and the tremendous size of her feet, which were encased in lacy ankle-socks and white patent leather shoes. A size thirty-seven, por lo menos, Lily thought.

"This is Irene Dos Santos," said Señora Gutierrez, the principal of Academia Roosevelt, the bilingual American school built with American oil money, which shone like a sparkling jewel in the sun above the filthy, poverty-stricken barrio of Las Ruinas.

Only the medium to very rich could afford to send their children to the prestigious Academia Roosevelt, and even then there was a long waiting list. To Lily's good fortune, her godfather was Alejandro Aguilar, media magnate and jefe of the regional television station TVista. Alejandro Aguilar was also on the board of directors at Academia Roosevelt, and so Lily's enrollment had been a foregone conclusion.

Señora Gutierrez was holding the new girl's hand. "I want you to take Irene to the fifth-grade homeroom and help her get oriented," she said to Lily, and to the new girl, "Irene, this is Lily Martinez."

Irene cast her eyes to the ground, where one self-conscious foot tried to hide the other one.

"Come on," Lily said, taking her hand and feeling superior in her skintight jeans and platform shoes, "let's go."

That was the first and last day Lily saw Irene in a dress.

"You looked so saintly," Lily said to her later, when they'd become best friends and told each other everything.

"Coño, its true," she said, "Mercedes made me wear that dress. You must have thought I was an imbecile." Irene always referred to her mother by her name, with an intrepid modernity that took Lily's breath away. Since no one, apart from the maid, was ever at the Dos Santos residence between three p.m. and eight p.m. or even later, Irene usually came back with Lily, and Lily's father would drop her home after dinner.

On most weekdays after school, Consuelo would make the girls sandwiches stuffed with the previous night's milanesas, before they rushed off to roller-skate at the Plaza Altamira.

"Cuídense bien, muchachas," Consuelo would say, kissing them both before they left, "and be back by seven."

"Your mother is such a great cook, and really sweet, tan linda," said Irene.

"I know," said Lily, "I don't know what I would do without my mother. Probably starve." And then they giggled in that hormone-induced borderline psychotic schoolgirl way.

Life at the Dos Santos residence and that at the Martinez residence was as different as night and day. At Lily's house people sat round the table together and talked about food, art, and politics, whereas at Irene's nobody sat at the table and the focus was on diets, fashion, cute boys, and the right combination of Johnson's Baby Oil and iodine to make the most effective suntan lotion.

Irene lived in a luxurious penthouse apartment with expansive terraces in the upmarket Urbanización of Prados, along with her older sister, Zulema, who was studying interior design, and her parents, Mercedes and Benigno.

In a large enclosure in the midst of the terrace garden, Irene kept a baby water boa as a pet. Sometimes, while she did her homework, she liked to hang it around her neck. Lily thought this wildly and wonderfully adventurous, though she herself was never brave enough to try it. The Dos Santos family had moved to Tamanaco from the capital when Irene's father, an engineering expert on earthquakes and landslides, was transferred by the Ministerio de Obras Públicas.

Mercedes and Benigno. A couple of such extraordinary incongruity that Lily was taken by surprise each time she saw them together, which was rarely. Benigno Dos Santos was a large man, bearded to disguise a weak chin, a polished passive-aggressive personality of few words who spent his time after office hours in his study with a view of the mountains, sipping vodka martinis and listening to Italian opera on the stereo. Which always seemed strange and disappointing to Lily, given that he was half Brazilian; Lily had expected Carnival in Rio. The voluptuous Mercedes, a mestiza of Chilean, African, and Guajiro descent, spent five days a week in the coastal town of Puerto, where she had a successful gunrunning business, a beach house, and a string of young, adoring lovers. Mercedes Dos Santos hated Pavarotti. Billy Ocean was more her speed.

"Pero, Benigno, why does your music have to be at TODO VOLUMEN?" she would yell when she came home on the weekend.

"Perdón, mi amor," he would say, cranking up the volume even louder.

Mercedes slept separately from her husband, in a room off the kitchen that was technically the servant's quarters but was actually the brightest and best-ventilated room in the apartment. No one was allowed to use the kitchen when Mercedes was home. The noise and smells bothered her, she said. This was probably why the Dos Santos family never sat down to dinner together. In fact, there was rarely any normal food in the house. At the Dos Santos residence everyone drank strong black coffee and dined at odd hours on expensive snacks—anchovies on toast, caviar on cream crackers, grapes and cheese, and their all-time favorite, sandwiches stuffed with Diablitos. That is, whenever Mercedes had remembered to stock the kitchen at all, which was about fifty percent of the time. The other fifty percent of the time, the refrigerator contained only beer.

In all likelihood, it was pure hunger that prompted Irene and Lily to fry bacon and eggs, purchased with their pocket money from the kiosk down the road, on the flat of an electric clothing iron in the bathroom. Somehow, these messy concoctions always ended up tasting more delicious to Lily than even her mother's cooking. Stomachs appeased, they would invade Zulema's closet and try on all her clothes, taking whatever they wanted for school the following day.

Mercedes Dos Santos, a devotee of the goddess Maria Lionza, believed in commemorating a girl's passage into womanhood with the onset of menses using rituals entirely of her own invention.

"Okay, muchachas," said Mercedes on the day Irene got her period (Lily was ahead of her friend by a month), "today, we are celebrating your womanhood. Ya son todas unas mujercitas. I'm going to teach you how to walk."

"Ay, don't be ridiculous, Mami," said Irene. "We know how to walk."

"You walk like boys," said Mercedes. "That is not the way for a woman to walk. A woman must walk like this." She strolled across the terrace, moving her hips in an exaggerated figure eight. "Vamos, muchachas, now you try it. Muevan las caderas."

They spent the afternoon swinging their hips around on the terrace until Irene said she felt like throwing up. Then Mercedes, in a rare display of maternity, put her to bed with a hot water bottle.

In the evening, Lily wandered into her mother's kitchen, swaying her hips in a figure eight and feeling very grown up—toda una mujer.

"What is wrong with you?" asked Consuelo, raising her eyebrows, and exchanging an amused glance with Marta.

"Nothing," said Lily, and went back to her room to practice the woman-walk.

When they were thirteen, Lily and Irene auditioned for the Roosevelt school play, since Irene thought she might want to be an actress when she grew up. That year it was *The Wizard of Oz*. They appeared together for two auditions—one to assess their spoken English-language skills, the other to determine their musical talent. Both girls were selected: Irene as Dorothy, and Lily as the Good Witch. Exuberantly, they embarked on a shopping expedition for red shoes in Irene's size, but they were unsuccessful in their quest.

"Let's look in my mother's closet," Lily suggested. Together, they foraged in Consuelo's closet until they found what they were looking for: a pair of old-fashioned but well-preserved red satin pumps lying inside a box that also contained some letters tied with blue ribbon. Irene wanted to read the letters, but Lily said her mother wouldn't like it. "Try the shoes on." They were a tight fit, but Irene managed to squeeze into them. Consuelo had gone to the grocery store, and they had to get back to the theatre for the dress rehearsal, so Lily said, "Just take them. She won't mind if we just borrow them; she never wears them. I'll tell her about it later."

The rehearsal went well, though Lily forgot one of her lines, and the director commented favorably on the red shoes. "Perfect," she said. "When the light shines on them, they look like rubies." Afterward, the girls took a taxi to Irene's, where they sat on the floor in the bathroom smoking stolen Astors from the silver cigarette case in Benigno's study.

"I'm bored," said Irene, after they had finished their cigarettes.

"Me too," said Lily, mirroring, as always, Irene's mood. "What shall we do?"

"Have you ever studied yourself aquí?" asked Irene, pointing to her vagina.

"Asco. Don't be disgusting," Lily said.

"No, I mean it," said Irene. "I do it all the time. You should try it. We can do it together, right now." Nothing embarrassed Irene.

"Forget it," said Lily.

Though Irene could usually persuade Lily to follow her lead, Lily had more conventional ideas of what was acceptable and what was not, and sometimes Irene went too far. Like the time they both had their periods during the same week. Irene had tried to convince her that if they mixed their menstrual blood together and buried it in the garden, they would be bound as sisters and their children would be hermanos.

Lily can't pinpoint when it all turned around—when they had exchanged roles and she, Lily, mutated fully from leader into disciple. Perhaps this gradual, imperceptible shift in the balance of power originated with Irene's discovery that she could fit perfectly into her sister Zulema's designer jeans, which were much more expensive and cooler than theirs. Irene wasn't selfish about her discovery, though, and readily lent Lily anything she coveted from Zulema's brimming walk-in closet. And Zulema didn't seem to mind, as long as they didn't choose anything she wanted to use on one of her dates the same night. Irene and Lily were the same size. Except for their feet. Only Lily could fit into Zulema's tiny shoes. Still, that didn't give her any advantage in the power equation. Irene had clearly become the controller in their society of two.

It was Irene who taught Lily how to French-kiss. They practiced on each other for three weeks before they were ready to try it with boys. And Irene tried it first. It was also from Irene that Lily inherited Elvis Crespo, a thirteen-year-old boy from the Prados neighborhood with jet-black hair and roguish grey eyes, who loved girls at an age when most boys still hated them.

"He's too young," said Irene. "I like them to be older than me. But he's a fantastic kisser."

Though the general consensus would be otherwise, it wasn't really Irene's fault that their Spanish teacher from the Academia Roosevelt caught Elvis and Lily with their tongues swirling around each other's mouths.

Meeting at the elevator in the lobby of Irene's apartment building one day after school, Elvis and Lily had pressed the penthouse button and agreed to kiss all the way up to the fifteenth floor. They were therefore unprepared when the elevator stopped, impromptu, on the fifth floor and the door slid open to reveal Señora Ramirez, who had been visiting her married daughter in the same building. Out of the corner of her eye, her mouth still locked on Elvis's, Lily saw Señora Ramirez raise her manicured hand to her own mouth, her eyes bulging behind tortoise-shell spectacles. "Ay, Dios mío," she exclaimed, just as Elvis, without taking his lips from Lily's, or removing his left hand from her bottom, reached to the side with his right hand and slammed the Close Door button with the heel of his hand.

"Mierda. That was my Spanish literature teacher," Lily said, laughing into his mouth. "Coño, Elvis, did you see her face? What if she's having a heart attack at this very moment!"

"Shut up," said Elvis, grabbing her hips with both hands. "We still have eleven floors to kiss."

Bursting with righteous indignation and concern for Lily's welfare, Señora Ramirez called the house the very same afternoon. It was Luz, Marta's daughter of the same age as Lily, who took the call. Luz had always been a tattletale.

When Lily got home and saw her mother's face, she knew she was grounded before she even crossed the threshold.

Irene emotionally rushed to Lily's defense when Lily phoned to whisper the news while Consuelo was in the shower.

"That bitch!" Irene yelled. "She's nothing but an old BOLSA FRUSTRADA. She probably hasn't done it in FIFTY YEARS. Listen, Lily, do you want me to come over and tell your mother it's a lie? I'll do it, if you want me to. I'll say I was in the elevator with you and Elvis, and that Ramirez is just one BIG FAT LIAR."

There were times when even Lily winced at the ferocity of Irene's language, when she was shocked by Irene's capacity for deception. But she knew the point was that Irene wanted to save her if Lily would let her.

"No," said Lily, "thanks, but I never lie to my mother."

"It won't be your lie," said Irene, who, Lily had observed, lied to Mercedes almost every time they had a conversation, "it'll be mine." And, for a moment, Lily was tempted, knowing that when her father learned of her French-kissing adventure—as he was bound to, since her mother told her father everything—she'd be grounded until she was an old maid. But Lily also knew that if she let Irene do this for her, she would never feel right again with her mother, and her mother would know. Consuelo always knew what Lily was feeling, sometimes even before Lily did herself.

"No," she said. "I'd rather get it over with."

"Okay," said Irene, "but call me back first thing in the morning and let me know what happened."

One thing about Irene, she always had to know everything. And Lily always had to tell her.

"Okay," she agreed. But over the weekend her mother and Marta watched her as if they had eyes at the back of their heads, and Lily couldn't elude their scrutiny long enough to make the call.

By Monday morning, Lily was enrolled in the school

attended by Marta's daughter, Luz. It was a convent boarding school in Valencia, two hours' drive from Tamanaco. Lily could still be in the Roosevelt school play, since it was only one night, and her parents didn't want to ruin it for the Academia Roosevelt, but that was it. She was no longer allowed to visit Irene, or to invite Irene over.

The next time Lily had the opportunity to speak with Irene was in the dressing room of the Carreño Theatre on the night of their first performance of *The Wizard of Oz*.

"They're sending me to a convent boarding school in Valencia where Luz goes," said Lily morosely, slipping into her white-witch dress.

"¡No puede ser!" Irene exclaimed.

"I'm not allowed to talk to you after the play is over."

"Ay, you poor thing. But don't worry, we can find a way, we can write letters."

At that Lily brightened slightly. "Don't forget to return my mother's shoes, or I'll be in even worse trouble."

Though not ordinarily one to place much stock in possessions, when Lily confessed that she'd lent the shoes to Irene for the play, Consuelo had been upset.

"I met your father in those shoes," she sighed.

The play received a standing ovation from an audience comprised predominantly of parents, teachers, and American consulate or oil company personnel. After the performance, as they were leaving the dressing room, Lily recalled her promise to her mother. But Irene said the red shoes must have accidentally gone back to the school with the costumes and that she would retrieve them the next day. Several days passed and, in Lily's presence, Consuelo phoned to congratulate Irene on her performance as Dorothy and to ask when she could retrieve her shoes, which, she explained, were of great sentimental value to her.

"I'm so sorry, Señora Consuelo," Irene said, "but they are missing. I've looked everywhere. My parents would be happy to pay for a new pair."

"That won't be necessary," said Consuelo.

It was Consuelo's idea to send Lily to the same school as Luz. Lily was certain this was because Luz was an incurable tattletale who could be counted on to report everything. She thought it hypocritical of her father, who didn't believe in a Christian God and had never stepped into a church after the day he married her mother, to endorse such a plan. And she said as much to Ismael, who conveyed her message to her mother, with whom Lily refused to speak. But Consuelo replied loudly enough for her daughter to hear, that between teenage boys with an itch in their pantalones and Catholic school, Catholic school was definitely the lesser evil.

From the age of ten until the last time Lily saw her at the age of fifteen, Irene thought nothing of walking around her family's penthouse dressed in bikini panties and a short, tight T-shirt that ended just above her belly button and said, *Mefiez-vous des enfants sages*. Dressed in this manner, Irene would sometimes wander into the study where her father sat drinking martinis and listening to opera at what Mercedes claimed was a thousand decibels above the human safety level. Climbing into his lap, she would wrap her arms around her neck and lay her head upon his shoulder. Benigno, clutching a vodka martini in one hand, would place his free arm around his daughter and bellow out the words to the music. This is how Lily found them when, after a gap of two years at convent school, she was finally allowed to visit Irene and invite her on a family trip to Maquiritare.

"She is with her father," said the maid. "Wait here."

Lily stood in the hallway while the maid knocked on the door of Benigno's study and called out, "La Señorita Lily, para la Señorita Irene." The door was ajar and from where Lily stood, she could see Irene with her father. She watched, mesmerized. Irene's profusion of hair swirled, obscuring the faces of both father and daughter from Lily's view. Long legs, his encased in brown silk pajamas, hers bare, ending in old-fashioned red satin pumps, creating a tableau of some mythical and wonderful four-legged life form.

Many years later, on a rainy Saturday in the month of August, Lily sought to re-create this image with Carlos Alberto. She made him pose in his pajamas on a leather lounge chair with a martini glass in one hand. She arranged his legs out in front of him.

"The things you come up with!" he exclaimed. But he played along anyway.

She positioned her husband's tripod and set his camera on automatic, before leaping into his lap wearing a T-shirt, bikini panties, and red heels. She flung her long brown hair about them. As soon as the flash went off, Carlos Alberto ran his tongue lightly along the nape of her neck and they made love right there in the leather chair. Afterward, Lily rushed the film to the photo shop downtown, which promised delivery of prints in two hours. She could barely contain her excitement while she waited for the chemicals to perform their magic. But her compositional masterpiece emerged from the dark room as a double exposure, with a close-up of her parents on their twenty-fifth wedding anniversary, their faces smiling radiantly, the figures of Carlos Alberto and Lily herself vaguely outlined, ghostlike, in the background.

The obstetrician confirmed Lily's pregnancy on the last day of October, one day before their birthday. They were born on the same day, Lily and Consuelo. And Lily could hardly wait to give her mother the birthday present.

"Mami!" she yelled, bursting through the front door, with Carlos Alberto close on her heels. "Guess what, Mami, buenas noticias, I'm going to have a baby!"

They had waited and wanted for so long and nothing had seemed to work. Not the beach weekends and sexy fantasies they devised to arouse themselves into a frenzy of passion. Not the fertility drugs. Not the humiliation of holding her legs suspended in midair for half an hour directly following intercourse. Finally, and in spite of Carlos Alberto's objections, she had gone to her godmother, Amparo.

"Don't worry, mija," Amparo had said when Lily told her she felt helpless. "These things have their own time. But there is no law that says we can't help speed them along." And she had handed Lily a bag of herbs. "This is Amantilla. Chew a leaf before you sleep with your husband. This one," she said, handing Lily another bag, "is Maca. It is for Carlos Alberto; he must take it as an infusion once a day. And this may sound crazy, mi vida, and I don't know why it is so, but making love on rainy days will improve your chances of conception."

"¡Feliz cumpleaños, Mami!" Lily shouted, racing toward the kitchen. "You're going to be an abuela!"

But her mother had not replied. How could she when she was lying unconscious in the garden?

"What is wrong with my mother?" Lily whispered when the elderly family doctor had finished his examination and given Carlos Alberto a list for the pharmacy.

"It is her heart," he replied with what seemed to Lily a preposterous calm. "Fortunately not a major attack, and she is stable now, but she'll need complete bed rest for a while."

Lily had the sensation of being swept away by a strong current. She could taste her mother's heart in her mouth: metallic, pulsating, blood red.

"You should notify your father," the doctor said.

"I would if I could, Doctor," said Lily, suddenly angry, "but he is somewhere in the Delta, and there is no way to contact him by phone."

"Your mother is lucky that you happened to arrive in time. Otherwise . . . well, she really shouldn't be left on her own in her condition."

When Consuelo was well enough to leave the hospital, Lily said, "You can't stay alone, Mami, while Papi roams the country looking for inspiration. You will have to stay with Carlos Alberto and me. . . . Coño su madre, why can't he stay in Tamanaco?"

"Don't judge your father so harshly, Lily," Consuelo said. "Can he help it if his work takes him away from us?"

"Mami, por favor, stop making excuses for him. Can't

a poet work from imagination and memory? Why can't he work from his studio at home like you do? He is seventy-five years old, and still he runs wild in the llanos and who knows where."

Consuelo turned her face to her daughter, but looked beyond her.

"It is who he is. And who he is, is the man I love. Do you know that every year since we met, he has written me a love song? Ay." Consuelo sighed, her tongue loosened by medication. "Cuanto lo amo. Even now, at this age, I long to wrap my arms and legs around that man and draw him into myself."

Lily had been shocked by the raw desire in her mother's eyes. The eyes of a woman still deeply in love with her husband of forty-one years.

Until that moment, Lily had never really thought of Ismael in any terms other than as her father. A father who shared himself with todo el mundo, a father more absent than present. On the other hand, when he was present, he had never failed to fill her days with wonder and adventure.

One day, he had brought her the moon.

It was a Sunday morning, the morning of her sixth birthday and her mother's forty-seventh. Lily heard a loud honking in the driveway and peered over the balcony to see her father smiling up at her from the window of a silver car with fins gleaming in the sunlight.

"Mami, guess what—Papi has brought home a car like a big fish!" Lily shouted.

A few minutes later, the three of them stood out in the

driveway surveying the Lancer station wagon. Ismael said he had purchased it secondhand on the meager salary doled out by the government Department for the Preservation of National Parks, Forests and Protected Areas where he worked to supplement the intermittent sales of his wife's paintings, infinite interpretations and permutations of the flowering passion fruit vine. Every available space in the house was crammed with her work, completed or in progress — a wild, violent collage of color and form that leapt out at the eye from every wall in every room. Not even the bathrooms were spared, which prompted Lily's godfather, Alejandro, to wonder how anyone could be expected to have a decent bowel movement while under such an assault. "Do you close your eyes when you sit on the toilet?" he asked, playfully poking Lily in the ribs.

Pointing to the car, Ismael turned to his wife and said, "Happy birthday, mi amor! Now you'll be able to do your shopping for the whole week at one time."

"You know I can't drive," said Consuelo, kissing her husband on the cheek.

"I will teach you," said Ismael. "Come, we'll practice right now."

For an hour, Consuelo practiced taking the car in and out of the driveway, while Lily watched from the window. Then Ismael drove them all to the Plaza Altamira, where they bought bread from the Panadería Sosa.

"Nice car," said Señor Sosa, coming out to admire it and running a gnarled hand along one of its shiny fins.

They ate the warm bread in the car, while Ismael drove. As they turned onto the highway and the car accelerated, Lily screamed with excitement and wet her pants. Then she cried, while her mother attempted unsuccessfully to console her. It was only when her father assured her that everybody peed in their pants their first time on the highway that her tears dried.

"What about Mami?" she asked, as they drove at a more leisurely pace through the gated residential park of Lagunita. Pulling up in front of the Aguilar mansion, Ismael whispered in her ear, "Mami has her own special powers. One of them is the power to hold her pipí even in the most dire of circumstances." When Lily laughed through her tears, he said, "That's better, we can't have you wet on both ends, can we? Now, we will clean you up and then your padrino and I have another special surprise for your birthday."

While Lily, wrapped in a giant beach towel and eating an arepa stuffed with Diablitos, sat on Alejandro's lap, Amparo threw her soiled clothes in the American-made washing machine. Within twenty minutes they were dry, and moments later Lily was dressed and on her way to the Lagunita stables with her father and godfather.

"She's groomed and ready, Señor Alejandro," said the stable boy when they arrived. Holding Lily's hand, Alejandro led her to a stall in which stood a magnificent silver filly, puffing and stamping her feet. "Señorita Lily, allow me to introduce you to Luna," said Alejandro.

"Ay, Padrino, she is the most beautiful thing I have ever seen!" Lily said, her voice trembling with both fear and marvel. "Where did you get her?"

"She is a gift to you from your father's friend, Diego García. But since you have no place to keep a horse, she will live here, in my stable. When you are a little older, your father will teach you to ride her."

Lily stared at her father. He was simply full of surprises that day.

Late in the afternoon Lily sat on the sofa in front of the black-and-white TV in the living room watching the one program her father allowed, *El Zorro*. "Mira, Papi," said Lily, "El Zorro's horse, Tornado, looks just like ours."

"Can you keep a secret?" Ismael asked.

Lily nodded solemnly.

"Well," said Ismael, "our horse looks like Tornado because she is the daughter of Tornado."

Lily's jaw dropped in admiration, because if her father's horse was the daughter of Tornado, it meant her father must be amigos with El Zorro. Then she frowned. "But, Papi," she said, "how can our horse be Tornado's daughter if she is in Padrino's stables and Tornado is inside the television?"

"Ah," said Ismael, "you're a clever one, aren't you? But there is an answer. And the answer is that El Zorro is a brujo with a magic horse who can be in two places at once. And how do I know this? I know because El Zorro is my secret identity. And it is only fitting that the daughter of El Zorro should ride the daughter of Tornado. Not only that, but your Tío Alejandro also has a secret identity; he is Speed Racer and drives the Mach 5." Alejandro Aguilar had recently replaced his red 1954 Corvette with the 1968 version in metallic blue.

"Ay, por Dios, Ismael," said Consuelo, who had come in during the revelation of Alejandro's secret identity, "don't tease her and fill her head with mentiras like that." But she was smiling.

Ismael turned to Lily, placed a finger to his lips and winked. And Lily understood that this meant the true identity of El

Zorro was a secret only she and her father and her godfather shared. She winked back and whispered, "Can we tell Mami the secret?" And Consuelo had rolled her eyes as Ismael replied in a stage whisper, "Only if she swears to keep it under wraps, and learns the secret Zorro Code. I'll have to teach the both of you."

Every day, when her father dropped her off at the Academia Roosevelt, Lily winked at him as she stepped out of the car and flashed the secret code, which consisted of writing a big *Z* in the air with the index finger of her right hand. She was almost nine before she understood, with the sorrow of one who discovers that it is the parents who put the Christmas presents under the tree and not San Nicolás, that her father was not really El Zorro—and that El Zorro himself wasn't even a real person. She was even more disappointed to learn that El Zorro wasn't even Criollo, but an import from gringolandia. But not long afterward, she discovered such a wonderful thing about her father that it didn't really matter that he wasn't El Zorro; she discovered that Ismael really *was* a brujo who could be in two places at one time.

For Lily's fifteenth birthday, Ismael announced a family trip to the jungles of Maquiritare during the Christmas holidays. He told Lily she could invite anyone she chose, and she disingenuously chose Irene Dos Santos. At first both her parents resisted, but later, yielding under their daughter's relentless onslaught ("You said *anyone*"), they agreed. After all, what real harm could come of it, with both girls under their direct supervision for the duration of the trip? But Lily's gladness at finally being reunited with Irene was marred by what she had seen, or thought she had seen, when she went to Prados to fetch Irene: her mother's red satin shoes.

Since traveling by road to Maquiritare would take days, the four of them — Ismael, Consuelo, Lily, and Irene — flew in a propeller plane that belonged to Alejandro Aguilar. The plane's choppy movements turned Lily's stomach and made her spew her lunch on the tarmac when they landed.

It was dusk by the time they were installed in their cabaña at the government-run tourist outpost in the province of Maquiritare. Everyone voted to have a dinner immediately and make it an early night. The girls slept in hammocks on the porch. But before they fell asleep, to make up for her humiliation on the tarmac, Lily whispered to Irene, "Tomorrow let's swim across to the island in the middle of the lagoon."

"I'll race you," Irene whispered back.

Early in the morning they took a hike through the forest and then a canoe trip through the estuaries with their Pemon Indian guide, and Irene seemed far more interested than Lily had thought she'd be, asking about the flora — what is this and what is that. And Ismael had obliged her, rattling off a list of names until Lily felt her head spin. "Perhaps I will be a botanist when I grow up," Irene said.

When they returned at two p.m., the girls were ravenous and ate two chicken sandwiches each. Afterward, Consuelo and Ismael withdrew to the cabaña for a nap, while Lily and Irene lay dozing in the hammocks on the veranda. Her eyes heavy, Lily said sleepily that they should forget about swimming to the island. "Besides, our swimsuits are inside."

"We don't need swimsuits to swim," said Irene, jumping

up and grabbing her by the arm. "Come on!" They stepped onto the sand, but it was too hot. Lily had her sandals, but Irene's sneakers were inside the cabaña. Not to be deterred, Irene walked along the stone pathway to the neighboring cabaña, which was rented out by a single man. She plucked a pair of flip-flops from the porch and waved them triumphantly in the air before slipping her feet into them. They were a perfect fit.

Together, the girls ran to the beach and stripped to their underwear. Wading in until the water reached their chests, they surveyed the distance to the island.

"It's not that far," said Lily, though she was starting to have her doubts.

"Bueno, gafa, what are we waiting for?" said Irene, throwing up the challenge.

Both girls had joined the junior swim team at Academia Roosevelt the year Irene decided she wanted to be a professional swimmer, and the team was a contender for the national championships. Lily was then transferred to the convent school, which had no swim team, and Irene had gone on to captain the Academia Roosevelt team to victory. Lily had concentrated on riding Luna who was stabled at the Valencia Riding Club, taking the first prize in three equestrian events for two consecutive years. But her blue satin riding ribbons had no relevance in the world she had shared with Irene before they were separated, and Lily wanted to prove that she was also still as good a swimmer as her friend.

They started swimming on the count of three, making rapid progress to the midpoint between the camp shore and the island, marked by a buoy. But it was a longer distance than it had seemed from the shore and, after a hundred and fifty meters, both girls began to tire, their strokes becoming uneven.

"¡No puedo más!" Irene panted, just as Lily felt her stomach cramp. She instantly regretted the chicken sandwiches consumed not half an hour earlier.

Treading water, Lily said, "I can make it."

"No you can't, you ate as many sandwiches as I did," Irene panted.

"Yes I can."

"You're lying."

That was how it started. There in the middle of the lake, Lily confronted Irene about the red shoes.

"You're the liar," Lily screamed back. "You told me my mother's shoes were stolen after the play, but I saw you wearing them when you were with your father in the study before you hid them behind the door. Además, I'm sure that charm bracelet you have been wearing belongs to Luz. I should never have invited such a ladrona mentirosa. I wish you were dead." Lily turned around, facing the distant shore where their swim had begun. Her arms, legs, and chest were aching. A few feet away, Irene was swimming toward her, her face furious, her arms slapping the water. The next thing Lily knew, Irene had seized her by the shoulders, dunking her, climbing onto her back, locking her legs around Lily's waist. Lily sank deeper with the weight. Twisting, she managed to slip from Irene's stranglehold, come up for air, and start paddling toward the shore. But Irene ferociously grabbed her by the hair and pulled her backward, her other arm clamped against Lily's windpipe. As Lily clawed at Irene's arm, the charm bracelet came loose in her hand. She clutched it in her fist, beating at Irene's arm that continued to press into her throat.

"Take it back," Irene yelled, as Lily went under again. "Take back what you said."

Just as Lily's lungs began their silent scream for release, she heard her father's voice. "Calma, mi amor. Remember what I taught you."

Summoning every reserve of strength she had left, she coiled and pushed, spun around in the water, drew her arm back, and hit Irene full in the face with the heel of her hand. Irene's head snapped back and blood spurted from her nose. Then Irene began to sink. Lily tried to reach out to her, but exhaustion made this impossible. And she, too, began to sink.

Lily said she remembered waking up in the hammock on the veranda of the cabaña, with Irene next to her.

"I dreamt that we were swimming in the laguna. We had a fight in the water and we almost drowned," she said.

"Don't be silly," said Irene. "Why would best friends fight?"

"I said I wished you were dead. But it's not true."

"It was only a dream. Forget it. Now, listen, I want to tell you a secret. Remember the guy I introduced you to that day we met at the Hotel Macuto last year? The reason I came here with you is because he's going to meet me here."

"When? When is he meeting you?"

"Right now."

"Now?"

"Yes, now. I'm supposed to walk about one hundred meters down the path into the forest. If anyone asks you where I am, say that I went for a walk, okay? Delay as long as possible."

"Okay."

"Promise?"

"I promise."

Irene embraced her, saying she would write when she and her indio got settled. And Lily watched her walk into the forest. Then she fell back asleep, waking only when her parents emerged from the cabaña just before sunset.

"Where is Irene?" her mother asked.

"She went for a walk."

"Why is your hair wet?"

Her father interrupted before Lily could answer. "Let her be, mi amor," he said.

Lily believed then that her father was special; that he could hear her thoughts and visit her dreams. She still believes it. That is why nearly twenty years later, as she fights against the doctor's recommendation of a Cesarean in the hospital room, she is not surprised to see her father appear like a vision, to find herself in his arms, being carried out of the hospital. And so, at the age of thirty-four, she is finally forced to acknowledge that there are times when her father's unpredictability has its advantages.

Carlos Alberto pulls into the driveway, and Marta, having returned an hour earlier to a mysteriously empty house, opens the door with a furrowed brow. Though visibly shaken she quickly takes charge, guiding Carlos Alberto, who is carrying Lily, to the living room sofa, where he sits, still holding her too tightly against his chest. Marta touches the bruise on Lily's forehead lightly, peers into her face. "What happened?" she asks.

Lily closes her eyes; the burden of explaining is beyond her. Carlos Alberto answers on her behalf, "She fell and hurt herself. At the hospital they wanted to deliver the baby by Cesarean section, to be on the safe side, but she refused. And then..." He gestures wordlessly toward her father, Ismael, who stands framed in the doorway.

Her mother says, "Lily wanted to come home and wait for Amparo to arrive before making any major decisions. It is only a matter of a day or two. In the meantime, Doctor Ricardo will come to check on her in the evenings. We'll make up the daybed in the living room so that we can keep an eye on her and she on us. Come, Luz, you can help me."

The living room is the hub of the airy modern bungalow she has designed for herself and Carlos Alberto. It is her second favorite room, after the kitchen, with a high ceiling and large French doors leading to the patio and garden. In the living room she will never be alone and she will be able to see and know what is going on in the house. She realizes her decision to leave the hospital is virtually incomprehensible to Carlos Alberto, who thinks that doctors know everything. But she is certain, from the way her womb had clenched at the word *Cesarean,* that the doctor is wrong. She might not have had the strength to convince Carlos Alberto to take her away, might still be there, might at this very moment be under the surgeon's knife, had her father not materialized out of nowhere, plucked her from the hospital bed, and simply spirited her out of the hospital. Suddenly, the thought of Dr. Ricardo Uzoátegui running after them waving assorted papers, in a panic over the breach in hospital check-out procedure, makes her want to laugh out loud, an impulse she controls out of loyalty to Carlos Alberto, who she is sure does not find any of this amusing.

◈

"Someone has cast the evil eye on you," says Marta, propping Lily with pillows on the daybed. "We must seek divine protection." She fingers the string of extended rosary beads she habitually wears around her neck. In the place where a crucifix should be, there is an image of Maria Lionza.

Lily smiles. Marta is never hesitant to include Maria Lionza in mortal matters. Her candles and offerings and spells for every domestic crisis and national calamity have been a peripheral part of the household life for as long as she has worked for Lily's family, a family whose primary religion has always been individual expression. It would not occur to anyone to ridicule Marta's devotion or interfere with it in any way. They indulge its marginally obtrusive manifestations in their lives—the rope of garlic hanging in the kitchen window, the small statuettes on their bedside tables, the burning of colored candles and herbs, the murmuring of incantations. Even Carlos Alberto has come to regard Marta's magical beliefs with indulgence and has, on occasion, been persuaded to carry a charm for protection in his pocket. Her diagnosis comes as no surprise to anyone.

"We will start a Novena to Maria Lionza this very night," Marta decides.

According to Marta, nine days before a baby comes into the world, its soul is born and wanders between the human world and the world of spirits, looking for the body it has been destined to inhabit. If the evil eye is cast before the soul finds its home, it continues to wander, lost between worlds. In order to guide the soul to the body, it is advisable to seek the help of Maria Lionza, for it is she who lights up the path for souls that are lost.

"How do we go about it, Marta?" asks Lily agreeably, glad for the distraction, but hoping that Marta's remedy doesn't involve anything grisly such as chicken's blood or pig's feet.

"Go about what?" says Luz, returning from the kitchen with her third beer.

Lily pats the side of the bed for Luz to sit next to her, then holds her hand up, saying, "Let's wait for Mami."

When Consuelo joins them in the living room moments later, Marta says, "Every night for nine nights, beginning tonight, we will say the Rosary of Maria Lionza and ask for her blessings." Luz, a self-proclaimed atheist, rolls her eyes and groans, but stops when Lily shoots her a beseeching glance. Marta ignores her daughter and goes to the kitchen to look for candles.

The sight of Carlos Alberto walking up and down on the patio is distracting, and Lily wants to divert him. When Marta leaves the room, she says loudly, "Carlos Alberto is the expert on Maria Lionza, aren't you, darling? Come and tell us about her."

Carlos Alberto stops pacing and returns to the living room, where he draws a chair up to the daybed. With Lily nodding encouragingly, he explains that unlike the traditional rosary, the rosary of Maria Lionza has seven decades instead of five. Each decade, he says, is dedicated to one of the seven courts of the goddess, which comprise a pantheon: the Court of Maria Lionza, led by herself; the Medical Court, led by an early twentieth-century physician; the Court of the Juans, composed of various members of popular folklore; the

Teacher's Court, led by a late nineteenth-century writer; the Black Court, led by a martyred African slave; the Celestial Court, led by the Madonna; and the Malandro Court, led by Yoraco, a rogue who steals from the rich and gives to the poor and has never been caught by the authorities. Each court has various subdeities, some real, some mythological, some even derived from comic-book characters. And since there is no central authority among believers in Maria Lionza, lesser deities are constantly added to the courts.

"Carlos Alberto!" says Luz. "How is it that you know so much about Maria Lionza? Could it be that the surgeon's son is a secret devotee?"

Though Luz is fond of Carlos Alberto, it is her nature to be provocative, and Lily wants to avoid an upset. "Don't you remember, Luz?" she says palliatively. "Carlos Alberto has been working on a novel about a girl who is possessed by the spirit of the goddess. And your mother has been helping him with the details."

"Of course I remember," says Luz, an avid aficionada of soap opera news. "It was a more literary version of his radio novela called *Maria del Sorte.* That new actress was supposed to read the role of Maria. If I recall, she was a blond bombshell and the casting director said she exuded sensuality, which is code for Big Tits. No wonder you became so interested in the subject, Carlos Alberto."

Two circles of red have appeared high on Carlos Alberto's cheeks. "My dear Luz," he says stiffly, "whether an actress is a bombshell or not is hardly relevant on radio. But for your information, I never had the chance to meet and personally observe the physical proportions of the person in question; I never even knew her name."

"Coromoto Sanchez, that was her name. Yes, I remember now," says Luz.

"Lo que sea; I couldn't care less," he says. "My interest in Maria Lionza stems from my research for my novel. And my present involvement in the novela business is purely financial. Some of us still have to earn money, you know; we can't sit around all day, listening to Passion Radio and waiting for someone to write the next episode."

He has touched a nerve, and now Luz is livid, her eyes flashing dangerously. Lily herself has never suffered from the Latin American addiction to soap operas; her father had forbidden them when she was growing up, saying they were for imbeciles who had no lives of their own—an opinion shared by her husband, who has never witnessed the enactments of his own scripts. But Luz is no imbecile, and her interest in novelas extends beyond that of spectator—she is a senior shareholder and coproducer at TVista. Before the discussion heats up further, Lily, who cannot bear quarrels, nervously interjects. "It's a good thing you are both so good at this tele-novela business. Because *Soledad* paid for the construction of this house, and *Amor sin duda* has paid most of our bills for more than two years."

Fortunately Marta returns with the candles and the discussion comes to a close. Though Luz and Carlos Alberto are still glaring at each other, they are quiet as she begins the rosary to Maria Lionza, which, Lily observes, is just like the traditional rosary if you don't pay attention to the words. Afterward, Marta says, "Now we must offer the baby's spirit a happy memory. Someone has to tell a story."

"Lily should do it, since it's her baby," says Luz sulkily.

Lily, who is relieved that Luz has decided to be participatory instead of disruptive, says, "All right, then. I will tell the story of how I fell in love." She eyes her husband mischievously. "You are not obliged to listen. Perhaps you'd like to find something more manly to do."

But Carlos Alberto says, "Show me the Criollo, man or woman, who can resist a good love story, and I'll show you a dead Criollo."

It is true that all through high school and even through college, Lily kept her word to her mother not to get into trouble with boys or allow them to distract her from her studies. Nevertheless, her fascination with them remained undiminished for the duration of her college education.

Between the beginning of her first year and the end of her senior year at the Universidad Central, Lily double-majored in architecture and in men. Handsome, intelligent, eminently eligible young men who believed they could change the world armed with their education and their wit, and with Lily beside them. When they held her close, undulating to an irresistible salsa beat, and raided her generous mouth with their tongues, she felt her body respond ardently, with a quickening of breath, an acceleration of the heartbeat, a fluttering in the lowest recesses of the belly. But when she examined her heart, she found it floating, a seagull on perfectly still waters. And so, on moonlit nights, when her enamorados pressed themselves hard and feverishly against her and moved their hands to her breasts, she reached and covered them with hers, entwined her fingers in theirs, and pulled them gently away. So tender and apologetic was the resolve with which she repelled their advances that never once was the sobriquet *tease* applied in her regard. Which drove her girlfriends crazy.

"How do you get away with it?" they asked, eyes large with admiration and envy. Lily did not think of herself as "getting away" with anything. And although she did not reflect on it at the time, she now supposes there must have been a number of boys taking a lot of cold showers.

In any event, it went on like that until her senior year in college. And then, one dazzlingly bright and crisp spring day, at a street café in the sleepy mountain village of Colonia Tovar, a beautiful stranger sat awkwardly across a table from her. He leaned in, elbows bent, his hands folded on the red-checkered tablecloth with the diamond-shaped mustard stain. And, as Lily observed him staring morosely into his coffee cup, a lock of tousled dark hair hanging beguilingly across one eye, the seagull took flight.

Everyone except Luz agrees that the baby is lucky to have such a poetic storyteller for a mother.

"You are most definitely your father's daughter," says Consuelo.

"Hah. There is no meat to that story, only bones," says Luz, taking a long drag off a cigarette.

"Ay, Luz," says Marta, "why do you always have to criticize?"

Luz shrugs her shoulders, ignores both her mother and the ashtray Marta has placed beside her, stands and flicks her ash out the window. At which point Dr. Ricardo Uzoátegui, who had examined Lily at the hospital, arrives, examines her again, and pronounces her better, but advises continued bed rest.

After dinner, Carlos Alberto takes up position at Lily's bedside, stroking her forehead until she dozes off. While she sleeps, a young mestizo boy with blindfolded eyes, and a smoldering fat cigar in his left hand appears to her in a dream.

"Have you seen my mother?" he asks.

He moves closer, until he is standing only a foot away. He holds the cigar to his mouth, inhales deeply, and blows out an enormous cloud of smoke into her face. He vanishes in the smoke cloud, which swirls, condenses, solidifies, and takes the form of her childhood friend, Irene. She is wearing the red shoes.

We had fun, didn't we, Lily? Gozamos una bola.

We did, whispers Lily.

We were fresh and fearless.

We were.

What happened?

I don't know.

Lily begins to cry. She cries silently and continuously, with her eyes squeezed shut, a steady stream of saltwater running down the sides of her face and dampening the pillow. Stricken, Carlos Alberto asks, "Where does it hurt?" But Lily cannot pinpoint the precise location of the wound, which is not so much a wound as a hole through which the remembered enchantment of her childhood slowly seeps. Right now, Lily misses Irene more than anybody in the world.

She can hear Carlos Alberto telling her mother that they should have stayed at the hospital. She can hear him slapping his hand against his head, as though her tears are somehow his fault and the fault of everyone on the planet. When Carlos Alberto has finally gone, cursing, from the room, and her mother after him, her father brings in some juice and spoons it into her mouth.

After a few sips, Lily finally speaks. "Papi," she says, "I have a wish."

"And what is your wish, my darling?" says Ismael.

"I wish to find out what happened to Irene. Will you help me?"

Before her father can answer, there is a shriek from the study, where Marta is listening to the radio. Luz, Consuelo, and Carlos Alberto come running from different parts of the house, thinking something has happened to Lily. But Lily points to Marta who now emerges from the study pale as chalk, wringing her hands.

"You'll never imagine what has happened!" Marta pauses dramatically while all regard her expectantly.

"What in God's name is the matter, Mamá?" says Luz.

"The statue of Maria Lionza in the capital—this morning it cracked in two! All the radio channels are carrying the story."

Like all plants, passiflora grown in a pot is likely to have the nutrients washed out of its soil during watering. If these nutrients are not replaced, the plant will die.

Efraín

On Monday morning, more than two hundred kilometers from the city of Tamanaco, Efraín rubs the sleep from his eyes as a beam of light from a hole in the palm-leaf roof of the hut falls upon his face. He tries to remember what he has been dreaming, but his awakening is too abrupt; a fragment, the image of a vast expanse of blue-green ocean, is all he can retrieve. He is disappointed, for he is fond of recounting his dreams in their entirety to his grandmother, La Vieja Juanita.

Sitting up, he swings his legs down from his hammock, his toes barely touching the dirt floor. He looks across the cylindrical one-room thatch hut and he is greeted by the familiar sight of his grandmother preparing breakfast on the wood-burning stove. Though there is no one in the doorway, he imagines he sees his mother in the open frame, brushing her long hair. Efraín forgives the sun for stealing his dream, as it is replaced by the vision of his mother's long mane spilling into the sunshine.

"Buenos días, mi cielo," says his mother-memory, turning at that moment, "and what did you dream last night?"

"I can't remember," says Efraín mournfully to his mother in his head.

"Don't worry, perhaps it will come back to you later. And, if not, there will always be other sueños." Her eyes are filled with love and tenderness, no longer the deep tristeza that had consumed her after they had fled Santa Marta.

It is almost two years to the day that, in the dead of night and with soldiers hot on their trail, they had made their way from the coast to Castilletes. In the terrifying pandemonium of flight, Efraín and his mother had been separated from Manolo at a river crossing on the border. They had traveled to a Guajiro refugee settlement near Escondido, where they had rested, but only for a few hours. The next day they left for San Felipe, where La Vieja Juanita waited to accompany them to their final destination—an illegal Quechuan hut in the Yurubí forest. But Manolo had never rejoined them, and after a year and a half of waiting, his mother, Coromoto, had gone to look for him. At least that is what Efraín believes. One day she was there, brushing her hair in the doorway, the next day she was not.

Neither Efraín nor La Vieja Juanita speak of those who are missing, for fear of jinxing their destinies. Yet, nameless, they are always present.

Efraín checks the position of the sun in the sky and concludes that he has overslept by more than an hour. On most days La Vieja Juanita wakes up first, Efraín last. Earlier, it had been his mother who woke up last because she worked nights as a bartender at a truck stop thirty-five kilometers away. Since there were no longer any buses plying her route by the time she got off work, a waiter called Gustavo would give her a lift on his motorcycle to the hole in the fence on the road past San Felipe that borders the Yurubí. Then, exchanging her sandals for the sneakers she carried in a fraying tote, she would walk for half an hour. By the time she got back to the hut, it would be nearly two in the morning. Even in his sleep, Efraín could feel her lips on his when she kissed him on her return. He misses her kisses.

"Levántate, muchacho," says La Vieja Juanita.

He climbs out of his hammock, goes outside. He pisses against the guava tree and walks back into the hut, where he sits on a stool next to the slightly lopsided wooden door held up on two sides by wooden fruit crates. It serves variously as a dining table, a cutting board, and the work space where his grandmother makes her delicate mobiles of papier-mâché. Suspended by nylon thread from pieces of natural wood that Efraín gathers from the surrounding forest, they are delicately crafted human forms with wings of exotic bird feathers, arms exuberantly outstretched, giving the impression that they are flying. No two mobiles are the same.

"Anyone would think this was a five-star hotel, the way you lounge about," says La Vieja Juanita. "I've been slaving at this maldito stove for over an hour." Efraín smiles at the daily refrain, inhales deeply the aroma of fresh ground coffee beans, shuts his eyes. A few minutes later, she places two fragrant cups of black coffee and two steaming bowls of Pizca Andina on the table. This is their usual breakfast before heading to Sorte, a favored tourist destination believed to be the home of the Indian goddess Maria Lionza. During the tourist season, which is most of the year, Efraín and La Vieja Juanita pack up the vibrant mobile representations of the goddess and her court and walk through the forest to the main road, where they catch a bus to the town of Chivacoa. There, they take another bus to the flea market at the foothills of Sorte Mountain, where they set up their stall made of cardboard. When they leave, Efraín folds the cardboard carefully and leaves it in the care of Fernando, the owner of the only place of business on this stretch with actual walls.

Though it is their only livelihood, Efraín is always sorry when La Vieja Juanita's works of art are sold at the flea market near Sorte, for they are far too beautiful to be given away for only three hundred bolívares. He thinks that most of the purchasers, with their absurdly festive tourist hats and fat wallets, don't appreciate the time, love, and skill that go into each piece, and he is sometimes rude to them. Then La Vieja Juanita makes him apologize. When he is silent and gloomy afterward, she ruffles his hair and changes the subject. She asks him to tell her his dreams.

Efraín can remember his dreams as long as they are not interrupted. Once in a while his dreams have a component of presentiment. According to La Vieja Juanita, this is a marvelous thing; it means he is in touch with the spirit world. La Vieja Juanita places great store in the spirit world. She says all Indian boys listen to the messages from the ancestors in their dreams and that is why they know who they are. "It is the mestizos who try to live in two worlds, white and Indian, who are in danger of losing themselves in the commotion of life."

"And what about your son, Moriche?" Efraín's mother had asked with a drop of acid in her voice. And La Vieja Juanita hadn't replied to that because the last they heard of Moriche, he was running guns and drugs for whichever side of the cross-border conflict—rebel or military—paid him the most, and even La Vieja Juanita had called him a malandro sin vergüenza.

Efraín's mother, who could never remember her own dreams, had said La Vieja Juanita's ideas were made of straw, that she should stop filling Efraín's head with fairy tales.

"Fairy tales?" the old woman had snorted. "And what about that time when he was three and refused to get into the bus because of his dream? Didn't that bus drive right off the road and into a ravine a few hours later? And wasn't everyone on the bus killed? Is that a fairy tale?"

"He was having a tantrum. He has never liked buses. It was just coincidence," his mother said.

"There are no coincidences," said La Vieja Juanita.

But Efraín's mother had not believed in the power of dreams any more than La Vieja Juanita believed in Maria Lionza. She had worried that her son's dreaminess would make him vulnerable and weird, and said she wanted his feet planted firmly in the world.

La Vieja Juanita had scoffed, "People live in the world they choose."

Efraín is not sure which world his mother had chosen.

One day La Vieja Juanita said her legs hurt and could Coromoto go to Sorte instead. And so Efraín accompanied his mother, which was completely different from accompanying La Vieja Juanita, who was a mostly silent traveling companion. His mother, on the other hand, liked to talk to him.

"When Manolo returns we will move to a city and I will go to the university. I think I would like to be a historian."

Sorte was congested because it was one of the feast days of Maria Lionza. A well-dressed woman tourist with European features approached their stall almost as soon as they had set it up. She couldn't make up her mind about which mobile she wanted.

"My daughter will kill me if I don't bring her the correct one to hang in the children's room. Why are they all so different?" she asked, and Coromoto explained.

"First of all," she said, holding up the mobile of a blond goddess, "Maria Lionza has more than one form. In this one, she is Maria, accompanied by two members of her court — El Negro Felipe, and El Indio Guaicaipuro. Together, they are called Las Tres Potencias, and they represent the nation and the three races that make it up — white, black, and indio."

"But I thought Maria Lionza was mestiza," said the woman, confused.

"She can be white *and* she can be mestiza. And she also can be india, or negra. More than one form, remember? When Maria Lionza is in her white form, she is depicted as a blond bombshell. When Maria Lionza appears in her mestiza form, she is equally voluptuous, of darker skin, but she is called Yara. Often she is depicted as an inversion of the best-known image of El Libertador, the one which is found in the middle of every Plaza Bolivar in the center of every village, town, and city. For example, Yara rides a tapir, El Libertador rides a horse; Yara is naked, Simón Bolívar wears an army uniform; she holds a human pelvis, he holds a sword. It's two sides of a coin — female, male; nature, civilization; birth, death...You see?"

"Dios mío, it seems very complicated!" said the woman, who clearly did not see at all. At which point Coromoto suddenly seemed to lose interest and began staring into the sea of brightly dressed tourists who floated past like large, colorful fish. Efraín held out different representations for the lady's closer inspection, and finally she selected the white version, paid for it, and went away. The customers that followed were less inclined to ask for explanations. Mostly they picked up the first mobile that attracted their fancy without really seeing it, nodding disinterestedly when Coromoto pointed out a special feature, their eyes already seeking out the next stall, the next tourist attraction.

In the glaring heat of the afternoon, when the flow of tourists began to dwindle to a trickle, Coromoto left Efraín in charge of the stall, saying "Ahora vuelvo." She walked toward a man standing near the shop that sold Pepsi and cheese tequeños. The man handed her something too small for Efraín to see, then both disappeared behind the shop. When she returned, her blouse was buttoned all wrong, her eyes had acquired a brightness that seemed somehow false, and she spoke too fast.

A few days later, when Efraín returned to Sorte with La Vieja Juanita, it was dull and slow at the stall. Taking pity on him, she said he could go and play until it was time to leave. Efraín used this opportunity to follow the man from the tequeño and Pepsi shop, who was heading over the bridge. His mother had forbidden him to cross the bridge to the foothills of the Sorte mountain, but Efraín could not contain his curiosity about the man, and so he followed him. On the other side of the bridge was a shrine of the author Andrés Bello, who, according to the words of a stone plaque at the foot of his plaster statue, belonged to the Maria Lionza court and was the saint of Arts and Letters. Scattered about the shrine were framed copies of diplomas from Marialion-ceros who believed they had received them with the help of Andrés Bello.

While he was reading the diplomas, Efraín forgot about the man he was following, and by the time he remembered, the man was gone. Following a group of Guajiro kids, pot-bellied and stick-legged, their hands and knees stained with the rust of the Yaracuy earth, he wandered into a small Mar-ialioncero camp at the mountain base, where a healing cer-emony was about to begin. At first he felt like an intruder, but the feeling evaporated when everyone there welcomed him, invited him to stay, offered him strong, dark coffee, and explained why they were doing this and that.

Efraín crouched on his haunches and watched while a man who said he believed there was a curse on his fields lay on the ground on a black sheet. Two young women and one old woman covered him up to his chin with a white sheet. In the dirt next to him, they drew lines in white chalk pow-der and lit candles of many colors. Across the middle of his body they laid two lengths of black ribbon and began smok-ing big handmade cigars. As they smoked, they chanted and blew the smoke over the man's body. Then they drenched the man in sugar cane liquor. When the man stood up, he smiled and paid some money to the women.

Efraín got up and walked a short distance to another camp, where a man stood within a chalk circle while a squat, bowlegged brujo called Banco smoked and chanted nearby. Several men dressed like gypsies tied the man in the circle upside down to a pole, using soft rope. They washed him in sugar cane liquor while the bowlegged man blew smoke on him. After he was released, he offered tobacco to the brujo.

At the next camp Efraín visited, there was another brujo called Banco, drinking from a coffee mug and speaking in a strange high-pitched voice. A dwarfish man with many tattoos stood by to refill the coffee mug as soon as it was emptied.

"What is he drinking?" Efraín whispered to the old man standing next to him, for he had observed that no one in the camps minded questions. The old man whispered back that it was rum, that no matter how much a Banco drank while in a trance, as soon as the spirit left the body, the Banco would be stone-cold sober. Only then did Efraín understand that all the Marialioncero brujos were called Banco, and he was quite pleased at having figured this out all by himself.

A few hundred feet away, on a higher level, eight people lay in a circle, their feet touching, like the spokes of a wheel. Efraín nearly jumped out of his skin when one of them, a mestiza girl, let out a couple of bloodcurdling shrieks. The presiding Banco, an enormous, bare-chested black man, spit on the ground and the screaming girl was suddenly silent. "Wash her," the Banco commanded. Three mestiza women from the crowd of spectators came forward. Together they lifted the girl, whose body was rigid, and carried her to the bank of the river.

Efraín had witnessed many similar ceremonies before he remembered the time of day. La Vieja Juanita would be angry if because of him they missed their bus. On his way back to the bridge he passed an old woman lying in a hammock under a ragged piece of tarp. She wore a dirty white cassock that was frayed at the neck. Mountain dust had settled into the wrinkles in her face. She stank of rum. She called out, *huiii, huiii,* and beckoned to him with her skeletal hand. When he approached her cautiously, she said:

"¿Qué quieres saber?"

He remained silent, shuffling his feet before her.

"Don't worry, there are ways to find the answer even to unasked questions," she said, and lit a cigar. After it had burned halfway, she threw it on the ground. It fell, spreading ash in a straight line before it, which fanned out like the wings of a small bird at the end.

"What does it mean?" Efraín asked, his voice hoarse with apprehension.

The old woman looked surprised. "If the ash falls in the shape of a sickle, it means your wishes for your future will be granted; if it falls straight, they won't. Your result is unusual, not sickle-shaped, not straight. I cannot give you an answer."

As he was leaving, she handed him two small golden feathers. "For you," she said.

"I don't have any money or tobacco to give you," he said.

But the old woman had fallen asleep. By this time it had begun to rain, and within seconds to pour. Efraín quickly tucked the feathers under his shirt and began to run toward the bridge. By the time he reached the crossing, the river was rising. He joined a stream of people rushing across the bridge. But, within minutes of his crossing, the rain stopped as suddenly as it had begun, the sun shone through the clouds, and Efraín was just in time to help La Vieja Juanita pack up for the day.

On the bus to Chivacoa, Efraín reached into his shirt and touched the feathers.

"And what did you learn from your trip across the bridge?" La Vieja Juanita asked.

Efraín was startled. How had she known? Dots of perspiration began to form on his upper lip.

"Anda, tell me. I won't say anything to your mother."

Taking a deep breath, Efraín said, "Besides Maria Lionza, the Marialionceros venerate Simón Bolívar very much, and the brujos say they can see him and have seen him many times. They paint his figure on wooden sticks, which they wave over people. They worship many other spirits whose names I cannot remember. The brujos are called Banco and everyone goes to ask the Banco what is going to happen: whether it will rain, or whether the crops will be dry or abundant, or whether they should put a curse on their enemies or not, things like that. Some people go to be cured of an illness or bad feelings. And the Banco says he will reply, after having a consultation with los espíritus. After that he blows smoke on them, or washes them with rum, or sends them to the river. And for this work they give some money to the Banco, or sometimes not money but tobacco. Sometimes the Banco is a woman who can tell about wishes and the future with her cigar ash."

"Ah. And did she tell you anything?"

"Yes."

"What?"

"She told me my future was neither straight nor sickle-shaped and gave me two Maizcuba feathers."

"Hah! What did I tell you—all these Marialionceros are bogus. Just like their false goddess."

Efraín, who knew he was not expected to answer, stared down at his feet. They rode in silence for the rest of the way.

How was it possible that La Vieja Juanita, who made more beautiful representations of the Immortals than any Efraín had ever seen, did not believe in them or their powers? Why did she believe that dreams were messages and Mamá not? He pondered these mysteries frequently, but never voiced his thoughts when his mother and grandmother were quarreling about worlds. He knew that when it came to such disputes between them, it was best to stay out of the crossfire.

In spite of her repeated assertion that dreams were nothing more than dreams, Efraín's mother had not been able to resist asking her son to recount them. When he did, she had listened to him, spellbound, like someone who is parched being offered a long, cool drink. She had been riveted even when the dreams were full of impossibilities, *especially* when they were full of impossibilities. Afterward, the light would fade from her eyes and she would say, "But you know it is only a dream."

In Efraín's favorite dream he is standing on a rooftop looking out at a mountain. He has climbed to the rooftop to escape the people on the ground. He can see them waving at him, urging him to come down. But he does not want to come down because the people talk too much, they have too many opinions that they all express at the same time. Their screechy voices hurt his ears. Efraín decides to ignore the waving people. He looks straight ahead instead of down. From his position on the rooftop, the mountain appears smaller, accessible. He is sure that if he takes a running leap, his arms will become wings and he will land on the mountain. But he always awakens before he can find out.

His mother had been frightened when he told her this dream, insisting that he must never, ever, climb any rooftops, much less try to jump from them. "If you do something like that, you will only break your arms and legs, and maybe your neck," she said. "Boys are not birds." She had been bothered for days about this dream. For weeks afterward, she would wake Efraín in the middle of the night to remind him about the dangers of jumping from high places.

The only thing that bothers Efraín about the dream is that he never found out whether he could fly to the mountain or not.

For the first year in his new home, some of his dreams had been nightmares. He never told his mother or La Vieja Juanita about them. Whenever he awoke from a nightmare, he would simply lie quietly in his hammock, clenching and unclenching his teeth. The nightmares involved mostly the same set of circumstances, with one variation. In one version, he was running hand in hand with his mother's boyfriend, Manolo, through the forest. Someone was chasing them, crashing through the undergrowth, gaining on them. He could smell his own susto. He worried that his own shorter legs would slow Manolo down. If they were caught, he knew it would be his fault, though Manolo would never say that. His chest hurt from the effort of running. Just as he felt his lungs could take no more, there would be a shot fired from behind. As Manolo fell, Efraín would feel his hand slip out of his father's. "Run, Efraín, run," Manolo would shout. That was the end of the nightmare.

In the other version he was running with his mother, and it was his mother who would be shot, just as they reached a river. "Swim, Efraín, swim," she would say, pushing him into the river just before she fell.

Luckily, the frequency of these nightmares decreased with time, and finally they stopped.

Although he is only eleven, Efraín understands that the

nightmares were because of their trouble with the militares. They had run like hell and they had escaped together.
Manolo urged them to get into the first car with La Vieja
Juanita, saying he would follow with Catire. But he did not
follow and Efraín's mother had gone to look for him, and
so far neither had returned. Because of this, every now and
then, Efraín feels a shard of misgiving pierce his consciousness. Because what if the dreams are true? If both his mother
and Manolo fell in the dream and disappeared in real life,
what did it mean? When these questions come to mind, he
tries not to think about answers. He has found that the best
way to achieve not thinking too much is with smoke.

Lately, Efraín has taken up smoking loose-leaf tobacco
with a little coca paste mixed in. The raggedy Guajiro boys
he sometimes hangs around with over at the Children's Park
in Chivacoa introduced him to it last year, on his tenth birthday. He meets them whenever he and La Vieja Juanita go
into town for supplies. The boys are older than Efraín, teenagers. Most of them, like Efraín, have never been to school.
None of them have regular jobs; they lie in wait for unsus-
pecting, gullible tourists and wide-eyed Maria Lionza cult
types, and offer to be their guides, carry their luggage, find
them a hotel room, whatever. The rest of the time, which is
most of the time, they hang out at the Children's Park, playing cards, or arm wrestling, or talking about girls. Way to
go, carajo, they say, when one of them tells of making it with
a girl or fucking a puta. Give it to me, they say, jutting their
hips and punching each other in the arm. It seems to Efraín
that their feeling of accomplishment is the same irrespective
of whether the act has been consummated with a girlfriend
or a puta. Sometimes the Guajiro boys refer to women in

general, and even to their own girlfriends, as putas, which only compounds Efraín's confusion. It seems to him that according to the Guajiro boys, the only women who are not putas are their own mothers. Mothers are out of bounds; none of the Guajiro boys talk about their mothers. Unless they are making a vow. When one of the Guajiro boys wants to convince someone that he is telling the truth, he swears on his own mother's eyes.

La Vieja Juanita thinks it is good for Efraín to be around other Indian boys; she lets him chew the fat with them while she shops. She knows about the tobacco but not about the coca paste. She has warned the older boys that if they give Efraín coca, she will make them impotent. Because of La Vieja Juanita's connection to El Negro Catire, the Guajiro boys do not question her ability to fulfill her promise; they never enlist Efraín's services in the cocaine business. They make him swear upon his mother's eyes that he will never breathe a word about the coca paste.

The Guajiro boys treat Efraín like a mascot, sending him on errands—to fetch them some soda pop or rolling papers from the kiosk on the corner. They are genuinely fond of him. Because they are fond of him, they have never told him the rumor. That before El Negro Catire found her and cured her, the hottest puta in Chivacoa used to be his mother; that for a gram of cocaine, she would give them a blow job. Besides, people who disappear are presumed dead, and even these boys know it is dishonorable to speak ill of the dead, not to mention bad luck.

Even though he hasn't been to school, Efraín knows how to read and write because his mother, who had studied through the tenth grade, taught him. When one of the older boys needs to write something, he is sure to ask Efraín to help him, even if it is only graffiti on the wall of the Mercado Costa. The Guajiro boys repay the favor by giving Efraín tobacco, coca paste, and rolling papers. They tousle his hair and tease him, asking what he thinks about women. The only women Efraín knows well are his mother and his grandmother, and while he is certain that the Guajiro boys don't mean *them,* he is not quite certain who they do mean.

The day before Efraín's mother disappeared, La Vieja Juanita said she had a plan to guarantee food on the table. Her plan was simple: Coromoto, who looked surprisingly like commercial depictions of Maria Lionza, would start having visions of the goddess in public and create a commotion. People would pay to talk to her, yes they surely would, the Marialionceros were ripe for a miracle.

Efraín's mother had scoffed at first, but La Vieja Juanita said, "Isn't it better than serving drinks to ruffians in a bar, Coro? Think of it as acting; pretend you are starring in a telenovela. If not for yourself, then do it for the boy." And she kept on about it until Coromoto had finally agreed, though Efraín thought it was mostly to make his grandmother stop talking.

The next morning, Efraín and La Vieja Juanita had traveled by minibus from Sorte to Chivacoa to make purchases from the only store open on Sundays where they could find the supplies required—feathers, beads, scraps of cloth, and natural dyes that La Vieja Juanita would convert into paint. She also selected some material—three meters of handwoven

Wayuu cotton—to make an appropriate costume for Coro-moto. The store was crowded, and it took longer than expected to collect their supplies and pay for them. The copper-skinned mestiza girl who was operating the cash register, and who Efraín thought was pretty, said there was news that more Gua-jiro rebels had escaped across the border. El Negro Catire was reported to be with the rebels and headed toward the West-ern provinces. Four rebels were accused of murdering twelve paramilitary troops in their beds, and it was certain the track-ers would try to hunt them down until they found them and killed them on the spot, without trial. Then the rebels would retaliate. It was all about land.

"It is the gringos who are adding fuel to the fire," opined the man in line behind Efraín and La Vieja Juanita.

"Those gringos," said the mestiza girl, handing Efraín the change, and a piece of candy gratis, "who made them the policía of the world?"

There were rumors that as a countermeasure to the antici-pated cross-border posse activity, El Presidente had ordered the Guardia Nacional to the Western provinces, that a cur-few might be imposed. Everyone was in a hurry to make their purchases and get home before dusk.

Night had fallen by the time the old woman and the boy reached the thatch-topped shack of their one room in the forest. But the moon was bright and as Efraín pushed the door, he thought he could discern the shape of his mother in her hammock.

"Mamá, we're home," he said, lighting a candle, which went out almost instantly.

"We made a killing today," said La Vieja Juanita, taking the matches from Efraín and lighting the oil lamp. "We will work late tonight and all day tomorrow. I plan to sell three times the number of mobiles," she said. "And tomorrow night, Coromoto, you will become Maria Lionza and make an appearance in Sorte."

"Guess what, Mamá," said Efraín, "you were right; on the way home I remembered my dream. It was about you and me and Manolo, about the time we went to Playa Azul and you taught me how to swim, remember?"

From the hammock there was no reply. There was no gentle rise and fall of the chest, no sigh of a breath. It was too still, too quiet. It was as if all the oxygen had been sucked out of the room.

Efraín ran toward the hammock in the corner of the hut, pushing the air in front of him as though it were water. In the hammock there was only a blanket.

"Mamá!" Efraín shouted, running out of the hut. But his mother was gone, and the only sound he could hear was the sound of his own breath quickening.

It was a bright summer day when they decided to take a trip to Playa Azul, a pristine stretch of sand on the Colombian coastline that received an ocean the astonishing color of Mexican turquoise. Efraín was only five, but he still remembers that day in particular because it was the day his mother taught him to swim. From the main beach, they walked along a narrow ledge on the outer side of a hill to a wide cove with giant brown-gray rocks on either side. With the exception of a few skeletal stray dogs and a lone fisherman, the cove was deserted.

They spread a blanket on the powdery sand and took off all their clothes, because Coromoto said there was no point to clothes on a hot, deserted beach. She was different then, daring and dynamic, infecting everyone around her with playful enthusiasm. She did not have two deep lines between her eyebrows. She laughed all the time.

"Don't you think he might be a bit young for swimming?" asked Manolo, who could float but could not swim.

"Of course not," said Coromoto, tossing her hair, bleached blond in places with agua oxigenada. When she tossed her hair that way, it meant that she had truth on her side and didn't give a damn who thought otherwise. "Before I met *you,* my love, and began this gypsy life, I lived in an apartment building that had a swimming pool and went to the beach every weekend. I was swimming like a fish by the time I was three. If Efraín is going to learn at all, he needs to start now. So, are you coming with us or not? We're wasting a lot of good waves."

"The view is better from here," said Manolo, grinning. "Besides, no man likes to be bested by his woman in any sport."

"Vamos, take my hand, Efraín, we'll go into the sea together, you and Mamá, and leave this scaredy cat to tremble on his towel all by himself."

Manolo pretended to shake in fear, then shouted, "But afterward I challenge you both to a game of football—two against one." Manolo was crazy about football and had tried, unsuccessfully, to persuade Efraín that football was at least as good a sport as swimming, if not better. Efraín giggled and took his mother's hand. Together, they ran naked to meet the blue-green sea.

"Let's live on the beach, Mamá," said Efraín afterward, his lashes crusted with salt.

"Manolo is the boss of where we live; you'll have to convince him about that," said Coromoto.

As it turned out, only a few weeks later, Efraín's family and other Guajiro farmers were accused of supporting members of the revolutionary armed forces and forcefully evicted from their lands by the government. By the time he was seven, they had been living in a beach town near Santa Marta for two years. Coromoto and Manolo helped run a small restaurant-cum-hotel called Lugar Perdido, part for pay, part for room and board. Efraín had always been a happy child, but he was even happier here than he had been on the farm, for here he had more children of his own age to play with. Still, he longed for a brother.

"Can I have a brother?" he asked his mother.

"Soon, mi amor," said Coromoto, "when we are settled in a house of our own, you will have more than one brother or sister."

"Yes," said Manolo, "we will have our own football team, why not?"

Coromoto was an exacting swimming coach, and Efraín could soon swim with a speed and strength that had her jumping up and down in the shallows and clapping each time he splashed his way out of the surf. Every day, after battling the waves for an hour, they would make their way back to the beach, where they would throw themselves on the wet sand, spent but exhilarated.

"I'll never be as good as you," he said. "I'm scared of the big waves and I sometimes get swept by the undertow."

"Your body is still much smaller than mine, corazón. You will grow bigger and stronger," said Coromoto. "Remember that with ocean swimming, respect for nature and your own natural instinct is even more important than strength. We'll try another way. During high tide, we'll start by going out into knee-deep water, then turning and facing the shore. As the waves pass by, I want you to jump into the white water and try to feel the wave pushing you along, without fighting it. Catching waves has a lot to do with being able to sense the right time to drop your body into the wave. By practicing, you train your body to sense the right time."

They had practiced for a week together before Coromoto said, "I think you have mastered the small waves. We will move out to waist-deep water and start again."

By the third week Efraín had progressed enough to swim outside the surf line, where his mother taught him to drop into waves by shooting out of the water like a dolphin and then, in a split second, turning his body and riding forward in the cup of the wave just before it broke.

When Efraín was eight, Manolo said to Coromoto, "Don't you think he's spending too much time splashing about in the ocean and less time doing something productive, like helping us peel the potatoes for the mondongo?

"Escúchame bien, amor," said Coromoto in her truth-is-on-my-side voice. "Learning how to swim is practice for learning how to live. Efraín is confident that no matter where he is, in a backyard pool, in a river or in the ocean, he can take care of himself. Good swimmers not only enjoy themselves and get wonderful exercise, they know when it's time to come out of the water. And they also know when it's wise not to go in. They know how to navigate safely through any watery environment."

"Hmmm. Then perhaps, my love, you should also be teaching *me* how to swim," said Manolo. "Some of our compadres in the rebellion are about to get into some very deep water."

After she disappeared, Efraín searched for his mother everywhere, in the bars of San Felipe by day, and in the forest by the light of the quarter moon. Of everyone he met, he asked the same question, "Have you seen my mother?" Those he approached felt sorry for him. Some, moved by the tremulous lips and the supplicant gaze, tried to pretend as though they believed in the possibility, taking note of his description, saying they would keep an eye out. But most thought it a cruelty to feed his hope, saying they were sorry and offering him a sweet or a glass of chicha or a compassionate pat on the back. What else could they do? People involved in cross-border politics went missing all the time, either because they were in hiding or because they were dead. It was nothing extraordinary; it was a fact of life: People disappeared.

La Vieja Juanita allowed him to carry on with his frantic search for two weeks before putting a stop to it.

"That's enough," she said one evening. "There is nothing else to do but wait; I need you to help me at the stall." And Efraín, waving his hand in refusal of the bowl of soup she offered him, tired beyond words, collapsed into his hammock and tumbled into the blessed oblivion of sleep.

He dreamt of his mother. In the dream he was swimming

in the river, and she was standing at the bank. She looked younger. He called to her to join him, she shook her head.

"But you are a swimmer," he said.

"You are a better swimmer than I," she replied. Then she waved and started to walk away.

"Where are you going?"

"To find Manolo, of course."

"Wait!" he called after her. But he could no longer see her.

Now, every night when he sleeps, he continues the search for his mother in his dreams.

Efraín finishes his breakfast, rises from the kitchen table and switches on the transistor radio. Tuning into the eight a.m. broadcast of *Buenos días guajiro* is a daily ritual. Apart from the daily news concerning tribal matters, *Buenos días guajiro* imparts useful information, such as the weather and the number of tourists expected on any given day in Sorte. During its broadcast, the anchors also randomly insert news from along the border about the rebel insurgency and military raids. They pass messages over the airwaves to the loved ones from those on the run. For some, *Buenos días guajiro* is a lifeline.

"This is *Buenos días guajiro* with today's news," says the female announcer. "On the other side of the border, twelve Wayuu men were massacred and thirty more disappeared, at least twenty of whom were children. There has been little mention of the massacre in the mainstream media, even though the final tally likely totaled more than forty victims.

According to humanitarian organizations, another three hundred Wayuu are on the run. Pablito says 'hola' to his mother, Inez, and that he will see her soon. Alberto has sent money for Carolina and the children to the usual place and asks that she collect it as soon as possible. Esteban wishes Graciela the happiest of birthdays and wishes he could be there."

Again, nothing about Manolo or Coromoto, or El Negro Catire. Catire must be hiding too, Efraín says, hopefully. But La Vieja Juanita carries on packing their lunch, behaves as though she is hard of hearing.

It is common knowledge that the militares from across the border have tried to make Catire disappear, sending secret task forces to capture him. But to their acute embarrassment and frustration, they can never find him. The international community has tried to bring pressure to bear upon the government in locating him, claiming that he is a guerilla leader affiliated with the rebels who is wanted for innumerable offenses, like stealing cars from rich people on one side of the border and selling them to rich people on the other side, to help fund the rebellion. They insist that he is in league with a guerilla sympathizer called El Malandro Yoraco, also known as Zorro, who delivers the money from the cars Catire allegedly steals and sells to the indio and mestizo poor.

Efraín has seen his grandfather on only two occasions. Both times he was driving a different expensive car without license plates.

Whether or not these stories are true, Catire has become a living legend, a folk hero to the Guajiro and mestizo populations on both sides of the border, a man they will protect even with their lives. As for El Malandro Yoraco, Efraín has never met anyone who has seen him; some think he was killed in a shootout with the militares, some believe he is still alive. Dead or alive, followers of Maria Lionza, whether they are white, black, indio, or mestizo, believe El Malandro Yoraco is an instrument of the goddess. Many revere him as a saint and pray for his protection, allocating to him his own court, La Corte Malandra, which is comprised of gangsters with names like El Ratón, Miguel Pequeño, Chama Isabelita, who run guns and drugs.

In addition, most Marialionceros are united in their belief that El Presidente is a believer in Maria Lionza and her pantheon, and that they are under his protection. Whatever the reason, so far the government has turned a blind eye to the alleged activities of both El Negro Catire and El Malandro Yoraco. The local authorities routinely give false information to the bounty hunters from the other side, sending them on elaborate wild goose chases.

Efraín hides his stash of tobacco, coca paste, and rolling papers in his back pocket. He likes to smoke when he takes his morning shit. When he smokes tobacco and coca he has visions. He does not tell La Vieja Juanita about them because then he would have to explain how they came to him. If she were to find out about the coca, she would become upset. Efraín does not like to upset her. She is already upset enough, even if she does not speak of it. The word in Chivacoa is that Moriche has also gone missing.

La Vieja Juanita tells Efraín to bring back some wood from the forest. As he walks through the forest, he collects one kind of wood for the stove and another kind for making mobiles, as La Vieja has taught him. He stuffs the wood in a large burlap bag. It is not long before his stomach begins to rumble. He finds a good leafy place, rolls and lights up his cigar. He pulls down his trousers and squats. He inhales deeply, letting the smoke out through his nostrils. While he empties his bowels, he blows smoke rings by making his mouth into a circle, watching the rings float upward, break against the leaves, dissolve into the air. The air grows darker and darker until it becomes a cave. Outside the cave some people are calling. Slowly, with animal caution, he steps, one foot in front of the other, closer and closer to the light. When he emerges, there is a roar from the people gathered outside in the clearing. Efraín can barely hear his own thoughts or distinguish them from the yells of the crowd. At first the noise is dissonant, garbled, but within seconds it is as though the people are shouting in one voice.

Maria Lionza, Maria Lionza, they chant, over and over.

Blinded by the light, Efraín holds up his hands in front of his face, then drops them to his sides as his eyes adjust. The crowd falls silent. He wants to ask the sea of expectant faces before him whether they have seen his parents. But when he opens his mouth to speak, no sound comes out. His mouth has dried up and so has his voice. The faces in the crowd, just moments ago alight with adoration, turn ugly. The shouts become vicious, enraged. Move out of the circle, they scream, charging toward him. His brow is bathed in sweat, his heart beating rapidly. He whispers his mother's words to himself: *You know it is only a dream.* The vision ends. Shaking his head like a wet dog, he picks up his bag of wood and returns to the shack.

"And now this, just in from the capital," the announcer on the radio is saying. "As one of our country's most venerated religious cult figures and national icons, Maria Lionza has inspired hope and granted wishes to devotees for over two centuries. But yesterday, hundreds of thousands of followers were shaken when the fifty-three-year-old statue of the mythical Indian princess cracked at the waist and fell backward, leaving her staring into the heavens. Fearful, thousands are flocking to Sorte to make offerings in the hope of appeasing the goddess....And now, stay tuned for another episode of *Los zapatos rojos,* courtesy of Passion Radio."

"We should do good business today," says La Vieja Juanita, switching off the radio.

On the bus to San Felipe, passengers are already buzzing with the news about the statue of Maria Lionza in the capital. Some believers say it is a sign that El Presidente and his socialist agenda have lost her approval. Others believe it is a clarion call for the spiritual renewal of all humanity. Or perhaps for repentance. They wonder whether a government plan to move the statue of the goddess from the Avenida Francisco Fajardo to the Plaza Bolívar has pissed off the goddess. "Con los santos, no se juega" is a common refrain. At one point a fiery dispute arises at the back of the bus between those who agree with the relocation and restoration plan as a symbol of fundamental change and those who oppose it. Those on opposite sides begin to roll up their sleeves, prepared to resolve the issue with their fists, if necessary.

"Epa," yells the bus driver, "why are you discussing as though you poor pendejos know what the gods are thinking and that you can influence the outcome?"

Efraín and La Vieja Juanita board another bus in Chivacoa. The bus is much fuller than usual at this hour of the morning—indeed, it is packed almost beyond capacity and they have to stand, pressed against others, in the aisle. When they arrive in Sorte, crowds of people are already thronging the shops and stalls and pouring across the bridge to the mountain. Efraín hastens to Fernando's shop to retrieve the pieces of cardboard and makeshift table that make up their own stall, while La Vieja Juanita waits with their bags, guarding their place from potential interlopers. When he finishes setting up the stall, Felipe Gonsales, a neighboring vendor who sells Maria Lionza rosaries and scapulars, walks over.

"Oye, Vieja, have you heard the latest?" he says.

"You mean about the statue? Who hasn't heard?" says La Vieja Juanita, pointing with her chin toward the crowds.

"No," says Felipe, "I mean about the boy."

"What boy?"

"Early this morning a boy is supposed to have emerged from the Lady's shrine right into the sacred circle of a ceremony dedicated to her. Quite a few people saw him. At first they thought he was just some brat fooling around, and they were angry that he had disrupted the ceremony. Some people are claiming that when they tried to grab him, their arms went right through him. Then the boy vanished into thin air. Now they are saying it is the boy in the legend, El Niño, the messenger of Maria Lionza. Hundreds are already on their way to Sorte to post a vigil in the hope that he will appear again. But the Bancos are saying that the next time he appears, it will be to El Presidente himself."

Efraín stares at Felipe as though he has seen a spirit while La Vieja Juanita snorts. "Those fakers and their followers must have consumed too much rum."

Felipe shrugs. Like La Vieja Juanita, he is there to make

money off the tourists. And anything that brings them to Sorte in droves is good for business.

This is certainly true for Efraín and La Vieja Juanita. The excitement about the statue is so great that within seconds of setting up their stall, they are mobbed. Less than forty-five minutes go by before their mobiles are completely sold out, and they are able to leave much earlier than expected.

In the evening Efraín decides to tell La Vieja Juanita about his vision but disguises it as a dream. When he finishes, she is staring at him as if she is experiencing a revelation. He has seen such a look on the faces of some of the Marialionceros just before they go into a trance, just before their eyes roll back into their heads and froth starts coming out of their mouths. He fears she might be on the verge of such a fit. Instead, she slams the table with her fist so hard it cracks the wooden plank lengthwise down the middle and makes Efraín jump. She laughs uproariously. When she laughs, the years fall away from her face. Efraín has never seen her laugh like that. He is both relieved and bewildered by her reaction. It is as though she has hit the jackpot.

That night Efraín dreams he is standing at the door of a room with people he does not know. Two men, one younger and one older, and four women of different ages. One of the women is lying on a bed. She is pretty, but her stomach is very fat. Another woman is sitting on the bed of the pretty fat one. The rest of the people are on chairs around the bed. The woman sitting on the bed, who is older than the woman lying down, but not as old as La Vieja Juanita, fingers some beads and begins to chant in a language Efraín recognizes as Carib.

> *Mábuiga Maria Lionza,*
> *Buíntibu Labu gracia,*
> *Búmañei abúreme binuatibu,*
> *Jeda su uriña,*
> *Biníua tiguiyé tin bágai.*
> *Sándu Maria Lionza,*
> *Lúguchu búnguiu,*
> *Ayumuraguaba uao gafigontíua urguñetó,*
> *Lídan ora úouve.*
> *Itara la.*

When the old woman completes the incantation, the pretty, fat woman says, "Who is that?" and points toward the door. Efraín moves into the shadows.

"Where?" say the others.

"Oh, I thought I saw someone."

The younger man goes to investigate. "It's nothing, mi amor, you are just tired."

"It must have been a shadow," says the pretty, fat woman, "Never mind, Marta, please go ahead." Then the woman sitting on the bed begins to tell a story. It is a story Efraín has heard before. It is the story of Maria Lionza.

A long time ago, to the Cacique Yare was born a beautiful daughter with green eyes like a cat. She was called Yara. On the night Yara was born, her father had a vision. In the vision, a monstrous snake consumed an entire village. The next day Cacique Yare summoned the tribal priest. The smoke-blowing priest told him that the color of his daughter's eyes was a signal of bad times to come. Furthermore, the priest said, sending a cloud of smoke into the chief's face and obscuring his view, if the green-eyed girl ever saw her reflection in the nearby lake, a giant anaconda would emerge from her mouth and bring death and destruction to the Caquetio tribes. Because of this, said the priest, the girl must be sacrificed to the Great Anaconda. But the Cacique Yare refused to kill his child. Instead he sent her to a secret place in the forest. For seventeen years, as Yara grew into a young woman, twenty-two guardians—eleven men and eleven women—watched over her. The guardians' most important job was to prevent the girl from ever reaching the water of the lake, where she might see her own reflection. But one day, after a heavy and gratifying meal, they fell asleep in the sweltering noonday sun, and Yara wandered away from them. She strayed into the valley and to the shores of a splendid lake with water like glass. With fascination, she observed her reflection in the water. As she watched herself in the water, her appearance began to change. She grew longer and longer and longer, until she had taken the shape of a giant anaconda. The snake kept on growing. It grew so much that it filled the lake, which itself overflowed and brought floods to the surrounding villages. Yara kept on growing. Her head remained in Acarigua, but her tail extended past Valencia and all the way to Tamanaco.

It is said that many years later, no one really knows how many, Yara shed her snakeskin and emerged once again as a beautiful young woman with emerald eyes. In her hair she wore a passion flower, a sign of her divinity.

(I thought it was an orchid, says the pretty, fat woman.)

(No, it is the passiflora edulis, which is sometimes confused with an orchid, says the woman telling the story.)

Anyway, while Yara gathered herbs and berries in the forest, she was discovered by a search party of Spanish soldiers who mistook her for Doña Maria Lionza, a Spanish lady presumed shipwrecked off the coast and rescued by local tribes. The soldiers attempted to detain her, shouting, "Maria Lionza, Maria Lionza," but she did not answer them. Instead, she called in a high singsong voice to a giant tapir that grazed nearby. When the tapir came to her side, she leapt astride it and disappeared into the thick of the forest. She rode into the Sorte Mountain, where she made her home, leaving the mountain only once after that, to meet with the conquistador Ponce de Leon, as an advocate for her people. Ponce de Leon fell in love with her and she with him, but it was an impossible love because of their opposing worlds. And so she returned to her world, leaving a piece of her heart with him and carrying a piece of him in her belly. It is said that she is immortal, that she lives in Sorte until this day, that she is known today as Maria Lionza, venerated by hundreds of thousands who call themselves Marialionceros. It is said that she visits the world by possessing a chosen woman with her spirit. It is said that one day she will send her son, El Niño, to deliver a secret message, and he will whisper it into El Presidente's ear.

The fruit of the passiflora edulis is sweetest when the skin is slightly shriveled.

Consuelo

Whatever challenges life has thrown at her, and no one familiar with the details will dispute that she has passed through some extraordinary ordeals, Consuelo has always landed squarely on her feet. According to Marta, it is because artists are especially beloved by the goddess Maria Lionza. Consuelo herself is wary of too much happiness, a tenacious seed sown in her in childhood by a cynical mother who had herself been abandoned at birth and who whenever anyone asked how her day was going, would invariably reply, "Pésimo." She had counseled Consuelo repeatedly that to expect the worst was to be well prepared for life. And so, the moment Lily slipped and fell on the kitchen floor, her thoughts were already anticipating the future, arriving at the culmination of a fast-moving event, an event in which her worst fears could be realized.

It was as though her mind had suddenly separated from her body. Even as she grabbed the keys to the young couple's Range Rover while Luz hurried to open the door for Carlos Alberto, whose arms were full of Lily, even as she helped him settle Lily with her head in his lap in the backseat, she was making a mental inventory of all the things that could go wrong. With her heart squeezing and her mind howling in alarm, it should not have been possible for her body to make itself climb into the driver's seat, for her fingers to turn the key in the ignition, for her foot to gun the engine in reverse, almost before Luz could pull in her foot and slam the door on the passenger side. They screeched out of the driveway at a speed that kept pace with her racing thoughts and made Carlos Alberto shout in protest, "Try not to kill us all before we get to the hospital." In response, her foot only pressed down harder on the accelerator, a robot foot powered by fear and the determination to overtake the future.

They sped past the Plaza and onto the Avenida Franco, where a terrific traffic jam forced the car to an abrupt crawl. Her eyes scanned for an opening in the left lane, and in the absence of one, she cut sharply in front of another car and sped onward to Los Aves Hospital. She parked haphazardly in the place for ambulances and ran behind Carlos Alberto, who was carrying Lily, through large and bloodied glass doors that Luz held open. In the emergency room, she stood like a startled deer, blood pounding against her temples, her breath coming in quick, jagged rasps.

A nurse arrived with a syringe to take some blood from Lily's arm and administer a tranquilizer because, according to her, Lily's pulse was too fast. Dr. Ricardo Uzoátegui, a former school friend of Carlos Alberto, rushed into the room, quickly examined Lily, and said: "We would like to conduct some tests to check on the condition of the fetus. You will need to admit her for observation." Luz, squeamish about hospitals since the surgery that had left her barren, said she would wait in the lobby.

Could a tranquilizer be good for the baby? Consuelo heard words of protest in her head but nothing came out of her mouth, which was dry as hay. *No se preocupe,* said the nurse, patting Consuelo's arm before wheeling Lily briskly away.

An hour later Dr Uzoátegui said the fetus was positioned with its head against the patient's kidneys. Although there was no imminent danger, to be on the safe side it might be advisable to perform a Cesarean section, he said. And later, if it should turn out that the patient's kidneys were bruised, peritoneal dialysis might be prescribed following the operation. This kind of dialysis could, he said, be performed at home, but under the supervision of a specialized nurse. Even though it was a completely hypothetical matter at this stage, he proceeded to describe the peritoneal dialysis procedure.

"A catheter is used to fill the abdomen with dialysis solution. The walls of the abdominal cavity are lined with a membrane called the peritoneum, which allows waste products and extra fluid to pass from the blood into the dialysis solution, taking on the function of the kidneys."

Although the features of her face were assembled in an expression of deference and attentiveness, Consuelo was rattled by the way Ricardo Uzoátegui, who had been best man at her daughter's wedding, kept referring to Lily as "the patient," as though he didn't know her personally, and to the baby as "the fetus," as though a baby were a thing. She was irritated by the way he seemed to want to apply all his medical knowledge to this one case, as if it were a contest he was determined to win. She was bothered by the way he was looking into the air as he spoke, rather than into the eyes of his friend, Carlos Alberto. She felt an almost irresistible urge to slap his freshly scrubbed face, to hear the clap of flesh smacking flesh, if only to feel and confirm the existence and solidity of her own hand.

"A natural delivery may not be advisable," Dr. Ricardo Uzoátegui continued, still looking not quite at, but in the vicinity of, Carlos Alberto. "We do not know the full extent of the effect the fall has had, and she is very close to her due date. In such cases, we find it best to operate. You will need to sign a release form."

Carlos Alberto took the doctor into the hallway, but Consuelo could hear. "What is the risk of surgery to my wife and child, Ricardo?" Carlos Alberto asked. His tone was polite but tinged with a hint of panic.

"Of course, with surgery there is always a risk, Carlos Alberto," said Ricardo Uzoátegui. "However, the risk of doing nothing outweighs the risk of surgery. With surgery, the odds are surely in favor of the patient. As for the fetus, we won't know until we see it. The heartbeat is not robust. I understand that there was some trouble conceiving, but in the unfortunate event the fetus is not viable, one might even consider a surrogate at some time in the future. Although it is not legal here, there is no reason one couldn't go elsewhere, the United States, perhaps. I would be happy to recommend a specialist there."

As though the baby might be expendable; a canvas to be painted over. No reason! No reason except that both parents wanted this baby in particular, and not some other baby grown in a stranger's womb. No reason except her daughter's wish to deliver this child the natural way. There was *no reason* for Ricardo Uzoátegui to talk about the baby in such a dehumanizing manner! And there was the cost of an operation to consider. Without Lily's income after she became pregnant, Carlos Alberto had struggled valiantly to meet the financial burden of supporting not only his wife but also two of his five sisters, at a time when the whole country was staggering under the crushing weight of recession and spiraling currency devaluation. His documentary film career was in shambles; all the financiers had vanished. In addition to teaching courses on film at the Universidad Simón Bolívar, he had supplemented his income by penning stories for the radio. Occasionally, if he was lucky, television producers would purchase the rights and convert his stories into screenplays. Consuelo had contributed whatever Ismael sent her to the Quintanilla household. Still, as the currency fell sharply against the dollar, inflation had risen exponentially. When Lily's filly, Luna, had developed an arthritic hip, they couldn't afford the treatment and it had been Amparo who paid. These days, they could barely pay their bills each month and frequently were forced to rely on the kindness of the Portuguese grocer on the corner of Avenida Benadiba and Cinco for credit. They were not insured. Where would they find the money for an operation?

The two men came back into the room.

"No Cesarean," Lily said.

Consuelo watched Carlos Alberto watching his friend Ricardo, who, perceiving silence as an agreement between hombres, began discussing preparations for surgery. His voice whirred on, an impassionate machine sound.

She heard Lily call out to her, but could not make her mouth respond.

"Shush, mi amor, your mother is right here, and so am I," said Carlos Alberto.

"I refuse to be cut open like a melon. I want to go home," Lily said, her voice trembling with rage.

Ignoring Lily, the doctor again aimed his words in the

direction of Carlos Alberto, insisting that Lily must not be moved.

"Take me home," Lily repeated in a categorical whisper, and began to cry.

Carlos Alberto's gaze darted agitatedly around the room. To Consuelo he had the look of a cornered animal. And she was suddenly incensed by her own timidity and fearfulness, by the palpitations of her heart. What was she afraid of? Wasn't she the woman who had captured the wildest man on the planet? Hadn't she pushed out a six-pound baby through an aperture the size of a pea? She was the mother, was she not? She could be the mother of everyone in the room, including this puny man-child with the pristine coat and superior smile. As the mother, she must take over, take a decision, overrule all other decisions. She must take charge of the future.

"Muchacho, look at me," she said to the doctor, reaching forward, taking his sparsely whiskered chin in her hand, turning his head to face her. "You know me. I am Señora Consuelo Martinez, the mother of this young woman who is the wife of your friend Carlos Alberto. From this moment forward, you will look at my daughter when you make recommendations regarding her treatment. My daughter's name is not 'the patient,' it is Lily, como usted bien lo sabe. You will address her by her name, and you will address her as if she has a brain. Lily is intelligent; she designs buildings on the rare occasions anyone has the money to build them these days; she will, I assure you, be able to grasp what you are saying. As for the baby, he or she has no name yet, but refer again to this child as 'the fetus' and I will remove that stethoscope from around your neck and throttle you with it."

Dr Ricardo Uzoátegui snapped to attention at the sound of the universal voice of mothers. And, incapable of enduring Consuelo's laser stare even a moment longer, he turned to Lily and looked into her eyes for the first time all morning.

"Is there something you would like to say, Lily?"

"If you don't mind, Ricardo, I would like to consult my godmother, Amparo Aguilar," said Lily, calmer, now that her mother had successfully balanced the scales.

"Amparo Aguilar," explained Consuelo for Ricardo's benefit, "is a licensed midwife."

Ricardo looked pained; he knew very well who Amparo Aguilar was. Amparo Aguilar was the bane of every obstetrician in the city. She was despised by the medical professionals of the mainland almost as much as the Cuban physicians who were scurrying about the country like cockroaches, dispensing free treatment and vaccines everywhere. Disappointed that the Universal Mother would consider such brujerías as those practiced by Amparo Aguilar on a par with his own scientific knowledge, he turned toward Carlos Alberto. At which point, Consuelo decided she must act swiftly. She must phone Amparo.

"All right, then, Ricardo," she said, "before we come to any decisions, would you be so kind as to permit us the use of a telephone?"

"I have one in my office, Señora," said Ricardo Uzoátegui, who had realized the foolhardiness of obstructing a tigress defending her cub. "First door to your left."

Consuelo, unsure of what influence Ricardo might exert on Carlos Alberto if left behind, and unwilling to leave it to chance, asked her son-in-law to accompany her. But before anyone could leave the room, before Carlos Alberto could agree or object, and as if in answer to an unspoken prayer, she saw Ismael, her beautiful Ismael, chiseled in the doorway. Without even a glance at Ricardo, or anyone else for that matter, Ismael strode into the room, gathered Lily in his arms, and walked out.

It was at this stage that Carlos Alberto began to dissent in a strangled voice, but Consuelo put a finger to his lips, caught him firmly by the arm. And together, leaning against each other more for moral than for physical support, they followed, down the long, white, antiseptic hallway, into the lobby, where Luz, surprised, joined the procession, out the hospital doors and into the bright afternoon. Ricardo Uzoátegui shot past Consuelo, Carlos Alberto, and Luz, gaining on Ismael, braying out hospital rules and regulations regarding patient discharge. But Ismael kept walking.

By the time they had all congregated near the car, which was covered festively in orange flower petals from the acacia tree above, Ricardo was winded and had lost all semblance of authority.

"Señor," he said to Ismael. "if you insist on taking her home, please ensure that she gets complete bed rest."

Ismael ignored the doctor, signaled with his chin to Carlos Alberto to open the back door of the Range Rover. When Carlos Alberto hesitated, Consuelo handed him the car keys and said, "Ricardo will come by to check on Lily later, won't you, Ricardo?"

Obediently, Ricardo confirmed, "I will come by after my shift to examine her, Carlos Alberto."

Consuelo observed with relief that Carlos Alberto seemed somewhat appeased. He thanked his friend, helped his father-in-law to settle Lily in the back of the vehicle, and handed the keys to Consuelo. But Consuelo, whose heart had not caught up with events and was still pounding irrhythmically, shook her head. "You drive," she said.

Twenty minutes later, as Carlos Alberto pulled into the driveway of Quinta Quintanilla, Consuelo realized her heart was no longer pounding, but dancing joyously to the beat of the love song Ismael had composed on the day Lily was born.

Minutes before her heart attack six months earlier, Consuelo had been sitting in her studio reading a review of her exhibition at Galería Venezuela:

> Sadly, Consuelo Martinez has lost her edge. Anchored in the complacent and tautological lexicon of the middle-aged woman, she has safely retired to the comfort of decorative artesanía of a kind popular with foreign buyers, Europeans and Americans, who pick it up in bulk and ship it back to their overpriced art stores — the kind of stores that also sell books on indigenous cultures, jewelry of silver and turquoise, handmade wind chimes and feathery dreamcatchers. The contrast between her insipid offerings and the powerful canvases of Antonio Bosca is like night and day.

Consuelo hadn't minded the critics' prosaic classification of her work; it had sold out, and that was what counted. For her, the paintings were mere reflections of her principal oeuvre — her family, immediate and extended, with her own heart pulsating at its core, fed and also consumed by the exigencies of loving and being loved. She might have preferred not to have been shown alongside, and compared to, the pretentious Bosca, who painted enormous psychedelic renditions of his own penis and called them self-portraits, but she knew it was largely the titillation of his work that had amplified the gallery's public exposure. She wondered how she might convince Carlos Alberto to accept some money from the sales without offending him. Suddenly, her head felt light, her stomach queasy. Her chest tightened, and there was a peculiar taste like boot polish in her mouth. Unsteadily, she made it inside to the bathroom and threw up in the toilet. That is all she can recall before she lost consciousness.

What she remembers after is lying in a blindingly white room while a white-haired man more or less her own age, with ruggedly distinguished features and carefully manicured hands, said he was Dr. Morales and that she was going to be fine.

After five days, before discharging her, he had asked her a number of questions, one of which was, "And are you and your husband sexually active?"

"Ay, Doctor," Lily had giggled nervously. "What a question! My mother is seventy-four years old!"

At this Consuelo had smiled in the manner of a conspirator at Dr. Morales and he had smiled back.

Ignoring Lily, he said, "Resuming sexual relations after a heart attack often involves more than the physical aspects of the stress on the heart. You should wait at least a month. And even then, it is not unusual for the patient or their partner to be at least somewhat fearful. Take it slow the first few times."

If Dr. Morales were before her now, Consuelo would ask him why it is called a *heart attack,* as if the poor heart were at fault. The heart is not the betrayer. The betrayer is time and the cumulative effect of shocks to the system. In her *heart,* Consuelo feels as young as a girl of twenty.

After Consuelo's release from the hospital, Lily had insisted on preparing all her mother's meals, shunning Marta's assistance, relying only on Consuelo's instruction. By the end of the first week, she had learned eight recipes — one for each day of the week, and one extra, just in case:

Sunday	Mondongo
Monday	Arepas con carne mechada
Tuesday	Sancocho de gallina
Wednesday	Arroz con chipichipe
Thursday	Repollo con sardinas
Friday	Pescado a la campesina
Saturday	Arroz con caraotas negras y plátano
Extra	Casabe

In spite of Lily's well-intentioned efforts, and her own desire to please, in spite of diligently adding her mother's secret ingredient, for two weeks Consuelo had not been able to stomach what her daughter cooked. The medication made her nauseous to the point where she could barely keep anything down, with the exception of chicken broth, unsweetened gelatin, lemongrass tea, and the diluted juice of the passion fruit. The last was prescribed by Amparo, for reigniting the zest for life.

After thirty days of Consuelo's convalescence, Ismael

had still not returned from the Delta. Sometimes she would awaken to the sound of her own voice calling out to him in her sleep. She would be embarrassed when Lily came running in to soothe her, as if their roles had been reversed and she, Consuelo, were the child now. But Lily could not sustain the role of mother to her mother for long. All of a sudden, tears would fill her long-lashed eyes and she would climb into Consuelo's bed. She would lay her head lightly on the pillow with her cheek against Consuelo's cheek. Then Consuelo would become the mother again, stroking her daughter's forehead as if she were a little girl who was having a bad dream.

"Ay, mi amor," Consuelo sighed one day, "if only I had been a much younger woman when I met your father, we would have more time together, you and I." Almost as soon as the words left her mouth, she was sorry to have said them. A solitary tear rolled down Lily's cheek and splashed right into Consuelo's heart where it formed a tiny saline pool of remorse.

"Can you imagine," she continued, smiling, trying to change the subject, "so far, I've only managed to teach you seven recipes." Lily had laughed through her tears then, because Consuelo's recipes numbered in the thousands.

"It doesn't matter, Mami, no matter how much you teach me, I'll never be as good as you." Lily placed her lips softly against her mother's cheek, curled her fingers in Consuelo's long hair, and they fell asleep like that together.

Consuelo had never been sick before in her life. For the first time she considered her own mortality and worried about the possibility that she might become a burden to her family.

"Listen, mi vida," she said a few days later, "I'm all right now. But if there should ever come a time when I am no longer myself, I want you to forbid any procedures that would prolong my life in a suspended state. I do not wish to exist as a vegetable. And tell your father I will be very angry if he defies me in this matter."

"Don't talk like that, Mami," Lily said, her mouth twisting, "nothing is going to happen to you."

Later, Consuelo felt ridiculous for having spoken so theatrically, for by the seventh week she had recuperated fully and begun a series of paintings of surrealistically enlarged hearts.

Ismael arrived, pregnant with the story of the campaign led by the Warao leader Carolina Herrera to stop a power line from passing through the tribe's rain-forest habitat. His new series of songs using the instruments crafted by the inhabitants of the Delta was incomplete, and he would need to go back. He would take Consuelo with him.

It was Lily who interrupted him, in an accusatory tone, with the news of Consuelo's heart attack. And though Consuelo felt well enough, and even eager, to travel with her husband, it was Lily who had not recovered from the heart attack.

"I want Mami to stay with me," Lily said to her father. "She is not in a condition to travel to el culo del mundo. What if something were to happen? No, no y no. Mami stays here. And you should stay too. Whoever heard of a viejo of seventy-plus years singing songs in the jungle?" Ismael had looked surprised, as if Lily had suddenly spoken in tongues; it was the first time she had expressed contempt for his life as a poet and musician.

Consuelo was as taken aback by her daughter's outburst at Ismael. But since Ismael said nothing to defend himself, she too said nothing, though she caught her husband's eye, signaled to him without words. For both of them, Lily came first. There had never been any question about that.

"You should go ahead without me," she said. And so, Ismael gently kissed his wife on the lips. He leaned toward his daughter, who offered him her cheek but would not meet his eyes. Then he turned away, walked out the door, got into his car, and drove away at his usual reckless speed.

Lily fretfully broke the silence left in his wake. "You see, Mami, how stubborn he is? Even now he will not give in."

Consuelo did not voice her suspicion that Lily might have wanted to force both her parents to stay in one place for reasons that had little to do with the state of her mother's heart. As the weeks and months passed, she did not say that she missed her husband every day and every night with every fiber of her being, or that she lived each day with the blade of separation in her heart. She did not confide to her daughter that when her heart finally did thump its grand finale, she hoped it would be while making love with Ismael, her long, full legs wrapped around his waist. She did not express any of these things because she had seen a bluish tinge to Lily's lip reminiscent of that terrible day when Lily had lost her memory.

For six months after she and Ismael had silently agreed to let Lily have her way, they had neither seen nor spoken to one another, and all her artwork during that period had been gloomy drawings of still objects in charcoal, reflecting the darkness in her heart.

Now that he is here in front of her, filling the air around

her with his essence, now that the tempest in the hospital is over, now that Lily is safe at home, Consuelo feels that she must ease herself into familiarity with her husband, gingerly, as though wading into ice-cold water. She finds she cannot bring herself to address him directly, as though a word or even a meeting of the eyes lasting longer than a few seconds would upset a delicate balance of her emotions.

And there is still Lily to consider.

Unsolicited, Marta has expressed to Consuelo her theory on the subject of Lily. According to Marta, Lily has only one problem: a paralyzing fear of losing people she loves. "And you know the source of it," says Marta. She means Irene.

Consuelo had met Irene's parents only once, at the only cocktail party they ever threw, when they first arrived in Tamanaco. And she had been surprised that Irene would be so readily allowed to spend Lily's birthday in distant Maquiritare with virtual strangers, strangers who had banned her from their home for nearly two years. Although she and Ismael had finally capitulated to Lily's request to bring Irene, Consuelo hadn't really expected Irene's parents to consent to it. But the afternoon before the trip, Lily had gone to Irene's house to ask their permission and returned with Irene. Consuelo had been flummoxed when she inspected the contents of Irene's suitcase—toiletries and makeup of a sort that should have belonged to a much older girl, string bikinis, designer jeans, dainty boutique T-shirts with sequins, and abnormally high platform shoes.

"Some of these things will not really be appropriate where

we're going, cariño," she said, pulling out the most irrelevant items and setting them aside. "I'm sorry if Lily didn't explain properly. You see, we are going to the jungle. You'll need more rugged clothes and shoes and you don't want to spoil these. Lily can lend you some things to wear on the trip." Then she remembered Irene's feet. "And perhaps you'll be able to fit into a pair of my tennis shoes," she said delicately, feigning a lapse of memory concerning the last time this girl had worn her shoes, her most cherished pair, and lost them.

"Thanks, Señora Consuelo," said Irene. "My mother packed for me. She's never been to the jungle in her life! She wouldn't survive a single day without her stereo and air-conditioning." Lily had grabbed Irene's arm and spun her in the other direction, away from Consuelo, and Consuelo had known it was so that her expression of pity would not register with Irene.

"Come on," Lily had said, "let's go to my room to get you some other clothes."

Throughout the journey and for the first twenty-four hours after their arrival, Irene had behaved like an angel, and Consuelo had been relieved. But although Lily had gotten her wish, Consuelo noticed that she appeared unnaturally subdued.

The day following their arrival, Consuelo and Ismael had woken from an afternoon nap to find Lily alone on the balcony with her hair wet. When questioned by her mother, Lily said the girls had taken a nap and then Irene had gone for a walk. So far, she had not returned. But it was getting dark, and they were responsible for the girl.

"Your father and I will look for her," she said. "You stay here."

As they walked toward the beach, she voiced her concerns to Ismael. "I know it may sound uncharitable, mi amor, but there is something strange about Irene."

Ismael said nothing for some time. Then he sighed and said, "I think that a girl who has been raised without a map, like Irene, is bound to be strange. But she is a child, and the strangeness is not her fault."

Irene Dos Santos. In Spanish it meant "Irene two saints," in Portuguese, "Irene of the saints." Either way, there was nothing saintly about the girl, Consuelo thought.

By nightfall Irene had not been found and the entire Maquiritare camp was searching for her. It was as though she had vanished into thin air. Lily was questioned again by her mother, and repeated that they had taken a nap and then Irene had gone for a walk. But two eyewitnesses claimed that although they had not seen either girl go into the water, they were present when Lily emerged — alone. In fact, no one had seen Irene at all since lunchtime. Consuelo began to have a strange foreboding and felt guilty for having thought so ill of the girl. After all, though she appeared older than her fifteen years, it was as Ismael said: Irene was really still a child.

By midnight there was still no sign of the girl and so Irene's parents were summoned by radio. They arrived the following morning by helicopter, along with two officers of the Guardia Nacional. Interrogation of other employees of the government-run retreat produced no results. But a search some hundred meters along the rough path into the forest nearby, hewn by the machetes of its Pemon inhabitants, produced signs of a scuffle. One blue flip-flop lay abandoned at a place where the path forked, but it was so large the Guardias were certain it could not have belonged to the girl. But nearby, there was also a silver charm bracelet, its clasp broken. But, as Irene, along with the Martinez family, had been on the path the previous day, she could have lost it then. The senior of the two officials conducting the investigation said that in all likelihood the girl had drowned, and Lily, unable to accept the loss of her friend, had blocked it from her mind.

Almost as an afterthought, he said there had been rumors of insurgents in the area, which raised another possibility: Lily was telling the truth—Irene had strayed into the forest and had been kidnapped, in which case the parents would no doubt receive a ransom note in due course. In the absence of clarity on the matter, with the help of the locals he attempted to drag the lagoon with fishnets weighted with stones. The only boats available were handcrafted Pemon canoes. They searched for four days but no body was discovered, which was not surprising in waters where the caiman patrolled the uninhabited mangrove shores in great numbers.

Consuelo, even after painting it, had never been able to completely exorcise the heartbreaking sight of Benigno Dos Santos holding his head in his hands, nor blot out the mind-piercing sound of Mercedes Dos Santos screaming her daughter's name.

Before that fateful trip, Irene had qualified in the nationals, led her team to victory, accepted the first-place medal on behalf of the team on national television, por Dios. How could she have drowned, when surely she was the stronger swimmer? Though profoundly grateful that her own child had survived whatever had happened in the water, to Consuelo it seemed as though Lily in the very act of surviving had conceded something, some part of her soul, to the other girl.

After they returned from Maquiritare, Lily had appeared to shrink, to become a diluted form of herself. And never, ever, would she acknowledge that the girls had gone swimming or that Irene might be dead.

At Alejandro's suggestion, but against Ismael's wishes, she took Lily to a psychiatrist, who suggested drawing as a therapy. But Lily, when encouraged to sketch her experiences at Maquirtare, had only drawn toucans and parrots, flat and cartoonish in their rendition. When after three weeks none of the psychiatric strategies had achieved the desired effect, that of clarifying or altering Lily's perception of what had transpired in Maquiritare, Ismael had said it was enough, that time and patience would be the cure. And so, for months, whenever Lily spoke of Irene in the present tense, everyone went along with it. After a while, Lily stopped referring to Irene at all, and Consuelo, assuming the chapter finally closed, was glad of it. But, mira! Irene has resurfaced in their lives, if only in their thoughts and imaginations, and so perhaps the cord was never really severed. Consuelo now regrets having returned Lily's box of childhood memories without going through it and checking for reminders of Irene. How could she have been so careless?

As if Consuelo has spoken her mind aloud, Marta shakes her head and says, "That Irene, she's the type to hold on even from the grave. If you ask me, this is all happening because of her."

"Don't be silly, Marta," Consuelo says, "we can hardly blame poor Irene for everything."

"Hummph," says Marta, throwing the black beans in a colander to rinse.

◆

"Escúchame, mi amor," Consuelo said on the day Lily got caught with her tongue throat-deep in the mouth of Elvis Crespo. "Maybe it is my fault you got into this mess. I'm quite a bit older than the other mothers, and I haven't spoken to you about relaciones between a man and a woman. I thought you were too young. In my day, girls of thirteen had no chance to be alone with a boy, and they certainly didn't know how to kiss with their tongues. And don't make big eyes, because la Señora Ramirez was adequately graphic in her description of what you and that young man were doing in the elevator."

Consuelo watched her daughter's face flush with a mixture of embarrassment and the memory of how crazy-hot and breathless the boy's kisses had made her feel.

"And, don't be angry with me for saying this, mi vida," Consuelo continued with velvet ruthlessness. "I know that Irene is your best friend and that you think the sun shines out of her culo. I know that the deranged way her family lives seems exciting and wonderful to you. And that you think Mercedes Dos Santos is the most sophisticated creature in the world. Much as you love your father and me, you hanker for a Dos Santos family life. But let me tell you something: Irene may teach you how to kiss, but she knows nothing of the passion that should make your soul fly when you do it. How could she know, when there is no one to teach her about love, pobrecita? The members of the Dos Santos family, for all their fancy modern ways, wouldn't know love if it jumped up and bit their faces. And love is the biggest adventure of all. When you find it, you must embrace it with your whole being and never hold back. But until then, muchachita de mi alma, keep your panties on."

Lily had cried and promised, and after a lukewarm resistance had adjusted well to convent school. Despite the intermediate tragedy that had been Maquiritare, she had completed her high school education with flying colors, she had graduated from college with honors and a degree in architecture, she had chosen an appropriate life partner, she had appeared to be in every way a well-adjusted, wholesome, happy woman, the envy of many mothers. But even so, Consuelo knew that in the few hours of memory that Lily was missing, something had been irrevocably altered; a shift in the structure of their family foundation, a pillar of confidence dislodged. Minus Irene, Lily seemed in some way less confident, less radiant than she might have been.

These are Consuelo's thoughts as she watches her daughter dozing on the daybed, oblivious to Marta's clashing of pots and pans in the kitchen. Lily tosses and turns, moaning softly. When Consuelo takes her hand in an attempt to comfort her, Lily cries out in her sleep, shakes her hand loose, defensively covers her belly. Carlos Alberto runs in to see what is wrong, sees that Lily is sleeping and that Consuelo and Luz are with her, returns to his relentless pacing on the terrace. Ismael is quietly writing verses at the kitchen table, respecting the void of silence and longing between them. Consuelo feels her throat constrict.

What if love is not enough?

The phone rings. It is Amparo returning their call. She will arrive from Miami tomorrow. She will bring a nurse.

Pending Amparo's arrival, Dr. Ricardo Uzoátegui has come each evening without fail. He examines Lily, takes her blood pressure, studies the output and color of her urine, which has been kept for his inspection in a jam jar. To the relief of everyone in the room, especially Carlos Alberto, he announces that over the past three days, her kidney functions appear to have returned to normal. Even so, he says, bed rest and observation are still recommended. Consuelo finds it maddening the way he uses the passive voice when making his recommendations, as though they come from some unknown but incontrovertible source, as though they come from God. But, at the same time, her heart goes out to him for coming all the way to check on Lily every day. He doesn't have to; it is not his job. She believes his intentions are pure, that he is only manifesting the symptoms of a rigid medical training. She can afford to be gracious because here in her daughter's house he is both overpowered and outnumbered; he can express but not impose his views.

"Maria Lionza, be praised," Marta mumbles, attributing the good news to the power of the Novena.

Luz, an unusual color high on her cheeks, offers Ricardo a glass of passion fruit juice from a tray, which he accepts gratefully and gulps down before appealing one last time to Carlos Alberto. Even under the best of circumstances, he says, delivery by a midwife is ill-advised in this day and age. The words make Carlos Alberto grow a shade paler, but he says nothing in response, merely nods, pulls out his wallet.

"How much do I owe you, Ricardo?" he says. But Ricardo Uzoátegui waves his hand dismissively.

Consuelo's heart hurts for Carlos Alberto, for the way he is ready to suppress everything he has learned, all his instinct to control the situation, in order to support Lily's desire to have Amparo deliver their baby. Consuelo could not have wished a better partner for her child.

"She's a very modern midwife, Ricardo," says Lily.

Ricardo Uzoátegui shrugs his shoulders, picks up his bag.

"In case you need to reach me," he says to Luz, who is nearest, handing her his card. Then, shaking his head, he turns toward the door. Luz hurries to open it for him.

"I think the handsome doctor likes you," Consuelo whispers to Luz after he is gone. "Did you notice how he blushed when you approached him with the tray?"

"¡Tonterías! You are imagining things."

"Did I imagine that the beverage you chose to offer him was passion fruit juice?"

"As if I believe in love potions. You are confusing me with my mother," Luz scoffs, but she is smiling.

Consuelo is glad because Luz has mourned the end of her failed marriage long enough. She hopes for Luz what she hopes for Lily, what she has had in abundance herself, someone with whom to share both the pleasures and pains of life. And god knows Ricardo could use a woman like Luz to bring him down from his high horse.

The previous night, Marta had announced that everyone needed to be better educated on the subject of Maria Lionza. So, instead of a happy memory, after the rosary she had recounted the legend of Yara, Maria Lionza's first incarnation. It had been,

Marta said, Luz's favorite bedtime story "until she got too big for her boots." Luz had sighed and rolled her eyes. But while Marta was telling the story of Yara, Consuelo had observed Luz perched on the edge of her seat, captivated, as if she were hearing it for the first time, her mouth open in wonder like a child. Perhaps, thought Consuelo, their nightly storytelling time together would prove to be as good for Luz as it was for Lily.

On this third night of the Novena, Marta begins by threatening San Antonio with kicks and blows because, according to her, he likes rough talk. It is, she says, the job of San Antonio to mediate with the goddess on behalf of anything that is lost, including lost souls, and it is best to have him on your side.

After seven decades of the rosary, Marta concludes with an exhortation to the goddess of the mountain to "inundate their minds with a river of happy memories." Then she says, "And who will tell today's story?"

There is a broad smile upon her face. Plainly, Consuelo observes, she is deriving immense enjoyment from her role as the mistress of ceremonies.

"I will," offers Consuelo.

"Make it a long one, Mami," says Lily. "I'm not sleepy at all, and neither is the baby, from the way he or she is punching and kicking."

"San Antonio had better sit up and take notice," says Ismael.

And then Consuelo tells of how it took Lily over nine years to come into the world.

With the exception of a brief stint in the rough and tumble neighborhood of Carmelitas, and in the absence of responsibility for anyone but themselves, Consuelo and Ismael had spent the first nine years of their marriage like gypsies, carrying little more than the clothes on their backs, relying on the kindness of those who harbored them in the course of their travels. Whenever they visited Tamanaco, they resided with Amparo and Alejandro, who would go out of their way to give them every comfort and luxury.

The village of the Que, located in the vast region of Maquiritare, was so small that it had never been placed on a map, and to get there they had to travel by water taxi canoe down a swift river the color of tea that emptied into a smallish lake in the middle of the forest. The lake was called Encanto, and it was filled with pink dolphins and sideneck turtles. It was here, in the forest by the lake, among the jaguar and puma, the blue and yellow macaws, the scarlet ibis, the purple orchids, that the couple spent most of their early married life, for it was here that the Que had built their huts and it was to the Que tribe that Ismael belonged.

While her husband went to the river to carve canoes or rode out on a hunt with his uncles and cousins, Consuelo spent her days with the women, hollowing calabash gourds, weaving geometric shapes into baskets, making handmade paper and natural dyes, items the Que bartered for cloth in the town of Santa Elena. It was here, in this remote part of the Gran Sabana, where she began to experiment, hesitantly, with the dyes she made with the other women, and to use them to record her experience. Her first subject was the fire goddess, Kawa.

According to the tribeswomen, the goddess Kawa had owned fire from the beginning of time. She hid it in her stomach and would not show it to anyone, not even her husband.

When her husband went out to hunt and she was alone, she would turn into a frog, open her mouth, and spit out the fire to heat her cooking pots. When her husband returned, hot food would be ready for him to eat. What Kawa did not know was that when her husband left the house, he turned into a jaguar, for he was the god of the hunt.

Initially, Consuelo painted on the inside of bark, or lengths of wood, or even on flattish stones collected from the lake bed, and only much later, when she had developed more confidence in her abilities, did she begin to draw and paint on handmade paper. At first her painting and drawing tools were feathers and sticks, but the Que applied their ingenuity to create for her special brushes made of horsehair and driftwood sculpted by the river. In the evenings she would join Ismael and their hosts for an exchange of stories and songs. She had never been so happy.

During that time, she and Ismael slept together outdoors in a single hammock strung between two trees with nothing more than the moon and the stars above their heads. Well, perhaps *slept* is a euphemism, Consuelo says, since they rarely slept at all in those days, whether they were in a bed or a hammock.

The only thing Consuelo missed in her life was a child of her own. After her first miscarriage, Ismael had rocked her in his arms and told her not to worry, that conception and birth were miracles that had their own time. And he had taken her to visit Amparo, who could always find a way to distract her. And because he filled her world with wonder and love, she did not dwell excessively on the absence; she rebounded quickly from the five miscarriages that followed, and the pangs of longing and loss she felt whenever she watched a mother with her child were brief.

Consuelo is positive that it was on one particular starlit night, in their ninth year of marriage, that Lily was conceived.

(How do you know for certain? We had so many such nights, says Ismael, smiling.)

(Tell my husband that it is because just as he was finishing off his business, and growling like a wild animal, I saw a starburst in the sky, and felt another burst inside me, says Consuelo.)

(Ay, Mami, not in front of the baby! I can't even cover her ears, says Lily.)

By the time she discovered she was pregnant for the seventh time, she had learned to keep in abeyance that bubbling stream of joy. But when she successfully entered her fourth month, her euphoria could not be contained.

Ismael went to Santa Elena and cabled Alejandro. Within days he had found a suitable duplex in the residential district of Altamira, since being pregnant had changed Consuelo's perspective on gypsy living, if only because she now hankered for a proper bathroom.

"It's a distress sale," Alejandro said excitedly, "it's going cheap for that locality."

The property had a large garden with fruit trees at the back of the duplex and a small rose garden in front. Consuelo was jubilant. Alejandro offered to advance the down payment. When Ismael declined, saying it was too much, Alejandro said, "Don't be a fool, hombre, it's not a gift. You'll be able to rent out the top half and pay me back in no time, with interest, if you insist."

The women in her new neighborhood came to welcome her with a Torta de almendras the day after she moved in. Consuelo served it immediately, accompanied by coffee, and the women stayed long into the evening, admiring her paintings, sharing recipes, gardening tips, and affectionate jokes about their husbands. The bond was sealed by six p.m., when the other women returned to their own kitchens.

Consuelo and Ismael now had, for the first time since their marriage, not only a home but a financial cushion, since within three days of their advertisement in the newspaper, an East Indian family of five fell in love with the first-floor rental portion of the duplex, and offered three months' rent in advance. Thus, the couple had officially joined the bourgeoisie, a social condition Consuelo enjoyed and Ismael good-naturedly endured, securing his first job as an inspector of national parks and forests so as to ensure a steady income. The ordinary trappings of middle-class living—refrigerator, stove, telephone, hot water in the shower, and a flushing toilet—which Consuelo had not missed during her nine-year honeymoon with Ismael, now seemed indispensable, and within days that other slapdash life in the wild seemed like a distant memory as she set about building her modern-day nest.

For the most part, with the exception of a need to constantly visit the bathroom, Consuelo enjoyed being pregnant, watching her body with awe as her stomach swelled, as her breasts grew to double their original size, as the skin of her face took on the luminescent sheen associated with pregnancy. She documented her bodily changes, week by week, standing before the mirror and drawing freehand on a notepad. From month four to month seven, she was ravenous for anything sweet and spent most of her time picking fruits from her garden and in the kitchen, where she would spend hours preparing exquisite delights for herself. Flan de auyama, Dulce de lechosa, Merenguitos con limón,

Jalea de mango. She must have perfected hundreds of sweet dishes during that period. But, she had to admit, the last two months of pregnancy seemed like an eternity. No longer able to muster the energy or the enthusiasm to cook, or paint, or tend her beloved garden, she spent hours lying on the sofa, a resplendent beached whale, talking to Amparo on the phone, joyfully expectant and nervous at the same time.

"How is it possible," she asked Amparo, "for this body of flesh and bone to stretch so much and crack open so wide as to accommodate the carrying and birth of a child?"

"It isn't pleasant toward the end," said Amparo cautiously, "but don't worry, we women are stronger than we think."

"I read in a magazine article that you forget the pain once it is over," said Consuelo.

Amparo snorted. "I suppose it was written by a man. No. What happens is this: you remember the pain, but your *forgive* it every time you look into your child's eyes."

"Amparo, what is an episiotomy?"

"Ay, no, por favor. Let's talk about something else. Let's talk about names. I like Azucena for a girl, and it's probably a girl judging by the way she hangs so low in your belly," said Amparo, who claimed she had learned this fail-safe method of discernment from her grandmother.

"Por Dios, Amparo! Azucena is a terrible name, it is a name for an old maid. Other children will laugh at a name like that," said Consuelo. Then, "Can you really tell whether it is a boy or a girl just by looking at my stomach?"

"Of course," said Amparo, whose grandmother had accurately predicted the sex of her own two children, Alex and Isabel. "Girls hang low, boys stay high. Promise me that I can be there when she is born."

"Promise? I insist!"

Ismael returned late at night from a three-day expedition to the Delta on the last day of October, one day before Consuelo's fortieth birthday. He curled himself around her on the bed, but not too tightly, since she had already told him that any sustained physical contact at this stage in her pregnancy made her feel unbearably hot and oppressed. In actuality, it would hardly have made a difference on that particular night, since Consuelo, who had taken a strong infusion of Manzanilla before bed, slept like a stone and was not even aware of her husband's presence.

Early in the morning on the first day of November, Consuelo awoke to a wet bed and contractions that were already seven minutes apart. She punched the slumbering Ismael in the small of the back with her fist, and he awoke with a start. "It's time," she said through clenched teeth. "We have to go to the hospital. Call a taxi and call Amparo."

"There is no time to go to the hospital," said Ismael, lifting her nightgown and peering between her legs. He ran up the stairs to the door that separated their own living area from that of their tenants from India, a Hindu man and his Muslim wife, both civil engineers working for an oil company. He pounded forcefully on the door calling out, "Nati! Nati!" The woman of the house, Nathifa Kalidasa, opened the door in her bathrobe and slippers and allowed herself to be firmly commandeered by the elbow, down the stairs to the apartment below. She followed Ismael into the bedroom, took one look at Consuelo writhing and moaning on the bed, and, without a word, ran to the kitchen to put on a pot of water to boil. She returned with an armful of towels, and a porcelain basin from the bathroom, which she set down on a chair. She approached Consuelo, took hold of her hand, wiped the sweat from her brow with the sleeve of her bathrobe, and began to sing alien words of comfort in a high sweet voice.

Ismael rolled up the sleeves of his pajama shirt and ran to the kitchen, returning with a clean, sharp knife and a bucket full of ice cubes, which he set down on the night table, before returning to the kitchen for the boiling water. He had forgotten to call Amparo.

"Let me help you up," he said to Consuelo. "You'll do better in a squatting position. Gravity will help you with your work."

"Don't TOUCH me, coñomadre," shouted Consuelo at her husband. "What do you know about delivering babies, eh?"

Ismael did not reply. He lifted his clawing, biting, howling wife, set her down on her feet, and pushed her into a crouching position at the foot of the bed. He placed her hands on the bedpost for support, put an ice cube in her mouth, and instructed her to clench it with her back teeth and breathe in short, quick gasps through her mouth. He wrapped some ice cubes in a washcloth, smashed it against the nightstand to crush the ice, and gave it to Nathifa, who held the washcloth to the back of Consuelo's neck.

An hour later, Consuelo was hurling abuses Ismael hadn't known were in her vocabulary. "Hang on, mi amor," he said, wiping his brow, "almost there."

Ismael crouched down. He slipped between his wife's straining arms, facing her. She spat in his face. He slid his hands under her, and she could feel a wriggling bundle, like a giant misguided mojón, moving wetly through her. Her stomach rippled, sending a searing jagged knife of white heat to her brain.

"Get it out of me," Consuelo yelled, falling back, and supporting herself with her elbows on the floor.

"Empuja," he whispered, leaning forward, his hands ready. Consuelo pushed so hard she thought her head would explode. She felt her bones unlock, separate in a massive rush of indescribable pain and pleasure. Then she was free.

"It's a girl!" yelled Ismael exultantly a moment later.

Ismael expertly severed and tied the umbilical cord, blew into the baby's mouth, and swabbed her with a damp towel. He swaddled her in a clean one and handed her to Nathifa, who had tears in her eyes. Kneeling in front of Consuelo, whose legs were still splayed open, Ismael waited for the afterbirth, which he placed in a bucket for disposal, then he gently removed his wife's blood-soaked nightgown. He washed her with another wet towel, helped her back into bed, covered her with a fresh sheet. Nathifa placed the baby against Consuelo's breast, and stood by, smiling. And when Consuelo looked into her child's eyes, her heart began to dance.

"Happy birthday, mi amor," said Ismael.

"I want to call her Lily," said Consuelo. "Lily Nathifa Martinez."

"Amparo is going to be furious that she missed the birth," said Ismael. "Are you sure you want to deprive her of being present for the naming as well?"

"We'll make her the godmother, as consolation. And Alejandro can be the godfather," said Consuelo with finality.

"Lily Nathifa Amparo Martinez? Are you sure?"

"Yes."

"And what consolation does your husband receive for all the curses he had to endure?" asked Ismael, smiling.

At that moment Consuelo couldn't remember cursing her husband. She couldn't remember the pain. In fact, she couldn't remember a time before the moment she held her baby in her arms.

"You mean *Papi* is the one who delivered me?" says Lily incredulously. "I never knew that."

"No," says Consuelo, "*I* delivered you, my darling. But it turned out your father knew a great deal about assisting, having once participated in a delivery in the jungle along with his friend Lucrecia, who was a midwife. Anyway, Amparo was so furious that your father forgot to call her, she demanded that he make it up to her. Which, of course, he finally did, by introducing her to Lucrecia. And that's how Amparo became a midwife."

Consuelo wants her daughter to understand the endurance and sacrifices love demands in return for the joy and ecstasies. There is another story that would illustrate her point. A story she has never spoken in words, though there have been hints of it in some of her early painting—a period Ismael calls her "brooding period."

Nine years before Lily was born was a time of unrest and trouble for the nation, and as far as the government was concerned, Ismael had become part of the trouble and unrest. When he disappeared in Tamanaco on the day of her birthday, Consuelo felt a terrible soul-shrinking foreboding. Every morning for three weeks, she left at eight and returned only at night. All day long, she scoured the city, searching in hospitals, police lockups, and, finally, the morgues. What she saw in the morgues made her blood run cold—grey, naked corpses, some without hands, or feet, or heads. Other bodies dark with bruises and burns. Sometimes the bodies were children. With haunted eyes she would tell what she had seen, while Amparo covered her shaking shoulders with a shawl and Amparo's husband, Alejandro, poured her a stiff drink. Finally, Alejandro learned through his secretary, Lily Percomo, that Ismael was being held in detention without charge at the Ministerio de Defensa.

Consuelo sought and received an appointment with Pedro Lanz at the Department of Security and Classified Information. She went to the Palacio Miraflores, signed her name in a registry, sat down in the designated area, and folded her hands firmly in her lap, expecting a long wait. She watched as, across the marbled hallway, a woman in a dark blue dress begged for an appointment and was denied. When the woman refused to leave, she was escorted off the premises by two soldiers, screaming, "I want to see El Mago, I want to see El Mago." Consuelo remembered with a chill in her spine that Pedro Lanz was morbidly known as the Colonel's magician for his ability to make men disappear. A few minutes later, another soldier approached her and asked her to follow him up an imposing stairway and down a long, wide hallway. When she entered the office of Pedro Lanz, he stood, looked directly into her eyes, and greeted her cordially, "Ah, Señora Consuelo, I must say that marriage has only enhanced your beauty. To what do I owe the pleasure?"

Dizzy with guilty gratitude that she had not met the fate

of the woman in the blue dress, Consuelo thanked Pedro Lanz profusely for seeing her on such short notice.

"I've always held you and your husband in the highest regard, Señora," he said, maintaining eye contact. "I am a great admirer of Ismael's musical and poetic talent. He is a genius—a true renaissance man." Pedro Lanz walked from behind his enormous desk to where she was standing, and, taking her solicitously by the elbow, drew her toward a red velvet upholstered sofa to one side of the room, saying, "I can never forget his role as one of the compadres who helped pave the road to power for this government, and indeed my own position in it. I assure you that I am not a man who ignores such debts. So, tell me, how may I be of service?"

"Señor Director, my husband is missing. He simply vanished nearly three weeks ago in Tamanaco, where we were houseguests of Alejandro and Amparo Aguilar. Since then, I have looked everywhere and contacted everyone I can think of. I don't know where else to turn," said Consuelo, moving ever so slightly away from him on the sofa, and turning toward him earnestly, in order to make it appear as though her intention was to have a better view of his face, rather than to alleviate her revulsion at his proximity.

"Claro, I understand," he replied, patting her hand. "After all, who can we turn to in times of need, if not to our friends? And I speak frankly to you now as your friend and not as a government official. As you know, I grew up with Ismael, who, like so many creative persons, was restless and never could stay in one place, or, for that matter, with one woman, ha ha, for long, until, of course, you came along, my dear. I don't want to appear indelicate, but even the best of men will stray from time to time and it is wise to give them a little extra rope." His tone implied that he knew this to be the case with Ismael and was breaking the news to her gently.

Consuelo could feel the blood flooding her cheeks at his reference to her husband's well-known and colorful history as a lady's man. It was difficult to keep her poise. "I am well aware of my husband's past, Señor Director. And though he is my husband, I have never curtailed his freedoms. During the year we have been married, he has had no reason, nor shown any inclination, to...stray, as you put it. He went to buy flowers for my birthday and never made it to the flower shop. This is why I am certain he has been hurt or detained against his will." *By you,* she wanted to shout, but stopped short just in time. Whatever you do, Alejandro and Amparo had warned, don't say you know he is being held at the Ministerio de Defensa. But of course Pedro Lanz knew what she meant even though she had not said it. For they lived under a dictatorship, and what was a dictatorship but a country without habeas corpus?

"My dear Consuelo, if he has been detained, as you put it, it is not by my order, though his political activities and affiliations are known to me," he said, smiling with his mouth but not his eyes. "Nevertheless, I assure you, I will make inquiries and do my best to get to the bottom of this matter." He rose, offering her his hand, signaling the end of the interview.

Consuelo leapt to her feet, the blood flooding her cheeks with crimson. "Excuse me, Señor Director, but I do not believe you."

As soon as the words escaped her lips, she regretted them. The reputation of Pedro Lanz was of a man who could inspire fear in the hearts of strong men using only his mirada, whose displeasure could have life-or-death consequences. Her knees began to tremble and her mouth went dry, but her eyes were blazing. To her surprise, he laughed.

"Caramba! I've always said that Ismael Martinez knows a high-spirited thoroughbred when he sees one, and you, my dear, are magnificent. I recognized this the moment I saw you that night in the home of Amparo and Alejandro Aguilar, and you scolded me for behavior unbecoming to a gentleman."

Consuelo's relief at the unexpected acquittal was so great that she absorbed the comparison between herself and a racehorse without offence. She went so far as to express her regret for having treated him so rudely at their first meeting. But Lanz waved off her apology with his hand and leaned so close she could feel his hot, stale cigar breath on her face. He was no longer laughing. A fat bead of sweat from just above his left eyebrow dropped into her lap as he whispered, "Instability in the country is growing as we sit here, you and I. Even among those in my own department, I cannot be sure whom to trust. I should be out doing something about that, yet I am here, listening attentively to your concerns. In the grand scheme of things, the absence of one man, while regrettable, is not a matter of such, shall we say, gravitas. So tell me, presuming I were able to help you, what would you give me in return?"

She would have given anything. She would have given her life.

Many days later, she sat in a hut in the forest and watched the door, willing it to open. When it did, and Ismael walked through it, her heart performed a *soubresaut*. She stood and walked to him, trembling. Without a word, they embraced. She did not know how long they stood there, pressed together, bone to bone. It was nearly dark when, reluctantly, she pulled herself away to put a pot of water on the wood stove to boil. While the room filled with steam, she gently removed her husband's clothing, wincing as she observed the bruises, welts, and burns on his back and buttocks, kissing each one with reverence. She could not bring herself then, or ever, to ask what he had endured in detention anymore than he could ask her what she had endured waiting for his release. Instead, she said to him: "You will never sing in public again. You must promise me."

Ismael had not argued that the danger was over, that under a new and democratic government, they would have little to fear, and political debate would become a matter of common public discourse. He had simply buried his face in her hair and said, "I promise you."

And so, gradually and tenderly, they moved beyond the unmentionable. Ismael continued to document his experiences and ideas through music and lyrics, work he gifted anonymously to musicians around the country, who would sing them as if they were their own. But the musicians all knew from whom the gift had come, for the words and music of Ismael Martinez could not be confused with those of any other artist. And without exception, those who performed his music would send him a portion of their profits.

After they left the Western provinces, Consuelo and Ismael had lived for a time on nothing but love, relying mostly on the kindness and hospitality of strangers. And, after his release from prison until the day Lily was born, whenever Ismael sang his compositions, it was for Consuelo's ears alone.

No, she decides, she will never tell anyone, not even her daughter, of the lengths she was willing to go to purchase her husband's life. It was a love sacrifice, yes. But it is not a happy memory.

In the afternoon, Consuelo pats her hair into place and smoothes the front of her dress, feeling more herself because Amparo has finally arrived. She had been addressing a midwife's conference in Miami on the day Lily had fallen. It took two days to reach her on the telephone, but as soon as she heard, she had cancelled her last lecture and taken the first flight back. That she has brought a nurse in tow is a miracle, since it is almost impossible to find live-in nurses in the city these days. And besides, who can afford them?

From the rattling of pots and pans in the kitchen, Consuelo deduces that Marta is not entirely pleased with this population invasion, with the extra mouths to feed, with the possible siphoning off of her authority. Consuelo can hear her grumbling to herself. She considers offering to help in the kitchen, if only to take her own mind off Lily and the baby. Cooking, the rhythm of preparing a meal for those she loves, has always been a source of joy for her, a creative act, like painting. She considers moving her easel outside into the garden. But the anxiety of the past four days appears to have stolen her inspiration as well as her appetite.

To her relief, Amparo's assistant, Alegra Montemar, has turned out to be a woman of cheerful disposition, with no residue of airs from her former life as a celebrity. Seamlessly, she has established herself as part of the household, coming forward when her services are required, melting into the background when they are not. Consuelo watches her as she enters the kitchen, instinctively deferring to Marta, only speaking when spoken to, offering to help with the washing. And Marta begins to thaw incrementally, to stop muttering under her breath.

After breakfast, with Alegra's help, Consuelo gives Lily a sponge bath and dresses her in a luminous sky-blue night-gown from her bridal trousseau. Luz applies a slight dash of rouge to Lily's chalk-white cheeks, which have never before known or needed the transformative powers of makeup.

"You look beautiful," says Carlos Alberto afterward. "Nobody would ever imagine you were sick."

"That's because she is not sick," says Amparo. "Pregnancy is a celebration of life."

Thank all the gods and goddesses of the universe for Amparo, thinks Consuelo. She can always turn any situation into a good time.

Indeed, Amparo's congenital happiness has flooded the house in a bubble bath of optimism and good cheer. Luz has turned on the radio and is dancing merengue with Ismael. Lily is watching and smiling. Carlos Alberto looks reassured, though he has yet to smile; Consuelo believes it is the sight of Alegra in her white nurse's uniform that reassures him. Earlier, she heard him on the phone, talking to his department at the University, saying that he had found a substitute to teach his classes for two weeks. She thinks he must be worried about money, and whether his employers will hold his job for him. These days, jobs of any kind are hard to come by. But if such are the thoughts on his mind, he is making a heroic effort to evict them. He asks to borrow Consuelo's sewing kit. Then,

spreading the contents on the dining table, he sits and con-
structs a red satin pillow in the shape of a heart, which he
stuffs to the brim with fragrant heads of honeysuckle—Lily's
favorite flowers. He places the pillow next to her bulging stomach, as close to the baby as possible, as though the strength of
his ardor might seep into the womb by a process of osmosis.

In the evening, Consuelo hears the ancient Lancer backing
out of the driveway, and calls out to Marta, "Ask my husband where he thinks he is going." But Marta cannot hear
her over the roar of the engine.

Concerned that he may feel he is no longer needed, that
he may be planning some new jungle expedition, that it
will be another impossible six months before she presses her
deprived flesh to his, she hurries to the door and signals him
to wait. Then she sends Carlos Alberto to accompany him.
One hour later they return, their arms full of paper bags, and
Consuelo's heart jumps with joy, as if it is her wedding day.

Of course love *is* enough; how could it be otherwise? For
the first time since he carried Lily out of the hospital, she
speaks to her husband without interpreters.

"I thought you might be planning to return to the Gran
Sabana," she says.

Ismael looks at her in a way she has missed every day since
they were separated by their daughter's decree, in a way that
still makes her legs quiver and her knees go weak, in a way
that starts a rumba in her womb.

"You, my darling, are my Gran Sabana," he says, taking
her into his arms.

The fruit of the passiflora edulis is used as a heart tonic and an aphrodisiac, its flower as a sedative, and its leaves to control muscle spasms and cramps.

Amparo

Amparo always felt her life lacked dimension until she became a midwife. Until then, she had defined herself as an adult in terms of her two primary roles: wife of the powerful and influential Alejandro Aguilar, and mother of rambunctious twins, Alex and Isabel. The fact is, Amparo had been fascinated with the business of birth ever since, at the age of nine, she had watched the birth of her bull terrier's puppies. As a child, so great was her desire to witness the miracle over and over again, she had rescued every pregnant stray she found on the road, creating a doggie birth center in her parents' garden shed, soothing her canine patients when they went into labor, squealing with delight each time a wet mongrel squeezed from its mother's womb. When her parents had had enough of being woken in the night by the cries of puppies, they told her sternly that she was not to bring any more pregnant bitches into the garden. But she had cried more noisily, and in a way more disturbing, than her charges until her parents surrendered on the condition that she agree to find homes for all the puppies and their mothers. Amparo diligently kept her end of the bargain.

Becoming proficient at delivering puppies was a stepping stone toward her ultimate ambition, which, she informed her parents, was to assist human babies into the world. But her science grades were so poor that not even her parents' considerable wealth and influence could procure admittance to any medical school, and her hopes in this regard were irrevocably dashed by the time she was seventeen. In any case, by then she had discovered boys — a passion that seemed to cure her of her disappointment in her own grades and, for a time, even of her obsession with birth. But it returned with a vengeance while she was pregnant with Alex and Isabel, and when they were born, despite the wracking convulsions of her womb, her screams were more of frustration than pain, because she could not have a bird's-eye view of their emergence. Afterward, she made her friend Consuelo promise that she could be in the room when Lily entered the world. But even here she had been thwarted, for Lily was born two months premature while she was out of town.

Next, she had volunteered at a local hospital, saying she wanted to assist with deliveries, but the hospital officials had told her that while they would welcome her help with the babies *after* they were born, *during* the birth only the doctors and nurses could be present. Foiled once again, she had finally given up, vowing to devote herself fully and exclusively to the role of wife and mother. It was a vow she fulfilled brilliantly and competently for a decade, when Ismael had introduced her to Lucrecia, a Guajira midwife who was looking for an apprentice.

Lucrecia was older than Amparo had expected, the skin of her face like soft, worn leather, her eyes acute in their perception. She made it clear from the beginning that position and wealth were of no consequence whatsoever, and Amparo realized she would have to use alternate means to make a favorable impression. As the wife of a powerful businessman, making favorable impressions had become one of Amparo's specialties, but she rightly sensed Lucrecia's immunity to her social charms and graces, and stood before her like an awkward schoolgirl, wracking her brain for a way to gain approval.

"Why do you want to become a midwife? What makes you think you deserve to bring babies into the world?" Lucrecia asked.

"I don't know whether I deserve it," Amparo said. "I only know that almost as long as I can remember, I have had no compelling wish to do anything else."

Though it seemed an eternity to Amparo, it took Lucrecia only seconds to make up her mind. She said, "Well, you're not quite what I had expected in an apprentice, but you have given me a straight answer, and you come highly recommended by Ismael. I'll teach you, but you should be prepared for a lot of hard work and mess you're probably not used to. Menos mal that you have maids and cooks to take care of your home and family, because from now on, you are going to be spending most of your time with me. You'll have to live in Valencia, at least during the week. And don't you come down there with your fancy outfits and high heels—the women I work with need to feel comfortable with you and you need to feel comfortable in order to work properly—bring loose-fitting clothes and flat shoes. And make sure you trim those claws. Long nails have no place in the birthing business."

"Agreed," said Amparo, weak with gratitude and relief that she at last had a foot in the door of miracles.

Oblivious to the scandal her newfound vocation would

incite among her social peers, she began to spend five days a week with Lucrecia in Valencia, an hour's drive away, returning to Tamanaco only on the weekends. In compensation for her absence during the week, she gave the cook the whole weekend off, insisting on preparing the family meals herself, calling her children into the kitchen to keep her company as she chopped, peeled, tossed, steamed, and broiled. Her exuberance was both evident and contagious, and, for the first time in years, Alejandro made himself unavailable to his office during weekends. He purchased matching red aprons and joined her in the kitchen, performing such tasks as she directed, mostly the washing up—just as he had done during the first year of their marriage, when they were nowhere near wealthy enough to afford a cook or a maid. In fact, the family now spent more time together than ever before.

For Alex and Isabel, this new lifestyle was something extraordinary, and they could hardly wait for the weekend to arrive. Though surely they knew they were deeply and abundantly loved by their parents, there had been little opportunity to spend time with them, except on holidays. They had never before seen their mother in the kitchen and had rarely been inside it themselves. To watch her cooking up a storm, while their father helped, kissing her each time he passed her on the way to the sink, to watch their parents laugh till tears spurted from their eyes—this trumped every other weekend activity, and the children began to make excuses when their friends called them out to play. During these boisterous kitchen reunions, they listened raptly while their mother recounted what she had learned each week—the use of gravity and bathtubs in birthing, how to turn a breach baby, the proper way to sever an umbilical cord, the unparalleled delight of ushering new life into the world, and the humbling privilege of laying a newborn upon the breast of the mother. So vivid and unusual were her descriptions, for each birthing story took unexpected twists and turns, that afterward the children, ordinarily fastidious and fussy in their eating habits, polished their plates with gusto, as though gobbling up life itself. Their flesh grew rosy and plump with contentment. As for Alejandro, a blaze of honeymoonish passion consumed him, and he couldn't keep his hands off Amparo when she was home.

And so it was that Amparo's life took an entirely new shape. She dropped out of society, appearing rarely, if at all, at her husband's business dinners, where she would be ill at ease, distracted, impatient to return to the fascinating business of bringing new life into the world. She studied diligently, learning everything the Guajira midwife had to teach her, all the while marveling at the sheer physical force of a woman's labor, with its attendant pain and joy. Amparo's teacher was a practical woman who, though she insisted that natural birth was best for the baby, found nothing edifying in pain for the sake of pain. She carried with her always a pouch filled with coca leaf, which she generously administered whenever a woman begged for strength and relief.

At the end of her third year as an apprentice, Lucrecia told Amparo she was leaving and would not be returning. "I have spent too many years bringing other people's children into the world. I have two sons; it is time I paid more attention to my own children." The prospect of working without the benefit of advice from her mentor terrified Amparo. Observing the panic in her pupil's eyes, Lucrecia touched Amparo's cheek, saying she had nothing more to teach her.

Amparo returned home with blessings and a suitcase full of medicinal herbs: Anamu leaves and Manacá root for stimulating the uterus, Pata de carnero for relieving muscle cramps, Abuta to regulate blood pressure, Anise to chew during labor, Sangre de grado to stop bleeding, Uña de gato for recovery from childbirth, Para toda to restore hormonal balance, Catuaba for stretch marks, Amor seco to increase breast milk yield, flores de naranja for soothing the mother of a stillborn, coca leaf for labor pain, Parchita to fortify the heart and ignite passion.

With exhilaration tempered by trepidation, Amparo began offering her services through bold advertisements in the newspaper. However, this move turned out disastrous. Threatened by even the smallest amount of competition, several leading obstetricians, encouraged, and some said financed, by the insurance companies, filed a criminal suit citing fraud and negligence, asking that the court intervene and obstruct Amparo from practice. It was a famous case, inflamed by thundering editorials in all the newspapers, mostly in support of the doctors, since much of their advertising revenue came from the insurance companies.

"We must fight back," said Alejandro, incensed over the ambush.

"But how?" Amparo asked, disheartened.

"With your own voice," said Alejandro, who by then owned a regional radio station in addition to a number of shares in TVista.

And so Amparo went to war with the Asociación Obstetra. On national radio, and then on television, to the charge that she was medically unqualified to deliver babies, Amparo said, "Pregnancy is not a sickness."

Over a period of two weeks, the tide turned in the court of public opinion; letters to the editor poured into the bureaus of all newspapers, an overwhelming majority in favor of a woman's right to choose a home delivery with a midwife over an expensive stay at the hospital with an obstetrician, usually male, who only arrived in time for the birth, and frequently not even in time for that. Hundreds of pregnant women demonstrated in front of the courthouse holding signs that said, "¡No somos enfermas!"

In the court of law, forty-eight women who had been assisted in childbirth by Lucrecia and Amparo testified on Amparo's behalf, and Alejandro's lawyers threatened to call another hundred or so if necessary. On the other side, the doctors and their insurance associates were unable to prove that pregnancy was a medical condition requiring medical intervention, except in special circumstances. Finally, the judge dismissed the obstetricians' case for lack of evidence, noting that as far as he was concerned, an oral undertaking by Amparo to refer her clients to a hospital in the event of medical emergency would suffice.

Amparo hired trainees, whom she paid with competitive salaries underwritten by Alejandro, until she broke even. She began earning a profit in spite of the numerous free deliveries she assisted for poor women. The trainees were predominantly social workers or emerging feminists, or single, unwed mothers from the barrio who were grateful for any kind of job that would help them to feed and clothe their children.

Long before the advertisements began to appear, long before the court hearing and verdict, long before the official inauguration of the first Amparo Birth Center, local society women learned of Amparo's foray into the business of birthing the usual way, by word of mouth, the story first transmitted in a horrified whisper by Lupe Neri, the wife of an oil baron and a retired opera singer. The news spread exponentially, and with each recounting the story took on ever more scandalous implications in the minds of the tellers. "¡Imagínate!" the listeners would invariably exclaim, eyes widening. "Has she taken leave of her senses?"

To the society women of Tamanaco, it was not clear what was more shocking, that any mother and woman of social standing would choose to get involved with such a messy, unmentionable negocio, or the idea that a woman would choose to go into any negocio at all, unless forced by desperately adverse circumstances.

Any scandal will automatically fade into oblivion, given enough time and incentive. In this case its demise was expedited by the fact that Alejandro and Amparo Aguilar had been the trendsetters and incontestable stars of society in Tamanaco for years. And the power wielded by Alejandro was such that no one could afford to ignore it. Besides, who would want to say no to their lavish dinners and fancy dress balls at Lagunita, attended by the most attractive people—famous actors, poets, artists, musicians, foreign dignitaries, ministers of state, and even presidents of the republic? Eventually society determined it was best to ignore, if not embrace, Amparo's chosen vocation.

In any case public attention was soon diverted by the unsuccessful suicide attempt of Passion Radio's most popular novela reader, Alegra Montemar. It seemed the man with whom she'd been having an affair had threatened to return to his pregnant wife, the daughter of Lupe Neri. The day the story hit the headlines, Lupe's daughter went into labor early, in the middle of the night. The frightened young woman had phoned her mother, and Lupe in turn had tried in vain to locate her doctor, who, it eventually turned out, was vacationing on the island of Margarita. Finally, in sheer desperation, Lupe phoned her old friend Amparo. Amparo, who was short of assistants that night, said Lupe would have to help. All night and part of the next day, while the young mother-to-be struggled, Lupe and Amparo took turns wiping the perspiration from her brow, assisting her in her ceaseless quest for a more comfortable position, until it was time to push. Then Amparo took over, coaxing her, guiding her, encouraging her, and finally catching the plump baby boy in her arms.

From the moment she set eyes on the wrinkly wet bundle of new life, Lupe's conversion to Amparo's methods of child delivery was complete. Not only did she begin recommending Amparo to all her friends with pregnant daughters, but she even asked whether Amparo would consider training her as a midwife. Before long, many bored society women had begun to take an interest in the business of birthing. They asked for and accepted jobs at the Amparo Birth Center, as secretaries, administrators, accountants, and, of course, midwife trainees. It took a good many years of hard work and hard knocks, but Amparo turned out to be an astute businesswoman as well as an excellent midwife and teacher. By the time she learned of Lily's pregnancy, there were Amparo Birth Centers in three major cities, which offered extended services, including day care for working mothers and shelter placement for homeless ones.

No matter how busy she is, Amparo never fails to blow a kiss to Ismael in her mind for making her dream come true.

Amparo always says it could only have been written in the stars that her best friend Consuelo should fall in love with Alejandro's best friend, Ismael, binding the four of them together in a rare and intimate alliance.

Alejandro Aguilar and Ismael Martinez had met at a meeting of a group known only as P.E., an underground movement of allied tribes whose objective was to oppose the dictatorship of El Colonel and its usurping of tribal lands and rights. Alejandro, an ambitious junior television executive for the government broadcast station at the time, had been trying to obtain an interview with any of the movement's leaders for months. But he had been unable to ascertain who they were, so closely was this secret guarded.

And then just like that, out of the blue, one of the leaders, Diego Garcia, turned up in his office (though Alejandro hadn't realized who he was at the time). By the end of the meeting, Diego Garcia had invited Alejandro Aguilar to an underground gathering of political dissidents.

Later, when Amparo asked him why, Diego Garcia could not explain what gave him the courage to take such a risk. After all, Alejandro worked as a reporter for a station controlled by the government. Perhaps it was because he perceived that this was a straightforward man, a man with certain sensibilities, a man who could imagine a world outside his own. A man, in fact, not unlike himself. Whatever the reason, Diego Garcia sought out the very man who was seeking *him* and said, "Hombre, I will give you an exclusive interview with the leader of P.E. if you will come with me to a meeting. But the condition is that you will have to come blindfolded."

The clandestine meetings of the P.E. movement were held with increasing irregularity in different locations around the city or on the outskirts, so as not to attract the attention of the government, which had banned public meetings. Alejandro could easily have given Garcia and his entire organization away, and taken out all the leaders of the impending strike in one devastating blow. And, to be sure, the thought that this may indeed be his patriotic duty did cross his mind. At the same time, Garcia, his concentrated essence of individuality and purpose, was a like a breath of fresh air and adventure, reminding Alejandro of his idealistic university days, before he settled for the uninspiring government-paid job at the only station available to aspiring television journalists.

Alejandro told Amparo that he didn't know why he agreed to Garcia's invitation any more than he knew why Garcia had invited him. And Amparo had known that this was something with which she could not help her husband. She simply held her breath as events unfolded.

Alejandro told his wife that Garcia was clearly a man of considerable intelligence and talent, besides being charismatic and persuasive, and that he wanted to understand what would induce such a man to choose such a life—always on the run from the authorities. Whatever the forces that finally compelled him to choose one course of action over another, Alejandro's decision to accept Garcia's proposal was one that would irrevocably change his (and by association, Amparo's) life.

On the appointed day, while Amparo watched from the doorway, Alejandro was collected from his home at nine p.m.

in a black sedan with darkened windows. He was driven, blindfolded, through the busy streets of Tamanaco for what seemed like a day, though in reality, he said, it was about an hour. When the car stopped, Garcia took Alejandro, still blindfolded, by the arm and led him up a rough and rocky path for about fifteen minutes, and it occurred to Alejandro that he might be walking to his own death. But the gentle pressure of Garcia's fingers on his elbow, whenever he stumbled, took the edge off his apprehension.

When Garcia finally removed the blindfold, Alejandro found that he was in a large clearing somewhere in the hills surrounding the city. The area was lit by kerosene lamps and candles, and he was standing amidst at least five thousand working men and women, a majority of whom represented the various tribes of the nation with banners—Guajiro, Wayuu, Warao, Pemon, Quechua, Puinave, Yanomamo, Que. He turned to his host, but Diego Garcia had disappeared. While Alejandro was still trying to get his bearings, a man at the far end of the clearing took up a microphone before a podium made of two wooden crates stacked on top of each other. Next to the podium were speakers and a small battery-operated generator. In front of the podium was a banner strung between two sticks that had been embedded in the earth. The banner had no words, only a painting of a vine with flowers that looked, to his untrained eye, like orchids.

A roar went up in the crowd, and Alejandro made his way toward the front of the crowd, observing with surprise that the man at the podium was Diego Garcia, who now held up his hands for silence.

"Save your applause and enthusiasm for our guest of

honor, a musician and poet who has given voice and vision to the resistance. I present to you Ismael Martinez!"

A mestizo man with strikingly handsome features, of spare and wiry build, came to the side of Diego Garcia to thunderous applause that seemed to go on and on, reverberating against the trees surrounding the clearing.

"Quiet, please!" said Diego Garcia, and Alejandro realized that Diego Garcia himself was the man in charge, for his words crackled like a whip and were like a command to the people packed into the clearing; almost instantly there was pin-drop silence. And, stepping smoothly into that expectant quiet, Ismael Martinez began to sing. His voice was melodic, mesmerizing, a sound even more captivating than the actual words of the song, and indeed it was the sound and feeling of the words that Alejandro would remember later — the roar of a river, the wind on his face, the smell of moist and fertile earth — and not the precise words themselves. Alejandro watched with rapt attention as Ismael invoked a simpler time when people sustained the land and took their sustenance from it. When he was finished, there was no applause. Instead, a collective sigh of longing filled the clearing.

Then it was again the turn of Diego Garcia to speak. He gave an abrazo to the singer before taking the microphone. In the commanding voice Alejandro found so seductive, he began. He spoke of his feeling of responsibility, for hadn't he fought alongside the incumbent president to overthrow the previous corrupt regime in the hope of creating a better future for the country? Only to find that the president had turned into his predecessor and betrayed the people. "And now, like his predecessor, he must be resisted."

"We have our battle cut out for us against the voracious

eaters of our lands and of our souls," he said. "But already there are other organizations that share our concerns about a common enemy. And together we can prevail. Together we will flood the streets, reclaim our rightful lands and our souls. Our resistance is like the wild passion fruit vine of the forest, beginning with a semilla watered by hope and strength, now growing exponentially, sometimes unruly, with tentacles that have taken unexpected detours, but all connected at the root. Soon our vine will bear fruit, and its fruit will be abundant." At this point, as cries of "Viva la resistencia!" began to fill the air, Ismael rejoined Diego Garcia on the stage with his cuatro and began singing in an exquisite soprano that made the hair on Alejandro's forearms stand on end. It was a ballad filled with yearning and pride, one he had never heard before, but felt as if he had known all his life. Within seconds everyone had joined in the chorus, "Como crecen las frutas de la enredadera." How they grow, the fruits of the vine. Some had tears streaming down their faces, and Alejandro was one of them.

Alejandro told Amparo that it was as though he had forgotten who he was, the enemy, an agent of the thousand-headed soul-killing terrophagus. All at once he felt on the side of the people in the clearing and, overcome with emotion at the conclusion of the song, he began shouting "Viva!" as wildly and enthusiastically as the others.

When Garcia made his way back to where Alejandro was standing, Alejandro clapped him vigorously on the back and said, "I feel that you and your friend have returned to me something I had lost; you must introduce me to this Ismael Martinez."

After the crowd had dispersed, the three of them—

Alejandro, Diego and Ismael—sat on the ground under the stars, drinking shots of agua ardiente and talking long into the night.

After that, Alejandro shared with his two new friends an intellectual love affair and boyish camaraderie that would last the rest of his life. The three met frequently under the Aguilar roof, sharing information, planning and plotting acts of resistance to the regime of El Colonel: Alejandro from within, Garcia and Ismael from the outside. Together, they founded the radio voice of the Guajiro resistance movement, *Buenos días Guajiro,* along the lines of Cuba's *Radio rebelde.* They used adolescent code names to communicate with each other. Alejandro was Speed Racer, Ismael was El Zorro, and Diego was El Negro Catire. It would have been comic, if their vocation had not been deadly serious, and even life-threatening.

After two aborted attempts, the P.E., along with allied movements, mounted an unrelenting street protest in every major city, paralyzing businesses and transportation. It was this third thrust that finally sent El Colonel fleeing into exile. But not before his henchman, Pedro Lanz, director of the Department of Security and Classified Information, almost made Ismael disappear.

A year after Consuelo and Ismael were married, Amparo received a cable from Ismael from a small town in the southwestern provinces. Consuelo had suffered her first miscarriage. Hoping that the company of her closest friend would serve as a balm for her sorrow, Ismael had decided to bring her to Tamanaco. They arrived in the month of October, and Amparo and Alejandro had welcomed them with open arms. Amparo allowed Consuelo nine days of tears, the time it took to complete the obligatory Novena for the unborn baby's soul, before instituting a regime of fun and happiness. It was not long before she had coaxed her friend into mornings of beauty parlors and shopping for pretty things, afternoons of movies and museums, evenings of boisterous card games, late nights of singing and laughing. Ismael spent most of his days with Alejandro at the office.

On the evening of November 1, he asked Alejandro to stop at a florist on the way home so that he might buy flowers. It was Consuelo's thirtieth birthday. Since there was no place to park anywhere near the flower shop, Alejandro dropped Ismael off and instructed his chauffeur to drive around the block a couple of times. After sixteen times around the block and still no sign of Ismael, Alejandro got out and went into the flower shop, but the florist said there had been no customers in over an hour. Alejandro used the phone at the flower shop to tell Amparo what had happened but urged her not to alarm Consuelo. He would wait at the florist awhile longer, he said.

"These men!" Amparo exclaimed to Consuelo with a lightheartedness she did not feel. "If it weren't for women they'd lose their own heads."

When the doorbell rang at six p.m., the maid had left and Amparo was in the shower. Consuelo ran to answer it. She barged into the bathroom, carrying a lavish bouquet of white roses, and stammering so badly that Amparo could not make head nor tail of what she was trying to say.

"Pero qué te pasa, Consuelo? Slow down, I can't understand a word."

"For me, from Pedro Lanz," Consuelo said.

When Amparo heard that, a chill of fear ran down her spine—for Ismael, for Consuelo, and indeed for them all. As director of Security and Classified Information, Pedro Lanz was in charge of his own section of secret police, a man believed to be so devoted to his job that it was claimed he slept with his eyes open. Certainly not a man to be taken lightly. To make matters worse, when Amparo had introduced him to Consuelo a little over a year earlier, Consuelo had reprimanded him for staring at her breasts and gone off to dance with Ismael. And it was not a matter of classified information that Ismael was no friend of the Department of Security and Classified Information.

"What shall we do?" Amparo asked, when Alejandro returned.

"We will make discreet inquiries," he said.

While Amparo took charge of the phones, Alejandro used his connections to obtain any information on the possible detention of Ismael. And Consuelo took to the streets, looking everywhere she could think of—military headquarters, police lockups, hospitals, mortuaries. Amparo knew she had every reason to be concerned for the life of her husband as well as that of Ismael. It was dangerous to appear to care too much about those who disappeared. After two tense weeks, she received the news she had been dreading. It was Lily Percomo on the line, an American woman who worked as her husband's secretary at TVista.

"Some Seguridad Nacional officials are here," Lily Percomo whispered into the receiver.

"Put me through to my husband," Amparo said urgently. The secretary complied, but, before Amparo could utter a word beyond hello, Alejandro said, "Polenta criolla will be fine for dinner."

"Está bien, mi amor," said Amparo, breaking out into a cold sweat, "I'll see you at the usual time, around seven?" *Polenta criolla* was code for an emergency. And *seven* meant that Amparo should send the kids to her mother's in Valencia.

"Seven, perfecto."

Amparo packed a suitcase and sent Alex and Isabel with the driver to her mother's. When she informed Consuelo of the situation, Amparo expected her to fall apart, but she was strangely composed. In fact, it was Amparo who was nervous, who would jump out of her skin every time the phone or the doorbell rang. Consuelo poured her a scotch and together they waited for Alejandro to come home.

Alejandro returned only at eight, his face haggard, his eyes grave. The Seguridad National men had interrogated him for three hours in his office on his connection with Ismael Martinez. Alejandro had maintained that his wife and the wife of Ismael Martinez were friends from childhood. Then they suddenly switched gears and grilled him about his car.

"That's a pretty fancy car you have. Where did you get that car?" they said, as if they didn't know already.

"I bought it from a dealer in sports cars."

"Really, and do you have a receipt for it?"

"As a matter of fact I do." After he showed them the receipt in his file, the tone of the interrogation alternated between chatty and menacing. Alejandro secretly recorded the exchange, pressing a button under his desk.

Are you aware that the dealer you bought your car from is trafficking stolen vehicles?...no...luckily for you we can't find the original owner of your Corvette and anyway it's not you we're interested in...you were seen having dinner at El Carrizo last weekend with Ismael Martinez who we believe is connected to another man we are very interested in...our wives are childhood friends...yes, so sad for your wife and your wife's good friend...she won't be seeing him for a while...arrested...¿qué dices hombre? there must be some mistake...no we don't think so or maybe you know something we don't...is it possible to contact him?...no of course not you cannot contact him, no one is allowed to contact suspected traitors to the nation...but, his wife, what is she supposed to do?...por supuesto it's a bum rap for the wife, these damn revolucionarios never think about their families never think they're going to get caught but they all do in the end and poof! keep your nose clean hombre.

When he came home, Alejandro played the recording for Amparo, and continued to play it in his head, over and over, especially the "poof," which had been punctuated by one of the Seguridad Nacional thugs making his hand into the shape of a gun and pointing it at Alejandro's head. They tried to evaluate his own performance, whether he might have slipped up anywhere, given unintended information, put anyone else under suspicion. Sleepless in bed that night, Alejandro told Amparo that the hardest part was pretending that he didn't give a damn about Ismael being arrested. And the feeling of powerlessness. Because even though he was a public figure with a certain amount of clout, even though he had maintained his friends in government, if Alejandro showed too much interest, too much concern, about what had happened to Ismael, it would be only a matter of time before the shadow of Pedro Lanz swallowed him as well. Political unrest was growing, crackdowns had become routine, these days no one was above suspicion.

The day after Ismael disappeared, police fired guns at students who were chanting, "Down with the dictatorship." While children were falling to the ground like rain, El Colonel appeared on television, telling the people how lucky they were to be living in an economic democracy. What he really meant was that *he* and his cronies were lucky, because they were indulged by the Americans in exchange for millions of barrels of oil each day. It was no wonder, said Alejandro, that El Colonel was completely enamorado with the gringos, who had already awarded him the Legion of Merit.

Lily Percomo, the American woman who worked as Alejandro's secretary, was married to Ralph Percomo, an attaché who worked at the American Consulate under the nondescript title Advisor, Foreign Affairs. Ralph Percomo and his wife were frequent social guests at the Aguilar residence. A cordial diplomat in public, Ralph Percomo was suspected by Alejandro of being an American intelligence operative. He was also a binge alcoholic. When he drank too much, he beat his wife, Lily, who he prevented from leaving him by locking up her passport. He always punched her in the ribs or stomach, never in the face, preferring not to review his handiwork the day after. When she arrived for work at TVista wincing, it was Alejandro who shut the door to his office and poured her a scotch. And it was Alejandro who twice took her to the hospital to wrap her broken ribs. Lily Percomo would do anything for Alejandro. And when she said she could find out where Ismael was being held, Alejandro believed her. After a few days, she said she had the information, but it was not good: Ismael was being held in the capital at the Ministerio de Defensa, an impregnable fortress from which no detainee had ever been released.

Alejandro went pale. "God help him," he said, before driving home with the news.

Lily Percomo phoned Amparo the next day, wondering whether they could have lunch together. There was such an urgency to her tone that Amparo, who was planning to make hayacas that day, changed her mind. "Bring your friend, Consuelo," said Lily Percomo. They agreed to meet at an open-air restaurant near Alejandro's office.

When Amparo and Consuelo arrived, Lily Percomo was already seated at a table, nervously smoking a cigarette. While they waited for their order of sandwiches and coffee, Lily Percomo began to describe her plan to free Ismael. It was stunningly simple, so simple as to appear desperate and even stupid. It was a plan Alejandro would never approve. Lily Percomo said her husband kept a box of official stationery locked in his briefcase. She said she knew where he kept the key. She would draft a letter to the Director of Security and Classified Information, Pedro Lanz, saying that Ismael Martinez was an American asset, an "information gatherer" whose information was culled, manipulated, and then disseminated through TVista to serve the incumbent government's interests. This would also explain any intelligence the government might have acquired regarding Alejandro's link with Ismael, beyond the friendship of their wives, and even, perhaps, the link with Diego Garcia. The letter would request Ismael's release, quietly, without any publicity.

"What about the signature?" asked Amparo. But Lily Percomo smiled and said she could forge her husband's signature, that she had done it before, on checks.

It would have to be hand-delivered to appear authentic; such messages would not be sent by post. And it would have to be done during one of Ralph's bimonthly trips to the United States. Lily Percomo said no one would question her if she personally delivered the letter to Pedro Lanz, as she had acted as her husband's courier on earlier occasions.

Consuelo listened without comment while Lily and Amparo discussed the timing of the letter's delivery. Should it be delivered immediately or just before the planned coup of the P.E. and its allies on New Year's Day?

The advantage of waiting, Amparo noted, was that even if the coup failed, as had the one before, there would still be so much confusion that Ismael might be able to escape the city before the women's duplicity could be discovered. But if it *were* discovered, Lily Percomo would be the first one incriminated. She would have to go into hiding once the letter was delivered. They would not tell Alejandro anything until it was a *fait accompli*; only then would they ask him to make arrangements to hide Lily until it was safe to spirit her out of the country, most likely via Curaçao. Lily would write a note for Ralph saying she was leaving him.

There were other valid reasons to deliver the letter later rather than sooner; it gave them more time to plan for contingencies and to better orchestrate an escape for Consuelo and Ismael, as well as for Lily Percomo.

Amparo said she had overheard Diego Garcia telling Alejandro that the P.E. had their own moles in the government, including a man in the Seguridad Nacional. If that were the case, surely Alejandro must be privy to information on Ismael's status, or could acquire it through Diego Garcia. Lily said Amparo would have to obtain this information from Alejandro. At which point, Consuelo finally spoke: "I would rather set myself on fire in front of the Presidential Palace than spend one more day doing nothing."

And so it was that they decided to implement their plan with immediate effect.

But that night, while Lily Percomo was in the process of stealing her husband's stationery, Ralph had woken up and surprised her in his study, the briefcase open before her. He had beaten her senseless. She was admitted to the hospital in a coma from which she would never emerge. Her husband claimed she had fallen down a flight of stairs. She died within a week. And Amparo confessed to Alejandro.

Since it could not be known how much information, if any, Ralph Percomo had been able to extract from his wife before she lost consciousness, for the sake of her safety, Alejandro wanted Consuelo to leave Tamanaco immediately. But Consuelo insisted she would not leave without Ismael, that without Ismael her life would have no value anyway, that without Ismael she would rather be dead. And no one, not even Amparo, could change her thinking on this. The next day, she phoned to make an appointment with Pedro Lanz. Her request was granted and she hired a taxi for the hour-long drive to the capital. She returned from the meeting in a subdued state, saying that she had appealed to his sense of honor. She said she had given her personal guarantee that Ismael would be no trouble to him in the future. He had assured her that he was a man of his word and had promised to help.

"There is hope," she said. "It is all I have." Amparo and Alejandro were torn between admiration for her resilience and pity for her faith in such a promise.

For nine more days they waited. During this time, there was no word from the mole at the Seguridad Nacional. They went about their business as usual, but their nerves were on the point of breaking. On the tenth day, a car with darkened windows was seen parked for several hours outside the Aguilar house. Alejandro said the situation was too dangerous, that Consuelo must leave the city because the government might try to use her against Ismael. He had hit on the only argument that could persuade her to leave the city, the terrifying thought that she might be the instrument used to break her husband. That very evening, Consuelo exchanged clothes with Amparo's housekeeper, covered her head with a scarf, and walked undetected to a taxi stand. Alejandro had instructed her to get into a cab with a particular license plate number. The driver had already been instructed to drive nonstop to the destination written on the paper Amparo handed him earlier in the day.

When they arrived in Yaracuy, the driver had refused payment.

"God bless you," said Consuelo.

"God, and the P.E.," said the driver, winking. And it was only then that she had noticed that the tattoo on his forearm was a passion flower.

A week later, on New Year's Day, thousands of people revolted against the dictatorship with the support of part of the Air Force, but the revolt was put down. A massive general strike followed within days. When the Navy joined the rebellion, El Colonel fled the country in a small plane in the early hours of the morning. All political prisoners were released. According to Consuelo, when she heard the news on the radio, she ran out of the safe house into the moonlight, laughing and dancing and crying all at the same time.

Years later she would name her only child Lily, with the English spelling, in memory of the woman who died trying to help her get her husband back.

Amparo is crazy about Lily, which is why she has moved, bag and baggage, along with her best nurse, the former radio and telenovela star Alegra Montemar, into the Quintanilla household. But also, it is because she wants to be a support to Consuelo, to make sure she is all right. It is always harder for a mother with an only child; there is nothing comparable to that depth of attachment. Lily is her world, and her anxiety about the delivery is palpable. Consuelo is depending on her, Amparo, who has never lost a baby or a mother. Her closest call, where she almost lost both, was eleven years earlier, when she had delivered the love child of a young mestiza woman called Coromoto. It was their friend Diego Garcia who had carried the woman in his arms, her body too thin for childbearing, her arms scarred with tracks, to Amparo at midnight.

"It's too risky, Diego," said Amparo. "Take her to the hospital."

"Amparo, the girl is destitute. No hospital in the city will accept her."

"No, Diego."

"Amparo, what do you think Lucrecia would do in your shoes?"

And still Amparo resisted, shaking her head.

"Let me put it this way, what would you do if you knew the child this poor girl was carrying is Lucrecia's grandchild? Lucrecia's and mine?"

So of course Amparo could not refuse.

They had settled the young woman, delirious and burning with fever, in a back room of the clinic. Two weeks later, when labor began, Amparo had struggled for hours trying to turn the breach baby. Every time she tried to reach inside, the woman would arch her back and emit a spine-chilling scream, and Amparo would have to stop. It was the only time in all her years of practicing midwifery that she thought she might lose a mother in the birthing process.

Amparo can still see the woman's taut and exhausted face before her. "No hospitals," she said through clenched teeth. "You do it."

It was too late to call an ambulance; it would be too dangerous to move the girl at that stage. For a moment, Amparo's mind went blank. As she struggled against the wave of panic, the words of her teacher came to her rescue.

"Indigenous people have been using coca leaf for centuries for medicinal purposes and in rituals. When a child is born, relatives celebrate by chewing coca leaf together. When a young man wants to marry a girl, he offers coca to her parents. Coca leaf is harmless when used in the traditional way. For the most part, it is used medicinally, mostly to dull hunger. But coca has another beneficiary use: it both hastens labor and eases pain."

Between contractions, she gave the girl an infusion of coca leaf. Then she handed her an entire bag of leaves to chew at will. During the next break between contractions, she smeared her hand and arm again with a mixture of aloe vera and olive oil. Closing her mind to the screams, she reached into the womb and finally coaxed the baby around. There had been a lot of blood—Amparo had never seen so much blood before or after this one delivery—and she had feared for the lives of both mother and child. The woman had a tear so long and so deep, it took Amparo half an hour to stitch it, and the baby was yellow with jaundice. The first twenty-four hours had been critical. But Amparo had used all her skill in treating them and they had survived. It was still ill-advised for them to be moved—and, in any case, where would they go? They made their recovery on a cot in the back room of the clinic. After eight days, a young Guajiro man with a perpetually running nose had come to take mother and child away. And Amparo had been relieved.

A few days later, when she had checked her supplies, she saw that her entire stock of coca leaf was missing. God only knows what happened to the woman and her baby in the end. She sometimes wonders about them.

Even though Amparo is a practical person, even after witnessing exactly one thousand six hundred and fifty-two deliveries, the marvel of birth has never failed to humble her. Three years earlier she had participated with reverence at the birth of her own granddaughter, and in a matter of days she will experience the joy of seeing Lily's baby come into the light.

Whatever eccentricities Marta might exhibit, she is certainly right about one thing; too much anxiety at Lily's bedside is not good for Lily or the baby so precariously lodged in her womb after so many years of trying. Even unborn babies need to be surrounded by joy and good cheer, much more so when their mothers are frightened of losing them. That is why she thinks Marta's Novena is a good idea. What harm could there be to mumble a few incantations and tell stories at Lily's bedside?

No harm at all.

Amparo is sitting in the study with her back to the door. She glances nervously over her shoulder to see if anyone is there, but they are all in the kitchen, listening avidly to a football game on the transistor radio. During commercials, they break into a heated discussion about football and why Venezuela has never made it to the World Cup.

"Who said that?" whispers Amparo to the air. The voice is familiar and unfamiliar at the same time. "Look at me, por Dios, talking to an imaginary voice! It must be senility coming on. May the Virgin protect me."

Your pale and tedious Virgin has lost her ability to imagine. She could never envisage such an extraordinary development. Now, pay attention, por favor, because there is something I need you to do. Go to the Quinta Consuelo. In the lower right-hand drawer of the dressing table in the master bedroom you will find a photograph. Bring it here.

"But what for?"

For remembering.

Amparo thinks her mind is playing tricks on her, tired out as it is from so much emoción, so much effort to create just the right atmosphere for bringing this special baby into the world. Of course it is just her apprehension about Lily, about the awesome responsibility of bringing Consuelo's grandchild into the world alive and well.

The evening before, after Ismael had taken off for his own house in his decrepit Lancer to get a change of clothes, Consuelo had suddenly sent Amparo after him.

"Amparo, please follow him home and bring him back in time for dinner," she said, "I don't think he's eaten all day."

"Of course, querida," says Amparo, although she does not understand why Consuelo does not go herself, take the opportunity to spend some time alone with her husband after being separated for the past six months. Now that they are together in their daughter's house, Consuelo's continued use of intermediaries between herself and Ismael seems crazy.

Crazy or not, it is the reason Amparo finds herself half an hour later ringing the doorbell of Quinta Consuelo, where Ismael and his wife had spent thirty-five years of their lives together.

Ismael opens the door with what Amparo has come to refer as his hard-boiled look. "I don't need any meddling mother hens around here," he says. But then his features soften, and she knows he is joking.

"Ismael, kindly address your complaints to your esposa. She sent me to make sure you are back for dinner," she says.

"Está bien, mujer," said Ismael. "But don't try to keep me there. My daughter's house is overflowing, and her sofa is not very comfortable for sleeping. I have been on the road for most of these past six months, sleeping on the ground in the open air. I am due a few nights of comfort in my own bed."

Amparo laughs, for Ismael is a man who is perfectly comfortable sleeping on the ground in the open air, and possibly even prefers it.

"Would you mind if I use your bathroom?" she asks. Ismael gestures politely toward the master bedroom.

In the bedroom, which is preserved in a state of disarray, Amparo notices that the side of the bed where Consuelo used to sleep is the only side that is rumpled. And her heart aches for Ismael. With all their bravado, men are lost without their women in the end. She is glad Alejandro went before her, even though she misses that old malandro so much it makes her teeth hurt.

At first she is unable to find the evidence that would vindicate the voice in her head. She is relieved and disappointed at the same time. But then her hand sweeps the back of the drawer, touches the pointy corners of a small box wrapped in paper. She pulls it out, takes it to the bathroom, and shuts the door behind her. In the cardboard box is a framed black-and-white photograph of the four of them—Amparo, Alejandro, Consuelo, and Ismael. It had been taken the night of their fifth wedding anniversary, Alejandro and Amparo's, the night Consuelo and Ismael first met. They were holding up champagne glasses and smiling. So young, so full of joy, of promise, with their lives ahead of them.

You remember?

"Yes, I remember."

You must tell the story to Lily.

Of course, Amparo knows this conversation exists only in her imagination. She must have seen Consuelo put the photograph in the dresser drawer at some point. But storytelling was as good an occupation as any other while waiting for the baby to come. Perhaps being compelled by a militant Marialioncera to dig for joy in their memories would be good for everybody. Luz, for example.

Life had given Luz some pretty tough knocks—the loss of her father before she was born, a difficult relationship with her mother, not being able to have children, her divorce. For a while, after she married Miguel Rojas, it had seemed as though Luz was finally going to be happy. But something had gone wrong; Miguel had left her. And although when he left her, he left her enormously wealthy, he also left her bitter. All Luz's toughness was just the veneer over her unhappiness, la pobre. Luz might be rich enough to buy diamonds at a time when most people could barely afford Harina P.A.N. But all the buying in the world could not cure loneliness.

The best cure for a bitter heart is to feed it with hope and possibility. And with that thought in mind, on the fourth day of the Novena to Maria Lionza, Amparo tells the story of how Consuelo Salvatierra fell in love with Ismael Martinez.

"Amparo and Alejandro Aguilar cordially request your company to celebrate their fifth wedding anniversary," said the embossed invitation. So, when she was twenty-nine, Amparo's best friend, Consuelo, attended a large dinner party at her home in the prestigious residential area known as Lagunita on a clear, star-filled night in June. And that is where she first saw Ismael Martínez—poet, composer, and revolutionary—just back from the Gran Sabana, where it was rumored he had been rabble-rousing with the Pemon tribes to block the construction of an oil field.

That Ismael, he was always up to something, raising hell of one kind or the other. There had been rumors of his involvement in working-class riots and plots to overthrow the dictatorship. And in those days individuals suspected of sedition usually disappeared or else were the victims of bizarre accidents, or inexplicable suicides.

But there was Ismael, acting as though he hadn't a care in the world. That night he was casually debonair in black trousers and a white shirt with the sleeves rolled twice at the cuff. He stood with his back against the terrace railing, his dark brown, wavy hair catching the silver light of the moon. He was facing Consuelo and Amparo, who stood just inside the French doors, surrounded by his usual group of revelers whenever he came to the city, which is to say, mostly women. He was playing the cuatro and singing. The song was "Flor de mayo," and the way he sang it could set a fire ablaze in any woman's belly. It is not an exaggeration to say that all the women were in love with Ismael Martinez that night, jostling one another in an effort to be closest to him, or in his line of vision, using every feminine trick in the book to capture his attention.

Consuelo and Amparo stayed where they were, observing the women surrounding the man. Like Amparo, like all the well-to-do, oil-rich wives in Tamanaco at that time, they were confidently slender and elegant, with perfectly coiffed heads. They wore imported lipstick and sported the latest fashions from Europe, all purchased with oil money. Amparo could tell that Consuelo, who was a big-boned woman with unruly black hair that fell to her generously rounded hips, felt immediately out of place, even though she looked spectacular in a low cut black dress and red satin pumps.

The song came to its wistful conclusion, evoking sighs of pleasure from the audience. Amparo thought: Ismael can make even these city slickers long for the Gran Sabana, even if they've never been there.

"Be careful with that one," she whispered in Consuelo's ear. "He has the soul of a llanero—a real heartbreaker. No woman can tame him. He belongs to every woman and no woman."

And just then, by some strange twist of fate, Ismael stopped singing and looked directly at Consuelo, who immediately became pale as a ghost and looked as though she might faint.

"I tell you, Amparo," she would say later, "it was as if he had grabbed my womb with his eyes and squeezed it."

But, to go back to the story, just as Alejandro instructed the band to play a bossa nova, a man called Pedro Lanz, who held an important government post and was visiting from the capital, approached Consuelo and asked Amparo for an introduction. Now, Amparo didn't like Lanz, for reasons she couldn't quite explain, for he was by no means an unattractive man and had impeccable manners. But, according to Alejandro, being nice to Lanz was good for business, and Amparo was nothing if not her husband's most effective public relations manager.

"But of course, Señor Lanz," said Amparo. "May I present Señorita Salvatierra."

"Un placer," said Lanz, politely offering his hand. But it remained hovering in midair, and Consuelo did not accept it. Amparo nudged her, thinking her distracted, but Consuelo, said, "Oh, was he talking to me? I thought he was introducing himself to my breasts."

Lanz's swarthy complexion went pink as if he had just been

boiled, and, for the first time Amparo's social skills failed her entirely. In any case, there wasn't a thing she could have done, since Consuelo was behaving as though both she and Lanz were invisible to her, and perhaps they were, because at that moment Ismael started walking toward them and Consuelo was watching him with her lips slightly parted, as if he were the only other human being on the planet.

"Buenas, Amparo; good evening, Pedro," said Ismael.

"Good evening, Ismael," said Pedro Lanz.

"Pedro and I fought in the last revolution together, did you know that, Amparita?" said Ismael. "But now he is a director and has become antirevolutionary."

"Ismael, you know I know nothing of politics," Amparo replied, while Consuelo began studying the area near their feet. Pedro Lanz must have realized he didn't have a hope in hell of redeeming himself with Consuelo. He politely extracted himself, saying he thought he would get something from the bar.

"Good riddance," Ismael said, eyeing Consuelo appreciatively. "Now this, Amparo, is a woman. Where have you been hiding her? I demand an introduction."

Amparo, like all the other women, was a little bit in love with Ismael, who, she was convinced, could charm a snake if he set his mind to it. Relieved by the precipitous departure of Lanz and happy for the opportunity to please Ismael, she said, "Ismael Martínez, this is my best friend Consuelo Salvatierra, from Valencia. We were in school together."

"In that case, I will have to visit Valencia more often," he replied, while Consuelo blushed all the way down to her knees.

Now, Amparo may have been fond of Ismael, but she was protective about Consuelo, and she didn't want him messing about and trampling the flowers in the garden of her best friend's heart. Besides, though Ismael could be considered among the best of the country's most important poets and musicians, he rarely had a céntimo to his name. On the other hand, one dance could hardly matter, and the two were unlikely to meet again. Still, she thought it best to caution him. "Cuidado, Ismael. Don't try to play the fool with her — she's not like the others. If you were to break her heart, Alejandro would kill you and I would let him." Alejandro had a reputation for a lethal left hook.

"I only wanted to ask her to dance," said Ismael, smiling disarmingly. "Do I have your permission, Amparita?"

Amparo looked at Consuelo, who continued to look at the floor. "Well, Consuelo?" said Amparo. "Would you like to dance with this good-for-nothing lout?"

"Yes," said Consuelo, without raising her eyes.

(And then what? says Lily.)

And then Ismael reached out, placed his fingers under Consuelo's chin, and lifted it until her eyes were level with his. Then he took her gently by the elbow and led her to the dance floor, where they began to dance. They danced so beautifully together, and all eyes were upon them. They continued to dance during the buffet, and during the serving of coffee and brandy. Finally, when all the other guests had left, Alejandro and Amparo went to put out the lights on the terrace, and through the French doors they saw a solitary couple, still swaying softly to the music of the moon. After that night, Consuelo and Ismael danced all night every night for a week. And on the eighth day of their acquaintance, they were married at a small chapel in Valencia, with only Consuelo's aged parents, Amparo, and Alejandro in attendance.

Amparo held a reception for them on the terrace where they had first met and invited all of Tamanaco society. All the women in attendance were dressed to kill in all the colors of the rainbow, as though, even after the fact, they might be capable of seducing Ismael back to his earlier ways. But Ismael didn't even look at them and in their hearts those women wore black.

"How did you achieve the impossible?" Amparo asked Consuelo later.

It seems that on the seventh day, Consuelo threatened to cut her hair fashionably short, as was the trend in the capital. Ismael told her he would never allow it, that he would keep watch over her night and day until she gave up such a silly notion.

"Well, if you're going to guard my hair twenty-four hours a day," said Consuelo, "I suppose you'll have to marry me."

And that is the reason Ismael gave up chasing skirts all over the country. It was to rescue Consuelo's abundant hair.

What is this thing with men and hair?

Amparo and the other women laugh and ponder this question for several minutes, but no one has an explanation. They regard Carlos Alberto questioningly, but he only smiles and shrugs his shoulders. They turn to Ismael for the answer. But he is asleep, snoring softly, on the sofa across the room; he has decided to stay after all. Consuelo is pressed up next to him, one arm across his chest.

"Look at them," says Luz, "they fell asleep during their own story!"

"That's because they are still living the story," says Amparo.

The corners of Lily's mouth are curved slightly upward in the beginning of a smile.

"I never knew that my mother could be so determined," she says, "I always assumed it was my father who called all the shots."

"Your mother, cariño, is no one's doormat," says Amparo. "It takes some nerve to rebuke a director for staring at one's breasts."

"Yes, I suppose that is true," says Lily. "I remember the time Señora Lupe asked why Papi was away all the time and Mami replied that it was because he was El Zorro, fighting against evil." She laughs heartily and the other women join her. Even Luz, who is mostly sour. Remember this, remember that, they say, their voices rising, their laughter getting louder and more raucous.

From the corner of her eye, Amparo sees Carlos Alberto regard them apprehensively, like a park ranger spotting dangerous animals that have rampaged into his camp in the night. But Amparo and the other women pay no attention to him; they are caught up with hilarity, slapping the table, roaring with laughter, tears streaming down their faces; they are celebrating the moon-dance life of Consuelo Martinez Salvatierra. And, as far as Amparo is concerned, this is the way it should be.

The capacity of the passiflora edulis to endure conditions less than optimum is often quite extraordinary.

Carlos Alberto

Sometimes, when women get together, they can summon up a cornucopia of joy that makes men, by comparison, appear clinically depressed. They can do this even during times of great hardship and duress. Just last night, Carlos Alberto had watched Luz, Amparo, Marta, and the nurse all congregated in a huddle around Lily's bed in the living room, laughing together with complete abandon, while Ismael and Consuelo slept on the sofa undisturbed. And, in that instant, he had been catapulted backward into his childhood, where he is a mere boy living among too many women and a man who doesn't talk to him.

Carlos Alberto has always found the intimacy between women both fascinating and unsettling. It is as though he is looking through the window of a club where he can never be a member, because it involves a comfort level and kinship that does not exist among men, except infrequently, out of necessity, such as among soldados during times of war, or perhaps among convicts in a prison facility. And he is filled with a certain wistful longing, an ache that seems to emanate in waves from the solar plexus, for this part of Lily he cannot own.

He has attempted to capture Lily in words, on paper. Not

only the way she looks, which always makes his heart skip a beat or two, or how she expresses herself to him. He has probed, with the tip of his pen, her fears, her thoughts, hopes and desires, her darkest secrets, just as he had done when writing the character of a woman possessed of the spirit of Maria Lionza, in his recently resurrected novel, based loosely on an old Cuban radio novela, *La reencarnada*. But Lily is nothing like the sinewy heroine of his imagination, with whom he has danced in his fantasies and whose fantastical character he has known intimately. The more he writes in his diary about Lily, the less he knows. Even now, after seven years of marriage. Perhaps it is as she accused him once (although she immediately apologized and retracted when shock froze his face): that it is more the idea of Lily than Lily that he loves.

To possess Lily entirely is a crazy, greedy, impossible desire; he realizes this. And how can he begrudge Lily her secrets when there are parts of himself that he has kept separate? He has, for example, never told Lily what happened with Miguel Rojas and how it changed him.

It was to the immense relief of Dr. Jorge Quintanilla when, after five daughters and a gap of four years, Carlos Alberto was born. Finally, he thought, a candidate for medical school. But there were periods during which his pride at having finally sired a boy was severely put to the test. For example: when Carlos Alberto was seven, he insisted on dressing like a girl. His older sisters were always piling onto one of the beds, lying against one another and laughing together.

He felt left out. He thought that if he dressed like them, he would be like them. It wasn't only because there were five of them and only one of him. It just seemed to him that it was clearly more fun being a girl. And his sisters didn't mind if he invaded their closets and came down to dinner wearing a dress and a pair of high heels. They didn't care if he painted his face with their cosmetics, as long as he put the caps back on. When he asked them to help him stitch a bit of lace onto his handkerchief, they thought it was great. "Ay, look at him, tan lindo," they would say.

"Carlos Alberto," said his mother, "please finish what is on your plate if you want to have quesillo for desert."

"My name is Lupita; Lupita Ferrer," Carlos Alberto announced in falsetto, daintily lifting a spoon of black beans and rice toward a petulant mouth slathered with his sister Celia's raspberry lipstick. "I am a movie star."

Dr. Quintanilla turned toward his wife, eyes bulging. "But, Maria Teresa," he exclaimed, "the boy is turning marico. He's a damn pansy."

"He'll grow out of it, Jorge," said Maria Teresa Quintanilla. But her husband wasn't convinced. Women surrounded the boy all day; he lacked sufficient masculine influence, in Jorge Quintanilla's opinion. And so, the day after he found Carlos Alberto cuddled up with his sisters on the sofa in front of the television and sniveling over the thwarted love of the gypsy character played by the sultry Rebeca Gonsales, he enrolled him in summer camp at the Club Carabobo, where many city boys from good families went, including boys from the prestigious Academia Roosevelt. Dr. Quintanilla felt certain that at Club Carabobo all detrimental feminine influences would be expunged from the boy's psyche forthwith.

"Pero, Jorge," said Maria Teresa, "he's only eight." She believed that Carlos Alberto was still too young to be sent away from home for a whole summer.

"Eight is old enough to start learning to be a man," countered Dr. Quintanilla. "With all of you on my back like this," he added, meaning his wife and daughters, "it's a wonder I haven't turned into a fag myself."

Dr. Quintanilla's idea of what made a man involved football and baseball, mountain treks in the Andes, relay swimming, and defending oneself from bullies, the last of which Carlos Alberto would learn to fully appreciate after Miguel Rojas discovered the lace handkerchief under his pillow. It belonged to Celia, his eldest sister, and had been liberally and clandestinely doused with her perfume, to remind him of home. When Carlos Alberto had surreptitiously tucked it away between his shirts in the suitcase, little did he know how much trouble it would bring him.

It was two weeks into the summer. Carlos Alberto had just been reprimanded by the swimming coach for lagging behind in the relay race, and he was eager to regain the security of his room, which he shared with one of the older boys, Miguel Rojas, who was fourteen.

All the younger boys had to share a room with an older boy. To keep them in line, said the coach. Miguel Rojas was the only son of Jaime Rojas, who ran a chain of supermarkets he'd acquired by a providential marriage to a Portuguese heiress, Lidia Costa. Miguel Rojas was an Academia Roosevelt alumnus and one of the richest boys in Tamanaco, if not the country. But being rich didn't seem to have enhanced his disposition, and Carlos Alberto took precautions to avoid drawing attention to himself and to stay out of the older boy's way as much as was possible in such close quarters.

"What have we here?" said Miguel Rojas, as Carlos Alberto entered the room, eyes already stinging with the tears he had not cried in front of the coach. Miguel was standing on his bed. Celia's handkerchief dangled from his hand. "Don't tell me I've been sharing my room with a mariquita."

"Give it to me," Carlos Alberto whined, making a desperate lunge for the handkerchief.

"No-no-no," said Miguel Rojas, whipping it out of the boy's grasp. "I think Coach would like to see this—this marvelous result of his training."

Carlos Alberto envisioned himself spinning wildly across the full topography of his utter humiliation. Coach's sardonic face, huge, looming above his own. The vicious taunts of all the boys in camp. His father's disgust when he learned of his son's disgrace. It was too hideous to contemplate. He couldn't allow it to happen.

"Please," Carlos Alberto whispered, "please don't tell anyone."

"And what," said Miguel Rojas, "will you do for me in return?"

"Anything," he promised, "anything you want."

Miguel Rojas sat down on the bed and indicated that Carlos Alberto was to stand in front of him. He obeyed, his heart pounding through his temples. Whatever happened, he told himself, he must not cry like a damn mariquita.

"Kneel down," said Miguel Rojas, as Carlos Alberto stood trembling but dry-eyed in front of him. When the younger boy was kneeling penitently as if before a priest, Miguel Rojas said, "Where did you get this handkerchief? And make sure you confess the truth, or you will be punished."

"It belongs to my sister," Carlos Alberto said.

"What is her name?"

"Celia."

"How old is she?"

"Sixteen."

"Is she beautiful?"

"Very beautiful."

"What color are her lips?"

"Pink."

"Eyes?"

"Brown."

"Does she have tits?" Miguel Rojas had his eyes closed during this part of the interrogation, as though trying to conjure a picture of Celia in his mind.

"Yes," said Carlos Alberto.

"Are they big?" Miguel Rojas asked, opening his eyes.

"I guess so."

"What do you mean, you guess so? Either they are big or not."

"They are big."

"How big?"

Carlos Alberto made a circle with his hands of about twenty centimeters in diameter. He was so busy trying to get the size right that he failed to immediately notice that Miguel Rojas had undone his fly. Carlos Alberto was afraid.

"Kiss it," said Miguel Rojas, his voice thick and strange. "This is what girls like."

Carlos Alberto did as Miguel Rojas said. Then Miguel

Rojas stepped back and began to rub himself. His face got redder and redder. "Celia, Celia, oh, Celia," he moaned, while Carlos Alberto stared in horrified fascination.

Afterward Miguel Rojas wiped himself with the handkerchief. "Here," he said, pressing the soppy piece of cloth into Carlos Alberto's hand, "give this back to your sister with the big tits."

In retrospect, Carlos Alberto thinks that perhaps Miguel Rojas did him a favor, for he never again wished to be like a girl. That part of him was gone forever, or else buried so deep he could no longer recognize it. After a week, he took up boxing, a sport he perfected year in and year out at summer camp, much to his father's delight.

"You see, Marité?" said Dr. Quintanilla, "All he needed was to be around boys."

Maria Teresa Quintanilla nodded and smiled at her husband, but sometimes he would catch her watching Carlos Alberto covertly with a worried frown creasing her forehead. Carlos Alberto's sisters were hurt when he shrank away from their caresses and refused to watch telenovelas with them. "Don't you like Lupita Ferrer anymore?" asked Celia, tousling his hair.

"Girls are disgusting," he said, violently pushing her hand away. "They are pigs." After that, his sisters left him to his own devices.

Miguel Rojas never bothered him again after he joined the boxing team. He had graduated from an all-boy high school and gone off to the Universidad Simón Bolívar by the time Carlos Alberto won his first state boxing medal at the age of sixteen. Dr. Quintanilla, glowing with pride (and possibly relief) presented his son with an expensively wrapped gift box in the locker room.

"Open it, mijo," he said.

Carlos Alberto, his face still throbbing from an uppercut to the left cheekbone and dressed only in the towel wrapped around his waist, tore off the paper and opened the box. He drew in a breath of surprise, wincing at the fresh pain in his side. But his pleasure at the contents of the box far outstripped his pain. Inside was a Rolleiflex 3.5F and a meter.

"¡Estupendo, Papá!" he exclaimed.

"I remembered how you used to beg me to let you take pictures with my old Zeiss when you were younger. I was going to give it to you on your eighteenth birthday, but I have decided you should have it now. You earned it tonight, muchacho." In his enthusiasm of the moment, he slapped Carlos Alberto roughly on the back, rattling his son's ribs so much he thought he would faint. Observing the wince, he ran elegant surgeon's fingers down Carlos Alberto's rib cage. Ruffling his son's hair, he said, "Looks like you might have broken one. But I'm sure your opponent is in far worse shape. Here, let me strap you up for the ride home."

While his father tied a bandage around his torso, they relived the match in detail up until the spectacular moment where Carlos Alberto had knocked his opponent out cold with a left hook he had learned from his father's golf buddy, Alejandro Aguilar, in the third round.

It was the first and only intimate moment he and his father had ever shared, as far as he can recall. Subsequent wins never brought on such a show of emotion and pride; they were expected. Dr. Quintanilla believed in physical excellence as much as he believed in excellence of mind and spirit. For him, excellence was the norm.

Carlos Alberto inaugurated his camera with photographs of his family members, secretly reveling in the unguarded private moments captured and suspended on celluloid. His sister Celia, combing her hair and dreamily staring out the window before her first date. His mother, laughing with abandon at his graduation dinner. His father on Christmas Eve, pensive at his desk. It became his primary hobby, at which he spent virtually all his free time. He numbered each photograph. In a notebook he wrote down the numbers and kept meticulous notes — the name of the subject, the date, the time of day, the occasion.

After a while, he began taking photographs of complete strangers on the street. In his notebook, he gave them fictitious names and began writing imaginary tales about them. And thus his love of stories was renewed from his soap opera days. Only now, *he* was the one telling the story. Despite his father's derision, it turned out to be his most valuable survival skill. In these days of economic hardship and incertitude, it is what keeps food on the table and turns the light-bulbs on.

A few days before he graduated from college with a degree in literature and a minor in film history, Carlos Alberto drove into the parking lot of the Supermercado Costa and reached into the glove compartment for his mother's grocery list. Just as he was about to turn into a parking space, a man driving a Jeep aggressively zipped ahead of him and took the place. Carlos Alberto lost his temper and leapt out of his car to confront the man. When he saw it was Miguel Rojas, a lethal icy calm descended upon him.

"Hola," Carlos Alberto said, "remember me?"

When Miguel Rojas simply stared at him with a benign bovine gaze that made him crazy with rage, he said, "I'm Celia, your marico friend from summer camp at the Club Carabobo. And you just took my space." Then Carlos Alberto beat the shit out of Miguel Rojas right there in the parking lot. In his memory the fight is a blur of fists — his own, hitting a body, *thump, thump, thump* — then a body hitting the side of the car with a sickening thud and slumping to the ground. He recalls launching several well-aimed kicks for good measure, before getting back in his car and driving away without the groceries.

To this day Carlos Alberto is not sure whether he has not told Lily this story because he is ashamed of what Miguel Rojas did to him or of what he did to Miguel Rojas.

When Lily introduced Carlos Alberto to her family over the Christmas holidays, there had been a bizarre and awkward moment. For, by a preposterous twist of fate of the kind that seems feasible only in soap operas, Miguel Rojas happened to be married to Marta's daughter, Luz. Carlos Alberto observed that marriage seemed to have made a better person out of Miguel Rojas, who judiciously behaved as though he were meeting Carlos Alberto for the first time, slapping him genially on the back in greeting, albeit a little too hard.

Carlos Alberto forgave him upon observing the tenderness he exhibited toward Luz and the gallant, if lumbering, way he helped clear the table on Christmas Eve. Who could have imagined that an ornery girl like Luz could work such a miracle on his childhood nemesis. In spite of the radical change for the better in Miguel Rojas and his manifest adulation of Luz, things hadn't worked out between the two, and Luz was now living in a luxurious penthouse apartment in Santa Fé, mooning about and feeling sorry for herself in the best telenovela tradition.

In direct contrast with the goings-on in his own family, where nothing truly extraordinary had ever transpired, there is always an air of high drama and the supernatural around Lily's people—especially, it would appear, during times of duress. One minute they might be arguing over politics at the dining table with enough passion to give themselves indigestion, the next they might be praying to a mythological fertility goddess and telling stories to an unborn baby! It is extraordinary.

When Carlos Alberto had started supplying stories to the television producers of soap operas for extra cash, he never imagined he might wind up living in one.

It is the fifth day since the statue of Maria Lionza broke in two, and everything related to the goddess has become a national obsession, fueled by an unremitting media frenzy. There are constant flash bulletins and updates, opinions are polled and dissected. Is the broken statue a metaphor for the political and economic divide in the country? Is it an omen, and if so, what does it portend? Should the statue be moved to a new location for repairs or should it be repaired on site? Who actually has jurisdiction over the statue—the Ministry of Art and Culture or the Municipality? Is the worship of Maria Lionza a religion or a cult? Clashes between factions with opposing views on these questions have broken out all over the country.

In a related story, the media is excitedly reporting that an apparition called El Niño is supposed to have materialized out of thin air before a group of Marialionceros in Sorte. Cut to a clip of the president, announcing the launch of a new educational reform campaign. The details of its aims are vague, but its slogan is : "¡El Niño, el Futuro!"

While Carlos Alberto is watching, the phone rings. It is a producer at TVista requesting permission to use segments from his documentary interviews with various Marialionceros as background on the evening news. Carlos Alberto is rendered almost speechless by the amount they are willing to pay for it: one million Bolívares. Seeing a chance to resolve all his financial problems in one fell swoop, he accepts their proposal on one condition: that they also give him a contract to conduct interviews with those claiming to have seen El Niño for a total of three million.

"And the copyright is mine," he says, nearly bowled over by his own audaciousness. Yes, fine, great, brilliant, says the British producer, we'll send the contract papers across by this afternoon. If Carlos Alberto believed in prayer, this would be its answer. And yet, what if something were to happen to Lily while he is away? Are three million bolos worth that risk? He is conflicted, thrown against the ropes of his own inner boxing match.

"Of course you must not miss this opportunity, mi amor," says Lily. "And take my father with you; he knows people everywhere."

"But what about you and the baby?

"Don't worry, it's only for a few days. I'll be fine here with all these babysitters." But Carlos Alberto thinks it is possible she is just being brave.

"You should tell a story to your baby before you go," says Marta, while Luz cackles wickedly.

"Why not?" says Carlos Alberto, glaring at Luz. "After all, storytelling is my métier."

So, on the fifth day of the Novena to Maria Lionza, Carlos Alberto tells of how much of an ass he was willing to make of himself in order to get Lily to notice him.

The first time Carlos Alberto saw Lily, she was standing at a honey stand on a cobblestone street in the German settlement of Colonia Tovar, which lies hidden in the mountains some 60 kilometers west of the capital.

Lily, whose name he did not know, of course, at the time wore a white sleeveless summer dress of fine muslin that fell beguilingly, ending in a flutter around her narrow ankles. Her small feet were delicately bound in flat bronze sandals with spidery straps. Her tiny round toes, with nails varnished in clear polish, were so alluring that he felt a desperate and urgent desire to place them, one by one, in his mouth. A slight chill pierced the air as afternoon moved into evening, and, tearing his gaze away from those succulent buds, he noticed little goose bumps standing out on her thin forearms. The sunset shone through her dress, outlining her slender thighs, the gentle curve of her calves. It caught wisps of her shoulder-length brown-black hair, spinning them into shimmering threads that swirled distractedly in the summer breeze. She was looking down, rummaging in her white crochet handbag, her lashes making dark quarter moons against the vanilla of her skin. Then, as she bent lower, digging deeper in her handbag, her hair fell across her face and it was all he could do not to reach out and brush it back. Finding enough change for the honey vendor in the bowels of her bag, Lily straightened before he could act on his insane impulse, tossing back her hair and revealing a few stray freckles on her nose.

(Not freckles, birthmarks, says Lily.)

Carlos Alberto followed Lily like a detective as she walked along the lanes of the village, hiding behind his newspaper when she stopped to window-shop. She made her way to the beveled lawns of the Fritz, a middle-range inn, but more expensive than his own, and sat down on a chaise lounge in the shade of a tree, next to a couple who looked to be around sixty-five years of age. The older woman was painting a watercolor with a child's paint set. The older man was strumming a cuatro and serenading her. Carlos Alberto decided these were the girl's grandparents. He was already making up stories about her by then, and he continued to do so throughout the afternoon from his perch on a stone wall in the sun.

So captivated was Carlos Alberto by this girl that when he returned to his room that night, images of her continued to flash through his mind. Even after several glasses of rum, even after he fell asleep, she continued to haunt him, appearing suddenly, unbidden, in his dreams and evaporating just as quickly.

On the second day of his vacation in Colonia Tovar, he awoke early. He shaved and dressed with lightning speed and rushed out into the misty morning, slipping and sliding through the damp cobblestone lanes to the grounds of the Fritz. Perhaps, he thought, he would be able to catch sight of her at breakfast. He found an inconspicuous corner table in the small wood-paneled restaurant the hotel management ran for its guests. When he ordered coffee, the waiter asked him which room he was staying in, and he was forced to confess that he was not a guest of the Fritz. The waiter's face took on a pained and offended expression.

"This restaurant is for guests only, Señor," he informed Carlos Alberto.

Carlos Alberto assured him that he was there to ascertain whether this was the hotel he wanted to stay in, that the quality of the coffee was very important to him in determining where he would stay. From his manner, Carlos Alberto doubted the waiter believed him—this was a family hotel, and Carlos Alberto was clearly a young man all on his own. It may have been the desperation in Carlos Alberto's voice that made the waiter decide to serve him a coffee. It was a much more expensive coffee than one obtainable at any kiosk in the lanes of Colonia Tovar. But it was worth it. For, a few minutes later, Lily entered the room, even more fresh and beautiful than he remembered. He remained with her—well not *with* her, but with her in view—throughout most of the day. It was a rather uneventful day, during which Lily made only one foray into the town, to purchase a cuckoo clock, for which the artisans of the colony are famous. It did occur to him that the real cuckoo was himself, or at least that is what his friend Ricardo would say when he returned to the city and recounted what he had been up to. But at that moment Carlos Alberto was ecstatic in his madness, and he could hardly wait to fall into bed so he could dream of the girl with the brown-black hair and rosebud toes. But again, he could not fall asleep without the aid of plentiful cups of rum.

The next morning was Easter Sunday. He wanted to attend the eight a.m. Mass at the chapel on the square because he thought he might see his fantasy girl there and perhaps be able to make her acquaintance. He stumbled, hungover, from the lumpy bed at the Viejo Aleman and made his way to the bathroom, where a leprous visage confronted him in the mirror above the washbasin. Could this be his face? He remembered having applied Coppertone sunblock at some point during the previous day. Clearly, the application had been uneven. And now his face was covered with alternately beet red and creamy white patches. This did not bode well for romance. He briefly considered makeup. Certainly, he had had enough experience with its application during his childhood. But there would probably be no shops open on Easter Sunday. He compromised with the Panama hat his father had given him, pulling it down low over his forehead, where the worst bits of seared flesh were localized. His sisters had always assured him that he was handsome in a roguish way. Now he looked like a gangster, but this was a distinct improvement over the unedited version.

After the Mass, the congregation spilled into the square. Carlos Alberto was relieved to notice that the object of his affection and heightened desire was without familial encumbrance. He was in the process of summoning enough nerve to approach her when he heard her cry out, her mouth making a surprised and exquisite circle of pain. She had twisted her ankle on the uneven cobblestones of the church square. Carlos Alberto sprinted to her assistance, solicitously guiding her back to her hotel, insisting that she put her weight on him as they went. She said she didn't know how to thank him. He responded by saying that he was completely lost in Colonia Tovar and didn't know where to eat, and that if she was feeling better by evening, perhaps she could accompany him to a decent restaurant. To his delight, she agreed.

As soon as he had her captive in a corner booth at the restaurant quaintly known as El pequeño Alemán, he wanted to come clean. Without prologue, he admitted to her that he had stalked her for three days since his arrival at Colonia Tovar. He confessed to her how he had completely humiliated and demeaned himself by lying and pretending to be lost, too ignorant to find a restaurant where he could get a meal and a cup of coffee, even though there was one on every street corner, all of which were fairly good. He said his friend Ricardo was a third-year medical student specializing in obstetrics who had a different woman on his arm each month, and was his love guru. He said Ricardo had told him that women love men who are lost, and that he had decided he had nothing to lose. As soon as he said all this, he regretted it; he was sure the girl would think him psychotic, or worse, pitiful — the biggest pendejo she had ever met. He became quiet, staring glumly into his untouched marroncito, as if his salvation resided in a demitasse.

"Well, it worked," she said simply, and began chattering away about the first time she had visited Colonia Tovar when she was thirteen with her school friend Irene Dos Santos. He didn't know it at the time, so easy was her banter, but she told him later that whenever she is nervous, re-creating her childhood has the salubrious effect of a tranquilizer.

A bit to his own surprise, Carlos Alberto doesn't feel stupid while telling this story to his unborn child. And while he certainly does *not* believe in Maria Lionza, a small secret part of him almost wishes he did.

"Incidentally, you never told me why you were so nervous that day at the restaurant," Carlos Alberto murmurs, later, just before falling asleep on the floor next to his wife's makeshift bed in the living room.

"Because I knew I was going to sleep with you," Lily says.

The first time they had made love, it had been unplanned, and Carlos Alberto had been afraid. He was so large and she was so small. He thought he might hurt her and she wouldn't want him again. But by the time this thought had completed itself, his body had taken charge and he was already pushing impatiently against a resilient barrier. Lily's eyes had been squeezed shut, her eyelashes wet, her breathing uneven. She cried out, but clenched him to herself, locking her legs around his back. "I'm sorry, I'm sorry," he gasped, his mind mortified, his senses bursting with delight. He sobbed as he plunged deeper and deeper, straining to reach the pinnacle, unable to pull back, to relinquish pleasure even at the cost of her pain. He felt himself a beast.

Afterward it had been Lily who was the consoler. She held his head against her breast, puffing pensively on an Astor, while the blood seeped into the sheets, and said, "If it had been up to my friend Irene, that barrier would have been broken a long time ago. My darling, I'm so glad I waited for you."

And with those words he became her slave. Months later, when she could not conceive, she said they should tell her mother. He had been appalled. "How can you discuss this most intimate thing with your mother?" he asked.

"My mother taught me that secrets are sicknesses," she replied. "When I need help and advice, I consult my mother. I can tell my mother anything."

"Anything?"

"Yes, mi amor. Anything and everything. You must get accustomed to that. In my family, we are constantly in each other's business."

Before long, Carlos Alberto himself was telling Consuelo everything, the words gushing from his lips like water from a broken tap. It wasn't so much that Consuelo had all the answers, it was just that he was finally voicing his questions. Questions had never been encouraged in his own family. In the Quintanilla household, only obedience and silent stoicism had been rewarded.

Dr. Jorge Quintanilla sold his home in Tamanaco and bought one in the hills of the Western province a few months after he retired from the cardiology department at Los Aves. But, almost before he'd had time to experience the freedom, and perhaps the boredom, of retirement, a sudden and massive stroke knocked him senseless on the golf green, and now he lay immobile in one of the beautifully appointed guest rooms, surrounded by medicine bottles and tubes, his eyes half open but unmoving, recognizing no one and no thing. He had turned into his own worst nightmare, for there can be nothing more galling to a doctor than for the doctor to become the patient.

They had already been married a year before Carlos Alberto took Lily to his parents' home. They arrived in time for lunch, a boisterous affair including his mother, his sisters, their spouses and children, during which, as usual, everyone spoke at once. Carlos Alberto was somewhat apprehensive about how Lily, an only child, would tolerate it. But she sat at the table, turning her head this way and that, trying to catch with her small ears all the words flying randomly around the dining room, smiling with delight. Later, they went to look in on his father. Carlos Alberto stood in the doorway watching his father's chest rise and fall. *Asshole.*

Unlike himself, who continued to stand rigid in the doorway, Lily was not revolted and not afraid to approach the shell of a man that had once been his father. She had bent down and kissed him lightly on the forehead. And Carlos Alberto thought how proud and relieved Jorge Quintanilla would have been, had he been able to see Lily, irrefutable proof that in spite of the choice to pursue a career in what he had oft referred to as "pansy work"—teaching and writing documentary film—his son was, after all, a man. For the first time, Carlos Alberto felt something bordering on pity for his father, an expert on hearts, who knew not his own.

The next day, they boarded the teleférico, which whisked

them up to 3,500 meters in a matter of minutes. Beyond
stood the snow-capped Pico Bolívar, swathed in clouds.
They held hands and were quiet on the way back down. The
crisp smell of snow had given them a sudden urge for ice
cream. And so, upon their return to the town, they stopped
by Helados Tibisay, famous for its unusual flavors, where
they surrendered to their childish fancy. Lily tried the celery,
while Carlos Alberto opted for black beans. From there, they
drove to Los Frijoles, their hotel, and spent the next three
days making love, interspersed with bouts of holding their
noses and blowing till their ears popped, in an attempt to
relieve the pressure from the high altitude.

On the fourth day they walked all the way to Laguna Vic-
toria, carrying a small but well-stocked picnic basket and a
blanket. Lily did not swim, but she said she would not mind
if Carlos Alberto wanted to take a dip. Carlos Alberto swam
with strong, smooth strokes, feeling the water ripple over
his back, oblivious to the fact that as his figure gradually
diminished from his wife's perspective, she was becoming
extremely agitated. When he turned back, she was waving
her blue and green silk scarf in the air, and when he reached
the shore, her eyes were rimmed in red and the features of
her face taut with an anguish he could not fathom.

"But, what is wrong, mi amor?" he asked her, the expression in her eyes wrenching his stomach with fear.

"You looked so small in the water," Lily said, forcing a
smile to blanched lips. And then, lying on the grass with
the dew seeping through the wool of the blanket, she lay
her head upon his chest and told her about her dream in
which she and her friend Irene Dos Santos had gone for a
swim in the lagoon too soon after lunch, developed cramps,

and drowned. Since then, Lily said, she was afraid of deep waters.

Early on in their relationship, there were occasions when Carlos Alberto considered the possibility that Lily may be "not all there" in a charming, nonthreatening sort of way, and he had strongly suspected that Irene Dos Santos was just a figment of her imagination. But this suspicion was laid to rest by his mother-in-law, Consuelo, who told him that Irene had been Lily's best friend in school. Apparently they had lost touch with one another at some stage during their school years, or so Consuelo gave him to understand. Precisely when and how this occurred continues to elude him. Lily herself has never discussed it and Consuelo, without his even noticing it, changes the subject whenever it comes up.

It occurs to Carlos Alberto that when women don't want to answer a question at a particular point in time, they somehow manage to make you forget you ever asked.

After a spirited discussion about the pros and cons of traveling to Sorte via Valencia or by the Nirgua mountain route, it is finally decided that they will go through Valencia. When Luz asks whether she can accompany Carlos Alberto and Ismael, he raises no objection, though he is not particularly keen on the idea. Luz can be such a pain in the ass. He thinks he knows why she wants to go: Valencia is where her estranged husband, Miguel Rojas, lives. Well, if Luz fancies the application of salt on her wounds, who is he to say no?

Ismael is quiet, as is Luz, who had insisted on driving. She steers Ismael's prehistoric automobile on the autopista at a speed that makes the hair on Carlos Alberto's forearms stand on end, and drives nonstop to the outskirts of Valencia. There, they have lunch and rest for an hour under the shade of an umbrella at an outdoor café. While Carlos Alberto is paying the bill, Luz tries to phone Miguel at a booth across the road. When she returns, her eyes are red, and both Ismael and Carlos Alberto discreetly pretend they haven't noticed.

As they set off once again, the car rattles uncontrollably, and Carlos Alberto regrets not insisting on bringing his Range Rover, given to him by his mother after his father could no longer drive. It was a sturdy vehicle, though some-what battered after being briefly commandeered by drug runners in broad daylight. "Get out of my car," they had said, one of them pointing a gun through the open window at Carlos Alberto's crotch. The police had found it later, abandoned in the hills of El Hatillo, one side riddled with bullet holes. Carlos Alberto thinks the bullet holes give the car character. In any case, who can afford bodywork these days? It is still a comfortable ride.

The Lancer has to be at least twenty-five years old by his calculations. He can already feel the impact of the shot suspension on his hemorrhoids. He voices his idea about stopping at a service station in Valencia. But Ismael and Luz exchange smiles as though he has just made a joke, and Luz continues driving at breakneck speed.

Around two p.m., Ismael takes over the wheel. Again, the drive begins in silence. The old man stares straight ahead as though there is no one in the car but himself. As for Luz, she is as reticent as the old man. Carlos Alberto begins to anticipate with something bordering on dread several days of silence interspersed with grunts of acknowledgement on whether to turn left or right at a particular juncture, or which truck stop to eat at. He is distracted from this train of thought as they enter the valley of Maraca.

Recently swept by a thundershower, the valley is at its lushest, reminding Carlos Alberto of why it is known among indigenous painters for its unique palette of greens and golds. Sugarcane in the fields is high. The breezes have diminished and a relentless humidity seems to press the air out of his lungs. Carlos Alberto hopes they will find rooms with air-conditioning in either San Felipe or Chivacoa, for he can afford the best as long as TVista is paying. They stop briefly at a small supply store along the highway. Like shopkeepers all over the country, this one, too, has become adept at disguising the holes on his shelves. When Ismael asks for a bag of wheat flour, the owner shakes his head.

"Wheat flour has all but disappeared from the shelves for two months now," he explains. "The little that gets into the state is being delivered directly to bakeries and pasta makers. Not much baking is done at home these days."

Ismael selects a bag of white cornmeal instead, which looks to Carlos Alberto as though it may have already exceeded its shelf life. This, he supposes, means that wherever Ismael is taking them first will involve cooking. He hopes he will not be expected to pull his weight in that department, since the only thing he can cook is steak, and the chances of obtaining good-quality meat on the road are unlikely. Luz purchases several packs of cigarettes and some mints. Carlos Alberto is suddenly aware that he has left home without his shaving kit. He buys shaving cream and a pack of disposable razors at a price that seems to him monstrous, double the price of such a purchase in the city. Ismael adds some rope and loose-leaf

Indian tobacco to the supplies. Carlos Alberto observes the selection of the tobacco with some puzzlement; as far as he knows, Ismael is neither a smoker nor a chewer of tobacco. When their purchases are complete, the shopkeeper invites them out back to a tarpaulin-covered patio for a drink of rum on ice. They accept.

"For a time, one thing we could still be thankful for was that the crazy love of crime besotting the country had not struck the Western province with the same intensity as in the capital," says the man, whose name, they have learned, is Mario Antonio Perez, Papy to his friends. "No longer," he continues, shaking his head mournfully, "what with this business of the rebels taking over some of the big cattle ranches and El Presidente turning a blind eye. That's what started it. Land reform. Now they all think they live in Cuba and that everything belongs to everyone. The situation is bad, and we expect it to get worse. One of the big supermarkets a block from my home was attacked at payroll last month by a bunch of indios. And just the other night, somebody tried to steal the metal nameplate of my apartment building to resell for scrap metal. He was heard at two a.m. by one of my neighbors, who got his gun and caught the guy. Big scandal in the street, people running around half naked, a couple of shots in the air for good measure, and after a few hours a police car finally came and took the thief. We couldn't find the sign, though we scoured the area." He shakes his head and sighs. "But look at me, giving such bad tidings to visitors! Pay no attention. Where exactly are you headed?"

Carlos Alberto says they are en route to Sorte.

"Paying a visit to the Lady and El Niño, are you? I doubt even they can help us now. If you are passing through San

Felipe, take care; car vigilantes propagate the latest racket there. You cannot park anywhere in the town without coming back to your car and finding a little cardboard on your windshield that claims your car is being attended. Some derelict Guajiro kid just pops out of nowhere to remove the card as you get into your car and of course you are expected to give him some money. My advice is, don't refuse, unless you want trouble. The street kids move in gangs." He continues for sometime in this vein, perfectly content to be the only one talking. Finally, he says, "Well, time for me to get back home, or the wife will have something to say about it. Good luck to you."

Luz says she wants to use the bathroom, but Carlos Alberto thinks she probably wants to make another phone call to her ex.

Finishing their drinks and thanking Papy, Ismael and Carlos Alberto climb back into the car, now hot-boxed from almost an hour in the full afternoon sun, and wait for Luz. As he fastens his seat belt, Carlos Alberto feels a wave of longing for those left behind, none of whom are ever at a loss for words.

From the day Carlos Alberto married Lily, though he has been polite, Ismael has barely spoken a word to him, which makes it exceedingly difficult for Carlos Alberto to discern whether or not his father-in-law likes him. So he is pleasantly surprised when, turning back onto the road to San Felipe, Ismael suddenly becomes a fountain of speech, embarking with gusto on a story about a road trip three years earlier. It was to the Indian settlements in the Delta, where he had gone on behalf of the Department for the Preservation of Parks, Forests and Protected Areas to investigate reports of unauthorized cutting of mangroves. Unofficially, he had gone to study the music and instruments of the Warao. His own face is illuminated as he describes the journey through the Delta, then another to Pemon country, the magnificence of the Tepuys, imposingly high mesas of up to 3,000 meters. Carlos Alberto watches, fascinated, as Ismael's craggy features, the deep wrinkles that make folds in his face, smoothen as he speaks. As they moved farther away from the city, Ismael begins to sing softly, almost under his breath, in a language Carlos Alberto had never heard:

Ihi kabo arotu ihi
Ihi tata arotu
Hi nasaribuna tane
Domo tuyu tuyuna
Hi nanoarate ine

"What is that language?" Carlos Alberto asks.

"It is Warao," says Ismael.

"What does it mean?" he asks.

" 'You are the lord of the skies, you are the lord of beyond, your voice is like the tigana bird, I call your name many times.' "

It is an astonishing transformation. And Carlos Alberto thinks to himself, Here is a man who belongs to the wild places.

Carlos Alberto knows that his father-in-law, a genetic blend of Spanish and Que, is quite famous for his cuatro playing and timeless ballad compositions, though his fame has never translated into financial security. He is aware that Ismael in his younger days had worked with the Indian underground organization, Passiflora Edulis, so named in honor of the legendary Spanish Civil War heroine Dolores Ibarruri, also known as La Pasionaria, who remained in exile in the Soviet Union. The P.E. (for the members were notoriously obsessed with secrecy and only referred to it by its initials until it had served its purpose and was disbanded) had joined the Junta Patriótica to overthrow El Colonel. Carlos Alberto even knows that Ismael had spent time in the unspeakable secret prison of the regime as a dangerous dissident for writing a song that had ignited the fire of resistance in the hearts of the people, and that he had been released only on the day of the uprising that sent El Colonel fleeing for his life. While conducting research on that brutal period in history, he discovered that Ismael is considered a kind of folk hero in some of the least expected circles. He had wanted to interview his father-in-law and record him singing his own music as part of a documentary, but when he brought it up, Ismael had declined crustily and without amplification.

Carlos Alberto thinks his father would have got on well enough with Ismael, who is definitely not a pansy by any social or cultural standard one may choose to apply. While he is by no means a heavyweight, he is tough and wiry, with a certain feral look in his eye. Other men would think ten times before opposing him. Because of his economy with words, he sometimes appears almost taciturn. Nevertheless, women fall for him, even at his age, which is seventy-five. Just the other day, Carlos Alberto accompanied him to the automercado to pick up a case of beer. The cashier, a sumptuous creature with sensuality oozing from her very pores, ignored Carlos Alberto completely and began flirting with

Ismael, as if he were Antonio Banderas. Ismael did nothing, as far as Carlos Alberto could see, to encourage the girl. In fact, he was rather gruff. Yet she appeared most reluctant to conclude the business at hand—that of ringing up the purchase—and went on chattering and blushing like a romantic schoolgirl.

From all reports, Ismael was an accomplished seducer in his youth. Carlos Alberto has even heard that Simón, another famous composer of ballads, had written at least one song with the exploits of Ismael in mind. It is quite possible. Not only does Ismael have a way with women, he is at ease around them. And yet he is, without question, completely devoted to his family. The thought that he and his father-in-law have at least this in common gives him the courage to start up a conversation.

"What made you decide to get married?" he asks.

"I met Consuelo," says Ismael, grinning.

"And what made you settle down in Tamanaco?"

"I promised Consuelo when she was pregnant with Lily." Ismael begins to hum "Caballo viejo" quietly to himself, and that is the end of that. The subject is closed. Luz sits staring out of the window, smoking a cigarette and twirling a lock of her frosty blond hair, humming fragments of the melody with Ismael. Then both bellow out the words of the chorus in harmony at the top of their lungs. Carlos Alberto thinks that Luz and Ismael are unlikely, but perfectly suited, traveling companions. He misses Lily.

"You are not really leaving me," she said before he left. "You can be anywhere and with me at the same time. Here, I bought you this journal for your birthday, but you can take it now to document your experiences along the way." She had motioned toward the bedside table, where a leather-bound A-4–size notebook lay. Deeply touched by her thoughtfulness, he had still insisted that he didn't really want to leave, that he was doing it for the money.

"I know that, mi amor," she replied.

"Don't worry, mijo," encouraged his mother-in-law. "My husband won't eat you for breakfast. His silence makes him seem much grouchier than he is." She patted his face. "Men have ways of connecting with their hearts, Carlos Alberto."

This alleviated his anxiety to a great extent, for Carlos Alberto thinks Consuelo must know a great deal about men's hearts if she could capture and keep the heart of Ismael Martinez.

After three hours of driving, of which Ismael now does the most since he is the only one who knows the final destination, they turn off the carretera onto a dirt road. After another forty-five minutes of bumping around, and just as Carlos Alberto is about to protest the choice of road — a rough-cut path, really — the speed with which they are attempting it, and the effect it is having on his back and hemorrhoidal ass, Ismael parks the car on the side of the road.

"I thought we were going to Chivacoa," says Carlos Alberto.

"Maybe tomorrow," says his father-in-law.

Without another word, Ismael gets out of the car, opens the rear door of the station wagon, which is now caked in mud, and beckons for Carlos Alberto and Luz to collect some of the bags and follow him through a hole in the fence near the road.

After half an hour of trekking on a rough path through what Carlos Alberto thinks must be some kind of national preserve or park, they arrive in front of the oddest dwelling he has ever seen. It is a sturdy circular structure with a conical roof, built of manaca palm wood and temiche leaves, bound together by rope. An oil lamp is burning in the cutout window, which has no glass.

A young mestizo boy — no more than ten or eleven years of age, perhaps younger — opens the door, his slight frame a silhouette against light behind him. A few moments later, a Guajira woman of indeterminate age, wearing a fraying dress of equally indeterminate color, appears at the boy's side and places her arm protectively around his shoulders. A broad smile breaks out across her face the moment she spots Ismael.

"Well, well, if it isn't El Malandro himself," she says. "It's been a long time, viejo. Bienvenido." Ismael embraces the woman and tousles the boy's unkempt hair, which looks like it could use a good wash. Clearly, this boy does not have older sisters, thinks Carlos Alberto.

"Carlos Alberto, Luz," says Ismael, "may I present to you my friends, Juanita Sanchez and her young grandson, Efraín."

Together, the five partake of a simple but generous dinner consisting of black beans, plátano, and rice, set on a knobby wooden table made of planks and cement blocks. The planks creak and wobble every time anyone shifts an elbow or passes a plate. During the meal, Ismael and the old Indian woman speak in a language Carlos Alberto does not understand. But it is apparent the old woman is upset by whatever Ismael is saying. Then the old woman apparently says something that upsets his father-in-law equally, for afterward he does not speak and stares off into space with a dark expression.

Carlos Alberto, uncomfortable with the ensuing silence, turns to Luz, but then changes his mind about starting any conversation with her, resigning himself instead to shoveling food mechanically into his mouth with a wooden spoon. When the meal is over, Carlos Alberto sees that the boy Efraín, who has been perched on Ismael's lap throughout the evening, has fallen asleep, his head lolling against the older man's shoulder, lips slightly parted in a half smile. The poor child will get a crick in his neck if he sleeps in that position much longer, Carlos Alberto thinks. He catches Ismael's eye and points to the boy. Ismael carries Efraín to a hammock in the corner of the room and Luz follows, taking off her long sweater and gently covering the boy. Then she climbs into the spare hammock and appears to fall asleep almost instantly. Funny, he would never have pegged Luz as the maternal type.

"Efraín made an appearance today; he is very tired," the old woman says in Spanish to Carlos Alberto. Carlos is about to ask Juanita Sanchez what she means by appearance, when he is struck by the realization that Efraín is the boy shown in a sketch on TV, the one they call El Niño. But before he can ask any questions, Ismael shoots him a warning glance. The old woman hands Ismael two hammocks and two light blankets, and Ismael beckons to Carlos Alberto to follow him outside. Together they select some sturdy trees between which to tie the hammocks. The hammocks are made of remarkably fine weave that feels almost like silk.

"Sleep well," says Ismael. "We'll talk tomorrow."

Carlos Alberto has never spent the night in a hammock. But that isn't what keeps him awake. Neither is it because this is the first time he has slept apart from Lily since they were married. It is because he is bursting with questions for Ismael, who, astonishingly, has brought them straight to the source of their quest. Here he had been worried that he was embarking on a mission that might cost him his job at the university, that he might well be risking everything on a potentially futile pursuit that would bring in little money beyond expenses from the television producers in the end. The old Guajira must be using the boy somehow to capitalize on the excitement about the statue, that much he has surmised, though he has yet to come up with an explanation for how she has conjured up the El Niño apparitions. But what he really wants to know is how Ismael is connected with these squatters in the middle of the forest. Without a doubt, Lily's father is full of surprises—a real aventurero! And what about Luz—Luz had behaved as though living in a shack in some forest was the most natural thing in the world. Who would ever have thought that Luz could go even a day without the beauty parlor and her telenovelas? No doubt, Luz was fitting into the adventure far better than expected, far better, in fact, than *he* was. She hadn't used the outdoor facilities before she went to bed. He wonders how she will react to the discovery that she will have to piss and shit in the woods for the duration of their stay here.

Poor pollination or insufficient watering can cause malformation in passiflora edulis. Attacks from pests can cause scarring.

Luz

When she was five, Luz announced that she wanted to be a gypsy dancer when she grew up. She arrived at this conclusion after her mother's East Indian friend from Trinidad, José Naipaul, took her to see a flamenco show. Afterward, at home in their one-bedroom apartment, she had demonstrated to her mother and brothers how a real dancer danced. With astonishing ease, her little feet replicated the stacatto steps of an accomplished flamenco dancer, while her fingers clicked away at invisible castanets.

"You must have been a dancer in your past life!" exclaimed José Naipaul, clapping wildly when she finished, and her mother had grabbed her in her arms and kissed her many times all over her face.

She had always been able to bring a smile to her mother's face when she danced. "You've got both Andalusia and Carib in your blood," Marta would say. But whenever her mother thought too much of her father, not even Luz's dancing could lighten her mood.

Even now, Luz loves to dance, especially salsa and merengue. When the music begins, she feels electrified, as though there is a lightning rod that begins at the top of her head and ends at her toes, illuminating and energizing her core.

Brava! Brava! Miguel Rojas would shout, when they were first married, spinning her triumphantly across the floor as her skirts flew up above her thighs. On the dance floor, Luz is a goddess and she knows it. Dancing is the only thing she is positive she can do better than Lily.

Competition with Lily has been the monkey on Luz's back for most of her life. Nothing really bad ever happens to Lily; it has always been enough for her to look lovely and fragile, for everyone to rally around her. This is the way it has been as long as Luz can remember. Granted, Lily might have hurt or lost her baby after the fall, which would have been horrible. But, Luz wonders, if the situation were reversed, and it were Luz's baby, Luz who needed comforting and mollycoddling, would everyone come running? Would Lily? Luz has her doubts.

Lily certainly hadn't come to her defense that time at the Hotel Macuto, had she? No, she had been so concerned about saving her own skin and the skin of her kleptomaniac friend, Irene Dos Santos. *You can't tell anybody, please, Lucecita, I beg you,* Lily had said, while Irene stood by, wary and silent like a cat, her small, bottle-green eyes hooded by dark lashes. It makes her positively ill to think of the way Lily always would get that cajoling, sugary sweetness in her voice when she wanted Luz to tow the line.

For a long time, even though the sheer force of her jealousy sometimes made it hard for her to breathe, Luz could not resist the desire to be loved by Lily. But Lily had never loved Luz that way, not the way she loved Irene, like a sister and confidant, a coconspirator in their exclusive adolescent club of discovery. Even afterward, even after Luz had presented her with the evidence that Irene was not a good friend, Lily had never turned to Luz. And when Irene drowned in Maquiritare, had Lily reached toward Luz? No, not even then. On the contrary, she had increased her distance. And for this, Luz has never quite forgiven her.

Luz was happiest after Lily joined her at the convent boarding school as the penalty for sticking her tongue in a boy's mouth while in the elevator. Not only because she had Lily mostly to herself for two whole years, not even because it meant separation from Irene Dos Santos, but because she felt it made them equals. Except during the holidays, when they returned to Lily's home, and she slept in the maid's room with her mother, where they resided at the pleasure of Lily's parents. Sometimes Luz pretended Lily's parents were her own and that her own mother was her maid.

"The maid will sign for it," she would say disdainfully to the postman whenever a registered letter arrived.

The first time Luz and Lily returned from the boarding school in Valencia was for Semana Santa. They were both fourteen. Consuelo embraced them both warmly at the door, took them by the arm, and pulled them into the kitchen, where Ismael, who had just returned from Maquiritare with fresh, handmade paintbrushes for his wife, was having his merienda. Ismael offered his face to Lily's kiss, a face that reflected pure joy at the sight of her, with eyes alight in a way that made Luz momentarily queasy with envy. Until he turned to her and said, "How beautiful you look, Luz, almost a woman. Soon we will have to contend with suitors beating at your door."

Luz blushed. Ever since she was little, Ismael had made her feel like the prettiest girl in the world.

"Can you keep a secret, Lucecita?" Lily asked, when they were alone in her room.

"Of course I can, don't be silly," said Luz with a forced laugh that thinly disguised her irritation.

"Okay," said Lily, "tomorrow morning, I'm going to tell Mami that we're going to the Hotel Macuto to sunbathe. Papi can drive us there."

"Right, so what's the secret?"

"Bueno, the thing is, I'm supposed to be meeting Irene, and my parents don't know. I haven't seen her since I changed schools, and I really want to see her. If you come with me, I won't have to lie—Mami always knows if I'm lying, don't ask me how, but she does. This way, it'll look normal if I say I'm going to the Macuto with you."

So that was the reason Lily had been so jittery! Luz was torn between feeling flattered and feeling abused at being made complicit in such a scheme. But in the end, the allure of partnership trumped her fear of collusion in a plan that could surely ignite the wrath of her mother and Lily's parents.

"Do you have a tanga?" Lily asked.

"No," said Luz, embarrassed. Her mother didn't allow her to wear the skimpy Brazilian bathing suits all the young city girls wore. *But Lily wears them,* she had complained. *Well, you're not Lily and you're not going to, punto final,* Marta had said. Luz had thrown her own unfashionable suit in the trash, preferring to own no bathing suit at all to making a fool of herself in front of other girls her age.

"That's okay," said Lily, "you can borrow one of mine."

The next morning, Ismael drove the girls to the Macuto. "Have a good time, muchachas, and call me when you're ready to come home," he said, pressing several hundred-bolívar notes into each of their hands.

"Gracias, Papi," said Lily, kissing her father on the cheek, before he drove away.

They found Irene waiting by the pool in her bathing suit, a fluorescent peach-colored tanga that enhanced her tan and showcased her streamlined torso, the perfect flat plane of her stomach, the sensuous curve of her full traffic-stopping breasts. Her long, straight hair was caught up in a simple but elegant twist and clipped nonchalantly in a way that Luz had often tried but which never worked because her neck was too short. The only physical feature Luz shared with Irene was a large and shapely bosom. Unlike Luz, who had been programmed by nine years of convent school to keep them under wraps, Irene flaunted hers, rubbing them with suntan oil repeatedly while three young, goggle-eyed waiters swirled about her.

As soon as Irene caught sight of Lily, she ran to embrace her with a squeal and kissed her four times on each cheek, making exaggerated smacking noises each time. "I've got a room, courtesy of the manager, who's a friend of my mother. Here's the key. Hurry up and change, Lily, the boys will be here any minute." Then, "Luz! How nice that you were able to make it." But Luz didn't believe that Irene was any happier to see *her* than she was to see Irene.

While Lily and Luz changed into their bathing suits, Luz said, "What did Irene mean by 'the boys'?"

"Luz," said Lily, "don't be a pendeja. What is the point of coming to the Macuto, putting on our bathing suits and lying around like wallflowers for the benefit of the waiters? Do you realize I haven't been near a boy for two whole years? I'm parched! But don't worry, I called ahead and asked Irene to arrange a boy for you too." Luz still remembers thinking that if it weren't for the overpowering influence of Irene, Lily would never have spoken in this way. Pretending to be so grown up and boy crazy. *Parched.* ¡Qué ridícula! Who did she think she was talking to?

As Lily hurriedly stuffed towels and suntan lotions into a tote, saying, "Let's go, let's go," Luz's heart began to hammer in her chest. She felt fat. Unsophisticated. Boring. What if the boy Irene had chosen for her didn't like her? And worse, what if her mother ever found out that she'd been preening around the Macuto half-naked with a boy? It could happen; the Macuto was a social center, hardly a place of discretion. How typical of Irene to choose a venue fraught with the danger of discovery. Wasn't it bad enough that Lily had been forced to change schools because of Irene? What was Lily thinking? They could all get in trouble. But if she backed out now, Lily and Irene would say she was coward, a prude, a complete pajuda. They would laugh at her behind her back and Lily would ignore her for the rest of Semana Santa. Maybe even for the rest of the year. Her thoughts raced frantically from one ghastly scenario to another, all of which ended horribly.

When the girls returned to the poolside, the boys had already arrived. To Luz it was immediately apparent from his possessive perch on Irene's lounge chair that the one with the distinctive Guajiro cheekbones was taken. "This is Moriche

Sanchez," said Irene, patting him on the head like a favored pet. "He used to love my mother, until he met me. We're going to open a restaurant together; I've decided I want to be a chef. Moriche, meet my best friend Lily Martinez. And this is Luz...what's your last name?"

"Galano," mumbled Luz.

"Mucho gusto," said Moriche, without offering his hand or taking his sly eyes off Irene. Luz guessed that he must be around twenty-two years of age. He was not handsome, though by no means repulsive; he reminded her of a hawk with his long beak of a nose. Luz recalled then that Lily had mentioned Irene's peculiar taste in boys, she said that even though Irene could have anyone she wanted with a snap of her fingers, she had always gone for odd-looking, sometimes even ugly, types. Boys who were also quite a bit older than herself. Boys who were men. According to Lily, Irene had once tried to sell her on the idea of men who were not in conformance with conventional good looks, but Lily's sense of aesthetic had recoiled at the idea.

"That's why we're never in competition," Lily had explained to Luz.

"And these two hombres," said Irene, nodding in the direction of the other two young men, "are Elvis Crespo, who has been caliente for Lily ever since he kissed her in the elevator of my building, and Elvis's friend and boss, Miguel Rojas, who, of course, is dying to meet you, Luz. He loves Cuban girls."

Smiling briefly and shyly at Miguel Rojas, Luz turned her focus on Elvis Crespo. So this was the elevator kisser. Elvis appeared much younger than the other two, and immediately Luz wished she were Lily so that she might claim this dark, compact boy with the wild hair and rascally smile that ignited an insurrection in her belly. Besides, she was sure Irene was being sarcastic when she said Miguel Rojas was dying to meet her.

Elvis grabbed Lily in his arms, raised her in the air, and swung her, laughing, in a circle. Tearing her gaze away from Elvis, Luz smiled at Miguel Rojas and held out her hand politely. Miguel Rojas smiled back and shook her hand with mock gentlemanliness, but not in a mean or depreciating way. He wasn't at all bad-looking, though she wasn't crazy about his hair, which was too closely cropped for her taste. He was on the stocky side, but she did like the way his torso tapered smoothly from his broad shoulders to his hips. And he was also better dressed than the other two. Expensively dressed. Even though she couldn't see his eyes through his Ray-Bans, Luz decided she could tolerate a day as Miguel Rojas's date.

"Let's order some drinks and snacks," said Miguel Rojas, when the boys returned from the changing room, all wearing boxer-style swim trunks. Signaling for the waiter, he said, "Three piña coladas for the girls, and three straight rums with lots of ice. And bring three plates of French fries." Luz thought it rather imperious of him to just order without asking anyone what they wanted, but no one else seemed to mind, and as the day wore on and numerous orders were placed by Miguel Rojas and consumed by all, she realized that the reason no one had an opinion about what to eat or drink was because Miguel Rojas always paid for everything.

After two piña coladas Luz found herself warming to the boy and also to the idea that he was rich. She closed her eyes and fantasized about dating Miguel Rojas, who would

provide her, in the tradition of Cinderella stories, with everything her heart desired, much to the envy of other girls. Not
that Luz had ever been treated as anything less than a full
family member in the Martinez household, but the fantasy
was too tempting to resist. After three piña coladas, she went
into the pool, floated on her back and smiled provocatively
at Miguel Rojas. When Miguel Rojas took the bait, swam up
behind her, put his arms around her, and pulled her toward
him, then turned and pressed her into a corner of the pool,
she allowed his tongue to travel across her lips, and thought
she might agree to marry him. After four piña coladas, she
felt dizzy and headachy, and when Miguel Rojas offered to
accompany her to the hotel room so she could lie down, she
said yes.

Luz had no idea how long she had been asleep when she
felt a sideways yanking at the crotch of her bathing suit bottom. She thought she was dreaming. Cymbals crashed in her
head each time she attempted to move it; her eyelids felt glued
together with cement. She lay still even when she felt little
bursts of pleasure on her stomach and realized that Miguel
Rojas was kissing her there. Slowly, tantalizingly, he moved
his lips lower, then lower. Her thighs tensed and Miguel
Rojas repositioned himself, above her, kissing her wetly on
the mouth, rubbing her gently with his finger where his lips
had been earlier. By this time her pleasure was so intense,
she could not have stopped Miguel Rojas from swirling his
finger in her most private place, even if she had wanted to.
But when he suddenly withdrew his finger and arched above
her, driving a hard rod against that barred passage, pleasure
turned into pain. Shrieking, she pushed at his chest.

"Coño, a virgin," said Miguel Rojas in a thick voice.

Groaning, he abruptly pulled away. Then he was kneeling, upright, rubbing himself furiously with his hand, his neck arched back, his face towards the ceiling, his hips jerking, his knees digging into her hips. A gush of liquid, hot, wet and thick, spurted on her stomach.

Luz was frightened. What if she got pregnant, was all she could think, as Miguel Rojas fell heavy and spent against her and the throbbing between her legs gradually subsided. She might as well kill herself if she were pregnant or her mother would do it for her.

"Are you okay?" he asked.

"Yes," said Luz politely, wondering how many would come to her funeral.

"Sorry," he said, wiping her stomach with the tail of his shirt, "you should have told me you were a virgin." Then he lay down against her, sex shrunken and soft against her side, his rum-infused breath blowing against her ear. Luz did not move until he began to snore. Then, carefully moving his arm, which lay across her hips, aside, she stood up and went to the bathroom. She peered fearfully into the toilet bowl through her legs at the urine that burned its way out of her. She wet a hand towel and wiped her sticky stomach, with another she washed between her legs. Then she lay down flat on the bathroom floor with her left cheek pressed against the cool tiles, her arms straight out in front of her.

Over an hour passed before she heard Irene banging at the bathroom door. "Open the door, Luz, te ruego," Irene was shouting, "I have to use the bathroom."

When Luz opened the bathroom door, Irene was leaning on it so hard, she fell into Luz's arms. Pulling back, Irene laughed and said, "My god, Luz, what happened to you? We thought you'd passed out from the booze in here." Luz looked over Irene's shoulder into the room. Miguel Rojas was gone.

"Where is he?" she said.

"Who?"

"Miguel Rojas."

"He's down at the pool."

"He did it to me," said Luz.

"What? Who did what?"

"Miguel Rojas. He did it while I was asleep." She searched for the vocabulary to describe what Miguel Rojas had done. She had seen dogs mating. She had seen lovers dissolving in one another in soft focus on the TV. What Miguel Rojas had done had been nothing like either, but still she wanted to hold him accountable for something, for making her feel heavenly and filthy at the same time. There must be a word for it. She began to shake uncontrollably and her nose began to run as if she were having an allergic reaction.

Irene was standing in the frame of the bathroom door, the light behind her, her face blackened by a shadow.

"Luz, what did he do?" said Irene, wiping Luz's nose with tissue, smoothening her hair, wrapping a towel around her shoulders, as if she were a mother soothing her child after a bad dream. Her fingers fluttered nervously around Luz's face and hair like butterflies. Luz felt calmer when she focused on the feel of Irene's fingers in her hair.

"He showed me his thing." She does not mention the disgusting glue on her stomach.

"Luz," said Irene, "tell me exactly what he did. What did he do after he showed you his thing?"

"He put his tongue in my mouth."

"Is that all?"

"Yes." Luz thought of her mother finding out and began to cry again. "Do you think I'm going to have a baby? My mother is going to kill me," she said. Her head still pounded from the aftereffects of too many piña coladas.

"Stop it," said Irene, "You're not going to have a baby. Babies don't come from tongues. Your mother is not going to find out anything unless you tell her." With evident relief, Irene pulled down her bathing suit bottom and sat on the toilet. She looked at Luz and two stern lines appeared on her forehead. "God, Luz, Miguel's a guy you barely know," she said as she peed. "Who told you to come up to the room with him? What did you expect? He probably thought you knew what you were doing."

Luz hoped Irene would get wrinkles on her forehead. "Make them go," she said. "Those boys, make them go."

Irene stared at her, as if sizing up the situation. "Okay," she said finally. "Have a bath; you'll be fine if you have a bath."

Luz showered, scrubbing herself almost raw with a pale blue pumice stone supplied by the hotel. When she emerged, a towel wrapped around her body, another around her head, Luz and Lily were sitting on the bed, conferring in lowered voices. They did not see her. There was no sign of Moriche Sanchez, Elvis Crespo, and Miguel Rojas. She went back into the bathroom and closed the door quietly. She put her ear to it.

Irene was saying, "Look, she's acting weird, and if she tells on us, there will be a lot of trouble all round. Mercedes has no idea I'm with Moriche, and if she finds out, she'll tell my father out of pure spite, and he will kill me for sure. And you'll probably have to become a nun."

"But what happened? Something must have happened."

"Ay, que vaina, Lily. He kissed her. And she's such a zana-horia that she thought she could get pregnant from it."

"Why did he kiss her?"

"Now you are sounding as stupid and immature as Luz. Why wouldn't he? He's a guy, isn't he? You should never have brought her, the little whining baby," said Irene, "but since you did, you've got to keep her quiet. You've just got to, Lily."

"Okay," said Lily, "calm down."

When she came back into the room, Luz pretended she hadn't heard anything. She couldn't exactly defend herself, since what Irene said was true: she had invited Miguel Rojas to the hotel room. Or had he invited himself? She couldn't remember. She couldn't remember because she had been drunk. No one had poured glasses and glasses of piña colada down her throat against her will, true. But Irene and Lily could have stopped her. Her mother would probably not see it that way, though. It was her own fault, acting like a little campecina slut, that's probably what her mother would say. So what was the point of telling? Even if Luz hated her guts right now, Irene was right.

Pulling her T-shirt over her head and zipping up her jeans, she emerged from the bathroom and said, "Where to next, chamas?" As though everything were normal.

"I know," said Irene, giving Lily a warning look, "let's go to the shopping arcade and find something really chévere to buy."

In the Macuto shopping arcade, they went into the jewelry store first. And there, on the display table, Luz saw a silver charm bracelet and wanted it. It had the tiny figures of Las Tres Potencias dangling from it — Maria Lionza, El

Negro Felipe, and El Indio Guaicaipuro. Luz thought her mother would love it; and it wouldn't hurt to have something to offer, something to temper the storm, in case it turned out she had made her mother into a grandmother. Looking at the label, she saw it was marked half off at six hundred bolívares. Just then, Irene picked it up and said, "I'm buying this bracelet."

"No," Luz said, "I saw it first." Suddenly, possession of the bracelet became the most important thing in the world.

Irene seemed about to protest, then changed her mind. "Okay," she said.

"Have you got any money? I don't have enough for this bracelet," Luz called out to Lily, who was looking at hair clips on the other end of the store.

"I've got three hundred," said Lily, looking at Luz. "Take it."

Her lips pressed into a thin line of concentration, Luz dug into the pocket of her jeans, retrieved the now crumpled bolívar notes Señor Ismael had given her, and completed her purchase while Lily called her father from the phone at the front counter and told him that she and Luz were ready to come home. Irene said she'd take a taxi back home. "Call me tomorrow, we'll make another date to meet with Moriche and Elvis before you go back to Valencia." Luz was clearly excluded from any future plans.

Before they went to sleep that night, Lily put her arm around Luz and said, "You're okay, right? You can't tell any-one what we did today, Lucecita, please, I beg of you. Because if you do, I'll be sent to the convent for the rest of my life, and Irene's father will put a bullet right though his own daughter's heart; you have no idea how tyrannical he is about her."

"Stop acting like an opera star. I won't tell anyone," said Luz. However, that was before she discovered that the bracelet was missing from her towel bag.

"She took my bracelet," she said to Lily.

"Irene? Don't be silly. She would never steal your bracelet. You probably left it at the store."

But Luz was certain that Irene was the culprit, and as far as she was concerned, the idea of Irene with a bullet through her heart was not a displeasing one.

At first no one was too worried when Luz went off her food on the fourth day of Semana Santa, two days after the outing to the Macuto. Perhaps it was a bug, they thought. But three days after that, on Easter Sunday, when Luz refused to get out of bed and dress herself, Marta threw up her hands in despair and Luz could hear her complaining to Consuelo in the kitchen. "I'll talk to her when we come back from Mass," said Consuelo. When they returned from the church, Consuelo came to the room Luz shared with her mother, carrying a bowl of steaming mondongo on a tray.

"Tell me what is wrong, Luz," she said, holding up a spoon of thick soup to the girl's lips. "I'm sure we can find a solution together."

But Luz had turned her face to the wall.

Lily came in next. "Mami says I'm not to leave this room without you. ¿Qué te pasa, Lucecita? Please tell me."

To this day, Luz doesn't know what made her say, "The bracelet," or why the loss of the bracelet symbolized everything that was wrong with her life.

Through half closed eyes, Luz observed that Lily seemed relieved and confused at the same time. "I'll ask Irene about the bracelet, if that will make you happy."

And just like that, Luz felt better. Without looking at Lily, she got out of bed, had a bath, combed her hair, pulled on a clean pair of jeans and a white shirt. She walked into the kitchen, sat down at the table and ate an enormous bowl of mondongo.

Luz was certain that Lily hadn't known what went on at the Macuto between her and Miguel Rojas, or later in the hotel room between herself and Irene. She knew it was irrational to blame Lily for something she didn't know at the time. But there it was, she couldn't let Lily off the hook.

It was a day before they returned to Valencia. Luz was on her way to the panadería and saw Irene and Lily talking just inside. She stood by the wrought-iron gate at the entrance and listened.

"I'm in a lot of trouble with Mercedes, chama," said Irene. "Apparently she suspected about Moriche and me. She went to the Macuto and talked to the management and the waiters and everything. She showed them a photograph of me. One of the waiters told her he remembered me, and told her that I was with two other girls and three guys. He told her we had a room and that one of the girls and one of the guys had gone into it together. He even told her that one of the other guys we were with was an indio. Coño, chama, he blabbed *everything* to my mother. So of course, she just *knew* the indio with me was Moriche. Pues, Mercedes threw a fit, armó un saperoco, and the result is that Moriche and I are running away together, as soon as we can figure out a way."

Luz is surprised when, instead of gasping with illicit excitement about Irene's plan, Lily says, "Luz was different after that day. I think it had something to do with Miguel Rojas. She got sick, she wouldn't eat, and that probably made Mami suspicious. But I didn't tell her anything and neither did Luz. I'm certain."

"Maybe, but she made sure to draw attention to herself. I knew we couldn't trust her."

"Don't say that."

"Listen, she's not so innocent. She's the one who took him to the hotel room, and drank like fifty piña coladas, which *he* paid for, by the way. What did she expect? So maybe he showed her his thing. Big deal. She got what she asked for. And it's not like she got pregnant or anything."

"Maybe he did what? You said he only kissed her—you acted like it was impossible that he could have done anything more." Lily's voice was rising in pitch and volume.

"*SHHHHHHHSH!* Listen," said Irene, "I said that because that is what you wanted me to do. You felt guilty for bringing her, for using her as part of the cover for meeting Elvis, and don't tell me it isn't true."

"It *isn't* true!" Lily whispered.

"Yes it is," Irene said, and walked out the gate, sticking her tongue out at Luz on the way out.

"Crybaby," she said.

"Thief," Luz replied.

Luz went into the panadería. As she walked past Lily, she stared at her triumphantly, but Lily did not meet her eyes. Lily had never been able to meet her eyes after that, always looking somewhere near the top of Luz's head whenever she spoke to her. Coward, Luz thought, but did not say.

When the girls returned to Valencia the following day, the equation between Lily and Luz had changed. Luz felt new, shiny and powerful, as if the act of eating and shitting out a large quantity of mondongo had cleansed her of what happened at the Macuto, while Lily was meeker and milder, a diluted version of herself. Lily was more careful now, palliating, as though Luz might be a ticking bomb.

Luz knew Lily felt guilty for using her as a beard to go out with Irene, and for exposing her to a situation for which Luz had been ill-prepared, and that's how Luz wanted her to feel. Irene hadn't been specific, and if Lily thought Miguel had put his thing in her, so much the better.

But power was not love. Lily still did not love her more than she loved Irene. And when she got to choose a friend to go to Maquiritare, it was not Luz she chose.

Though Lily had temporarily lost her mind after the bad business with Irene in Maquiritare, she had recovered and rejoined the convent school a month later, where she would graduate with Luz three years later. And during this time Luz developed a fondness for measuring her own happiness in terms of before and after Irene.

A few days after graduation, and after returning to Tamanaco, Luz unpacked and unwrapped the clay image of a dancer she had made in school. Carrying it carefully, she went out to the patio, where Consuelo stood at her easel painting the light through the trees in watercolor on paper.

"I made this for you," she said, offering the dancer to Consuelo in cupped hands.

"Thank you, Luz," said Consuelo, laying down her brush, "it's lovely. Come, let's put it on the side table in my bedroom." When they went into the bedroom Luz placed the clay dancer on the table. And that was when she saw the bracelet. Just casually lying there on the floor, almost under the bed. What was it doing there?

She picked it up and held it up to the light. "I remember this bracelet," she said. Consuelo took it from her and put it in the drawer of the bedside table.

Consuelo sighed. "We found it in Maquiritare years ago. It must have belonged to that poor girl. The Guardia Nacional said they had no use for it. I meant to return it to her mother, but it slipped my mind." If at all it was necessary to refer to what happened in Maquiritare, to the disappearance of Irene Dos Santos, everyone referred to her as "that poor girl" and to the incident as "the accident," though there was an unspoken agreement not to make any reference to it at all, however veiled, in Lily's presence. "It must have fallen when I was cleaning out the drawer. Don't tell Lily. I'd rather she not be reminded of what happened."

"The bracelet is mine," said Luz. "I bought it for my mother."

Consuelo tried to reason with her. "Luz, if Marta wears it, Lily will see it."

"Irene stole it and I want it back," Luz insisted.

Consuelo sighed again. "All right. Perhaps she won't remember it. But if I give it to you, you must promise that you won't tell Lily where you got it."

"If she notices it, I'll say I bought it recently." But as much as Luz loved Consuelo, envy and hatred got the better of her, and she could not resist dealing Irene one last blow.

That's how Luz explains to herself now what she did then: as getting even with Irene.

Lily lay on the bed reading a magazine, when Luz entered and said, "I want to show you something." She pulled up the sleeve of her blouse to display the bracelet.

"That's nice," said Lily.

Luz thought Lily was protecting Irene, that she had to be pretending not to remember what happened *before* the accident. Her promise to Consuelo flew out of her head. "Apparently your mother found it in your hand after the accident."

"What accident?"

"When Irene drowned." Luz could almost hear the whoosh of an ax cutting through the air, and a wicked thrill of delight danced in her belly.

Lily's eyes began to lose focus, her lips to drain of their color, her fingers to pick like birds at invisible bits of lint on the bedcover.

And Luz was suddenly afraid. She had gone too far.

"Epa, I'm just kidding around," she backpedaled furiously. "I bought it for my mother. She loves anything with Maria Lionza on it."

"Which shop?" The color was beginning to return to Lily's lips.

"Oh, it was just a souvenir seller who had set up near the panadería," said Luz, eager to step away from the precipice, to reverse her betrayal of Consuelo, to erase the past few minutes.

"I'm sure she'll love it, Luz," said Lily.

The bracelet flashed shiny and bright against the palm of Luz's hand. When she presented it to her mother, she had been so pleased, just as Luz imagined she would be. But the satisfaction of finally seeing the bracelet on her mother's wrist had come at a cost. After she insisted on claiming the bracelet and demonstrated her disregard for the potential consequences of such an act, Consuelo, whose love she coveted almost as much as her mother's, had never looked at her in quite the same way again; a crack had formed in the cup of her love for Luz.

As it turned out, and in spite of the bad beginning, Miguel Rojas was quite taken by Luz and went to ask Irene for her address. Irene was persuaded to part with the information only after being bribed with a box of imported Swiss chocolates and first-rate seats for the Gloria Gaynor concert at the Poliedro. But being one of those for whom out of sight is out of mind, he stuffed the address in his wallet and forgot about it, until, a month after she graduated from high-school in Valencia and returned to Tamanaco, he looked at the security camera feed from his executive office at the largest of his supermarkets and saw her pushing a grocery cart down the cereal aisle. He dug frantically into the pockets of his wallet until he retrieved the address, written on a page of notepaper that was frayed and yellowed with age but still legible. Then he went to the flower section of the Supermercado Costa and filled his car to the brim with roses of all the colors available. Even Marta had been impressed.

"Now that is how a boy should treat the girl he loves," she said.

Miguel Rojas courted Luz every day for a whole year. They never spoke of that day at the Hotel Macuto, and throughout their courtship Miguel Rojas was the perfect gentleman, never forcing even a kiss. The first time they kissed, it had been Luz who held him by the collar, pulled him toward her, and offered him her lips.

When she was admitted to the hospital for an emergency appendectomy, he was seated by her bedside when she awoke and her hospital room was filled with roses. And a few months after that, exactly two years after her graduation from high school, he asked her to marry him.

The year they married it was discovered that the surgeon who had performed the appendectomy had accidentally cut something he shouldn't have. Because of this, the peritoneal lining had looped around her right fallopian tube, causing cysting and infection. The infection had spread throughout her abdominal cavity. Miguel flew Luz to a specialist in Miami who conducted another exploratory laparoscopy and told her she would require more surgery, but he would not be able to give her any guarantees. The Miami surgeon took the right ovary and tube, removed cysts from her womb and from the left ovary, cutting part of it away. He noted that the left tube was damaged by scarring from the infection and decided to take everything out. Again, when she awoke Miguel was by her side and the smell of roses suffused the air in the room. After he told her the news that she would never be able to conceive, he held her tight against him while her tears soaked the front of his shirt. He told her it didn't matter.

Although she came to accept that no child would ever emerge from her womb, she could no longer bear the smell of roses. And when Miguel made love to her, she often wept. After some time, he stopped making love to her and moved into the guest room and she did not ask why.

A few days before their ninth anniversary, Miguel said he wanted a divorce.

"Because you want children?" she asked.

"No, Luz," he said. "You know it isn't that."

"What then?"

"Luz, we don't even sleep together anymore."

"Pero te quiero."

"You love me like you would a father or a brother, not a lover."

When Luz tries to recall the exact reason she said yes when Miguel asked her to marry him, she cannot remember it. Could it be that she had been merely flattered to be the beneficiary of the kind of attentions customarily bestowed on the beauteous Lily? Or perhaps it was the awed expression on her own mother's face when confronted with the fact that Luz was being wooed by the Supermarket King of the country. Though she had grown to love him, he was right—it was akin to the love of a friend, a father, a brother, a love without ardor. When she realized this, she felt like an impostor and was almost relieved that the charade was over.

Even their divorce had been devoid of passion. Miguel gave her an enormous settlement that included the penthouse, stock in TVista, sole custody of their beloved Japanese Spitz, Muchacha, and more cash than she could possibly spend in her lifetime. She was free, she could do anything she wanted, she could rely upon him if she needed anything, he said. But after the divorce was final, she found herself missing married life with a keen, sharp longing that sometimes made it difficult to breathe. She missed the feeling of walking into a dinner party with her arm linked to one of the most powerful men in the room, and the way other women's heads would turn as they entered. She missed the warmth of his body next to hers when she woke up in the morning. She missed being adored.

But did she miss Miguel himself? Was it love or loneliness that made her want him back?

She had tried dating, but was clumsy and awkward at it because the only person she had ever dated was Miguel Rojas, and even then he had done all the work. Besides, she thought of herself as damaged goods; a woman who could not bear children, who would want a woman like that? And then there was her wealth to factor into any romantic equation. At the back of her mind was always the question of whether the man across the table from her at the restaurant was after her money. It was all too difficult and not worth it, this search for a partner, the investment of her time, when she would probably find out in the end that the guy was already married, or boring, or stingy, or weird. She hadn't the energy to start all over again.

She took to waking at noon and moving from her bed to the divan in the TV room, where she would watch telenovelas all day with Muchacha on her lap. She loved the way that in spite of all odds, in spite of the most exaggerated difficulties and tribulations, and opposition from a whole cast of characters, the male protagonist was always a high-minded stud who would fight tooth and nail, defeat his enemies, and win his woman in the end. She knew it was cliché and inevitable, but thrilled anyway when the lovers ended up together at the end, passionately embracing, kissing and rolling about on luxurious outsize beds or on a blanket under a flowering tree. Real life could rarely compete with that, and for this reason telenovelas had her vote. The heady power of making everything come out impossibly right in the end is what motivated her to become a producer at TVista. The station was happy for the fresh infusion of currency, always in short supply these days, and the union was successful. When she insisted on editorial control, the executives readily conceded. It was not a foolish decision on their part, either, for Luz had demonstrated time and again her capacity for choosing winners and staying on budget, steadily rising in their esteem, her influence growing beyond even her own expectations. Where the business of telenovelas is concerned, she is the station's goose with golden eggs.

In terms of the present, it means she is in a position to help Carlos Alberto, whom she both loves and hates like a brother, and who, in her opinion, has written some of the best telenovela material ever. In fact, it had been Luz's idea to have Carlos Alberto's stories, which he had been selling for a pittance to the radio, adapted for television. And she can hardly wait for his latest one, *Fantasmagórica,* about a tragic and beautiful woman who doesn't know she is dead from drowning and haunts the living in their dreams, giving them advice and altering the course of their lives. If Carlos Alberto knew that it was she who had made the calls to TVista, first about having his radio scripts converted into telenovelas, and most recently regarding his documentary of Marialionceros, he would be furious. And so, as much as she would like him to know of her munificence, he must never find out. So quaint and proud he is, just like his sensitive but sexy male protagonists. She is not enamored with the fact that there is something of Lily in all his heroines, evidence that year after year, no matter how fantastical his stories, his love for her is most real.

She craves such a fairy-tale love in real life. But what she craves most is a belly like Lily's, ripe with the fruit of passion.

Camped at the Quintanilla residence since the day Lily fell, Luz watches her with both fascination and distress. The distress is amplified by the recent demise of Muchacha, who had taken the place of a child in her heart and whose absence is a raw and throbbing wound. She had come home one evening from a producers meeting at TVista to find the little dog whimpering and squirming in her wicker bed. Her hind legs had collapsed and trying to stand sent her tiny body into spasms of pain. Luz spent the night weeping and dialing Miguel Rojas's empty apartment, with Muchacha clasped against her breast, her little doggie heart fluttering against her own.

"Brave girl, Muchacha, my beautiful little princess girl," she murmured, hoping against hope that the veterinarian would have a magic cure come morning. But the inexplicable nerve damage was grave and irreversible; there was no cure. And so she was forced to look into her dog-baby's eyes reassuringly while the sedative was administered before the lethal dose to stop the heart. Now she can barely stand to be in her own apartment where reminders of Muchacha haunted nearly every room, which is the real reason she continues to camp in her mother's room at the Quintanilla's.

"You should adopt a child," Marta says. "God knows you have enough money to raise a football team of them."

Luz says she will consider it. But the mere idea of initiating the process all on her own makes her feel tired and lost. Even as she procrastinates, she knows time is passing her by and that if she doesn't hurry up, she will end up adopting her grandchild, rather than her child. Still, she would rather wait, she decides, until she finds the right lover, the right companion, the right father for a child. For Luz it is all or nothing, just like in the telenovelas.

The day before the statue of Maria Lionza broke, Luz had been sitting on the sofa eating dulce de leche straight out of a can and crying over a photograph of Muchacha with *La Traviata* playing full blast on the stereo. Her taste for opera had been aroused when she and Lily were around twelve and her mother's friend José Naipaul had taken them to see *Madame Butterfly*. In the car, on the way, he had told the girls that the opera was all about passion, that people who witnessed it for the first time either loved it or hated it, that it was best to find out how one felt well in advance, to avoid embarrassment or even shock later.

"My lover took me to the opera on our first date," he said. "I had never experienced the opera before then, and nearly jumped out of my skin with delight during the first aria of *La Boheme*."

Lily had made fun of *Madame Butterfly* and of José with Irene the next day, both of them clasping each other, breaking into high-pitched wails, and collapsing on the bed in spasms of breathless hilarity. Luz had pretended to agree with them, and laughed and shrieked, too, but secretly she thought the opera was the most beautiful thing she had ever seen or heard. Of course she still thinks it's unfair when Pinkerton takes advantage of the oriental girl. On the other hand, the oriental girl is a geisha, so how innocent could she be? She thinks perhaps it is true that even a tragic love affair is better than no love affair at all. But she is too fearful to test this belief firsthand. In any case, such a story would never work as a telenovela.

When the Lancer sputters and chugs to a stop at a gas station at the outskirts of Valencia, and Luz places the call to Miguel, it is a woman who answers the phone. The voice sophisticated, assured, smooth as silk. So, no, she can't pretend it is the maid. Luz says she is an old friend from Tamanaco, just passing through, and hangs up before the woman can ask for her name. She is relieved and grateful when Ismael and Carlos Alberto, her traveling companions, do not ask questions.

As if intuiting her need for distraction and focus, Ismael asks her to take the wheel of the old Lancer again. And she is grateful. As they head full speed away from Valencia, she notices the white-knuckled grip Carlos Alberto has on his knees, and succumbs to a childishly cruel pleasure. Ismael, who also notices, tells her to slow down, and she behaves herself until an hour later when Ismael takes the wheel for the last stretch.

Luz has always felt the highest regard for Ismael. And this is not so remarkable, since he is really the only father she has ever known. Her own father died before she was born. She doesn't remember him, feels no connection with the faded black-and-white photograph in her mother's room at the back of the Quintanilla house. When she was growing up, she used to pretend that her real parents were Ismael and Consuelo. And that her mother was just the maid. She told strangers that her name was Luz Martinez and practiced this signature in secret. Until the day Consuelo gave her the bracelet. After that she had felt too guilty to use that name.

In the photograph, her father is dressed in country clothes, a cap on his head, the visor casting a shadow upon his face. Because of this, and because the photograph is so old, she cannot fully distinguish his features. Every morning she searches her own face in the mirror for signs of his, mentally subtracting those features clearly inherited from her mother, until her own face blurs before her. It is a useless exercise, she knows, but it has become a compulsion, this search for a reflection of her father in herself.

In the jungle shack where she, Ismael, and Carlos Alberto take up residence there are no mirrors. After dinner the first night, she had been somewhat distraught to learn there wasn't even an outhouse and applauded herself for having had the presence of mind to conduct all her bodily affairs at their last truck stop, electing not to tackle the bush until daybreak.

In the morning, Luz awakens with an involuntary jerk and nearly topples out of her hammock. She looks at her watch. Six a.m. She cannot remember when she last woke up this early. Gingerly, she sits up and takes stock of the cramped surroundings. The stark poverty of the room, which seven hours ago had appeared so enchanting in candlelight, stands exposed by day. The moldy bamboo and thatch that form the dome, the dirt floor, the wobbly makeshift table, the threadbare bedsheet that had protected her from the onslaught of mosquitoes in the night. Her gaze moves to the primary source of light, the cutout window, where the figure of a naked woman with arms outstretched floats in midair. At first she thinks she is hallucinating, then she remembers how it is that her hostess earns her living. It is a mobile, but the most beautiful one she has ever seen. She must not leave without one. Better yet, she will buy as many as she can carry, for they will make exquisite and original gifts.

Except for Efraín, who is still asleep, there is no one else in the room. But the door is wide open, and she assumes the others are somewhere outside. Efraín's eyes move rapidly under eyelids fringed with thick, dark lashes. A solitary teardrop glistens at the edge of one eye. The fragile delicacy of his features, his utter defenselessness, whatever the dream that has produced the tear, all this squeezes at her heart.

"Buenos días, Señorita," says Juanita Sanchez, coming through the door, her arms full of firewood. She is followed by Ismael and a puffy-eyed Carlos Alberto, who take their places at the table. "I trust you slept well and have an appetite for Pizca andina."

"Very well, thank you," says Luz, swinging her legs out of the hammock, feeling for her sandals with her feet, and stepping right onto an iguana's head. She shrieks.

Efraín sits bolt upright, rubs his eyes, sees the iguana, jumps out of his hammock and grabs the offending creature. He takes it outside, and when he returns he smiles at Luz. It is a big, crooked-toothed smile that makes him look alluringly impish. Luz, recovered, smiles back.

"Show the señorita where to do her business, Efraín, and take a pail of water so that she can wash up," says Juanita Sanchez, turning on the radio.

Carlos Alberto grins wickedly at Luz, and she knows he thinks she won't last the day. In fact, she was thinking that ruefully to herself, as she observed the welts where the mosquitoes had feasted on her blood, but the smug look on Carlos Alberto's face has just inspired her to stick this adventure through to the very end. Grabbing some tissues from her purse, she follows Efraín outside.

"Don't worry, Señorita, I'll take you where there aren't any snakes," says Efraín sweetly, while Carlos Alberto chortles into his coffee cup. Luz shoots him a withering glance as she takes Efraín's hand and walks more boldly than she feels out the door and into the dense forest.

Midmorning, after a breakfast more hearty than any she has permitted herself in years, Luz asks Ismael whether there is a defined plan for the day. Carlos Alberto, who already has his video camera slung around his neck, points it at Efraín, but Ismael steps in front of him and places his hand over the lens. Juanita, who has already begun to preen for the camera, begins to argue with Ismael, but Ismael gives her a warning look. She abruptly stops arguing and tells Efraín that they need more firewood. Efraín looks at his grandmother in surprise, then at the stack of firewood in the corner, then at Luz. Luz, realizing there is going to be a discussion over the filming and that Ismael does not want the boy to be a party to it, holds out her hand to Efraín, saying, "Vamos, Efraín, show me how to find wood in the jungle." Efraín, tilting his head and smiling in that crooked-toothed way that had taken her heart hostage at first sight, picks up his machete and sack in one hand, and offers Luz his other. And together they go into the forest.

They walk between the trees, following a faint path of previously trampled leaves for several minutes. They reach a small clearing, where Efraín begins to cut wood while Luz places it in the sack. When the sack is full, Efraín says, "Would you like to see the nest of a Maizcuba?"

"Yes," says Luz, "I certainly would."

"We can leave the sack here and collect it later," says Efraín.

"Let's go, then," says Luz.

Efraín leads her out of the clearing, where there is no path, cutting his way through the overgrowth, and Luz momentarily wonders how they will find their way back. But the boy is so confident, turning every now and then, and smiling at her encouragingly, that her misgivings are quickly allayed. Of course he knows his way, she thinks, this forest is his backyard.

After several minutes of walking, they come to a stream, and Efraín stops, putting his finger to his lips and pointing up in the branches of a tamarind tree. "Do you see it?" he whispers.

But Luz is looking somewhere else, to a place her nose has led her eyes, a pungency, faintly nauseating, on the other side of the stream, almost directly across from where they stand. She sees the boot of a man. The man is lying face-down on the bank covered in mud and leaves, arms out-stretched. Below him lies a woman; the upper half of her body is in the stream, her face appears to have been eaten by wild animals, her long hair floats in a fan around her on the water. Further on, two others, both men, one lying on his side, the other on his back. Efraín follows her gaze and begins to scramble through the water toward the bodies. Luz reaches out to restrain him, but he is already halfway across, leaving her no choice but to follow.

Efraín stops near the woman and stares, his eyes growing wider and wider.

Then his frail body crumples in a faint and he falls backward into the stream, in almost the same position as the woman without a face.

Luz, holding her breath to avoid the stench, gathers Efraín in her arms and lifts him. Carrying him, she crashes back across the stream and, with a strength born of pure adrenaline, runs through the forest, concern for the boy her only compass. When she reaches the clearing not far from the hut, she falls on her knees still holding Efraín and begins screaming for help.

Minutes later, Ismael comes running into the clearing with Carlos Alberto close on his heels.

"There are four dead people by the stream. Efraín saw them and fainted," says Luz, her breath coming in gasps. She is on the verge of fainting herself.

Carlos Alberto lifts the boy from her arms and they return to the house. While Luz pulls off Efraín's wet clothes, Juanita holds guanabana leaves to his nose to revive him. Carlos Alberto grabs his video camera and he and Ismael head back to find the place by the river Luz has described.

The senior producers at TVista are of the opinion that footage of three dead Guajiro males and one female of mixed race wearing rebel armbands, three shot three times in the back, and one in the stomach, is too politically sensitive to air.

"Too sensitive?" Luz argues over the smelly pay phone at a corner store in San Felipe. "Why shouldn't cross-border executions of the poor be news?"

"Luz," says Enrique Alonso, her boss, "when did you of all people turn into a champion of the so-called disenfranchised? Forget it. Leave it to our illustrious leader to dole out bread and bricks to fuel the fires of social justice. Our job is to keep the public entertained and happy. Right now people are hooked on this El Niño character. We get hundreds of calls every day since the first story aired. That's the story we want."

"I can't believe you!"

"Believe it. Listen, Luz, it is imperative that you stick to the original plan. Since the day before yesterday, El Presidente is putting out the story that each morning he receives an important instruction from El Niño, who whispers it into his ear while he attends morning Mass—the first was he should form an alliance with China, the second was that he should make a book by a Jewish intellectual mandatory reading in schools, and the latest is that he should nationalize the airwaves. The public is lapping it up, and my instructions from above are to demystify the rumors. Just get us the kid. If you don't we'll send someone out there who will."

Luz finds she doesn't care that her opinion regarding what constitutes real news has been overruled by her superiors. Certainly not enough to argue, which would be pointless, anyway. All she cares about is getting back to Efraín, who has been in what appears to be a semicatatonic state ever since he saw the dead people by the river.

"They won't air it," she says to Carlos Alberto, who is waiting in the car.

"Well, I guess that's the end of my big break," he says, sounding almost relieved. But then he looks depressed.

"What is it?" Luz asked.

"Perhaps my father was right; what sort of man supports his family with soap opera scripts?"

"The best kind," says Luz, smiling.

"What is the best kind?"

"The kind who knows how to tell the story of a woman."

Of course the story of the executions of four people in the woods would have aired in the days of Alejandro Aguilar. And even today, it would have aired if the senior producers and executives, all big businessmen who hated El Presidente and his protectionary policies toward the masses, had known that one of the dead men was the infamous Negro Catire, whose real name was Diego Garcia; yes, they would have fallen all over themselves to publicize such a victory over the most pernicious of thorns in the side of capitalism. But they wouldn't obtain that information from Luz or Carlos Alberto. Because, over the past twenty-four hours, there has been an unspoken agreement between them that the true identity of El Niño will never be revealed for public consumption.

"We would make terrible journalists," says Carlos Alberto, smiling.

"Yes, but we'd make excellent bank robbers," says Luz.

"Have you noticed you've started to drive as though you're at the wheel of a getaway vehicle?"

Early the previous morning, before she left with Carlos Alberto and Ismael for Yaracuy, Luz did something she knew was bad and for which she now feels guilty. All the others in the Quintanilla house were asleep—even the nurse, Alegra, who was snoring softly in the leather recliner in the living room. Luz drew another chair next to the daybed where Lily lay, placed her lips near Lily's stomach, and whispered the true story of the Macuto and the silver charm bracelet. It took over half an hour, during which Lily, deep in slumber, did not stir even once. When Luz finished, she was so tired she could barely keep her eyes open.

"How's that for a story, baby?" she murmured.

As she dozed off, her head resting against the side of Lily's daybed, she felt a repetitive pat on her shoulder and heard a voice, softly crooning her to sleep. From the time she was a child, Lily had always patted her on the back and sung to her when she was unhappy or upset or couldn't sleep. When Lily started singing to her, Luz tried to open her eyes, but her eyelids were too heavy.

"I'm so sorry Luz, please forgive me," she thought she heard Lily say. Except it sounded like Irene.

As Luz drifted deeper into sleep, she felt the light feather touch of a kiss brush across her lips, like a summer breeze. And then fingers, playfully pulling at her toes. And the thick, dark thing that had clouded her spirit for so many years began to lift and dissipate in the predawn light.

She awoke to her mother's touch upon her shoulder.

"You need to get up and get ready if you are going with los señores," said Marta.

"It was so strange, Mamá," said Luz. "I dreamt that some-one was pulling my toes."

"¿Ah, sí?" said Marta. "Pretty soon it will be me pulling your toes if you don't get up and get going." Luz regarded her mother with sleep-filled eyes and a smile, thinking that the one thing she could be certain of was that her mother would never change. But then Marta unexpectedly reached down and hugged her roughly. And for the first time in years, Luz did not pull away.

Now, as Efraín mourns the execution of his family in his dreams, while she rocks him in her arms, she thinks she may have discovered something about a mother's love. She wishes she could tell him it is only a dream.

Passion fruit mousse is easy to prepare. Cut in half lengthwise and scoop out the seedy pulp with a spoon. Boil down to obtain syrup. Serve cold, like revenge.

Marta

When Marta dreams, she is back in Cuba. In some of the dreams she is a young child, sitting at the table with her parents, eating a steaming plate of yuca, rice, black beans, and fried plátano. In other dreams she is a grown woman sitting in a cafetería called La Esmeralda with Humberto. Always, when she visits Cuba in her dreams, she is happy. It is only when she is awake that Cuba becomes the enemy.

Marta's understanding of, and interest in, politics is limited. As far as she is concerned, a good leader is one whose enemy is her enemy. And though she loves Ismael like a brother and savior, she still thinks he was crazy to have fought against El Colonel, who not only opposed the Communist leader of Cuba but gave Maria Lionza the recognition she deserved, raising her status to that of a national symbol. Wasn't it true that his government was blessed by the goddess, that people were safe in their own houses and on the streets? These days no one can walk in a public place without fear of atracos, or park a car in front of a restaurant without wondering whether it will still be there by the time the meal is over. El Colonel had been a real Presidente, not like this one, who behaves like the primogénito of the island tyrant, constantly running there like a propio payaso to seek his advice, and importing his vile ideas to the mainland. No wonder the statue of Maria Lionza has broken in two.

Marta was one of the first of an estimated seventy thousand Cubans who migrated to Venezuela during the revolution. Why she left her home and her dashing revolutionary husband of only two years, Humberto Galano, never to return is a question she has been asked by employers, friends, acquaintances, and even total strangers. Over the years her answer has evolved. At first it was because Humberto was involved so deeply with the revolution that it put their lives in danger. He insisted that it was best and safest for her to remain in exile until Cuba was free—which, he said confidently, was only a matter of a couple of years at most. Then it was because once every two years, when Humberto came to visit her in her adopted country, he left her preñada, and she was either pregnant or nursing whenever the opportunity to return arose. Then it was because of the children, because of financial security, for in the early years, one thing was clear: she and Humberto could not support their growing family in Cuba under the crushing economic conditions that prevailed. Then it was because of democracy; it was better, Humberto said, to wait until elections were held and a democratic government was in place. Finally, it was because her husband was dead.

Most recently Marta has taken to saying that it is not a question of why she left Cuba, but why she will never return. Then, relishing the expectancy in the eyes of her interrogators, especially if they are prorevolution, as so many are these days, she says, "Because He [she can never bring herself to say the name] finds it more expedient to sacrifice others for the revolution than to die for it himself." She says the last word as if it should be accompanied by spit. No. She cannot return, she says, because the only way to return is with a sharpened machete for cutting a smile in His thick neck. And then her children would lose a mother, as well as a father, before it was time.

Although she is seething with rage over the present, Marta often remembers her childhood with longing.

"Do you suffer from terminal nostalgia? You were dirt-poor, it couldn't have been that great," Luz snapped at her once, as though she were jealous of it, this period in her mother's life when she did not exist. It is true that Marta prefers the past to the present. Her family had been poor, but they had been happy. It had been another time, another place. But when you have perfection, the gods remind you what it is like not to have it. Now she is rich, or at least her daughter is, which amounts to the same, but neither is happy.

For generations, Marta's Andalusian ancestors had endured the cruelest forces of history in conditions of unrelenting scarcity. Their only escape was through making love and the telling of stories, stories about themselves embellished by their hopes and wishes, stories in which they had the power to create a miraculously happy ending, even if happy endings were rarely a part of real life. Marta's mother, Maria Inocenta Usoa, was especially gifted in the art of invention, and it is from her that Marta developed her taste for exotic cuentos. When Marta was a child Maria Inocenta had held her daughter spellbound with accounts of the long winters she spent growing up as a poor peasant in Andalusia, an experience made beautiful by the embellishments she added to her tales.

The only daughter, among many sons, of a farm laborer, Marta's mother had fled Spain at the age of sixteen, just two years before the military coup that would spark off a social revolution. A cousin who planned to get out on the next boat claimed that it was easy for young women to find positions as housemaids in the New World, a better prospect than waiting to be raped by insane revolutionaries.

"That damned Basque woman will be the death of us all," she said in reference to the Marxist revolutionary Dolores Ibarruri.

With tears in her eyes, Maria Inocenta accepted the small money pouch that contained the sweat of her father, her mother, and her brother and crossed the Atlantic Ocean, as thousands of poverty-stricken Spaniards were doing, their hearts nearly bursting with hope of a better life and the means to send money to their families in the old country.

Maria Inocenta's arrival in the port city of Havana was dramatic: the flimsy craft that was carrying her from the ship to the shore capsized, sinking all her belongings in the bay, including a few ropes of smuggled Andalusian chorizos.

She was illiterate, but whatever she lacked in education she compensated with fearlessness and spunk. What she did not know when she left Andalusia was that Cuba was suffering an economic recession almost as severe as the one in Spain. Like so many other European refugees whose hopes were soon dashed on the shores of the New World, Maria Inocenta did whatever had to be done to survive, including, it turned out, trabajo de jintera. After striking out at all the fancy restaurants where she had begged, once even on her knees, to be given work as a waitress or cook, she finally knocked, her stomach rumbling stridently with hunger, at the door of Las Quince Letras in the San Isidro district of Havana.

"Do you know how to please a man?" asked her prospective employer, Señora Conchita Ramos, one eyebrow elevated. She was wearing a Chinese silk kimono, open almost to her navel, and held a slim cigar in her hand, which she brandished with a certain flair that to Maria Inocenta, dazed by hunger and exhaustion, appeared impossibly exciting and attractive. She had never seen a woman with so much confidence. But what appealed to her most was the fact that Señora Conchita appeared extremely well fed.

"Back in the old country I was the favorite girl in the most famous and busy brothel in the city of Granada," said Maria Inocenta, even though she was a virgin and had never even lain eyes on a city before arriving in Havana. She could not be sure at the time whether Señora Ramos hired her because she believed her story, or because she liked her, or because she simply wanted a fresh face. And what did the reason matter? She had a roof over her head and food in her belly. She would not die like a dog on the streets.

Devoutly Catholic and hence resistant to the loss of her precious virginity, she insisted that her specialty was hand work. And, upon hearing this, a sensation both sharp and sweet struck a chord in the breast of the jaded Señora Ramos. This dark Andalusian beauty, with her quick wit and defiant youth, reminded her of herself in years gone by. And so she told Maria Inocenta that she could stick to hand work but would have to undergo training in mouth work as well. She could keep her virginity until she turned eighteen, and then they would see.

Las Quince Letras was a high-class establishment. The wealthy and exclusive clientele of Señora Ramos followed her rules, paid her extravagantly, and behaved like gentlemen. In turn, Señora Ramos could afford to take excellent care of her girls, and it made business sense to protect her investment. Maria Inocenta was given free room and board, lovely night-clothes made of lace and silk, and an evening gown for each day of the week. Plus, she was allowed to keep forty percent of her earnings, better terms than any other whorehouse in the city, half of which she dutifully sent back to her family in Spain. In her spare time she helped out in the kitchen, and it was there in the brothel kitchen that she learned how to cook and discovered she had a knack for it.

Life was almost too good to be true, until the night one of the clients broke the rules and impregnated her. It wasn't all his fault; Maria Inocenta admitted later that she was as much to blame as he, having somehow lost herself in a world of the senses while entertaining the young man in a game of strip poker, where the rule was that the winner not only got to choose the clothing item to be removed but to remove it. When his hand gently slipped into the waistband of her silk underwear and then slid slowly down into *that place,* she swooned, and before she knew it he was inside the forbidden gate.

Señora Ramos, who had grown maternally fond of Maria Inocenta, said she could continue working as a hand-and-mouth girl because, believe it or not, there were some men who would pay a great deal to be so serviced by a beautiful pregnant woman. She said Maria Inocenta could keep the baby, that a baby would bring joy to all the members of the household. She would treat it as her own grandchild, she vowed. But Maria Inocenta thanked her benefactress for her kindness and said she would leave the brothel and take her chances, because what kind of life would a baby have in a brothel? Conchita Ramos was disappointed but not in the least bitter, and she did what she could to help.

Only barely beginning to show, and on the recommendation of a friend of Señora Ramos, a rum baron who frequented Las Quince Letras, she applied for a job as an assistant cook in the household of the rum baron's niece, a villa in Calzada del Cerro.

"I write down the menus in the morning. Can you read?" the woman asked.

"But of course! I have a high school diploma from the old country," Maria Inocenta replied with confianza, though she had never been to school and could barely scratch out her own name with a stick in the dirt. In reality, she had simply memorized some important phrases found on the menus of the most popular restaurants and made them into pictures of lines and curves and dots in her mind. Sofrito. Rabo encendido. Picadillo. Lechón asado. Dulce de leche. But take the letters apart and she would have no idea what they represented. However, so convincing was her pronunciation that it never occurred to la Dueña that she was faking it. She got the job and moved into a small but well-ventilated room at the back of the house.

In spite of her disreputable beginnings in the new world, and the illicit seed in her womb, Maria Inocenta had remained throughout a staunch Catholic. She wanted to baptize her child and so, before the Mass one Sunday, confided this desire to the elderly parish priest, Padre Delgado. He listened quietly while she told him that her husband, a fisherman, had drowned off the coast, victim of a terrible storm. Afterward, he advised her to come regularly for instruction and promised to help her. But to her mala suerte, a gentleman frequenter of Las Quince Letras had recognized her at Mass and, indignant at watching her receive the Host with the same mouth and sip the Blood of Christ with the same lips that, only a few days before, had caressed his manhood, had waited until she left and done his sacred duty by informing the priest. When she returned the following day, Padre Delgado scolded her for telling such monstrous lies. He said she had severely jeopardized the safety of her soul. He said that under the circumstances, and until she had confessed and been purified of her sins, he would not be able to baptize her child.

Maria Inocenta was a girl who had never learned to hold her tongue. She tried to explain that if she had always remained virtuous, she would be dead. No one, she said, could fill their belly with chastity and honesty. For her, living on the streets was the reality she faced and against which she fought so that she could meet her basic needs, and now the needs of her child.

"Which is better for the soul," she asked the priest, "giving a man five minutes of pleasure and telling a small mentira here and there that hurts no one, or living on the streets and starving like an animal?"

The aging priest, who was essentially a kindly soul, though somewhat restricted in his ability to express it by his doctrine, had felt pity for her plight but insisted that she renounce both men and lies. He said it was most definitely better to starve and die than to lose one's soul to the devil. Then he prescribed a penance of three rosaries per day along with her promise to visit each person to whom she had told a lie, confess to them, and apologize. He said that given her unmarried and sullied state, she would not make an appropriate mother and that when the child was born, she should give it up for adoption. He said that although her own soul had a stain on it, there was still a chance for the newborn.

As though, Maria Inocenta said later to Marta, this old childless padre with his poor, shriveled private parts could know anything about the soul of a mother, whoever she may be and however she may have come to be with child. For that matter, what could any man know about it? Only a woman could understand what it means to carry new life in her body for nine months. She decided that to bring her child safely into the world, she would tell any lie that would keep her alive. From then on, she gave up the idea of baptism, and directed her prayers exclusively to la Virgen de la Caridad, patroness of Cuba. La Virgen, blessed be her name, was a woman who would understand, and it was La Virgen alone in whom she would confide and from whom she would seek solace.

Meanwhile, she continued to work in the home of the wealthy Trujillo family, where she met the man who would become her husband, Ernesto Torre.

Ernesto Torre was the gardener for the Familia Trujillo. He nurtured and talked to his thriving plants, flowers, and bushes as though they were his babies, and this is what Maria Inocenta first loved about him. When she offered to take his lemonade to him in the garden one midmorning, the elderly head cook had smiled perceptively and handed her the tray. And that is how their courtship began.

Ernesto was the first to notice when Maria Inocenta

began to show and immediately asked her to marry him. He claimed he did not object to raising another man's child as long as he could have Maria Inocenta by his side. He would raise this child as one of his own, and he expressed the hope of having many. Together they saved their money, until, in Maria Inocenta's sixth month, they calculated they had enough to purchase a small plot of land. They found one near Matanzas, where they grew black beans and yuca, and where Marta was born—kicking and screaming, according to her mother—on an Easter Sunday.

Marta remembers the details of her mother's stories better than the details of her own childhood. Of her childhood, she mostly remembers sensations. The succulent taste of black beans and yuca. The wind on her skin when she climbed the mango trees with her sister, Yolanda, and their two younger brothers, Angel and Lucio. The rich smell of her father's tobacco pipe.

She knows, looking back, that her family was poor, barely eking out a living on their crops, but poverty is not what she remembers. Since she had never lived any other life, never had any source of comparison, how could she have known the difference between poor and rich? Love and warmth is what she remembers, with one hot day blurring into another, and another.

The only sequence of events in her childhood that stands out with clarity in her mind is the time she traveled to Havana with her mother and they visited the big fancy whorehouse, Las Quince Letras, though of course she hadn't known it was a whorehouse at the time. She must have been around nine years old, the eldest of four children. She remembers all the women in the big house, beautiful women wearing beautiful clothes, fussing over her, taking turns holding her on their laps, and calling her "little pecado de juventud," with tears in their eyes. She remembers the soft rustle of silk and the heady smell of perfume. She remembers Señora Ramos feeding her delicious chocolates, the first she had ever tasted, and handing her mother a packet with money in it. She remembers her mother's desperate gratitude, and that her father had been angry when they returned and had thrown the money on the floor.

Maria Inocenta's ability to inspire confidence in her eldest child about her origins must have been extraordinary, for Marta feels no shame about her mother's story or her own illicit conception, and tells of it often. Carlos Alberto had been so taken with the story that he asked and received her permission to turn it into a telenovela. It was called *Soledad,* and Marta had watched the dramatization of her mother's early life with pride and fascination. That the names were changed mattered nothing; on the contrary, being privy to the secret of the story's origins was a titillating enhancement to her viewing experience.

Marta likes to say that just as Abraham and Sarah exploited and abused the slave girl Hagar, so too her mother had been exploited and abused by Churchgoing people who took advantage of her. Her mother was like Hagar. The spring she found in the desert, where none existed before, is what enabled Hagar to survive. This is how Marta sees her mother: as a woman who miraculously found a spring in the desert.

She acknowledges that it was the fierce determination and force of her faith in La Virgen de la Caridad that had empowered her mother, who could neither read nor write, to make a way out of no way. In the depth of her soul, though she knew not how to articulate it, Maria Inocenta had understood the essence of theological ethics from the sidelines, and the role the Church has played in keeping the poor in their place. Maria Inocenta's response, to rely on a female deity that always provided the psychic resources to meet the harsh realities of life, made complete sense. She composed no grand thesis on the subject but taught her daughter this concept via her oft-stated aphorism: "La Virgen, she is not like the Church. She squeezes, but she does not choke."

It was in that spirit that Marta had put Humberto's life in the hands of La Virgen de la Caridad. But to her profound shock, La Virgen had betrayed her, failing in her mission to protect Humberto from the paranoiac wrath of a tyrant.

Maria Inocenta had written to her grieving daughter, saying that everything in life was part of a divine plan, and Marta knew that her mother believed that it was Humberto's lack of faith in a power greater than the revolution that had contributed to his destruction in the end. But Marta thought that her own fervent faith and thousands of Novenas should have softened La Virgen toward her husband, who, in spite of his atheism, was a good and compassionate man. Marta never told her mother that she had subsequently acquired a more benevolent and powerful patroness who did not insist on martyrs, for it would surely have broken her heart. So Maria Inocenta had gone on consoling her daughter with holy pictures, reminding her to say a prayer on the feast days of various incarnations of the Virgin, especially that of Caridad. And Marta had gone on letting her mother believe that she continued to be faithful.

Maria Inocenta's life had drawn to a close two decades ago today. And on the seventh day of the Novena to Maria Lionza, Marta remembers to thank Maria Lionza for her mother's vibrant life.

Everyone present has already told a story, Consuelo, Amparo, Lily, and herself.

"Someone will have to go again," she says.

"You tell, Marta," says Lily. "The last time you told us the story of Maria Lionza. This time why don't you tell us your own story and how you came to this country?"

And so Marta begins.

When Marta was fourteen, the villagers of Matanzas became fearful that their lands would be snatched away by a powerful sugar farmer they called Papa Grande. For a time, Papa Grande alternately threatened and wheedled, and finally doubled and tripled his offers, making it difficult for small farmers to resist his advances. Marta's father, one of nine farmers who had managed to survive Papa Grande's onslaught for a whole year, was on the verge of capitulating when the intrepid Humberto Galano arrived in Matanzas.

Humberto Galano was the first communist Marta had ever met and the most beautiful and electrifying man she had ever seen, with his red, wide mouth, laughing eyes, wild, curly hair and large gesticulating hands that seemed to have lives of their own. He was part of the Sierra Maestra movement and had come to Matanzas to help the small farmers resist the sugar baron. Son of a wealthy banking family, he financed much of his activity with his inheritance, which he had received at the age of twenty-one, when his idealism was at its peak. He brought twenty armed men with him to help in the resistance, and he stayed until his mission was accomplished two years later. Then he asked Ernesto and Maria Inocenta Torres for the hand of their eldest daughter, Marta.

It had been a strange courtship. Humberto seduced the farm girl with quotes from Marti. He wooed her with stories about the leader of the revolution, about his courage, about how he defended the poor and strove to release them from misery. And the way he spoke, the way his eyes shone, made her want to embrace his struggle, for on some level she realized that he and it were one and the same. She wanted to prove to him that she could contribute in some measure to his cause, even though she didn't understand it, even if it only meant following Humberto to the ends of the earth, if he would let her.

Ernesto and Maria Inocenta recognized the call of love in their daughter's eyes. Humberto had impressed them with his selfless work on their behalf, and they had grown to love him. They agreed readily to the union. There was neither time nor money for a wedding, and, in any case, Humberto was an atheist. But to please Maria Inocenta he promised to say a prayer at the shrine of the Blessed Virgen de la Caridad before taking Marta with him to a village in Oriente province, where he had a modest house.

In Oriente, Humberto continued his work as an advocate for agrarian reform, offering assistance to other groups of small farmers in the surrounding areas.

By the end of their first year together, Humberto had also become a courier for the Rebel Army. Now the couple's nights were frequently broken by sudden clandestine meetings held by candlelight. While the rebels pored over rough maps, discussing whether they should camp here or there, attack first in this place or that, Marta cooked and served them platters of food, hoping to fill the hungry hollows in their cheeks, and cups of rum or hot coffee until, thanking her profusely, they dropped, exhausted, on mats on the floor, or left under cover of night to prepare for another day of battle with the enemy. It was during this time that Marta saw Che, who was already a legend throughout the Americas. He arrived on the back of a donkey, his figure drooping. He was smaller than she had expected, and seemed fragile. She mentioned this to Humberto. But Humberto told her later there was nothing fragile about Che. He was as tough as steel and an inflexible disciplinarian. According to Humberto, any and all disorderliness of men in his charge was severely punished by Che, because La Disciplina was critical to a guerrilla's survival.

"He doesn't even take a lover," exclaimed Humberto, with admiration coupled with disbelief, "that's how dedicated he is to the cause."

Marta replied that while Che was undoubtedly handsome, he was also apparently sexless. Unless they were blind, men generally observed Marta, who was full-bodied and sensuous, with a great deal of appreciation. "He didn't even notice me," she said.

"Just as well," said Humberto, patting her bottom. "I wouldn't want that kind of competition."

When Humberto began traveling as a courier for the

Revolution, he shaved and dressed in faded but clean country clothes. A knife hung from his belt and he carried a gun. During his travels he often slept in ditches by the side of the road, pulling a broken tree branch over himself for camouflage. Weeks later it would be another Humberto who returned to her with clothes tattered and filthy, hair long and scraggly, a deeper line etched in his forehead. He left Marta alone for weeks at a stretch with only a semiautomatic rifle as company. She was good with it, for he had taught her to shoot. But it was then that she began to hate the Revolution a bit.

After a particularly lengthy absence, Humberto returned with horror and revulsion in his eyes. On the way home he had seen a murdered woman in the tall corn grass near Guisa. "Her skirts were above her waist," Humberto told his wife, "her left leg bent at an impossible angle, her eyes staring without sight at the summer sky."

It was after he saw the dead woman that he decided to send Marta to the mainland. She did not want to leave him, and she begged him to come with her. They could start a new life together, she said, a life away from all this killing. But in her heart she knew he would not be tempted away from his grand mission, and in the end, because she loved him, she had no other option but to accept his verdict that discipline and sacrifice came before personal desire in times of revolution.

"Then let me stay," she pleaded. But he said he must not be distracted in his work by a constant concern for her safety.

As yet under the influence of her mother's beliefs at the time, Marta, too, continued to set great stock in La Virgen de la Caridad. Humberto had indulgently allowed her to erect an altar in their home, though he said he didn't care for the idea of a virgin staring down at their bed while they made love. He made her move it to the kitchen, where Marta prayed daily for the success of the Revolution. It was later, after her husband was assassinated by the Revolution, a perfidious beast that consumed its own children, that she eschewed La Virgen de la Caridad and Cuba forever. In exchange, she pledged her allegiance to her adopted country, and to Maria Lionza.

Marta was frightened and alone when she arrived in Venezuela with her small, worn suitcase. But the thought of her mother's bravery when faced years ago with similar circumstances steeled her backbone. She was determined to be open to face anything and everything head-on during her exile from her homeland. After spending a week with a friend of her husband's in a horrid, filthy place called Petare, just outside the capital, she saw an ad in the newspaper for a room to rent in the nearby city of Tamanaco. The ad read "Gentleman preferred." But she went for the interview anyway because the rent was cheap, and she was confident of her powers of persuasion. After taking three different buses, she found herself standing dubiously in front of a dilapidated building near the Sabana Grande. Taking a deep breath, she marched into the building and took the dirt-stained stairs to the second floor. A man in a bathrobe opened the door of the apartment. The place was as gaudy as anyone could imagine, and everywhere there were images of Marilyn Monroe — on the shower curtain, the lampshades, the toaster. There were three men living in the two-bedroom apartment. A couple and a friend who lived on the sofa in the living room. The second bedroom was the one available for rent.

At first the atmosphere was uncomfortable. But when the residents invited her to have a drink with them at the kitchen table, she accepted, and after a toast and a couple of sips, everyone relaxed.

Gentleman preferred, explained Pepe, the man in the bathrobe, was a kind of code, since they couldn't possibly have advertised for a man of their persuasion publicly without being arrested, beaten, or killed. The inhabitants of the flat were the most genuine and attractive personalities Marta had encountered since her arrival on the mainland. After establishing that she did not care a whit what they did with their night lives, they invited her to move in.

Living with them was an education in and of itself. Pepe, who had originally leased the apartment, was Puerto Rican. He slept till noon, and at night he put on extravaganzas in some of the seediest bars in the poorest and most run-down areas of the city. These were outrageous, colorful, highly staged erotic shows in which he played many different roles. He had hired a group of women dancers who formed part of his popular burlesque escapades. Pepe conducted his rehearsals in the afternoons, and it was not unusual for the living room to be filled with half-naked girls who politely covered themselves.

The man who slept on the sofa in the living room was José Naipaul, a tattoo artist from Trinidad and a devotee of Maria Lionza. At first, Marta was baffled by the Maria Lionza pantheon, a celestial court of disembodied spirits of people, real and imagined, native warriors, ex-slaves, political leaders, writers, doctors, crooks. Even Simón Bolívar was there, reputedly very useful when seeking employment with the government, and other things, too.

Marta spent most of her time after work chatting with José Naipaul and learning from him how to make mouthwatering Indian curries with aromatic herbed rice. His tattoo business was far from flourishing, and to pay the rent he also drove a taxi around the city. On weekends he took people on tours to Sorte Mountain, where the biggest shrine of Maria Lionza was located. A believer in Maria Lionza more for the romanticism of it than anything else, José told Marta to think of Maria Lionza as the Mother Mary of the marginalized, especially the mestizos.

"Maria Lionza is not dead," José had insisted. "All Marialionceros speak of Maria Lionza in the present tense, because, according to them, she is immortal."

The complexity of the belief system and the ever-expanding pantheon of the goddess made Marta's head spin. There were so many Immortals who belonged to one or the other of the seven courts of Maria Lionza. José explained that each court was led by one of the more important Immortals, starting with Maria Lionza herself. Marta knew what the most important of them looked like because most of them were figures of either history or legend, and statues and figurines representing them were to be found everywhere at Sorte and in the perfumerias and the tiendas dedicated to the goddess all over the country.

Marta accompanied him to Sorte on occasion, though she was not yet a believer then. She was lonely for Humberto and the company of men in general, having spent so much of her life surrounded by Humberto's compadres, who had been, for the most part, male. So her association with José afforded her both a safe way of passing time with a man, as well as an exotic, strange, and colorful experience. It was only later, after she had rented a small one-bedroom apartment in La Florida, when her boys, Juan Pedro and Jorge Luis, were lost and then found, that she believed.

She had been shopping in the familiar (and cheaper) district of Sabana Grande with her boys in tow, when she realized she couldn't see them. Dropping her bags of purchases on the street, she had hurriedly retraced her steps through the busy marketplace, calling out their names, stopping people and shouting in their faces, "Have you seen two boys, have you seen my boys?" For two hours she combed the streets and bylanes, then, frantic, she ran to her old apartment. Only Pepe was at home. He had danced till dawn in a cabaret the night before, and at first he ignored the bell, pulling the bedclothes over his head. But when he realized it was Marta, pounding and screaming, he leapt out of bed with bloodshot eyes and ran to open the door. Then, still in his pajamas, which consisted of boxer shorts and a tight woman's T-shirt that ended above his belly button, and shoving his feet into furry bunny slippers, he grabbed her hand and, together, they rushed back to the market. Compassionate shoppers and shopkeepers spread the word about the missing boys, and soon shouts of "Juan Pedro! Jorge Luis!" could be heard on every lane, but to no avail. It was as if the boys had simply evaporated into the air.

Finally they went to the local police station for help, but when the police saw Pepe, they laughed their heads off and said maybe the children had run away in fear of this fag. Don't worry, they said to Marta, whose swollen eyes reproached them, boys run away all the time, but when their stomachs hurt from hunger, they return to their mothers. By this time,

José, who was returning to his apartment for his wallet, which he had forgotten on the dining table, had heard the news on the street. He ran up the steps of the police station, taking them two at a time, and nearly collided with Marta and Pepe as they emerged. Marta collapsed in his arms and began to weep uncontrollably. "Mis niños, mis niños," she wailed, while Pepe stood by, shoulder hunched in defeat, tears and mascara making tracks down his face.

"Stay here," said José, and ran back toward the apartment. A few minutes later, he pulled up in his taxi. They drove to the capital, twenty-five kilometers away. Stopping opposite the statue of Maria Lionza on the Avenida Francisco Fajardo, he said, "Go and tell her about your boys." At that point, such was Marta's derangement and desperation, that even if José had said, "Climb up a tree and screech like a monkey," she would have complied. As if there were no cars whizzing by at a hundred kilometers per hour, she had charged across the highway without stopping or looking. Standing before the statue, she had prayed with all her corazón. Give me back my boys, she said over and over, with her head in her hands.

When she raised her head, a woman handed her a flyer. One side had a likeness of a bald monk in brown robes holding a child; the reverse had a child figure in a blue cape with a shepherd's staff in one hand and a little basket in the other.

When Marta returned to the taxi and showed the flyer to José, he told her that many Catholic saints were included in the pantheon of Maria Lionza, and that those on the flyer were representations of San Antonio and El Santo Niño de Atoche. Both, he said must be approached in different ways. According to José, in order to get San Antonio's immediate attention, it would be necessary to scold and threaten him, and in extreme cases such as Marta's, bind his statue with rope and place it in a dark place, until that which was lost was found. To appease El Santo Niño, he said, she should fill a small basket with dried grasses, candy, toys, rum, and cigars. Next, she should write a letter to El Niño, asking for the return of the boys. Finally, she must carry this basket offering to high ground, where she should offer prayers and light candles. Under José's careful tutelage, Marta complied with all the requirements, trussing her porcelain statue of San Antonio and locking him in her cupboard. Then, accompanied by both Pepe and José, she hiked halfway up the Avila mountain to present her offering to El Niño. When they returned to her apartment in La Florida, it was dusk, but even in the dim light she could make out the figures of the policeman and her two boys, standing by the entrance to the building. "They were playing poker with a drunk in the back of a bar," said the policeman.

"Why didn't you answer when so many were calling out for you?" Marta shouted, while the boys hung their heads and stared at the ground.

"They had lost their watches in the game, and were afraid to come out until they had won them back," said the policeman.

Marta thanked the policeman, knelt down, and drew the boys into her arms, burying her face in their hair. "Never do that again," she said. Then she raised her hand and whacked them, one after the other, on their cheeks, which turned strawberry red with the force of her delivery. Afterward, while Pepe pressed ice packs to the weeping boys' cheekbones, and José began to prepare dinner, Marta went to her cupboard, withdrew the statue of San Antonio, gently untied him, and returned him to his rightful place on the altar in her bedroom. Then she sat on her bed, held her hands to her face, and wept with gratitude. She wept so long and so hard that by the time she returned to the living room, her nose had taken the shape of a potato, giving her a cartoonish appearance. Pepe had put on a record by Tito Puente and was dancing wildly with the boys. Marta allowed herself to be drawn into the middle of their mad gyrations and, with her hands on her hips, twirled and whirled around while José applauded from the door of the kitchen. By the time dinner was on the table, her nose had returned to its normal size, and the aromatic scent of José's famous pasticho set her mouth watering.

The following day, Marta allowed José Naipaul to give her a tattoo of Maria Lionza on her back. Her conversion was complete. The figures on the altar stand were increased by two: Maria Lionza and El Santo Niño de Atoche. Over the years they would swell to a battalion.

"Your collection of religious iconography has multiplied tenfold," observed her husband the last time she saw him. He told her he had been made the manager of the National Factory of Sanitary Fixtures in the city of La Esmeralda.

"Then I can come home?" she asked.

"Not yet, not yet," he said. He seemed distracted. And later that night, while he panted and labored over her in yet another desperate farewell, she prayed to La Virgen de la Caridad to keep him safe.

When she discovered she was pregnant, she hoped the baby would be a girl because she thought a girl would be less likely to ever become a revolutionary.

Humberto Galano died in prison before Luz was born. He never saw his daughter. It was through her friends in Petare that Marta received the news that he had been executed as a traitor to the Revolution, several months after the execution occurred. He had refused to be blindfolded, they said. He died like a man, they said, their voices laden with pride. As though this was better than living like one.

Six months pregnant, Marta walked to the liquor store down the street. She purchased a case of the cheapest rum and paid a delivery boy five Bolívares to carry it to her apartment. She drew the frayed curtains of all the windows and proceeded to get very, very drunk. Night and day, she sat in a chair by the darkened window, rousing herself briefly twice a day when the boys said they were hungry, reaching into her purse for the amount it would cost to buy two perros caliente at the kiosk next to the liquor store. This is how José found her after two weeks. Horrified, he packed Marta and the boys into his taxi and drove full speed to Sorte. Within twenty-four hours, Marta had been successfully weaned off alcohol by a clever Banco, who, after covering her belly with red cloth to protect the unborn child, prayed over her and forced her to drink rum "blessed by the Goddess" all day and all night without respite, waking her when she dozed and pouring it down her throat, refilling her stomach with it when she vomited. Until she had had enough rum to last her lifetime and beyond. It was the second time Maria Lionza had come to her aid, and she would not forget it. When she returned a few days later, her landlord was threatening eviction as her rent was over a month overdue. She applied for another housekeeping job and, despite her pregnancy, was hired by a cousin of President Marcos Perez Jimenez.

Marta was not the sort to tell her problems to people she'd barely met, and she didn't know what made her tell her new employers about her predicament with the rent and the pregnancy. But it was the right decision, because they immediately offered to advance the money. They even paid her hospital bill when she delivered a baby girl, whom she named Luz, a beacon shining out from the darkness of her loneliness.

The following year, when the rent was suddenly raised exorbitantly, her employers helped her make arrangements to put the boys in boarding school in Valencia, and invited her, along with the baby, to live with them in their home.

Although she felt appreciated and loved, although her existence and that of her children was secured, although she had a new country and a new life, she continued to quietly mourn Humberto. Her grief, at first a large, dark cloud that dimmed her senses, over the years condensed into a small black stone that settled, hidden but never forgotten, in her heart. And she never failed, once a week, to make an offering to the vengeful spirit of La Negra Primera, petitioning for the painful and humiliating demise of her husband's executioner. Sooner or later, her petition would be heard, of that she was convinced. She would continue praying for that day to come until it did come.

With the ouster of El Colonel, her employer, who had benefitted financially from his blood ties with the president, had fled to Spain, and she was forced to look for alternate employment. After several days of pounding the pavement, going door-to-door in the residential areas of the capital and hearing a series of *no thank you*s, she finally sat, exhausted and dejected, at an outdoor table outside the Panadería Sosa, wondering how on earth she was going to keep her children in boarding school. A woman holding a young girl by the hand, a child no older than Luz, who was five, approached her tentatively and smiled. "All the tables are taken," she said. "Would you mind if we joined you?"

"Please do sit down," said Marta, smiling at the little girl.

"I'm Lily," said the child. "Don't you think my name is pretty?"

"It surely is," said Marta.

"Please allow me to buy you a coffee," said Consuelo.

An hour later, she had become an integral part of the Martinez household.

Since her daughter married a millionaire, Marta no longer needs to work for anyone. Still, she can't imagine leaving Lily. Luz doesn't see why not. But hadn't Consuelo and Ismael built a cottage for her in their very own garden, where she had lived with her family until the boys had joined the military and Luz had married?

"All I'm saying is that you don't have to *work* for them," says Luz. "You could live in your own apartment and visit them whenever you like."

"No. I can't live in my own apartment. What would I do there?" It isn't as though Luz is offering to share her own flat and companionship. And who wants to cook for one?

That enormous penthouse and all that money Luz got

from Miguel Rojas, what good has it done her? is what Marta wonders. Luz doesn't know that Marta has refused to accept a salary ever since the Quintanillas began having financial trouble, and Marta doesn't plan to tell her. Luz gives her far more than she can spend, so where is the need of a salary? In fact, if Marta were Luz, she'd use the money to help those less fortunate — perhaps doing something for someone else once in a while would put a smile on her face. But no, she just lounges around, gobbling up chocolates and watching telenovelas half the day. Is she blind to the way people all over the country are struggling?

Ay, Luz. Perhaps it is as the Banco of Maria Lionza once told her: in her bones, if not her mind, Luz knows that her mother had cursed her at birth.

The truth is that her last, and what should have been her easiest, delivery almost killed her. Twelve hours after her water broke, she lay writhing on a cold metal table. Her legs, jammed into stirrups, trembled with fatigue, while her belly convulsed without end. In the brief moments between contractions, she could see José Naipaul's face pressed white against the small rectangular window in the door to the delivery room.

As her blood pressure mounted, so did her rage against Humberto. He had done this abominable thing to her and left her to fend for herself. She swore to the white ceiling above her that she would have killed him herself if he had not already been dead. Dr. Campos, the hospital's obstetrician, who was also a surgeon, conferred loudly with a nurse, as though Marta were not in the room, as though his voice did not need to compete with Marta's screamed curses. Or at least she was trying to scream, but her throat was so parched that what emerged sounded more like the croaking of a frog.

"Let's move her to surgery," said Dr. Campos.

"Yes, Doctor," said the nurse. And Marta wanted to kill her for having such a smooth, flat stomach, for even having the capacity of speech.

"Why did you wait so long?" she gasped, as the nurse approached her.

"Dr. Campos said he would prefer a natural delivery," said the nurse.

"Fuck Dr. Campos and his preferences. And fuck you. And fuck this brat who is trying to kill me," growled Marta, just before she lost consciousness.

"You always take up for her," Luz said to Marta, on the day she turned nine and her mother made her share with Lily her American Barbie doll collection, which had grown to twenty, due to the largesse of José Naipaul. And, thinks Marta, perhaps it is true. Lily is not complicada, she does not baffle. Lily is like a serene, dark pool, with waters that rarely ripple. Marta's relationship with Lily has always been unperturbed, easy, sane. Whereas with Luz, Marta has always felt she must be prepared for battle, to defend her position. Luz makes Marta feel like she must guess the weather of tomorrow and always be wrong.

Marta has done the best she knows how with all her children. It isn't that she doesn't love Luz or that she wouldn't walk through a thousand fires to save her were it ever necessary. It is just that . . . Marta can't understand why Luz hoards her hurts as if they were treasures. The way she still holds a grudge about that doll, even though it was almost twenty years ago! Marta decides the reason she and her daughter cannot have a decent conversation is weariness, pure and simple. She is weary of Luz and her constant dredging up of what she considers to be her mother's past misdeeds. She is tired of her judgments and blackmail, of her ceaseless barbs and unquenchable demands for validation twenty-four hours a day. She wants Luz to grow up and stop being mad at her brothers Juan Pedro and Jorge Luis for being born first. And now that Lily needs her family and friends more than ever, she wants Luz to give up her silly childhood rivalries. But instead, Luz is jealous. It seems to Marta that Luz is jealous of anything that isn't about her.

Gracias a la Reina Maria Lionza, the boys had never given Marta much trouble, except for the time they were lost. Even between the ages of twelve and seventeen, when their hormones rage out of control, the boys had been easier. Consuelo and Ismael had helped her put them through a government-subsidized boarding school, and they had grown up into strong and principled men without untoward incident, except for a few broken bones along the way, as with all young boys. Bones are easier to mend than hearts. Luz, well, it was as though she'd been born with a broken one.

Marta loves her daughter. But she doesn't always like her. That's the truth of it, though she wishes it weren't.

Because of their proximity in age, Marta had entertained fantasies that Lily and Luz would be like sisters, since neither of them had one. She wanted them to relive what her own sister and she had growing up in Cuba. Until she married Humberto, Marta and her sister Yolanda had done everything together, shared everything. Even after Marta had fled to the mainland, the sisters wrote to each other every month. But Marta never saw two girls more opuestas than Lily and Luz, as different in their likes and dislikes as chalk and cheese. If it was the weekend and Lily wanted to go to the park, well, then, Luz wanted to go to the zoo. It had to be her way every time, and there was no compromising, otherwise there would be hell to pay. And, while this may be a good quality in a businessman, it is no asset in a woman, is what Marta thinks. Which makes Luz furious. But then, everything makes Luz furious. According to her brother Juan Pedro, Luz is just mad at the whole world and wants the world to know it.

From the time she was five, which is when Señora Consuelo had offered Marta a job, Luz was always watching to see whether Lily got a larger piece of chocolate, more ice cream on her plate, a better birthday present. Neither of them could ever finish a whole banana when they were little, so Marta used to cut one in half. Once, Luz complained that whenever Lily was around, her mother always gave her, Luz, the culo of the banana.

"What do you mean, the culo of the banana?" Marta asked, astonished.

"You always give her the top part and me the bottom," Luz accused.

"Ay, por Dios. What are you talking about?" Marta had been so upset, so…baffled by her daughter. But La Señora had only laughed and cut up another banana. She gave Luz the top part. She handed the culo to Marta.

"Give her time, Marta," said Señora Consuelo, "she'll grow out of it."

But, so far, thinks Marta, Luz hasn't grown out of it. And now she fears that it is Luz herself who has cast the evil eye on Lily. Not on purpose, of course, that's not how it works; most people aren't even aware that they are doing it. And Luz, whatever her faults, would never deliberately wish Lily harm, but the evil eye is cast when one person covets, even unconsciously, the life, looks, possessions of another. Years ago, Luz had been envious of Irene's hold over Lily, and look what happened to *her*. That Luz is envious of Lily's pregnancy is clear to Marta, and it is impossible for her to ignore the fact that when Lily had slipped and fallen six days ago, it had been right after Luz entered the room. This is why she is relieved that Luz decided to accompany Carlos Alberto and Ismael to Sorte. But Luz's absence is only temporary, and Marta is not sure what will happen when she returns. And so these days she prays to Maria Lionza, not only for the safe delivery of Lily's baby, but for the delivery of Luz from the sickness that is envy. In return she offers to give up her petition of revenge against her enemy.

Marta wonders whether there might be an advantage to having children late in life, although it is generally considered dangerous because the later you have them, the more likely they could turn out mental. She once saw an older woman—forty-five or so—in the grocery store in La Esmeralda. She had her child by the hand. Marta saw that the child had slanty eyes like a Chinese person, and her tongue was hanging out of her mouth. It scared her half to death, because she was thirty-six at the time, and pregnant with Luz. What if my baby comes out like that, she had thought.

When she was growing up, it was considered best to get the childbearing over with when you were young. It was unthinkable for a girl to remain unmarried out of choice beyond the age of twenty-three. There was none of this modern nonsense about how women had to fulfill themselves intellectually and have careers before they settled down to have their babies. In those days, until the Revolution, the roles were clear—women stayed at home and had the babies, and the men brought home the bacon. Everyone had their work cut out for them, knew what it was, and nobody was traumatized about it. But today's women are having their babies later and later. Marta read an article in her favorite magazine, *Mujeres,* that said there was a woman in the United States who had a baby at fifty-five. Her daughter couldn't have one because there was something wrong with her insides, so this lady decided to have one for her. Fifty-five! Imagine! The woman's daughter said she wanted a "natural child." But it seems to Marta that there was nothing natural about any of it, because the mother had to use her twenty-eight-year-old daughter's egg and grow the egg outside of her body in a petri dish. Then the daughter's egg had to be planted in the mother's womb at a later date. Even though Marta no longer attends the Church, she can see why His Holiness, the Pope, would be against such a procedure, because if people are going to grow babies in dishes and grandmothers are going to start giving birth to their own grandchildren, where is the line to be drawn?

Consuelo says that because of her age, which was forty when Lily was born, the first thing everyone did was count all the baby's fingers and toes. Then they closely examined her genitalia, because sometimes, when the mother is too old, the baby is born with both sexes. But, gracias a Maria Lionza, Lily was perfect when she was born.

Marta sometimes used to worry that it would be a problem for Lily to have a mother old enough to be her grandmother, but Lily and La Señora, they were always like two peas in a pod. And Lily never gave her mother any trouble. At least not after she was separated from that little demon, Irene Dos Santos.

"Don't say that," says a voice in her ears.

"Ah, it's you, isn't it, still causing trouble in this house," Marta says. "Why don't you show yourself?"

But there is no response and Marta knows the reason why: it is far easier to get rid of a ghost you can see than one who hides in your ears.

The wild passiflora edulis found in the rain forests of South America are hardy vines that are able to endure the onslaught of pests and extreme weather.

Ismael

While Carlos Alberto stands on the bank of the stream looking on, his mouth slack with shock, Ismael smothers his nose in the left sleeve of his jacket, and with his right hand turns the man nearest to him around. It is one of Diego's twin sons, he cannot tell which. The young man's lips are blue, his brown eyes staring. Fumbling with one arm, the other still held against his face, Ismael unbuttons the man's denim jacket and pulls up his shirt. The bullet to the back has traveled through the body and exited from a place just above the sternum. The wound is pale and clean, its blood having emptied into the stream. He can barely bring himself to look at the others. Another youngish man might be the second twin, but his state of decomposition is further along, and Ismael cannot be sure. Only Juanita would be able to make an identification. The remaining two bodies are of the woman without a face, and his beloved friend, Diego. All four have been dead at least two days, he concludes.

Two by two, Ismael and Carlos Alberto drag the bodies to a flat area at the top of the stream's bank, wrap them in the bedsheets they had brought with them, and drag them through the forest back to the hut.

La Vieja Juanita weeps inconsolably, wailing that they should be buried where they belong, on the other side of the border, alongside her sister Lucrecia. When she is finally and quietly exhausted, Ismael suggests they put the dead to rest near the guava tree, but Efraín begins to scream hysterically, his shrieks growing louder and more piercing by the minute. Only when a whiff of urine from the tree assails his nostrils does Ismael realize the boy must have used that place to relieve himself. "All right. Not near the guava tree," he says, and the boy stops screaming. He takes off his shirt, rolls up his pants, grabs the only shovel, and begins to dig in an open space behind the hut, away from the guava tree. The grueling rhythm of this labor cuts his grief into manageable segments. *Plunge, scoop, dump…plunge, scoop, dump.* Diego Garcia had been shot in the stomach. *Plunge, scoop, dump…plunge, scoop, dump.* It would have been a slow and excruciatingly painful end. *Plunge, scoop, dump…plunge, scoop, dump.* Diego's executioners must have wanted atonement for his sin of eluding them for over forty years. *Plunge, scoop, dump…plunge, scoop, dump.* This would explain why the others had all been shot in the back and through the heart. *Plunge, scoop, dump…plunge, scoop, dump.* If one is going to die, it is better to die instantly than to watch life's blood seep slowly into the earth. *Plunge, scoop, dump…plunge, scoop, dump.* We honor the spirits of the dead by remembering them and making their families our own. *Plunge, scoop, dump…plunge, scoop, dump.*

The last time Ismael saw Diego Garcia, they had argued furiously, after Ismael had asked what the difference was between Diego and his enemies now that the end had come to justify all means. They had not met again. But he had not forgotten his promise to take care of his family. Of Diego Garcia's family, only Efraín remains.

Diego and Ismael had first met, when they were both in their thirties, during the pandemonium of a government raid on a peasant uprising against the encroachment of the latifundios on tribal land in Yaracuy. Ismael had been leading the crowd with energetic songs of resistance, accompanied by a sha-man musician known as Antonio Lorenzo, when the sound of sirens and bullets filled the air. People screamed and scattered. Ismael covered his face with his jacket, jumped from the podium, slipped, and fell to his knees, cracking one of them sharply on a stone. Staggering hurriedly to his feet, one hand holding the jacket over his face, the other flailing out in front of him, he began a limping, loping blind run, tripped over a man who had fallen, regained his footing and kept going. A couple of meters out of the range of the tear gas, he looked back over his shoulder and saw a policeman with a club heading for the fallen man. But he was closer than the policeman. Pivoting, his knee sending bolts of lightning pain to the center of his brain, he doubled back, and grabbed the man by his arm, yanking him to his feet. "Follow me," he yelled.

"I can't see," said the man.

"Here, hold on to my sleeve and run with me."

Bound by the single-minded goal to escape police brutality, they had raced neck and neck, zigzagging across the public square of Simón Bolívar in the town of Barquisimeto as bullets whizzed past them, heading for the street. Grabbing the man's hand, Ismael veered toward a moving bus, yelling "¡Socorro! ¡Policía!" which in those days of rebellion was not a call for assistance from the police, but meant one was being chased by them. The bus screeched to a halt while the men jumped in and took off again just as quickly.

Inhaling sharply, Ismael held out his hand and introduced himself.

"Diego Garcia," said the man, grabbing Ismael's hand in his own. "Thanks for saving my ass back there."

They took the bus to the outskirts of town, where they got off and ran across a fallow field and into the woods. They slept without dinner on their jackets on the ground under the trees and awoke ravenous. They considered approaching a farm they had passed while crossing the fields the day before to solicit a few eggs, but they decided it was still too dangerous for them to be seen in the open. Ismael, trained in wilderness survival by his Que family, went deeper into the woods and returned with some berries and edible wild mushrooms. But he had been unable to find a water source and, finally, it was thirst that drove them midafternoon into the open and across the field to the farmer's door. The farmer was a mestizo who supported the tribal cause, as did all the small farmers of the area who were being eaten up by the caudillos. "I sent my workers away after one of them was severely beaten. They are trying to get rid of all the campesinos. They threaten us and burn our vehicles. If I miss this harvest, I'll have to sell my farm to them."

He told them the police were still looking for all resistance organizers and that they should not travel by daylight. He gave them as many water bottles as they could carry, along with some bread, dried fruits, and strips of smoked venison. He also gave them a flask of homemade agua ardiente. When they thanked him for his generosity, he waved off their gratitude. "It is I who must thank you, who are risking your necks for total strangers." There was nothing more to say. Silently, they shook the farmer's hand and returned to the woods under cover of darkness, and on the way Ismael caught and skinned a rabbit with his pocket army knife, which he roasted slowly over a wood fire for their dinner.

"Would you like to hear a funny Guajiro story?" asked Diego, wiping his mouth on his sleeve and smacking his lips in appreciation of a tasty meal.

"Sure," said Ismael. A sense of complicit camaraderie had grown between them in the hours they had spent together in hiding.

"Around the time of the elections, the white politician, hoping to gain some extra votes from the indigenous tribes, flew his helicopter over the forest where the Guajiros had made their home for generations. Spotting a village in a clearing, he instructed his pilot to land in an open field. The pilot did as instructed, but the people of the village ran into the forest. So the pilot took the helicopter up again, and hovered. The people came out, waving and pointing at the air. Once again, the pilot attempted to land, but the people all ran into the forest. This happened two or three times, and finally the politician said to his pilot, 'Drop me off in the clearing and take the helicopter away, pick me up again in half an hour.' The pilot did as he was told, and the politician stood in the clearing, smiling, while the people of the village peered at him curiously from behind the trees. Then the leader of the tribe said to his people, 'Look, the giant bird has gone, but it has left its shit!'"

They had laughed with belly-shaking abandon, until tears squirted from their eyes. "I swear to you that story is true," said Diego.

Then Ismael told a story about the time he was working in a camp housing displaced Warao families following a flash flood. Ismael had been interviewed by a journalist, and a photographer had taken his picture. The next day the newspapers had printed the photo with a caption that read, "Warao man surrounded by his extended family."

When it was Diego's turn, he told about the time he accidentally came upon a border posse, whose members had contracted an infection from poison ivy while defecating in the forest and were seeking relief by soaking their enflamed posteriors in the river. They had tried, half-heartedly, to run after him bare-assed, yelling curses as he disappeared into the forest. And so they continued swapping stories, embellishing and exaggerating for effect, and shaking with laughter. Slowly, the stories grew more serious. In the pitch-black of the moonless night they shared their hopes, their dreams, their loves, and, Diego, suddenly serious, said, "If I had a family and anything were to happen to me, you would be the kind of man I would want to look after my children."

Several years later, after they had brought a group of refugees across the border, including two women and one child, an operation that had involved fighting off soldiers back-to-back with pistols at the river crossing, Diego, who by then did have children, had repeated that sentiment.

"You are far too stubborn to die young. It will be your children who will be looking after you," said Ismael, smiling.

"I'm serious." Diego's mood had been dark.

"Of course, hombre," said Ismael, patting him on the

back, "don't worry, it goes without saying." Only then had Diego's good humor returned, and, raising a jam jar filled with rum, he toasted the revolution with a bawdy tune.

As long as Ismael had known him, Diego Garcia had been a large-hearted man with a fighting spirit, whose fiery love of rebellion against any authority had trumped all other loves. For Diego, resistance was not a means of achieving freedom; it *was* freedom. Fortunately—or unfortunately, depending on one's perspective—this was a passion he was able to ignite in the hearts and minds of many, including his sons.

There was only one time that Diego ever fought another Guajiro. The man was a drug and gun runner who had escaped the clutches of the militares so many times that the people called him Aceite; he lived in the village of Ladrones, a village he had himself founded, located on the northwestern border. It was here to the village of Ladrones that illegals came to learn the arts of pickpocketing, grifting, car hot-wiring, and so forth, before moving to the cities. And it was here that Diego himself had recruited his best drivers to move the cars he stole from the cities, on Ismael's tip-offs, or those prematurely "scrapped" by Alejandro's company.

The story was that when Aceite's unmarried daughter, a traveling midwife, came to visit him, he had lost his temper and thrashed her within an inch of her life. It was because of a gift of two gold bracelets she had received from a client in gratitude for the safe delivery of a baby boy, a gift she refused to hand over to her father. Aceite had beaten the girl black and blue with a horsewhip and, as she lay nearly unconscious on the floor, he had shattered both her wrists, on which she wore the bracelets, with blows from a hammer. Aceite claimed that keeping such an extravagant gift was a humiliation and disrespect to her father. And as far as he was concerned, the only humiliating would be performed by *him*. Of course, Aceite had not reckoned with Diego Garcia, who came to hear the story from the very man who had given the girl the bracelets. After beating Aceite almost to a pulp, Diego had carried the midwife, whose name was Lucrecia, out of her father's house and taken her to the nearby town of Valera, where a doctor set the bones in her wrists. Then Diego took her home and cared for her until she was well enough to fall in love with him.

Though Diego's tryst with the midwife Lucrecia had been brief, it had resulted in conception. Lucrecia, possessed of a roving and revolutionary spirit as fiercely independent as that of her lover, was prepared to birth a baby but not to raise one, much less two, for it turned out she was carrying twin boys. She gave them unnamed to her elder sister, Juanita, to bring up as her own. Juanita, widowed and childless, had named them Manolo (after her late husband) and Moriche (after her father). She had mothered the boys and loved them to the best of her ability, but Moriche, the secondborn, had the temperament of his namesake and had fought her from the start, seeming to perceive even as an infant that she was not his real mother and thus without rightful claim to him.

There was no Guajiro community on either side of the border that was immune to the lure of Diego's call to arms. When Manolo was sixteen, he ran away to join his father in the guerilla struggle for the rights of his people to their land and way of life. Juanita could not prevent a son from join-ing his father's call, but she was determined that Moriche not follow suit. In an effort to shield Moriche from the fate of Manolo, Juanita had explicitly forbidden Diego to recruit him. Her effort, however, had ultimately been in vain, for Diego was a hero, and trying to prevent any young Guajiro from revering him would have been like trying to blot out the light of the sun from the sky.

Diego, out of respect for Juanita's wishes, had assiduously refused to admit Moriche into the revolutionary army. But Moriche, who thought it was merely a matter of proving his mettle, was not to be deterred. He had tried to establish his value and resourcefulness by intrepidly running dangerously large caches of guns and drugs across the border at the age of seventeen. He arrived at one of Diego's moving camps in the middle of the night, offering a share of his profits as funding for the rebellion, but Diego had refused his money and slapped him, saying it was blood money, that Moriche had brought shame upon his own name and risk to those who fought in the rebellion, that he should stop playing peligroso games and go back to his mother. This had the unfortunate effect of a challenge to Moriche's young manhood. Embittered, he had become a mercenary, peddling his wares to the highest bidder and keeping the money for himself. His influence grew in the dark underbelly of the drug world that had no borders, and so did his fortune, which he squirreled away in banks under different names in two countries. In the end his father had come to him for help to secure the release of a group of rebels held by the militares near the border town of Arauca. And after that the line between good money and bad money had been blurred for the resistance fighters.

Though it was thought by many that Diego Garcia, like all pure revolutionaries, was incapable of romantic love, Ismael had heard that his reaction to Lucrecia's accidental death by a stray bullet during a skirmish with the militares had been that of a madman. From all accounts, he had begun taking ever crazier and exaggerated risks in his cross-border activities, taunting and provoking his foes as though he actually wanted his life to be given a punto final, dragging his sons and even his daughter-in-law down with him.

When Ismael's arms begin to strain and ache beyond endurance, Carlos Alberto quietly removes his shirt, takes the shovel from his father-in-law's hands, and continues to dig. Ismael, sitting exhausted on the ground, watches his boxer muscles ripple, the sweat pour down his torso, and he is overcome by affection for this strong, gentle man who has married his daughter. It takes two hours to make four shallow graves. They lay the bodies to rest in the graves without coffins. When the dead are covered with dirt it begins to rain lightly. Efraín's face contorts violently before becoming flaccid again. It is all right to cry, says Luz. But Efraín mutters that the drops on his cheeks are from the rain and brushes them aside roughly with his fists. He will plant flowers, he says defiantly. Then his eyes glaze over, his body goes limp, and he does not speak again.

"I'm taking the boy, Vieja," says Ismael.

Juanita emerges momentarily from her veil of sorrow to say, "You cannot have him."

"It is Diego's wish, as I told you the day I arrived."

"To hell with Diego, his wishes, and his endless revolution. The boy is my grandson."

"He is Lucrecia's grandson. And you have allowed him to draw too much attention to himself."

"He has a gift. Why should it be hidden?"

"Such a gift untrammeled and exposed to the public will surely destroy him."

"And who will teach him and raise him to manhood? Not you, surely; you're as old as I." Juanita's voice is tired and Ismael knows her defiance is half-hearted, hollow, unsustainable.

"I will raise him," says Luz. Ismael hadn't realized she was listening from the doorway. He looks into her eyes and wonders whether a motherless child and a childless mother might not be the right combination under the circumstances.

Juanita lies down in her hammock, turns her face to the wall. "The little bastard is cursed. Only bad things happen around him. Take him then, and leave me to mourn my sons in peace."

And so they begin the drive home to Tamanaco, Luz in back with the unresponsive boy's head in her lap, Carlos Alberto at the wheel, and Ismael in the passenger seat, staring out the window and humming a song called "Consuelo," which he had composed for his wife on the day they were married.

They arrive in Tamanaco in the cool of the summer afternoon. And when they turn into the driveway Consuelo is already standing in the middle of the garden waiting for them, surrounded by roses, her hair blowing in the breeze. After the initial reunion jumble of hugs and kisses, Luz collects Efraín from the backseat of the Lancer and carries him to her own bed, while Carlos Alberto, his arms around Lily, quickly recounts their adventures in telegraphic hushed tones to an astounded audience.

This excitement, it seems, is all that is required for Lily to go into labor. Amparo and Alegra fly into action, joyfully barking out orders and assigning roles to everyone. Lily's labor progresses into its fourth hour, but the business of birthing is not enough to dissuade Marta from commencing the eighth Novena to Maria Lionza promptly at eight p.m. Afterward, Ismael is enjoined by Lily to tell a story. In increments, between his daughter's contractions, pulling and tugging at the memories, forgetting in the heat of the moment to edit the happy from the unhappy, jumbling everything together, Ismael sings his story to his daughter.

Before he met Consuelo, the only thing Ismael enjoyed as much as music was diversity in women. Every woman had something alluring and irresistible that caught at his belly like the claw of a jaguar. With this one, it was the sharp angles of her shoulder blades that moved him to tears. With that one, it was the curve of a calf descending into the fine art of an ankle that made him ache with yearning. With another one, it was the composition of the foot with delicate arches and toes like ten delicious little shrimp that took his breath away. The swells and curves that rose and fell along the terrain of a woman's topography made him want to take up sculpting—in order to mold over and over again the balance and counterbalance of women's bodies, to re-create the juxtaposition of breasts, the roll of derriere, the differential between waist and hip, the outline of thigh, the sharpness of hip bone, the soft swell of the pelvis, mysterious repository and origin of life. Unfortunately, sculpting was not among his many talents, and his creations were monstrous, the precise opposite of what he meant them to be.

Immune though he was to deep and binding attachments of the heart, there was nothing devious about his love affairs. He made it a practice to make love only with those women who made the first move, warning them in advance that the only promise he could make to them was that he would leave. The terms of the contract were always clear, and it never occurred to a single one of his lovers to stake her claim to him or keep him longer than he wanted to stay; it was his very wildness that made him so attractive to them, and they were happy merely to be among those with whom he had dallied for a time.

All that changed the moment he locked eyes with Consuelo the night of Alejandro and Amparo's fifth wedding anniversary. All other women suddenly paled in comparison, and he could imagine himself with no one but her. It was as if he had been struck by a thunderbolt, every cell of his being electrified at the sight of her. He wanted to bury himself forever in her hair, which swirled, curled, cascaded from her delicate and perfectly formed skull, obscuring or framing the features of her face as she moved, playing hide and seek with the nape of her earlobes and neck.... What wouldn't he give to drink from the triangle at the base of such a neck, so perfectly cupped by bones of exquisite delicacy? Without waiting for permission, his heart pledged its allegiance to Consuelo, and he could hardly believe his good fortune when hers returned the favor.

When they were first married, Ismael, who had never

before been responsible for the safety and security of anyone but himself, had at first yielded to the opinion of the majority that the jungle was no place for a woman. He began to search for a place to rent in Tamanaco so that Consuelo could be near Amparo and Alejandro, and have the pleasure of their company while he was away, for of course it did not occur to him to give up his nomadic ways, and neither did it occur to Consuelo to expect it. Though his heart was captive, his wandering soul was not. And though the length of his travels was greatly reduced, his life as a married man was not so different from his life as a bachelor. Instead of returning to many lovers, he now returned only to Consuelo. Similarly, in what Amparo said was the quintessence of hubris, the fact of his marriage failed to temper his bold politics of resistance to an all-powerful regime. Once a friend and an ally of the incumbent, he saw no danger to himself or his beloved; friends could disagree and still be friends, he argued with an idealistic innocence that confounded Amparo. Or at least that was the substance of his argument until some other "friends" began to disappear, but by then he would be in too deep and it would already be too late.

His income from public performances and sales of his handcrafted cuatros was irregular, but it was enough to afford a small rented apartment in the rough and tumble neighborhood of Carmelitas. At least this was its reputation, the newspapers said as much — nearly every day there were noticias about some robbery or stabbing or drug arrest, and editorials on the government's "determination" to restore law and order. It was a determination that resulted in a type of reverse ghettoizing of the cities and their environs, where the rich were permitted to create vast prime property enclosures for themselves, with high walls and gates and rigorously policed by contracted guards, while the poor were left to fend for themselves in the overcrowded neighborhoods of the inner cities.

On a busy street in Carmelitas he found an affordable one-bedroom apartment, where the mostly mestizo neighbors were friendly. The women brought the newlyweds baskets of fruit, steaming pots of food, small items of furniture they could barely spare. The men brought their tools and set about repairing the leaky kitchen sink, the broken window, and the busted light socket in the living room. Lacking cross-ventilation, the apartment was almost unbearably hot during the day, making the use of clothing an unthinkable torment, though it cooled to a tolerable temperature by late evening. The kindly neighbors from the other side of the street, who caught sight of the couple's daily naked parade past the solitary window in the living room, kindly advised them to wet a bedsheet and place it over the window "so that they would not feel the heat so much." And Ismael, assured that Consuelo would be safe amidst such generosity and solicitude, had continued to travel around the country, carrying his song of resistance to the inner recesses of the nation, returning to Tamanaco every few weeks with a renewed vigor and inspiration that manifested in the marital bed, a double feather mattress on the floor of their bedroom.

As soon as he walked in the door, he would pick up Consuelo and swing her in the air, bury his face in her bosom. Then, in a flurry of purpose, as though he might forget what he had seen, he would sit down at the all-purpose card table near the window where the light was good and begin to write, until Consuelo, impatient, would pull him away from the table and into the bedroom.

Already popular in the neighborhood, for anyone who can sing melodically while caressing the strings of the cuatro is always abundantly feted among the people, Ismael had rounded up his musician friends, organized a concert in the Plaza Bolívar, and donated the proceeds for a center in Carmelitas that rehabilitated local dropouts, a feat that elevated him to new heights in the eyes of the community. To show their appreciation, the men from the neighborhood kept an avuncular twenty-four-hour watch over Consuelo when he was away.

Consuelo declined Amparo's invitation to stay with her when Ismael was gone. She, like Ismael, thought the newspapers exaggerated, or focused too much on poor neighborhoods like Carmelitas, or even made things up. She read aloud to him with surprise about the fulano who had been taken into custody for beating his wife, after the police had heroically entered the dangerous neighborhood of Carmelitas and subdued him. She was acquainted with the protagonists of the story, she said; she knew through her new friend Maria Pagán, who was a writer and ran the small secondhand bookstore down the street, that the police had been called but had arrived hours after the wife beater's own neighbors took matters into their own hands, gave him a walloping he would never forget just to show him what a walloping felt like, and broke his right arm to make sure he would remember the lesson when he awoke sober.

"Why do the newspapers print such lies?" she asked.

Ismael replied that making an example of crime in Carmelitas was more publicly acceptable than investigating the exclusive residential communities where the powerful committed their own abominations from within their gilded ghettos.

They might have gone on living in Carmelitas forever, had Ismael not been home on the day a shot rang out, and the slender man in a suit who was walking toward Consuelo as she returned from the grocery store, fell to the ground, dead as wood, his eyes staring into the sky, blood pouring from his temple onto the sidewalk.

"He was only a few meters away from me," Consuelo told him, when she reached the apartment, pale as a cloud. Her tone was calm but her teeth were chattering uncontrollably. She said the word on the street was that the dead man was a political dissident who printed pamphlets for the Communist party and had been taken out by the secret police. At that moment, Ismael changed his mind about living in Carmelitas for even one more minute, and they moved into Amparo's house until they could make other arrangements.

After a few days, Consuelo said that what she wanted most in the world was to be always at his side, and if that meant following him into the jungle, well, she was ready. And Ismael had looked deep into the autumn-speckled eyes of this woman who communed so completely with him heart to heart, whose unwavering gaze spoke so eloquently her love and trust, and he thought, Why not?

Ismael was not so much defined by his early formative years as liberated from them when his father, Don Rafael Medina Martinez, began to speak in a tongue no one else could comprehend with a person, or persons, no one else could see. Don Rafael's siblings had him committed to an asylum in the town of Las Tres Marías, where he would live out the rest of his days in the company of ghosts. His remaining days, as it turned out, were numbered to sixty-nine, the amount of time it took for a small bleed in one of the blood vessels in his left temple to become a torrent.

Since Don Rafael had not had the foresight to make a will, assorted family members, which included not only his three brothers and two sisters but also aunts, uncles, and second cousins once removed, upon receiving word of the demented patrician's demise, took it upon themselves to carve up the assets expeditiously on a first-come, first-served basis. The division was an acrimonious one, with accusations and litigations that would span several generations, but at the time in question they all agreed on one thing: the inheritance rights of Don Rafael's five-year-old son Ismael, born of an embarrassing (to them) union with a woman of impure blood, must be neutralized by the immediate burning of his Catholic baptismal certificate, to be followed by an expunging of the Church records in the parish of Las Tres Marías. So anxious were the relatives to eclipse the evidence of his paternity that the child might have been out on the street were it not for Don Rafael's sister Estrelina Aguamar, an aged widow and devout Catholic, with skin the color of grapefruit. She insisted that the boy must complete his Catholic education and took it upon herself to pay for his schooling and boarding in the Don Bosco lyceum of Las Tres Marías until he turned sixteen.

"It is not the child's fault that his blood is tainted, and it is our duty to ensure that he does not grow up like an animal," she decreed.

The others concurred piously with the noble thought, especially since Estrelina had been the one to take charge and have Ismael's baptismal records erased with the compliance and complicity of the parish priest of Las Tres Marías. They were lavish with praise when Estrelina, who had invested her sizable widow's wealth judiciously, announced she would be footing the poor little bastard's bills.

The truth of his birthright and dispossession would become known to Ismael many years later, piecemeal, from his Que family and through accounts told in the village closest to the Medina Martinez estate known as Santa Elena. But whether his course had been altered by design or by destiny mattered little, for he felt no connection with that former life or with those who had played a role in it. He could remember only vaguely the man and woman whose genes he bore, dim figures made out of smoke that hovered benignly in the loft of his memory. The only characteristic Ismael believes he inherited from his father is the ability to fall instantly and irretrievably in love.

Don Rafael Medina Martinez was a distinguished gentleman, of medium build and an enviable head of wavy, jetblack hair, who had inherited his wealth and property from his father, who had inherited it from his father, a former colonel who had won it from another colonel in a card game. He had completed a degree in medicine, as was the practice for a proper Señor, though it was not the practice for landed gentry to vulgarly put their degrees to any use. With the exception of the years spent obtaining his degree, he had lived in the estate mansion known as Cabeza de Carnero all his life. Solitary and ascetic in character from a young age, by the time he was forty-five he remained unmarried, a condition that had pleased his relatives enormously. When by the age of fifty he remained a bachelor, it seemed certain that the status quo would be preserved and the only question was to whom the estate would devolve. Since his intentions had not been made known to them, his siblings and their spouses jockeyed for position, visiting him dutifully on the holidays with gifts of potted meats, cheeses, and sweetbreads, and fussing over him in an apprehensive manner that more often than not drove him to the sanctuary of his stables. This gave his siblings the opportunity to rummage about in the study in search of a will, but they never found evidence of one. In the frenzied competition for his affections, they would redouble their efforts, arguing over who would sit at his right hand at the dining table, who would pour his sherry or coffee, who would accompany him for his nocturnal walk in the garden, until it was, to Don Rafael's relief, time for them to return to their own homes. Every year they played this game, bowing and scraping in his presence, but, in his absence, as his eccentric habits augmented, they could not resist mimicking his peculiar and fastidious mannerisms. As soon as he left the room, their very faces would change, slyly spewing defamations and untruths about him with each other. It was understood that he was to be tolerated because of the *money*. And so it went year after year, until the day Don Rafael fell madly in love.

A man of discipline and scrupulous habit but not of imagination, every morning Don Rafael would perform his ablutions and emerge from his room at precisely eight a.m. impeccably dressed in his riding attire, punctuated by his signature cravat the color of wine. He would breakfast frugally on fruits and nuts before riding out to inspect his properties, which consisted of two hundred acres of timber forest and another two hundred of rubber plantation, returning by one p.m. to lunch on a single filet of fish, half a tomato, and a light chicken broth, then retiring for a siesta till four. From four to six p.m. he would attend to his property accounts. Promptly at six, he would pour himself a glass of sherry from the decanter in the library, select a book he had read before and would read from it again until eight, at which time the standard dinner of finely chopped boiled vegetables and beef roast cut as thin as cloth would be served and polished off with a small bowl of quesillo, accompanied by a demitasse of strong dark coffee. His day ended with a brief walk in the garden to hasten digestion, followed by bed. And so it went, with one day melting into another, for weeks, months, years, until the morning he rode out with his trusted foreman, Anastacio, to inspect the eastern side of the timber forest, which bordered a stream that separated his property from the small settlement on the other side. The settlement was inhabited by a branch of the Quechuan tribe, who were known as Que. For generations there had been an unspoken understanding that neither the white man nor the Que would cross into the other's territory, and the stream marked the boundary of their agreement.

That day on the opposite side knelt an Indian girl of no more than fourteen years of age. She was collecting large smooth stones from the stream's bed, which Don Rafael knew would be heated on a fire and used to assuage the pain of muscle fatigue, having observed this practice among some of his workers. Her head bent, focused on her task, the girl did not notice Don Rafael's approach. Stricken by an inexplicable and gripping urge to see her face, he dismounted, signaling to Anastacio to remain where he was. As he stepped into the mild current of the stream, the girl started, then leapt to her feet, covering her face with one arm as if to avert a blow, as the stones scattered to the ground from her lap.

"Iman sutiki?" He asked her name gently. Slowly the girl dropped her arm to her side and looked at him with a face so fresh and vibrant with youth that a covetous spear of desire pierced his breast. He reached out his hand, which she took, tentatively, in hers. He smiled, she smiled back. Hand in hand, they approached the girl's father who was also the tribal leader.

"Munaycha ususiyki," he said, which meant "Your daughter is pretty," and was the traditional way of asking a father for his daughter's hand in marriage. The girl's father, impressed with the whiteskin's facility with the language, smiled and nodded. And when Don Rafael led his child bride back to his horse and lifted her up, she went with him willingly.

This is the story as told in the town of Santa Elena. In the Que version, the girl was captured, bound, and trussed like a wild boar, clawing and biting, and taken to Cabeza de Carnero, and she never smiled again. But the stories again converge on the following points:

Don Rafael had loved the girl, whose name was Luna, with passion but without understanding, as if she were a beautiful but mysterious figure in a painting to which he was drawn inexplicably, an object with which he could not bear to part. It was this lack of understanding that led him to re-create her in the mold of his fine lady ancestors whose majestic portraits hung on the walls of the Cabeza de Carnero mansion in gilded frames. He called for a tailor from Las Tres Marías to make petticoats and corsets and dresses. He gave instructions to the servants that her abundant hair be pulled tight and away from her face, tamed into an enormous bun that made her head appear too big for her body. She was bedecked with family jewels that had been taken out of their boxes after many years, and her feet were bound in elegant slippers. Within a year she bore him a son, who was christened Ismael in the church of Las Tres Marías, but who she called by a secret Que name that meant "moonlight," and with whom she played as if with a delightful toy, being only a child herself.

One evening when Ismael was four, Luna bent to kiss him and went for a stroll as usual. She was never seen again. Don Rafael found her dress and petticoats lying in a heap on the edge of the forest, then farther down the path her corset and hair clips. Finally, her satin slippers were discovered on the bank of the stream where he had first seen her. With seven of his men, armed with rifles, he crossed for the second time the unspoken boundary into the Que settlement in the desperate hope that he would find her among her people and take her back. But the elder of the community, held up his hand and said with a sadness that left no doubt, "She is as lost to us as she is to you."

Her disappearance marked the beginning of Don Rafael's end, for it was then that he began to consort with ghosts.

Here, the Que version has something to add. On the day Luna vanished, children playing near the stream on the Que side claimed to have seen, only for a moment amidst the trees, a creature with the head and torso of a woman and the body of a tapir.

Ironically, it was his education at Don Bosco that equipped Ismael for a life far richer than his paternal relatives could have imagined, since riches for them were appreciated exclusively in terms of acres and bank balances. While in his last year at the lyceum, a young priest lent Ismael the novel *Cantaclaro,* by Rómulo Gallegos, about a singing cowboy with incurable wanderlust in his heart, which sparked in Ismael the irrepressible urge to follow suit.

Upon passing out from the lyceum, his aunt Estrelina (though he was never allowed to address her as "Tía") gave him one hundred bolívares, a new suit of clothing that included shoes, and a letter of recommendation in which Ismael was portrayed as an orphan and she his benefactress, all of which was delivered by way of her houseboy, for she had no wish to look into his eyes as he went off alone into the world. But instead of looking for work in the town of Las Tres Marías as expected, Ismael had other ideas. He gathered his belongings—a small valise containing his few articles of clothing, his school certificate and letter of recommendation, a rosary, and his precious copy of *Cantaclaro,* which his teacher had bequeathed to him as a parting gift—and set off in search of his mother's village. He arrived after a day and a night of walking on dusty roads and through the forests. Dusty and parched, he was welcomed by a laughing group of people who looked familiar, and they celebrated his arrival as if they had been waiting for him.

And so, albeit a bit late in the day, Ismael was finally taught the things a Que man needs to know: how to hollow a log and make a canoe, to dig for roots, to build a hut, to hunt and fish, to craft and play the cuatro, to compose poem-stories with featherpen and cocksblood. Most importantly, he learned to safely cross the smoke bridge between reality and dreams.

His last lesson would serve him well in difficult times, not the least of which was the six weeks he was under detention in the Ministerio de Defensa, not so much for perniciously interfering with the oil companies in the Delta, an insurrection of unarmed indios swiftly and brutally put down, but for writing a song that had incited even soldados to rebellion, a danger far greater to the regime. In the end his incarceration and punishment had been an exercise in futility and meaningless cruelty, for "Como crecen las frutas de la enredadera" was a song that could not be unsung.

At first his interrogators in the secret prison at the Ministerio de Defensa behaved in a faux-friendly manner, complimenting him on his musical talent and legendary cocksmanship, and even humming a few bars of "Como crecen las frutas de la enredadera," before saying they just had three simple questions, and if he would oblige them with the answers, he would be home in time to celebrate the birthday of his lovely wife.

The first question was: "What is the real name of El Negro Catire, and what is the name of his organization?" Followed by, "Who are the organization's other leaders and sympathizers?" And finally, "Where can we find them?" But, receiving no answers to their unimaginative queries, they began the slow and inevitable tightening of the screws.

The tightening of screws was figurative at first; with each passing day, the interrogations became longer, the light on his face brighter, the interrogators' voices louder, the questions became statements of accusation alternated with threats, the water glass now conspicuously absent. When these measures failed to produce the desired effect, they soon moved on to something else. On several occasions his head was submerged in a metal bucket filled one day with icy water, one day with hot water, one day with their own piss. From such immersions, they graduated to beatings, electric shock, sleep deprivation, isolation in a space the size of a child's crib. And finally to the use of a contraption simply known as El Vicio, in which the tightening of the screws became real.

"White men go crazy because they attempt to discover the secrets of life without crossing the smoke bridge to ask the blessings and guidance of the Great Maizcuba," said Ismael's grandfather nine days before his initiation.

"Who is the Great Maizcuba?" Ismael asked.

"The Great Maizcuba is Imawari, the creator bird of the dawn, and without his permission, you can neither cross the abyss of nothingness, where a hungry caiman lives, nor escape the claws of the jaguar of knowledge that awaits you on the other side."

According to his grandfather, Imawari resided in the House of Tobacco Smoke, made out of solidified smoke in between the waking world and the dream world. To prepare for his initiation, Ismael received many days of instruction from his grandfather. He had memorized the steps:

1. Present his grandfather/teacher with a gift of tobacco.
2. Smoke a cigar with his grandfather/teacher filled with special leaves that were meant to "open the chest."
3. Fast for five days, smoking at mealtime instead of eating, and lighting cigars from a virgin fire, communing only with the insect spirits.
4. After five days of fasting, observe a month of silence, and avoid strong odors.
5. Swallow the two sacred sticks presented by his grandfather/teacher.

Then it would be time to bathe in the river before undergoing nine days of fasting and chanting. After that he would enter the smoke hut, where he would smoke incessantly from an enormous cigar and drink ayahuasca at prescribed intervals. He would do this until he entered the world of dreams, where he would blow, with the help of the elders, a smoke bridge that led to the edge of the world. He had been warned that to interrupt an initiation dream is to sever the soul from the body, and to prevent this, his grandfather and several of the other elders would not only smoke with him, but they would anchor him to the earth with their hands and with their spirits.

On the day of his initiation, Ismael's grandfather offered his final advice: "Before blowing the smoke bridge you must first ask the blessing of Imawari. While crossing the smoke bridge, walk carefully with one foot in front of the other and your eyes straight ahead. Do not look down. When you arrive on the other side, you must blow smoke in the jaguar's face, and pass quickly to the edge of the world. Crouch and pound the earth three times to signal your arrival. Only then will Imawari assign you a toll price that will allow you to roam the waking world through your dreams."

Moments after the tibia bone of his left leg cracks, he goes to a different place. A land of verdant hills and sunny valleys. He can see Consuelo running toward him and his heart rejoices. His tears, earlier of pain, now of elation, irrigate the rough terrain of his soul, which during consciousness had been a desolate, barren wasteland. Joyfully he cries out, and flowers of every hue and variety fall from his lips and to the fertile ground where they begin to bloom. And when he opens his hands, which had been clenched tightly in fists, sunbirds fly out of his open palms and soar high into the air. There is thunder in his heart. He longs unbearably for her lips, her eyes, the touch of her fingers on his skin. There is fire in his bowels, his loins, his throat; a wave of emotion rushes over him with deafening speed. And when she is finally in his arms, he thinks he must seek death to end a joy that cannot be borne. But then Imawari flies overhead, casting a golden shadow, and his spirit is restored.

"Look to the north," says Imawari. And Ismael obeys, even though taking his eyes off Consuelo means returning to the place from whence he has come.

"Mierda, you're not supposed to kill him, they want him alive," said the stockier of the two interrogators, who Ismael thought of as el Gordo y el Flaco.

"Shut up, marico, he's still got a pulse," said Flaco.

Ismael observed the scene from the dream world as a military doctor was summoned to examine the prisoner slumped in the iron chair.

"You're not going to get any more out of this one," the doctor said. "He'll have to be admitted to the infirmary if you want him to stay alive."

After he was released from the infirmary, Ismael was placed back in a cell with another prisoner, where he awaited further interrogations that never came. "The reason," whispered his cellmate, whose jaw hung crazily to one side from his last beating, "is because they've decided to execute you for treason. Or it could be that you won't even get a kangaroo court and will simply disappear." So Ismael began to wait for his execution or disappearance, which never came, either.

The fact of the matter is that no one had the stomach to order the execution of a figure as popular and respected as Ismael, the beloved composer whose song "Como crecen las frutas de la enredadera" during the months of his incarceration, had come to rival the national anthem — certainly not El Colonel, who had begun to face insubordination and outright insurgency in his own ranks.

"Fool!" he had thundered when informed that the interrogators of Ismael Martinez had been unsuccessful in their endeavors despite the use of all tactics at their disposal. "Have I not brought unprecedented wealth, progress, and stability to the nation? On my watch, the welfare of the state always takes precedence over the whims of its people. Without me, this country would just be another banana republic. This resistance, were it to succeed in its effort for regime change, would only come to the fate of the one before, and the one before that, and the cycle would repeat itself. That cannot be allowed. Ismael Martinez is a symbol of the resistance; a symbol that must be broken or destroyed." This is what his interrogators told their captive, for by then they had developed a fearful admiration, bordering on reverence, for the unbreakable Ismael Martinez, and were unwilling to pursue further interrogation, lest any one of them be the ones accidentally responsible for his death. And now, whenever they took him to the bloodwashed interrogation room, they locked the door and let him sit quietly in his chair, while each of them took turns screaming, making it into a contest about who could make the most spine-chilling sounds.

As for Pedro Lanz, even were he to defy pure common sense, his own self-preservation instincts, his feelings of loyalty to his former school friend who had begun to visit him in his dreams—even were he to disregard all that and give the order of execution, it was by no means a certainty that the guards would carry it out. He could not be sure who among them had not been contaminated by the resistance, which had spread like a bushfire, raging from city to city, town to town, village to village, and even through the forests, consuming everything in its wake. Pedro Lanz was a man whose decisions and orders were designed to achieve a particular result, a man who did not like waste, particularly the waste of a good man, a man whose composing ability and lyricism, though clearly subversive, was nothing short of a maravilla. What a great advantage it would have been to have such a man on the side of the regime. Pedro Lanz could discern that the writing on the wall of time was not in the government's favor, that its days were numbered. Besides, he had given his word to Consuelo that he would do "everything in his power" to secure the safe return of her husband, and he was nothing if not a man of his word, though when he gave it, it never crossed his mind that Ismael would resist every conceivable method of persuasion. Well, not *every* method; Pedro Lanz had never used the one method that would have broken Ismael in seconds: He had never arrested or threatened to arrest Consuelo. On the contrary, he had relaxed the surveillance on her the day before she disappeared from Tamanaco. He had done this because he too had the ability to fall in love at first sight, as he had on the night of the fifth anniversary of Amparo and Alejandro Aguilar, the moment he saw Consuelo.

On the morning of the most violent and well-orchestrated popular uprising in the history of the nation, before leaving for the plane that would carry him into exile, the last order Pedro Lanz would give as director of Security and Classified Information would be to free Ismael Martinez.

Ismael was alone in the cell, his cellmate having been executed three days earlier, when the only guard who had not yet deserted his post opened the cell door. "Hurry up, get going, and buena suerte," he said, before racing down the steel grey corridor, ripping the regime's insignia from his uniform and flinging away his cap as he ran, with Ismael close on his heels.

Once there was a norteamericano, a black man, who said he had a dream. But it was not a dream. It was only a fleeting vision; a vision that dims and brightens in the never-ending battle between the few who have everything and the many who are tired of being left behind to suck the bones at the empty banquet table.

Following a spate of random school kidnappings in Tamanaco, Ismael had taught Lily certain maneuvers that would enhance her chances of escaping the grasp of a predator. Once she had succeeded in loosening the grip of an attacker, her father said, she should run like hell, shrieking like a siren, to attract as much attention as possible. Lily was best at slipping out of a neck lock, but that was on dry land, with her feet on the ground. From his dreams he could see his daughter struggling in the water with Irene and called out to her. With seconds to spare, Lily followed her father's instructions, coiling first and then jackknifing out of Irene's grasp. Irene lunged toward her again as if in slow motion. "Hit her," said Ismael.

He had been warned by his Que grandfather of the dangers of intervention from the dream world in the course of real-life events. "There is always a price to pay in such an exchange," his grandfather had warned. Ismael knows that Lily has already paid with a part of her soul, that he and Consuelo have paid with the pain of their own separation and the anguish of watching their child battle the unnamed fears that have prevented her from embracing life to its fullest. And Irene had surely paid. And now Efraín; he too is paying with the loss of his entire family. Perhaps finally Imawari would be sated.

"Dios, mío," Lily exclaims, "I just realized...the boy Efraín, he has Irene's eyes!"

"Stop talking and push," says Amparo. And a few seconds later the first granddaughter of Ismael Martinez bellows her way into the world.

For the first time in months Ismael and Consuelo fall into each other's arms and into the same bed, too exhausted even for speech. But even in their sleep, their bodies call out to each other, and they awaken in the early hours of the morning to the relentless, involuntary movements of their hips. Laughing, they succumb to that primordial command. The silk of Consuelo's nightgown slides from her body like a sigh. He kisses her; her legs lock around his back. Their lovemaking is long, luxurious, and wanton. And, at dawn, when there is a light knock at the door, they hold their hands to their mouths like randy teenagers who have made too much noise.

"Come in," says Ismael, covering their nakedness with the sheet.

It is Luz. "I'm so sorry to disturb you," she says, "but we cannot find Efraín."

Instantly, Ismael is on his feet, pulling on his trousers, running out the door, with Consuelo close behind him. Marta and Amparo are searching the house while Lily anxiously clutches her baby in the living room, Alegra at her side. Carlos Alberto is scouring the garden compound. "He couldn't have gotten over the wall or out the gate," says Carlos Alberto when Ismael joins him.

Having run out of places to look in the house, all, including Lily with her infant, come out into the garden. They are all talking at once—who was the last person to see Efraín, what time, how could this happen, and so forth.

Then Ismael observes the ladder against the back wall

of the house and looks up. Efraín is standing at the highest point of the roof, right at the edge, his arms outstretched like a bird, his eyes wide and glazed as though sleepwalking.

"He is on the roof," says Ismael. Immediately Carlos Alberto and the others follow the direction of his gaze and there is a collective gasp.

"Poor child," says Carlos Alberto, "it is too much for him; he has lost his mind."

Luz begins to wail.

"Quiet, Luz," says Ismael. "He is dream-walking; we mustn't do anything to startle him. Someone please get me my pipe and pouch of tobacco."

Standing in the garden below, Ismael lights his pipe, inhales deeply, closes his eyes. As he enters into a trance the sounds of the world fall away and there is only the smell of rich, full-bodied tobacco. In his mind's eye the edges of the world soften, a resonance fills the sky, there is a hovering wind, the air assumes a ponderous density, and in his mouth he can taste metal. He is on the edge of the world of dreams. Through the dim gray light that filters through the membrane between the real world and the dream world, he can see Efraín outlined some distance before him instead of above him. Pushing away the membrane like cobwebs, he sees that the boy is standing on a cliff at the edge of the abyss. Across the gaping hole, and through a blue diaphanous mist, he can distinguish a female form. At first it seems as though she is beckoning to the boy, but then he realizes she is waving him back from the edge of the abyss. Efraín stands with his legs apart, his face upturned, and his arms outspread as he sings, "I can fly." In each hand he holds a small feather. As Efraín tilts precariously forward, the woman's gestures become more frantic. Ismael sucks deeply from his pipe and begins to blow a smoke bridge but he is too far away. He runs forward, blowing as he goes, but even as he gathers speed, he knows he cannot save the boy from tumbling into the abyss nor even keep himself from falling, for he has not asked Imawari for permission. And yet he leaps into the air, stretching and reaching to grab at Efraín's shirt collar. It is a leap of faith. The sky opens in a livid sear, and a tremendous wind begins to blow, scattering debris in his face. Then, he and the boy are free-falling, hurtling toward the jaws of the great caiman. All at once, a great vine made of smoke unfurls beneath him and wraps itself around his waist, hoisting him, along with the boy, to safety. A gourd adorned with Maizcuba feathers drops at his feet. It is his grandfather's rattle. Efraín crumples to the ground and Ismael lifts him into his arms. As if from a great distance Ismael hears his grandfather's voice: "Who knows the line between vision and madness, between dreaming and waking, or whether there is a line at all?"

When Ismael opens his eyes, he is on the roof with the boy in his arms. Efraín, now awake, is clinging to his neck, and those below are whooping and cheering. Except for Luz, who is laughing and crying.

"You see that, Efraín?" he says. "That is your family."

It is possible to grow passiflora edulis even from cuttings, layers, and grafts.

Irene

In her dream, she is riding through the forest on a giant tapir, when she sees Lily standing, bewildered, in a clearing.

"Vamos, vamos," she says as the tapir, over which she has no navigational or speed control, rushes through the clearing. As she passes Lily, she reaches out, expecting her to grab hold and hoist herself onto the tapir. But Lily hesitates at the critical moment, and the chance is lost. Then she is blinded by a flash of light, her neck snaps back as if she has received a blow to the chin, she falls backward, her back bending at an entirely impossible angle. The dream shifts. In this dream she is swimming. Arm over arm, pummeling the water, and with each breath, just before she dips her head to exhale, she sets her sight on the shore. Then a cramp makes her jack-knife. The sandwiches. Why had she eaten so many? The cramp recedes but her leg and arm muscles are spasming. Treading water she shouts to Lily, "I cannot keep this up much longer. I want to go back."

"I can make it," Lily shouts back.

"No you can't."

And suddenly, for no good reason at all, midway between the shore they had left and the shore to which they were heading, hundreds of meters away from either, they get into a fight about it. Liar, liar, they are both yelling, a short burst of adrenaline rage propelling them toward each other. Then they are hitting and pulling each other's hair, scratching and screaming out every remembered hurt, every offense — you did this, you did that. Take it back, take back what you said, she says, climbing onto the other girl's back. And Lily, spluttering, still screaming, goes under. Moments later she receives a kick or punch to the chin, she too goes under. She is swallowing a lot of water. She can't see Lily. The water has closed over her head. Time grinds to a standstill. She knows she is drowning but is strangely detached from it. Suddenly someone is grabbing her by the hair, an arm goes under her chin, someone is pulling her in to shore, then pounding on her chest.

No, she wants to say. I am *not* dead. I am alive. The moment the water gushes from her mouth, she opens her eyes. An older man, older than her father is staring at her, relieved.

Where is Lily? he asks.

Lily? she says. She can feel the fear clutch at her throat. *The other girl,* he says, *the other girl in the water.*

There is no other girl, she lies.

She remembers Lily's face floating above hers, eyes wide open, hair spread out like a fan of snakes. There had been something piercingly beautiful about watching Lily breathe water.

She awakens to the morningsong of the golden-winged Maizcuba with Manuel snoring lightly next to her, his hand heavy on her hip. Gently, she removes the hand. Raising herself to a sitting position, she studies the photograph on her bedside table, which her lover has mounted expertly, presenting it to her last night, on the eve of their first anniversary together. It was taken in the magnificent Tepuys, where they had vacationed last month.

In the photograph, she is standing on an enormous boulder that is suspended in the crevice between two mountains cut of Precambrian rock. Five hundred meters below runs a stream that flows into a lake. Her feet appear much smaller in proportion to her body, much daintier than they actually are. Her face has been darkened with a fake shadow because her frozen smile in the original photograph had reflected her unmitigated terror. Tricks of the trade, said Manuel.

A photographer by profession, he had insisted that she stand with both feet on the boulder because that would make a more dramatic picture. It is important to him that his pictures have drama. Though she is no stranger to drama herself, these days her role of choice is that of spectator. When she had hesitated, he had been exasperated.

"It's been there for thousands of years, and hundreds of people have stood on it before; why would you imagine it might fall now?"

Perhaps because deep down she still believes that everything she imagines can become a reality?

When she reaches into herself to find that quintessential core, she pulls out a fistful of sights, sounds, smells, tastes, emotions, that shift like tiny pebbles in the palm of her hand.

The only bedtime stories she ever heard had been

those her father—her real father, not the reticent cuck-
old, Benigno—would tell her about a magical place near
Soledad in the state of Anzoátegui, where he had grown and
lived in a big extended family on a hacienda called La Mariposa that hugged the border of the River Orinoco. A place
where everyone was as easy on a horse as in a bed; where
work, food, and play were shared; where every evening, after
dinner, his uncle Rainaldo would bring out his cuatro and
all the family would gather in the courtyard to sit on the
wooden stools and wicker chairs. And Rainaldo would begin
to sing, and all would join, their voices carrying high into the
clear llanero sky. And his grandmother's eyes would fill with
tears each time Rainaldo sang his signature ballad, "Maria
Luna," about a campesina who fell hopelessly and forever in
love with a fidalgo, for it reminded her of her own story. And
every summer the women and children would travel to the
north of the state to the beach town of Conoma, where they
would remain for three weeks, to fortify themselves with the
medicinal salt of the sea. And one evening his mother lost a
diamond earring in the sugary sand at Isla de Plata, and his
aunt threatened San Antonio before digging her hand into
the sand and pulling out the solitaire, which shone in the
moonlight like a star in the palm of her hand.

She doubts that her father had any preconceived notions
about acquainting his daughters with their llanero heritage;
more likely he was homesick.

She was three when the family made their one and only
trip to Soledad from Caracas. The airport was a makeshift
shack, and their suitcases were unloaded onto the tarmac. It
was hot and sticky, and the air smelled like slightly wilted
flowers. Her father's brother Rainaldo was there to pick them

up in his faded blue truck. Just beyond the airstrip, they had stopped at a local bar. She and her sister were given a limonada, the adults drank beer. What she remembers most about the drive to the hacienda was the incredible expanse of green for as far as she could see. Even at that age, it had made her heart beat faster.

The trip from the airport had taken over two hours. When they finally arrived, her grandparents, aunts, uncles, and cousins had covered her in kisses and all the aunts and uncles had taken turns holding her on their laps.

So, her best and truest memories are of La Mariposa, of the heat, the smell of beer and fresh air, the laughter and the excited chatter of her father's enormous family, and the sense of being enveloped in a big love blanket, of the hot summer breeze, and her grandmother's chickens, of the enormous dining room where twenty-eight people—aunts, uncles, cousins, and farmhands—congregated. And of Señor Camacho, her grandfather's foreman in his pristine white shirts with the sleeves rolled to his elbows, who taught her how to swim in the river. And of her grandmother's maid, Maria Pagan, who would take out the evil eye whenever she got too cranky.

Her biological father's name was Pedro Lorenzo, and he had been her mother's first love. But she never mentioned this to her Jungian therapist. Even with him, whom she later trusted the most, there were still a few details she held to her chest, a few truths she wasn't giving up, a few secrets she would keep.

Her earliest recollection of Pedro Lorenzo is of his breath, pungent with tobacco and coffee, as he kissed her good-night, and the roughness of his unshaven cheek before he left for work at dawn.

"Good morning, Princesa," he would say.

Except for the Mariposa stories, the rest of her memories are not as vivid; they are a blur of loud voices, anguish, angry silences, a rare and curious laugh like the bark of a small dog. Besides this, she remembers only one other thing about Pedro Lorenzo: he had liked to tease. Usually, he overdid it.

After that first and last magical trip to La Mariposa, Pedro Lorenzo gave her a glossy picture book with many animals in it. Every evening, when he came home from work, he would sit with her on the living room sofa, the book spread open on his lap and he would teach her the names of all the animals. He also taught her the sounds the animals were supposed to make, except he mixed them all up so that she thought the zebra said "meow," the lion, "moo," and so forth.

Mercedes said it was cruel and told him to stop. But Pedro Lorenzo thought it was hilarious. He'd trot out his toddler animal expert whenever he had his business friends over for dinner and make her stand in the middle of the living-room floor with everybody watching. Then he'd ask her to recite the names of the animals and their corresponding noises, the way he taught them to her.

"And what does the (rooster/dog/pig) do, mi amor?" he'd prompt.

When she obliged, proud of herself, Pedro Lorenzo would bark-laugh and his guests would join him in hilarity, while his child stood, bewildered, a questioning half smile on her face.

When she was five, just before he disappeared forever, he came home in the evening with his face bloodied.

"See what Mamá did to me?" he asked, a strange, brooding humor in his eyes. "This is what happens to you when you argue with Mamá."

When, at the age of ten, she blamed her mother for bashing up her father and driving him away, Mercedes told her not to be ridiculous. "Your father had too much to drink and slipped on the gravel in the driveway, the pendejo. Good riddance to that asshole."

The night before he left forever, he said to Irene, "Try not to be your mother when you grow up, Princesa. Be my princess forever."

A tall order, considering she never saw him again.

A year later, her mother met Benigno at a bar in the Hotel Macuto, who, she said assuredly, if slightly drunkenly, was a real man, with a real job, who could take care of a real family. Unlike Pedro Lorenzo, she meant. The loser, she called him. The girls were forbidden to speak of him, much less refer to him as their father. That Benigno Dos Santos was incompatible in every conceivable way with her mother, and for that matter with herself and her sister, did not seem to factor into Mercedes's thinking. Nor the fact that at the age of forty-five he had never been married. Nor the fact that he loved his adopted daughters more than he should have.

When Irene turned fifteen, Mercedes had thrown a party at the penthouse she shared with Benigno.

"Fifteen is an important benchmark in the life of every

young Latina girl," she said, though she was unable to explain precisely why fifteen was the magic number. Her mother invited only adults, her own friends, to the party, including someone called Lourdes, a lesbian sporting a crop of bleached blond hair who looked much younger than her thirty-five years. Lourdes brought her own bottle of Cuban rum, which she shared clandestinely with the quinceañera, pouring it into her Coke bottle under the table while stroking the girl on the thigh. When the birthday girl threw up all over the ceremonial cake trimmed with cherry-red hearts, her mother sent her to bed and carried on partying with her friends.

The next day Irene wrote a letter to her best friend, Lily, who was in boarding school in Valencia. Lily, who had the parents and family she coveted. She wrote the letter in such a way as to make her own life seem the better one, more fun, more chimerical, more adventurous.

Caracas, February 1978

Hola, Lily. Prepare yourself. I have a lot to say.

I'm skinnier, I cut my hair chévere and I don't like Carlos anymore. You know why? Well, I'm skinnier because I don't have your mother to cook for me. And besides, I don't have time to eat. I work in Zulema's boutique after school and I get fifty bolívares every Thursday. I cut my hair because it bored me to look at the same face every day in the mirror, and also to punish my father for grounding me last Saturday. My father hates short hair on women. But

I think it looks fantastic. And I don't like Carlos anymore because he's too clumsy and he suffers from a severe lack of coolness. See, I went to the airport with him to pick up my sister and on the way back he crashed the car. I saw this car veering ahead of us on the autopista and I said, "¡Frena, frena!" and instead of braking, he accelerates. And so we crashed. Then two hours for the police to come. Then finally the whole thing got fixed because Zulema paid the cops off. So then we were all hot and sweaty and decided to stop and have something to drink, and when he asked me what I wanted, HIS SALIVA CAME OUT. I couldn't stand it and I started laughing and he was embarrassed. Then, on the way back from the airport, he kept grabbing my hand because he wanted to tell me something and his saliva came out again and I felt like diving out of the car. So I go, "¿Qué te pasa?" and he goes, "Nada." And this scene was repeated about ten times until we arrived in front of my building and finally he goes, "I like you and I want to keep seeing you." But that saliva thing was in my mind and so I smiled and said "bye" and scrammed. Then I was thinking the whole night: that Carlos, so cute and such a good body and such a pendejo. And I never went out with him again.

Okay, now to Ricardo who is twenty-four years old. Bueno, he really is cool. We went out on a lot of double dates with Zulema and her boyfriend. And I liked him so much. But... he went to Brazil, and do you know when he's coming back? IN TWO YEARS. I cried when we said good-bye at the airport. We got there real early and he embraced me in some corner of the airport and French-kissed me for a long time. And he got out some keys and scraped

$R + I = AMOR$ in the cement floor. He kissed me some more and I cried. And he took off his cross, put it around my neck and said, "Te quiero," and I cried even harder. He said he would write and always remember me and love me. And that when he came back, I would be a woman, etc, etc. Just before he got on the plane, he gave me a big French kiss in front of my sister and everybody. Well, that was the end of that. Boo hoo. That's the way life is and you have to learn how to face it. Or else you'll be jodida.

Now to Diego. Remember him? I was going out with him when you were with Elvis. He wrote to me from his college in the U.S. saying he loved me forever. I wrote him back some bullshit that I'm waiting for him, etc. He hasn't replied. Better. I hope he forgets me.

Now to Alejandro. I'm back with him. He kept bugging me so much and swearing he loved me. And because I was depressed about Ricardo, I decided to console myself with him. And that's why my father grounded me — he says Alejandro is too old for me. Imagínate.

Well, now to myself again. On Friday I went to El Poliedro to see Gloria Gaynor, a gringa black singer. She sang this song called "I Will Survive" that really resonar with me. Paco and I went down and danced near the stage. And I was so happy. Last week I went to the movies with Alejandro, and his sister Dolores and her boyfriend Esau. And after the movies we went to two parties. After the two parties, we went to the Reflexions discothèque. After the Reflexions, about 4:30 a.m., we went to our houses to get our bathing suits and drove to the beach!

Now to my sister. There was a big fight in my house between my sister and my dad, because she defended me *about Alejandro. And my father threw Zulema out of the house, and now she lives with her boyfriend, Max.*

Oh, and I forgot to tell you: Alejandro and I did coca and it was really fantastic. You have to try it. By the way, my mother has a new boyfriend. He's nineteen. Ha! He's younger than my *boyfriend! He could* be *my boyfriend! And guess what: he's a Guajiro !!!*

Love you always,

Irene

P.S. I guess there aren't any boys where you are. You poor frustrated thing.

P.P.S I haven't worn my tanga bathing suit because my culo is too white.

P.P.P.S I hope you come back soon.

P.P.P.P.S I love you and miss you. I mean it.

Reading the letter again so many years later makes her laugh so hard that tears stream down her face. Even though she knows it isn't funny. Zulema is the only one who really looked after her — or tried to, at any rate.

Benigno had been annoyed that Zulema and Max had taken her along with them for a weekend at Colonia Tovar. Zulema was teaching her younger sister how to be a whore, he said at the top of his voice. The way it all started was this:

Max, in one of his benevolent avatars, offered to take Zulema to Colonia Tovar, and since Irene was standing around at the boutique when he made the offer, he chivalrously invited her to come along. They drove up into the mountains on Good Friday, arriving around nine p.m., and checked into the hotel they always stayed in called El Pequeño Aleman, where they gorged on strudel and thick German sausages. The thinness of the mountain air had made them ravenous. Max and Zulema had gotten into a minor argument over dinner about the exact pronunciation of Peugeot, which Max owned and was thinking of replacing with a Saab. Max said it was pronounced "peyott" and Zulema, who had studied French in high school and spent a summer in Paris, said Max was a barbarian. The issue was settled by a Swiss-born waiter who gave the word a different intonation from that of either Zulema or Max. Both were thoughtful after that. Irene was grateful that Max had refrained from baiting Zulema further with some of his usual sexist remarks. (Zulema liked to pretend she was something of a feminist, but since her teens she had never been able to live a week outside of a relationship, and, now in her twenties, never had a relationship with a man who could not support her in style; and she never worked except for fun.) Irene had been in a hurry to get to her room before any untoward incident could ruin the evening. Pleasantly sated and somewhat stupefied by the heavy German meal, they left the restaurant and walked to their cabañas, which were side by side. Just before they separated, Zulema had kissed her sister and whispered that they would go for a walk around the shops in the morning before Max, a very late riser even on working days (he owned his own box-making company) got up. She said they could meet for coffee around eight.

The next morning, when Zulema joined her at the restaurant at eight-forty, Irene thought her sister looked tired.

"Didn't you sleep?" she asked.

"Sure. After I ate all the chocolate Easter eggs out of the guest basket," Zulema smiled.

"So, what's the matter, then?"

"Bueno. I'm pregnant. And I haven't told Max yet because he doesn't like children." Zulema's face began to crumple, but then she regained her poise and put on her happy voice. "It is nothing for you to worry about, mi amor. Everything will work out for the best."

They wandered through the cobblestone streets of the town and bought a handmade cuckoo clock and six jars of honey.

When they returned to the Pequeño Alemán, Max had already paid the bill and was standing outside the lobby with their suitcases. He said his sister in Caracas had phoned to say his apartment had been burgled. They got into the Peugeot, which Max drove down the mountain like a stunt-man, squealing around curves, honking and overtaking anything in his path, as though getting back to Caracas more quickly would counteract the fait accompli of the burglary. Irene had clenched her hands tightly in her lap the whole way down, while Zulema stared out the window, humming tensely and out of tune.

When they arrived at Max's residence in Cumbres de Curumo, the place was crawling with cops. Zulema announced immediately that she was going to lie down. Irene stood in the spacious living room, shamelessly making eyes at one of the youngest cops, while Max charged about, trying to assess his losses.

It turned out that, besides the usual—TV, stereo, computer—most of the silver had been taken. Max paced up and down, ticking off items on a sheet of paper on a fancy clipboard and pursing his lips in a way that made Irene think his mouth resembled nothing so much as a dog's asshole. How could Zulema bear to kiss that wrinkled asshole mouth, she wondered. The cops said they'd try their best, but in all likelihood the silver would have already been melted down by now. At which point Zulema emerged from Max's bedroom to say that all her jewelry had been taken, and Max said, so what, since most of it was junk. "Who cares about those peroles?" he said.

Strangely, the only item removed from the ultramodern, heavily mechanized kitchen was an antique earthenware pot, which Max had purchased for a bomb from an archaeologist's assistant at Hato Viejo. Could the thief be an indio? Who else would attribute value to such an item? Irene mentioned the possibility to Max, who ignored her, because, after all, she was just a girl. She repeated her theory to one of the cops, who listened politely, looked at her intently, and said, "To me, it looks like a job by a Guajiro called El Malandro. He always takes the cars."

Max's second car, a fully loaded, custom-accessorized Jeep with huge wheels, was gone. But, although the keys were still in the ignition, this Malandro character hadn't wanted her sister's beat-up, but beloved, Corvair. Too bad, she thought. If he had, it would have given Max an excuse to buy her sister a better car.

In the middle of everything Zulema had blurted out right in front of the cops and neighbors that she was pregnant, then promptly burst into tears. And Max had told everyone except Irene to leave, had shut the door, had taken Zulema in his arms, and said, "Let's get married." For all his assholish ways, the fact was Max loved Zulema and would always take care of her. And Irene felt glad about that. But her gladness had been short-lived, because, as soon as they got home, Benigno threw Zulema out of the house for taking Irene to Colonia Tovar with Max. Irene was forbidden to see her sister.

"Yes," said Zulema, as she walked out the door with her last suitcase, "take it out on the minor child, the only person in this family you can forbid anything. But just remember, she is not your blood, she is ours, mine and Mami's."

"That's the pity," Benigno shot back, "the poor thing is related to two of the biggest putas in all of Caracas."

Two months after her sister had been banished, Irene was admitted to a mental health facility for the first time (but not the last) with what they had said was a cocaine-induced "fugue." She was subjected to a straitjacket, tranquilizers, and seemingly endless sessions of hide-and-seek with a ferret-faced psychiatrist known as Dr. Estrelina Uzoátegui. Terrified and terrorized by the paradigm shift—the sudden and never-before-experienced policing of her thoughts and restriction of her movements—she took some solace in making fun of her doctor's faint but discernible mustache and hair set in wings that pointed upward. "Dr. Beethoven, I presume," she would greet her, which did not win her any favors.

But for Lily, for Lily alone, for even the *thought* of Lily, Irene had cloaked her fears in high-spirited abandon and mirth. Lily's name did not feature on Benigno's list of "real people" in her life, which was required by the hospital as part of the data on patients suspected of suffering from too much imagination. Which was why her handlers had tried their best to convince her that Lily was only a figment of her imagination. She wrote many drafts of many letters to

Lily, which she asked her jailors to post. Whether or not they posted the final editions to the address she gave them, she has no idea. The point is, at fifteen, she was already an adept storyteller long before she ever considered taking it on as a métier. She kept the drafts but only two remain.

A few months after she was released from the hospital, she accompanied her mother to Puerto. Tiring of the responsibility after two days, her mother went off to have a Brazilian bikini wax, granting temporary custody to her hombre of the moment, a hard-boiled Guajiro drug and gun runner in his twenties called Moriche. Since there was nothing to do in Puerto besides go to the beach, that was what they did, scanning the sand for a clear space, running hand in hand to claim it when they spotted it, spreading their outsize beach towels on their small half moon of powdery sand, rubbing Johnson's Baby Oil mixed with iodine on each other, leaping over dead jellyfish as they ran to the sea, hugging and laughing while the big waves crashed over them in an explosion of foam. Afterward, her mother's lover ordered dozens of fresh raw oysters with lemon juice from the roving beach vendors, which he fed to his young charge, while she braced herself on her elbows and slurped greedily from the shell. Some of the juice dripped onto her bare stomach, collecting in the concave of her belly. Laughing, Moriche dipped his finger into the little puddle and tasted it. When she giggled, he bent his head and licked her belly button.

He was very interested in her family and most particularly in her father, Benigno. What he did for a living, where he worked, what kind of car he drove, that sort of thing. Irene was fed up. "You seem more interested in my father than in me," she said.

"Only because he's your father," he demurred.

The next day, Mercedes took one look at her daughter, who was looking at Moriche, and said they were leaving.

When she returned with her mother to the capital, it was nearly Semana Santa. Lily contacted her on a pay phone from the panadería near her house every day, and they had clandestinely arranged to meet several times, always successfully. They had even spent a whole day together at the Hotel Macuto, and she had been in a state of elation all week. But when Lily returned to convent school in Valencia, Irene's euphoria evaporated as suddenly as it had appeared. Besides, her mother had found out that Moriche had followed them to Caracas from Puerto. She knew all about the Macuto rendezvous and threatened him with the direst of consequences. With both Lily and Moriche gone, she felt dead.

"Buenas tardes, Señora Crespo, may I speak with Elvis?" The receiver was hot in her hand and her heart began to beat more rapidly as the viper rose in her throat. It had been three days since Moriche had been banished.

"Hola, Elvis, it's Irene. Listen, I have to talk to you about something as a friend. It's about Lily. The day we all met at the Macuto, after you guys left, she made fun of you behind your back, saying things like, 'He kisses like a fish,' and 'He walks like a faggot.' I really felt bad for you."

She held her breath and pinched her thigh until he responded the way she knew he would....

Yeah, for sure, she can be a real frigid bitch. I just thought you should know...So, you want to come over and hang out? I'm here all alone, even the maid has gone out....Don't worry,

you can confide in me, I'm like a tomb, pana... You're coming?
Okay, see you later. Ciao....

An hour later she clasped her legs around her best friend's
novio, and while he strained against her, she stared over his
shoulder and tried to remember the precise number of oysters Moriche had fed her in Puerto.

Often she cries in her sleep. And sometimes her dreams tell
her it is the salt of the sea she tastes on her lips. That it is the
sea breeze that ruffles her hair. That it is the sand that causes
her toes to curl. That it is her Guajiro lover who leaps out
from behind a coconut tree, grabs her by the waist before
she can run, drags her into the water, deeper and deeper. She
struggles pretend-angrily, banging her fists on his chest.

He says, "You are like a sparrow, so tiny and soft and fluttering." He smiles. Then he scowls. "Look at this crap all over
the beach. It's getting so you can't even find a decent place
to sit in the sun." She looks around and notices for the first
time that the beach is heavily littered. Plastic bottles, cigarette butts, condoms. Three stray dogs snarl over someone's
leftovers, a half-eaten sandwich and an apple. The owner of
a nearby restaurant shack runs out and whacks at them with
a stick, shouting, "Fuera, fuera, animales de mierda."

"He should be hitting the humans who left the garbage, not
the dogs," says Moriche. The dogs are spoiling her moment.

"Don't look at them, look at me," she says, cupping his
chin in the palm of her hand, gently turning his face toward
hers. He smiles. When he smiles, the suntanned skin around

his eyes crinkles. His smile is a lighthouse and, basking in its beam, she thinks she is in safe harbor.

Caracas, May 1978

Dear Lily,

I'm writing to tell you that Elvis has turned out to be just like every other asshole guy. He actually tried to do it with me the other day, making cutie eyes and saying he was so lonely. Anyway, I thought you should know that he obviously isn't faithful to you. It's not really my business, but you know how much I care about you and I don't want you to get hurt. You should definitely dump him.

Now, I have a lot of other things to tell you. Remember the Guajiro guy I introduced to you at the Macuto when you came down for Semana Santa? The one who was my mother's lover. Anyway, one day when my mother wasn't there, he surprised me in the kitchen alone and told me he loved me. And I told him I loved him too. I mean, I suddenly realized that I loved him right then while we were standing in the kitchen together. All of a sudden, he grabbed my you-know-what, and then pulled me to him by the hips and French kissed me. WOW. We went into my mother's room next to the kitchen (she still uses the cachifa one) and we did it like three times. I love him! I love his brown hair, his brown eyes, and his incredibly bueno body. He picks me up from school every day on his motorcycle and you should see the looks on the faces of all those Roosevelt bitches. Women just love him and he makes eyes at practically every female that passes in front of him, and of course I die of jealousy, but he tells me that I'm the only one he really wants. The big problem is: he hasn't officially broken up with my mother yet, and even if he does, can you imagine the peo if she finds out about him and me? But maybe she'll be the one to break it off because my dad has threatened a divorce if she doesn't give up her place in Puerto and come live in the city permanently. And you know what else I found out? Please don't tell ANYBODY, only between you and me. Besides the gun business, she's started dealing coca. Moriche told me and he knows it for a fact because he supplies her. The last time I was in Puerto there were some really scary characters hanging around her cottage, and one of them, this guy in a military uniform, practically tried to rape me. But Moriche gave him a huge coñazo on his jaw and my mother started screaming in his face and so he left. I don't know what to think about it all. What do you think? Please write back soon. A really big letter. Are you coming back to the city in November for your 16th birthday? I hope so.

I love you. Your friend always,
Irene.

She had never been a good judge of character. And most of the characters in her life weren't exactly pillar-of-society material. So though it pains her, it does not really surprise her to think that it was Moriche who tipped the insurgents off that she would be in Maquiritare that Semana Santa, that it was Moriche who orchestrated the kidnapping in the forest.

When she left Lily on the veranda of the cabaña, her heart was pounding with the excitement of seeing him again. But instead of Moriche there had been four guerilleros dressed in military fatigues who grabbed her roughly by the arms and covered her head in a black cloth so dense she thought she would suffocate, or that she and her abductors would live like fugitives in the jungle for what seemed like an eternity with only cocaine to pass the time and stanch their hunger when they couldn't find food, or that they would force her to swear her loyalty to the revolution one hundred times a day, or that one of them would prick her finger with the coke-cutting blade and press it to a sheet of paper, leaving an ugly stain over a strange insignia that looked like a passion flower. She hadn't expected there would be a ransom note.

Finally Moriche returned, but not as her knight in shining armor; instead of rescuing her, he said, "You have to go back. Otherwise they won't give us the money."

"No," she said.

"You have to do it for us, for me." Wheedling.

"No," she said.

He had raised his hand and she had run into the night.

When she ran away, she stayed on the run. She was nearly three months pregnant by the man she was running from. She ran and ran until she reached a road, and there she hitched a ride on a pickup truck in the caravan of a traveling circus. She climbed onto the back and sat down next to a man with wild hair and green eyes, who, she learned, was a member of a flying trapeze troop.

"What's your name?" he asked, and she felt it was more out of politeness rather than inquisitiveness.

"Coromoto," she lied. She had always wished her name

to be different, and now there was nothing to stop her from assuming the name of her choice.

"Like the Indian chief!"

"Yes," she said.

The circus people were kind. They gave her some cash and a list of people to contact in Barquisimeto if she needed a job. The first name on her list was a man called Catire who had a car-repair shop. She couldn't imagine what kind of job would be available in a car-repair shop for a girl like her, a broke and pregnant runaway, but the circus people swore by the proprietor, saying he had connections everywhere.

When she arrived at the shop, which was located in the seedier section of the city, she asked one of the mechanics for Catire. He pointed her gruffly toward the back of the shop, which was much larger than it seemed from the road, and she made her way through a maze of vehicles in various stages of repair, stepping around oilcans and toolkits and over the legs of men whose upper torsos were hidden under cars, until she reached a room of glass in which she saw a middle-aged mestizo man talking on the telephone. He seemed deeply involved in conversation. As she stood, hesitantly, near the glass door to the glass room, he looked up, saw her, and beckoned with his hand for her to come in. He hung up the phone.

"Bienvenida," he said, smiling.

Since her circus friends had told her that there was nothing that could shock Catire, and no problem he couldn't solve, she told him everything. "I won't go back."

"Your arrival is timely," he said, when she had finished. "I have business to attend to on the border, and I have been looking for someone to attend to the office while I am gone."

She worked for several months in the glass office taking phone calls and writing down messages, suspecting that her "job" had been invented on the spur of the moment and grateful for it. Catire would disappear for long stretches of time, and when he returned the furrows in his brow would be deeper. Every evening she returned to a convent, to the nuns who had taken her in on Catire's recommendation. She was polite and respectful and said the rosary with her benefactrices daily, but they watched her with concern, for it seemed to them that that she was restless and merely biding her time until her baby was born. She had agreed that the baby would be put up for adoption; she had met the prospective parents, a simple, working-class Catholic couple. Unfortunately the baby did not survive more than a few days.

The day after the burial, she sat on a bench waiting for the bus to take her to the convent after work, as she had done every day except Sunday since her arrival in Barquisimeto. The bus came and went, and then another and another, and still she sat on the bench. And when a middle-aged man in a car slowed down and offered her a ride, she said yes. He was on his way to Sorte, a kind of pilgrimage, he said, for favors rendered by the Lady. When they stopped for gas a few hours later, he offered her some cocaine. "To keep us awake for the drive," he said. She took it. And that was the beginning of an endless spiral of drug consumption, withdrawals, and more drug consumption.

Eight years later, she was picked up outside a restaurant in Chivacoa for offering oral sex in exchange for money, disturbing the peace, and being under the influence of illegal drugs. As she was disoriented, the police handed her over to the poorly equipped and understaffed psychiatric ward of a government hospital, where she was admitted. She was seven months pregnant, and even if she had been coherent she would not have been able to say by whom. The effort of her resistence to the hospital staff induced a premature labor, and a baby was delivered and put up for adoption the very next day. Her agitated and disoriented condition was diagnosed as schizophrenia. She was wrongly administered a drug that put her into a catatonic state. Fearful, the hospital transferred her to a mental health facility, where she remained in a catatonic state for eleven years.

When she became catatonic, she entered a state of profound indifference along with a slowing down to the point of immobility. Although seemingly unresponsive and soporific to those trying to elicit a reaction, in fact she can recall her experience as one of reacting normally and appropriately but in glacial time, where others appeared to be moving too fast. At the same time that her physical life came almost to a standstill, her interior life accelerated to the speed of light; she began to live entire lifetimes in the span of a single day, most of the details of which she can remember even now. She tried on the skins and breathed through the lungs of men, women, children, young people, old people, middle-aged people, married people, single people, widows, heterosexuals, homosexuals, prostitutes, priests, athletes, poets, painters, musicians, revolutionaries; people who were beautiful, ugly, brave, timid, sad, joyful . . . Lovers who tasted like oysters and seaweed and salt.

Like a latter-day Maria Lionza, she lived a thousand lives, with all their attendant joys and sorrows, ups and downs, successes and failures. And she died a thousand deaths. All in a period of one year.

Toward the end of her first year as a catatonic, she discovered that a part of her always remained separate and independent from the life she was leading in her imagination, a part that behaved like an omniscient scriptwriter, and that by rescripting her choices, she could alter the course of her destiny. In other words, she could be both the scriptwriter and the scripted; she could be in two places at once. She became enamored of a particular incarnation, that of a mother and wife whose name was Coromoto. She took refuge in that role and decided she would stay in it until she ran out of ideas, or until Coromoto died of old age, whichever came first.

No physician could explain it when, after eleven years, she was abruptly catapulted into the world of the asylum. Physically she emerged hardly the worse for wear, the passage of years imperceptible in her countenance. Incredibly, she had the muscle tone of a professional swimmer and hardly required any physiotherapy at all. But she was not happy to be back; she missed her other life so terribly and desperately that she begged her doctors to administer to her the drug that had induced her catatonic state. And when they refused, she had tried to bribe one of the physiotherapists with sex. Though sorely tempted, for he found her heartbreakingly beautiful, he was an upstanding fellow and told her that even if he wanted to help her, it was impossible, for the drug had been taken off the market.

For nine days, she refused to leave her bed, shutting her eyes tightly, willing herself to sleep, hoping to find her lost life in her dreams. Sometimes this was possible, if only fleet-ingly. But her body put up a resistence; cramps from being too long in the same position, and the relentless pressure of the mattress, neither of which had affected her while cata-tonic, conquered her in the end. She sat up, swung her legs gingerly over the side of the bed, stood, and took her first hesitant steps in eleven years.

It took several months, but eventually she began to accept and participate of her own accord in the routines and activi-ties her doctors prescribed. But she was often disoriented and vacillated between social and antisocial.

On sociable days, to distract herself *from* herself, she often felt inclined to elicit personal information from her fellow inmates. These she would document in the notebook with the leather binding her sister had sent her for Christmas, then rewrite them as her own. She even documented the utterings of the one they called El Cantante, who went about wearing operatic makeup and belting out songs in the style of Carlos Gardel, a tango singer of the thirties. Sometimes El Cantante would stab himself in the chest with a pencil for effect and then he would be carried away, waving his fist emotionally in the air and bellowing to the tune of "Cielito lindo," "Ay, ay, ay, ay, I'm dying, I'm dying!" Around him, she composed a tale that had to do with transvestite bar dancers.

On antisocial days, she read everything she could get her hands on—novels, history books, magazines, newspapers, even gardening tips. She was particularly taken with a chil-dren's book containing legends and descriptions of foods and customs attributed to the different tribes of Venezuela. Of the legends, her favorite was the legend of Coromoto, name-sake of that other Coromoto, the one of her dreams.

One day, while the Cacique Coromoto was crossing a stream, he had a vision of a woman of astonishing beauty who beckoned to him. At that moment a mestizo called Juan Sanchez, who was a friend of the blancos but also of the indios, passed that way and the lady disappeared. The Cacique Coromoto recounted his vision to Juan Sanchez, who told the Cacique to gather his tribe at the end of eight days near the stream, which is when he would pass that way again. At that time, he said, he would teach them how to become purified for the lady. Coromoto consulted his medicine man, who thought it was a trap. That night the beautiful lady appeared to Coromoto in his dream. Coromoto drew his spear and raised it up against her, but the lady approached him without fear. With his hand he tried to push her away, but she walked into his hand and disappeared, and in the palm of his hand her image remained. When he awoke, there was no image on his hand, but he discovered that everyone in the tribe had had the same dream. The next night the lady appeared again in his dream. Coromoto told her that if she was a friend of the white man, she should not visit him again. The next day he gathered his people and told them they must move deeper into the jungle. But Juan Sanchez, who was listening from behind the trees, alerted the blancos, who surrounded Coromoto's camp before dawn. The people were all captured except for Coromoto, who escaped into the forest. The blancos pursued him, but just before they could capture him, he was bitten by a snake and died within minutes. On the palm of his hand, there appeared an image of the lady.

*   *   *

How she wishes she could be the Coromoto of her dreams again. To retrieve the life she lost. To love and be loved by a strong and good man. To hold her son against her breast and feel the beating of his heart. To recapture, even for a day, those carefree times under the palms in Santa Marta.

With the years that passed came more enlightened methods of therapy. The last psychiatrist in residence had been a Jungian, a mestizo import from Cuba who saw no conflict between the world of dreams and reality, as long as, he said, one maintained an awareness of one's own level of consciousness.

"Think of dreams as just another kind of reality," he said. "It is not so much what you believe but whether your beliefs are a help or a hindrance to you."

Under his tutelage, she progressed incrementally toward the metaphorical light at the end of the tunnel (which meant, as her doctor repeatedly reminded her, toward a functional reality of her own that she could tolerate). Unlike his predecessors, Dr. Martinez saw role-playing of the kind she had engaged in all her life as having a useful function in maintaining mental equilibrium.

Sometimes he would play Benigno. Sometimes she would sit on his lap.

"So, having parents like Benigno and Mercedes, do you think that's what made me loca?" she had asked the Jungian, still relishing the power of secrets.

"Nice try, but too easy," he had replied.

At the interview to evaluate her petition for release, the Jungian doctor said, "You are still sometimes a niñita in your woman's body. Have you decided what you would like to be when you grow up?"

She thought it over. She would like to be a daughter who can manage to make it to her own father's funeral, instead of sitting around drunk on agua ardiente and high on cocaine in a dirty bar downtown. She would like to be a mother not compelled by circumstances of insanity to give up her child for adoption, too stoned to notice he is gone, never to see him again or know his destino. Possibly, she said, she would like to be older, with all her trials behind her, sitting in her garden on Año Nuevo, a good man by her side. Definitely, she can see herself as a doting grandmother, with laughing, equally doting grandchildren at her knee, drinking fresh passion fruit juice, her favorite as well as theirs. But since it is not possible to will into *this* existence *that* son, *that* mother, *that* wife, *that* grandmother, requiring as it does a rewrite of the past or a fast-forward to the future, not to mention an unavoidable dependency on the collaboration of others, she will settle for being a grown woman who can wear red shoes and get away with it. In short, she will settle for being herself: Irene.

Her words and good humor had seemed to satisfy the release board, and they let her out to try her way in the world. By this time, she was already thirty-five.

Her first impulse as she embarked on this new chapter was to find Lily. But though she scoured the city white pages of the moth-eaten directory at the halfway house where

Dr. Martinez had secured her a room, she could find no trace of her former friend, nor even of anyone who had known her. Disheartened, she sat at the card table that served as both dining table and writing desk, tapping her foot to a jazz rendition on the radio of the song made famous by Judy Garland— "Somewhere Over the Rainbow"— the song she had sung to a crowded theatre hall as a schoolgirl, a song she had practiced with Lily.

Or had she?

Could it be that, as with so many other characters that have populated her thoughts and dreams, she has simply invented Lily Nathifa Amparo, whose name means "Pure Pure Sanctuary"? All the evidence— or lack thereof, actually— might seem to point in that direction. Yet, her memories of Lily are the most vivid, standing out from most of her recollections of life before the asylum.

It is, of course, entirely possible that Lily and her family, like so many others, weary of an unforgiving political and economic climate that ground their dreams to dust, had migrated to some small town in North America or Europe, or anywhere they could maintain the fiction in their minds that to exchange their homes and traditions for security is a fair trade.

Or could it be she, Irene, who is imaginary? Perhaps we are all God; perhaps no one would exist if someone else did not dream them into existence.

Now there is a thought the Jungian would appreciate.

❖

It was her outpatient therapist, Lucrecia Usoa, who, quite accidentally, while substituting for a colleague on holiday, discovered that Irene's mother, Mercedes, had admitted herself to the Serenidad Old Age Home in the hills of El Hatillo several years earlier. She suffered from Parkinson's.

"They say she doesn't recognize anyone now. I can go with you, si quieres," said Lucrecia Usoa. Irene was certain that not even Lucrecia's reassuring presence would be able to shield her from the unquenchable nature of her mother. She was wrong. When she arrived, her mother, a shell of her former self, looked right through her as though she weren't there at all. Irene sat in front of her, held tight her trembling hands in an attempt to still them, and blurted out the heartbreak of all she had lost — her lost years, lost time, lost loves. She apologized for running, for her own lunacy. But Mercedes only stared at a place somewhere over her head, her lips moving soundlessly, as if in silent prayer. Then, loosening her hands from Irene's grip, she stood and tottered over to her dressing table, where she began to fastidiously rearrange and meddle with the items on its surface. Folding and unfolding a washcloth, mixing her tooth powder with water from a jug, dabbing rose water behind her ears. There was a statue of the Virgin Maria on the dressing table. No Maria Lionza nonsense here; the place was run by nuns. She stood up to leave. Mercedes took no notice. Irene did not return, for there was nothing to return to but ashes.

It was also Lucrecia, after reading some of her stories, who said she had a good ear for the cadence and mannerisms of speech and suggested that she try her hand at scriptwriting. So she gave it a shot, completed a script about a family like the one she would have liked to have had, sent it off to the biggest telenovela-producing station. And then she waited for three months.

When a letter from the station arrived, she tore it open with clumsy, trembling fingers.

Your script has been rejected. Too raw, too weird, with too many old people. Too much narration in the background. We make telenovelas, not art films. We're in the business of happily ever after. We fabricate dreams.

The rejection continued:

For future reference, there should be only two central characters destined to fall in love, and everything in the story should revolve around that. Make them young, more contemporary, give them sexier names... Consuelo and Ismael are too antiquated; our viewers don't want to see old people in love. It's a turnoff.

That's how they talk over at the big, corporate TV stations. Though apolitical as a rule, she thinks it will serve the bastards right if the government shuts them all down.

She is neither able nor willing to comply with the terms of the TV producers, to rewrite the beings culled from the imperfect, twisted, but nevertheless beloved, fragments of her own psyche and experience. While she has no issue with fantasy per se, she cannot write lies or characters who have no souls. In her present life she can no longer pretend that everything crazy is exotic, she cannot ignore the elephant in the room, and when confronted with ugliness or pain or misery, she does not turn away. Her tenacity over the matter of editorial control has paid off and she has successfully sold for radio eight starter scripts, known as *enredaderas* because of the vinelike nature of their narratives, which can be continued by other writers into infinity, or as long as the audience's love and attention holds.

The first, *The Fall of Maria Lionza*, she dedicated to Lily after seeing her in a dream. It received widespread acclaim in a public survey among novela aficionados and ran for six months. The next was called *The Boy Who Thought He Could Fly*, followed by *The Dancing Heart*, then *Opening the Door of Miracles—A Midwife's Story*, *Diary of a Writer in Love*, *Daughter of the Revolution*. The latest, *Dreamwalkers*, whose protagonist is gifted with the ability to enter the dreams of others and change their destiny, has been on the air since last September. And she is already midway through another, *Incarnation of a Princess*.

No matter how many times she hears it, she is always thrilled when a new novela is announced with a dramatic flourish: "This is Passion Radio with another hot-blooded tale from the pen of Coromoto Santos." Coromoto Santos is her nom de plume.

It is public radio, not television, and it pays far less, but the fruits of her labor are read to the audience precisely the way they are written. And once her starter script has been enacted on the radio, she is happy, and perfectly in harmony with the idea that someone else will carry on what she has begun. Every now and then she tunes in to see what has happened to this character or that, and, more often than not, she is delighted. She loves writing for radio. Radio scripts are far more equitably balanced in terms of narrative and dialogue, inviting the audience to participate in their own unique visualization process. There is no question that radio allows for a much more intimate storytelling experience than television. She has voyeuristically watched people in cafés, or through the windows of their parked cars and living rooms, turn on the radio, close their eyes, and be transported to another place, another time. Public radio is far less glamorous than television, but the scripts are unadulterated, allowing for a more equitable balance between dialogue and narrative. It is literature. She likes that.

Long live public radio.

The Jungian had warned her against indulging her inclination toward magical thinking. But as for the fate of the corporate TV stations, it amuses her to flirt with the idea that her wish is being granted. One by one, they are having their leases revoked by the government. Students take to the streets, protesting in the name of freedom of speech. She believes in freedom of speech, of course. But she will not be joining the protests in the streets. In her catatonic period, she had lived the life of a revolutionary and died for it. She remembers the experience quite vividly, and as far as she is concerned she has already paid her karmic dues toward society in this regard. In this, her current and chosen life, she is responsible only for herself, and that responsibility is great enough, sometimes almost too great.

These days, says Lucrecia, you have to take care to differentiate between dreams born of your own subconscious that lead to awareness, and fantasies handed to you on a platter that lull you into a stupor. You have to be on your toes when it comes to discerning what is real.

For Irene this sometimes seems an exhausting and overwhelming task, mitigated only by her love for Manuel and his for her. How fortunate she is to have seen him sitting moodily in a café on the corner of Benadiba and Cinco and caught his eye, how fortunate that he took out his camera and asked her if she would mind if he took her picture, how fortunate that she, normally so reticent with strangers, had agreed to accompany him to his studio.

When she thinks about it, it is a miracle that more people aren't flocking in droves to the nuthouse. She supposes they go to Sorte instead. Or, for those who can afford it, to the banks of the River Ganga in India, whose muddy waters, it is said, can wash away even the most tenacious of ills.

Lucrecia says there are those in the mental health business (for in this crazy world, craziness has become a business) who believe that blurring the line between what is real and what is imaginary is perfectly legitimate, even outside the realm of fiction. One of Lucrecia's collegues at the halfway house where Irene used to live teaches a self-brainwashing technique to his patients, a complicated business involving the monitoring and conscious adjustment of one's eye movements, which can be used to convert unacceptable memories into acceptable ones. In other words, they alter the facts. Of course, writers of novelas can do this automatically, without coaching. They write the world the way they *want* it to be at that moment. It is a heady thing, dreaming up worlds, kneading them like pastry dough, folding them over on themselves.

The day before the last of the private television stations was shut down, she watched a rerun of an American talk show dubbed in Spanish, where the female host asked her celebrity guests, "What do you know for sure?"

The only thing Irene knows for sure is that she is done with running. She will stick it out till the end, clinging to her own small slice of life, a life she had so long resisted and later fought demons and hellfire to keep. She will plant her vine and nurture its fruit. She will graft it with budding hope for herself and Manuel, for her country and its people, with all their attendant complications and contradictions, races and beliefs, secure in the knowledge that even in this, the so-called real world, there is a place for magic, that it is possible, sometimes, to pull starlight out of sand, to reach into the sky and bring home the moon. She will write her radio tales and blow into the mouths of her characters the hot, sweet breath of life and passion. She will do what she has always done, only now she will draw an invisible line in the invisible sand to demarcate where these lives end and hers goes on. She will stand on the foundation of the new life she has fashioned, trusting that it will not crumble beneath her feet, and believing that her story, *this* story will continue.

And now Manuel is kissing her, sucking softly on that tantalizingly tender place just under her ear, the place that gives her goose bumps.

"Perdóname," he says about the photograph of her frozen terror on the rock, placing it facedown on the bedside table.

"For what?" she asks, and means it.

Acknowledgments

This book was several years in the making, during which I received sustenance from many quarters. I am deeply indebted to:

Sonia Anderson, best friend, touchstone, and co-custodian of memories.

The late Consuelo Perez, who was the inspiration for the character Consuelo in the novel.

My agent, Ellen Levine, for her judicious editorial feedback, patience with my process, and diligent efforts on my behalf.

My editor, Selina McLemore, and her assistant, Latoya Smith, for their belief in this book and painstaking attention to detail. And the people at Grand Central's art department, who created a wonderful cover.

Women who have been readers and brutal critics when necessary: Andrea Bachigalupi Boyle, Ginu Kamani, Mafalda Mascarenhas, Nell Sullivan, Antonia Van Becker, Swatee Kotwal, Shobhaa De, Lea Rangel Ribeiro, the late Dixie Engesser, the late Frances Bregman.

Men who get me and my writing, have read for me enthusiastically, and have made crucial observations that helped flesh out my male characters: Victor Rangel Ribeiro, Sudeep Chakravarti, Remo Fernandes, Maitreya Doshi, Avtar Singh, Akash Timblo, Cecil Pinto, Apurva Kulkarni, Stan Kugell, Sergio Mascarenhas, Desmond Fernandes.

Milana, who contributed a swimming club membership that helped alleviate writer's cramp and carpal tunnel syndrome.

Mario, for being my biggest cheerleader and helping to finance the lean periods.

Che, Maximiliano, and Oliver, my doggie foot warmers.

Maria Lionza, irrespective of whether she is fact or fiction.

And Venezuela, my home away from home.

Extract from "The End of the Colombian Blood Letting Could Begin in Washington"

On November 9, 2006, the Revolutionary Armed Forces of Colombia-Peoples Army, (FARC-EP) sent an "Open Letter to the People of the United States." It was specifically addressed to several Hollywood producers and actors (Michael Moore, Denzel Washington, and Oliver Stone) as well as three leftist academics (James Petras, Noam Chomsky, and Angela Davis) and a progressive politician (Jesse Jackson). The purpose of the open letter was to solicit our support in facilitating an agreement between the U.S. and Colombian governments and the FARC-EP on exchanging 600 imprisoned guerrillas (including 2 on trial in the U.S.) for 60 rebel-held prisoners including 3 U.S. counterinsurgency experts.

FARC-EP

Founded in 1964 by two dozen peasant activists, as a means for defending autonomous rural communities from the violent depredations of the Colombian military and paramilitary, the FARC-EP has grown into a highly organized 20,000-member guerrilla army with several hundred thousand local militia and supporters, highly influential in over 40 percent of the country. Up until September 11, 2001, the FARC-EP was recognized as a legitimate resistance movement by most of the countries of the European Union, Latin America, and for several years was in peace negotiations with the Colombian government headed by President Andrés Pastrana. Prior to 9/11 FARC leaders met with European heads of state to exchange ideas on the peace process.

—*James Petras, November 20, 2006*
(http://petras.lahaine.org/articulo
.php?p=1684&more=1&c=1)

A Goddess, a Snake, and a
Double-Edged Sword

In early June 2004 drivers on the Avenida Francisco Farjardo in the city of Caracas witnessed a strange and disturbing sight: the landmark statue of Maria Lionza, commissioned from Venezuelan sculptor Alejandro Colina, had cracked in two. The torso of the goddess had fallen backward, leaving her staring helplessly, arms outstretched, at the heavens. Oddly enough, according to news reports, this occurred a day after authorities announced the completion of restoration treatment. The imposing fifty-four-year-old monument of reinforced concrete, which normally stands 11.2 meters high, had not been moved for the restoration process, and was surrounded by scaffolding at the time of the collapse, creating a surreal cagelike effect. According to a BBC news story, "When Venezuelans awoke on 6 June to find Maria Lionza broken at the waist, interpretations and conspiracy theories abounded. Some said the goddess had broken in two deliberately in order to warn Venezuelans about the danger of their deeply-divided nation" ("The Goddess and the President," BBC, June 21, 2004).

Having grown up in Venezuela, for me this story became the irresistible seed material for a novel.

For centuries, Maria Lionza, a mythological Indian princess/goddess, has captured the imagination of the Venezuelan population, and the number of her supplicants is estimated to be in the hundreds of thousands. Given strong impetus in the 1950s by dictator Marcos Perez Jimenez, who made Maria Lionza a symbol of national identity, the cult has been officially recognized and sanctioned by subsequent democratic governments of Venezuela—even though the existence of Maria Lionza herself has yet to be authenticated by scholars of the period—and she is still considered to be the patron saint of the nation. The mythical origins of Maria Lionza, handed down by oral tradition, are lost in time. The version I have given in the novel is an amalgamation of several of the most popular stories of her origin.

Though believed to have many incarnations, the goddess is generally depicted in two forms: (1) as Yara, naked, riding a tapir and holding a human pelvis in her upstretched arms; and (2) as Maria, a mestiza Virgin Mary figure wearing a blue mantle over her head and shoulders. Maria Lionza reigns over her subjects from the Sorte Mountain in the state of Yaracuy along with a pantheon of deities that includes real and legendary characters from Venezuelan history. Officially known as the Maria Lionza National Park, Sorte is frequented by large numbers of pilgrims and tourists, particularly on weekends and holidays.

The primary deities in the goddess's pantheon, which is divided into "courts," include "El Libertador" Simón Bolívar, the man who fought for and won the independence of many Latin American countries; "El Negro Felipe," a black man who is said to have fought with Bolívar in the Independence Wars; and "El Indio Guaicaipuro," who is believed to have fought against the Conquerors at the time of the Conquest. When Maria Lionza, El Negro Felipe, and El Indio Guaicaipuro appear together to mediums, they are called Las Tres Potencias (the Three Powers), representing the three races that make up the Venezuelan population.

There are numerous other subdeities such as the writer Andrés Bello, and even a notorious criminal known as El Malandro Ismael, whose veneration is outside the realm of traditional perceptions of "goodness" and "morality."

In her Indian avatar, Maria Lionza is depicted as the reverse of the most frequently represented image of Simón Bolívar: she rides the gentle tapir, he rides a stallion; she is nude, he wears an army uniform; she holds a symbol of life (a human pelvis), he holds a symbol of death (a sword).

Catholicism is the predominant religion of Venezuela, and a majority of Marialionceros are Catholic. Although the Catholic Church frowns upon the worship of the pagan goddess, it has abandoned efforts to eradicate the cult. Maria Lionza's devotees come from all races and classes, but she is especially revered among the poor.

To my knowledge, no Venezuelan radio novela or telenovela has been written specifically about Maria Lionza or her incarnations to date, which is quite extraordinary, given that she is the emblem of all the hopes and aspirations of Venezuela's masses. I myself have used the myth primarily as signifier and anchor in *The Disappearance of Irene Dos Santos.*

Kidnappings, forced disappearances, and assassinations orchestrated by revolutionaries, crime bosses, the secret police, or international mercenaries have long been a part of the Venezuelan story. In 1976, when I was in high school,

William Niehaus, an American businessman and the father of a former schoolmate, was kidnapped by the Grupo de Comando Revolucionario, the guerilla wing of the Liga Socialista, and held for over three years. Around the same time the charismatic media personality Renny Ottolina, beloved by the masses, was killed after deciding to run for president as an independent, just three months before the elections. The crackdown on the drug trade in Colombia has forced much of it across the border, and these days Venezuela is a very dangerous place to travel. The nexus between drug running and gun purchase by groups such as FARC continues.

The roots of the popular Latin American serial novel extend back to the days of the Cuban "radio lectores," readers hired to read social realist novels of the nineteenth century to workers in cigar factories. With the advent of radio was born a genre of melodrama that depicted social ills in a more popular and less literary format. It was called the culebrón ("snake") because of its tendency to go on extending itself as long as the audience for it existed, and it was the precursor of the telenovela. Not surprisingly, the telenovela's global export came via Cuban exiles at the end of the 1950s and early 1960s, many of whose writers and directors fled to Venezuela, Argentina, and Mexico.

It was in Mexico that a new form of serialized storytelling emerged. It was pioneered and developed by Miguel Sabido for Televisa, where he was vice president for research in the 1970s. The essence of what is known today as the Sabido Method was the use of the soap opera to educate and encourage social change. Using the classic literary device of character growth, Sabido developed the process of character transformation in a way that was television-specific and tackled sensitive subjects such as sex, abortion, family planning, and AIDS in an accessible manner. It was a new communication model that has had enormous global impact, one that has been adopted and adapted all over the world. Obviously, such a mechanism for influencing the masses can be a double-edged sword....

Venezuela, one of the world's major oil-exporting nations which also boasts one of South America's largest, most abundant rain forests, has one of the most vibrant cultures I have ever experienced. The country is currently engaged in a fascinating political experiment, and on this subject it is a country deeply divided. I have met some who are passionately for it and others who are vehemently against it. I have no idea how it will turn out, but it promises to be a wild ride.

—*Margaret Mascarenhas, August 2008*

Discussion Questions

1. Maria Lionza is an actual cult figure in Venezuela. How does the goddess Maria Lionza function as a symbol in *The Disappearance of Irene Dos Santos*?

2. How does the passion fruit vine work as a metaphor in the novel?

3. How much of the ethos of Venezuela has the author been able to convey through the lives of her characters? Has it changed your perception of that country?

4. How does the author juxtapose magic against craziness, ghosts against hallucinations, lies against truth, prorevolution against antirevolution, socialism against capitalism?

5. Are the protagonists of the first eight sections of the novel real, figments of Irene's imagination, or characters she has written into her radio novelas? All of the above?

6. If we live in someone else's dream/imagination, is our reality as real as that of the dreamer/writer? Is the author suggesting that it is possible to dream something/someone into existence?

7. What does Irene lose and/or gain by becoming "well" and reintegrated into society?

8. Is it possible for the South American radio novela format to serve the purpose of promoting social change? If so, why would radio be a more useful tool in this endeavor than television?

9. The themes of revolution and resistance—the ongoing battle between the people and their leaders—are integral to the story line of the novel. Among the nine primary characters, Ismael, Consuelo, and Amparo are the most overtly "revolutionary"; Lily, Coromoto, Efraín, and Luz are neutral; Marta is opposed to revolutionary ideology; while Irene appears ambiguous. What might be the author's intent in representing all these worldviews?

Una diosa, un serpiente y una espada de doble filo

En junio, a principios de de 2004, los conductores en la Avenida Francisco Farjardo en la ciudad de Caracas encontraron una vista extraña y perturbante: la famosa estatua de Maria Lionza comisionada del escultor venezolano Alejandro Colina, se había partido en dos. El torso había caído al revés, dejándo la diosa mirando desamparadamente al cielo con los brazos extendidos. Lo raro es que, según las noticias, ésto ocurrió un día despues de las autoridades anunciar que el processo de la restauración de la estatua estaba completa. El monumento imponente de 54 años, hecho de concreto reforzado, que normalmente tiene 11.2 metros de alto, no había sido movido durante la restauración. A la hora del derrumbamiento la estatua estaba todavía rodeada con andamio, creando la impresión surreal como si fuera encerrada en una jaula. Según una de las noticias del BBC, "cuando los venezolanos se despertaron el 6 de junio para encontrar Maria Lionza partida en la cintura, interpretaciones y teorías de conspiración abundaron. Algunos dijeron que la diosa había rompido en dos justo para advertir a los venezolanos de los peligros de una nación profundamente dividida." (BBC, La diosa y el presidente, 21 de junio de 2004)

Yo pasé los años formativas en Venezuela, y para mí, esta historia se ha convirtido en la material irresistible de una novela.

Por siglos, Maria Lionza, princesa india de mitología local, ha capturado la imaginación de la población venezolana, y el número de sus supplicantes se estima en los centenares de millares. El ímpetu fuerte en los años 50 dado por el dictador Marcos Perez Jimenez, hizo de Maria Lionza un símbolo de identidad nacional. El culto ha sido reconocido oficialmente y sancionado por gobiernos democráticos subsecuentes en Venezuela aunque la existencia de Maria Lionza misma jamás ha sido autenticada por los académicos del período, la todavía la consideran como santa patrona de la nación. Los orígenes míticos de Maria Lionza, transmitidos por la tradición oral, se han perdido con el tiempo. La versión descrito en esta novela es una amalgamación de las varias historias populares sobre su origen.

Aunque tiene muchas encarnaciones, la diosa generalmente aparece en dos formas: (1) como Yara, desnuda, montado sobre un tapir, sosteniendo en los brazos una pelvis humana; (2) como Maria, una imágen de la Virgen de los Mestizos, con una capa azul cubriendo la cabeza y los hombros. Maria Lionza reina sobre sus súbditos desde la montaña Sorte en el Estado de Yaracuy junto con su panteón de deidades, incluyendo personajes verdaderos y legendarios en la historia venezolana. Conocido oficialmente como el Parque Nacional de Maria Lionza, Sorte es frecuentado por una gran cantidad de peregrinos y turistas, particularmente los fines de semana y los días de fiesta.

Los deidades primarios en el panteón de la diosa, que se divide en "cortes," incluyen El Libertador Simon Bolivar, el hombre que luchó para, y ganó, la independencia para muchos países latinoamericanos, El Negro Felipe, un hombre negro conocido por haber luchado junto con Bolivar en las guerras para independencia; El Indio Guaicaipuro, quien se cree haber luchado contra los conquistadores. Cuando Maria Lionza, El Negro Felipe, y El Indio Guaicaipuro aparecen juntos a los medios, se les llaman "Las Tres Potencias", representando las tres razas de población venezolana.

Hay muchas otras deidades secundarias, como el escritor Andres Bello, y un criminal notorio, conocido como El Malandro Ismael, cuya veneración está fuera del reino de opiniones tradicionales sobre "lo bueno" y "la moralidad."

En su avatar indio, muchos representan a Maria Lionza como el revés de la imagen más popular de Simon Bolivar: ella montada sobre un tapir apacible, él montado sobre un garañón; ella desnuda, él vestido en uniforme del ejército; ella sujetando un símbolo de la vida (una pelvis humana), él sujetando un símbolo de la muerte (una espada).

El Catolicismo es la religión predominante de Venezuela y la mayoría de Marialionceros son católicos. Aunque la iglesia Católica no condona sobre la adoración de la diosa pagana, ha abandonado el intento de suprimir el culto. Los devotos de Maria Lionza vienen de todas razas y clases, pero es venerada especialmente entre los pobres.

A mi conocimiento, no existe ninguna radionovela o telenovela venezolana especificamente sobre Maria Lionza o sus encarnaciones hasta la fecha, cosa extraordinaria, dado que es emblema de todas las esperanzas y aspiraciones de las masas de Venezuela. He utilizado el mito sobre todo como una ancla en *The Disappearance of Irene Dos Santos*.

Los secuestros, las desapariciones forzadas, y los asesinatos orquestrados por los revolucionarios, los jefes del crimen, el policía secreto, o los mercenarios internacionales han formado un gran parte de la historia venezolana. En 1976, cuando yo estaba todavia en colegio, el Grupo de Comando Revolucionario, facción guerrilla de la Liga Socialista, secuestró al padre de un compañero de clase, William Niehaus, un hombre de negocios americano, y lo guardaron cautivo por más de tres años. En esos tiempos, Renny Ottolina una personalidad carismática de televisión, muy querido por las masas, murió en un acidente de avión después de anuciar su intención de postular para Presidente independiente de otras partidos. Su muerte occurrió apenas tres meses antes de las elecciones.

Las medidas enérgicas contra el comercio de la droga en Colombia lo ha forzado a través de la frontera, y hoy en día Venezuela es un lugar muy peligroso para viajar. El nexo entre el comercio de la droga y la compra de armas por los grupos tales como FARC continúa.

Las raíces de la novela serial latinoamericana popular se rastrea los tiempos de los "lectores de radio" en Cuba — lectores empleados para leer las novelas sociales y realista del siglo 19 a los trabajadores en fábricas de cigarro. Con la llegada de la radio nació un género de melodrama que representaba los males sociales en un formato más popular y menos literario. Se llamaba el "culebrón" debido a su tendencia a ampliarse con tanto de que existieran las audiencias, y era el precursor de la telenovela. No es sorprendente entonces que la exportación global de las telenovelas fue vía exilios cubanos por los fines de los años 60 y del principio de los años 60, pues, muchos que de escritores y de directores cubanos huyeron a Venezuela, a la Argentina y a México.

Fue en México que una nueva forma de contar historias en serie apareció, iniciado por Miguel Sabido para Televísa donde él era vicepresidente del departamento de documentación en los años 70. La esencia de lo qué se conoce hoy como La Metodología Sabido, fue el uso de la novela para educar y para creer el cambio social. Usando el dispositivo literario y clásico que se trata del desarollo del carácter, Sabido utilizó un proceso transformativa del carácter de una manera especificamente modelado para televisión, abordando temas sensibles tales como el sexo, el aborto, la planificación familiar, y la SIDA de una manera accesible. Fue una nueva forma de comunicación que ha tenido un impacto global enorme, una forma que se ha adoptado y se ha adaptado por todo el mundo. Obviamente, tal mecanismo, utilizado para influenciar las masas, puede ser una espada de doble filo....

Venezuela es una de las naciones del mundo que luce en la exportación del petroleo También dispone una de las selvas más grandes de Suramérica. Este país tiene una de las culturas más vibrantes que he experimentado en la vida. En este momento es un país comprometido en un experimento político fascinante, y por eso, es un país profundamente dividido. He conocido a algunos que están apasionados por este experimento, y a otros que están vehemente en contra. No tengo ninguna idea cómo termina esta historia, pero promete ser un viaje espectacular.

—Margaret Mascarenhas, agosto de 2008

Para discuitir

1. Maria Lionza es una figura de un culto que existe actuelmente en Venezuela. ¿Qué simboliza la diosa Maria Lionza en *The Disappearance of Irene Dos Santos*?
2. ¿Cómo funciona como metáfora la vid de la passiflora en la novela?
3. ¿Es que la autora consigue creer el genio real de Venezuela a través las descripciones de la vida de sus caracteres? ¿Ha cambiado su opinión sobre ese país?
4. ¿Cómo es que la autora yuxtapone la magia con la locura, fantasmas con alucinaciones, mentiras con la verdad, pro-revolución con anti-revolución, socialismo con capitalismo?
5. ¿Es que los protagonistas de las primeras ocho secciones de la novela son verdaderos, unas quimeras de la imaginación de Irene, o caracteres que Irene propia ha escrito en sus radionovelas? ¿O, todo el antedicho?
6. ¿Si fuera posible que vivimos en los sueños/la imaginación de otros, sería nuestra realidad tan verdadera como la del soñador/ escritor? ¿Sugiere el autor que es posible soñar algo/alguien hasta que comienza exitistir en realidad?

7. ¿Qué pierde y/o gana Irene "curarse", y integrándose de nuevo en la sociedad?

8. ¿Es posible que el formato de la radionovela sudamericano asiste enn promover el cambio social? ¿Si es así, por qué sería la radio un instrumento más útil en este plan que la televisión?

9. Los temas de la revolución y de la resistencia—la batalla entre la gente ordinaria y sus líderes—son integrales al argumento de la esta novela. Entre los nueve caracteres primarios, Ismael, Consuelo y Amparo son los que son pro-revolución más abiertamente; Lily, Coromoto, Efrain y Luz son mas o menos neutrales; Marta se opone a la ideología revolucionaria, mientras que Irene parece ambigua. ¿Qué podría ser el intento de la autora en representar todos estos puntos de vista?

About the Author

MARGARET MASCARENHAS is a consulting editor, columnist, and novelist. She is the author of *Skin*, published by Penguin India in 2001, also published in French translation by Mercure de France in 2002, and in Portuguese translation by Editora Replicacao in 2006.

An American citizen of Goan origin who grew up in Venezuela, she currently resides in Goa, India.

For more information please visit http://mmascgoa.tripod.com/